"TOM DORCHESTER JUST BLED TO DEATH. ALL AT ONCE."

"How?" asked Slater.

"I don't know," said the doctor. "I've never heard of anything like this before in my life."

"Guess," insisted Slater. "Give me something to go on."

"Poison," answered Payne, his voice flat. "And from the looks of him, there was very little time between contact and death."

"That's incredible."

"By the way, Jack, I don't think you should mention this to anyone. Not yet, anyway. There's no sense in alarming people."

Slater took a last look at what was left of Tom Dorchester. It was like something out of a horror movie, and he knew the image of that bloody, oozing corpse would haunt him forever . . .

CHRISTOPHER HYDE

JERICHO FALLS

AVON
PUBLISHERS OF BARD, CAMELOT, DISCUS AND FLARE BOOKS

JERICHO FALLS is an original publication of Avon Books. This work has never before appeared in book form. This work is a novel. Any similarity to actual persons or events is purely coincidental.

AVON BOOKS
A division of
The Hearst Corporation
1790 Broadway
New York, New York 10019

First Avon Printing: December 1986

This one is for Mariea, who gave me the idea,
and for the other women in my life,
Lucinda Vardey, Carolyn Brunton, Lee Creal,
and Linda Turchin.

PART ONE

CHINOOK
Friday, October 31

In the event of a CHINOOK alert, members of the unit shall be contacted immediately and any and all leaves will be canceled. Officers of the unit will report to ComDiv HQ within two hours of the alert for briefing. If there is no stand-down from the alert within twelve hours, the alert will automatically escalate to BLACK ROLLER status and officers should consult their manuals for further instructions.

—Lt. Col. James H. Wright
Commander, Special Unit 7
AMCCOM
Rock Island Arsenal
Rock Island, Illinois
Section 1, Number 1, page 5
BM-31-210

CHAPTER ONE

6:00 P.M.

Autumn had come to the White Mountains of New Hampshire, and the hills surrounding the town of Jericho Falls were patched in a dozen shades of red and gold. The last days of summer were long gone, but the earth-warm colors blazed defiantly against the cold white months of winter lying just ahead. It was October 31, and in a few hours the bright, late afternoon sky would darken to ash.

Even before the sun would fully set, shadows would fill the small, bowl-shaped valley, bringing on an early dusk, and the crisp evening breeze would ripen with the scent of birch smoke and the faint dark tang from the thin layer of rime covering Drake's Pond.

Along the tree-lined streets of Frenchtown and River Park, the dry, dying leaves would rustle softly as the costumed children— ghosts and goblins—ran from door to door, their bulging loot bags crammed with molasses candy, peanuts, and sticky confections of a dozen different kinds manufactured by the ladies of the Orpheus Society Women's Auxiliary and sold to raise funds for the restoration of the Earl Alexander Coolis Memorial Bandstand on Constitution Common.

The trees would whisper their warning of things to come, but children young enough to believe in Halloween are too young to know that the living nightmares of the adult world rival anything their innocent imaginations can conjure forth, and no one, young or old, had any way of knowing that for most of the citizens of Jericho Falls, this Halloween would be their last.

* * *

Karen Slater stomped back and forth across the worn, creaking boards of the tiny, old-fashioned bandstand, hands jammed into the pockets of her bright orange, quilted ski jacket, her angry breath sending ragged puffs of steam into the cold, late afternoon air. Most of her long, dark brown hair was tucked up under the white, knitted tuque on her head, but loose strands had escaped, framing her pink-cheeked, oval face and adding to her wild-eyed look.

"Sometimes this town just makes me want to scream," she muttered.

Normally, without the furious scowl, she was willing to admit that she didn't look half bad—now that the last of the baby fat had gone, and if you were willing to overlook the fact that her legs were too skinny and her boobs too small. But right at the moment, she couldn't have cared less what she looked like.

"Derek's got the flu or something. If it wasn't for that, we'd be all right," said Billy Coyle, seated on the short flight of rotting steps leading down to the patchy, fall-brown grass of the Common. He was sixteen, a year older than Karen, as blond as she was dark, and undeniably the best-looking senior at E. A. Coolis High School. Dressed in a designer pea jacket, tailored cords, and handmade cowboy boots, he was like something out of a fashion magazine; if it weren't for the fact that his father was Luther Coyle, Jericho Falls's blowhard mayor and perennial pain-in-the-ass head of the Chamber of Commerce, Billy would have been perfect.

Karen snorted, then trudged back across the bandstand to the steps. She sat down and slipped her arm through Billy's, briefly pressing her cheek to his shoulder.

"It's not Derek," she said finally. "We shouldn't have to depend on him. I mean, it's not like this is the fifties or something."

"It's always been the fifties in Jericho Falls," said Billy, laughing. "Nothing ever changes here, you know that."

"Sure I know it. That's what I mean. Just look at this place." She waved her free arm in the air in a sweeping gesture, frowning as she looked around the perimeter of the Common.

Once upon a time, Constitution Common had been the center of Jericho Falls, and it was still the town's heart, even though the business district had spread well to the east along Mountain Creek and the river as well as down the "Strip" created by the 115A extension. You shopped the Strip if you were a French-towner looking for cheap work clothes or a fast snack at Arnie's Flameburger, and you went to Main Street or Waterhill if you wanted J. C. Penney or Kinney Shoes, but the Common still had class.

The Common consisted of a score of buildings arranged in a long rectangle around the bandstand and the park, wide sidewalks beneath rows of elm and maple as old as the town, with John Stark Hall as the crowning glory. The hall was a Greek Revival municipal building, complete with fluted white columns, porticoes, cupola, and clock, built in 1858 to replace the burned-out old courthouse and named for New Hampshire's greatest hero, Colonel John Stark of the Revolutionary War and the man who'd given the state its motto, "Live Free or Die." Beside it was the redbrick Volunteer Fire Station, the Police Station, and the Jericho Falls Savings and Loan at the corner.

On the far side of the Common was Merchants Row, a cheek-to-cheek collection of stores and offices, bracketed on the corners by the Victorian sprawl of the Old Empire Hotel and the ugly, one-story, flat-roofed Woolworth's. Across the street from Woolworth's was the Bo-Peep Grill, a hangout for the youth of Jericho Falls for almost fifty years, and beside it, so overgrown with ivy that the brick was almost invisible, was the Murray, the town's one and only movie house, open Tuesday, Thursday, and Friday evenings, and Saturdays for the matinee trade.

"Hicksville," breathed Karen. "Sometimes I feel as though I'm suffocating here."

"It's not that bad."

"Sure." She grimaced. "It's okay for you. You get to go to New York and Boston four or five times a year. My daddy never goes anywhere."

"Three more years and you'll be in college. That's not so long."

"Right. But that doesn't help us now, does it?"

"No, I guess not," agreed the young man. He turned his head and found himself looking at the stores on Merchants Row, Have-lock's Pharmacy in particular.

"Maybe you could just walk in and buy them," suggested Karen, following his gaze.

"Not a chance," Billy answered, painfully aware of the denim leg pressed against his thigh. "Mr. Havelock would be on the phone to my old man in about five seconds if I did. No way."

"Maybe we should get Bodo to do it," said Karen, nodding her head toward a stoop-shouldered figure a few dozen yards away slowly making his way along the sidewalk.

Bodo "Born Dopey" Bimm was in his late thirties, had the mind of a six-year-old, and bought his clothes from the sale bin at Bargain Barney's on the Strip. He worked nights at the Gas Bar beside the Slumber-King Motel on the edge of town, and he was so dim-witted you had to make your own change when you got your tank filled.

No one had the slightest idea where Bodo had come from or where he lived, and no one cared. Bobo Bimm was as much a fixture in Jericho Falls as the clock on Stark Hall or the swimming hole at Drake's Pond.

"He'd probably come back with an armful of rubber gloves," said Billy, watching as Bodo crossed Grand Street and went into the Bo-Peep.

"So what do we do?"

"Nothing. Without Derek there's just no way."

"You sure you don't have any left?"

"No. We used the last one the night your dad had to take that guy down to Concord, remember?"

"Yes," said Karen, "I remember." Like all the other times, it had been nice, but not the way they made it sound in books. She was beginning to think that she was frigid, but it excited Billy and that was enough—at least for the time being.

"You sure it's not okay?" he asked. Karen shook her head.

"No. I'm right in the middle of my cycle. It's too dangerous." She twined her fingers into his and kissed him softly on the cheek. "Will you come anyway?" she asked. "I'm only baby-sitting until nine-thirty; the Crawfords promised they wouldn't be any later than that. We could do . . . other things, you know, and anyway, we could go to the party together later."

"Okay," said Billy. "I guess we don't have much choice."

"Shit!" Karen whispered, huddling down beside her boyfriend as a familiar blue Ford sedan pulled into the square. The car turned into one of the reserved angle parking spots in front of Stark Hall. Karen peeped over Billy's shoulder and watched as a tall, dark-haired man wearing a brown-leather bomber jacket with a wool collar climbed out of the car and trotted up the short flight of steps to the police station.

"It's Daddy," Karen said. "He'll have my ass for breakfast if he sees me here. I was supposed to go right home after school to do my homework." She waited until her father disappeared into the building and then stood up. She bent down and kissed Billy firmly on the lips, her cool tongue darting briefly into his mouth. "Seven o'clock," she said quickly. "The baby's out like a light by seven-thirty. We'll have a couple of hours, okay?"

"Okay," Billy said. Karen kissed him once more, then she quickly ran across the Common. Billy Coyle waited for a few seconds more and then stood up. He stared at the front of Havelock's Pharmacy, frowning sadly, and then turned away.

The Jericho Falls Police Station was a squat, two-storied stone building that had once been Buller's funeral parlor, and no amount of halfhearted renovation over the years had been able to brighten the gloomy interior. The front part of the building held the business offices, and the long rear section, once the "preparation room," had been converted into a makeshift cell block and morgue, unnecessary ever since the construction of the Medical Center. On bad days during the summer you could still catch a whiff of formaldehyde in the air, and more than one drunk drying out in the cells had insisted that the place was haunted by the ghosts of former clientele.

Jack Slater, Kancamagus County Sheriff and chief of the six-man, one-woman Jericho Falls Police Force, unzipped his jacket as he went through the heavy wooden doors of the station then on through the glass swinging door leading to the offices.

The front room was small, made even smaller by a waist-high counter running from one side to the other. A bank of fluorescent lights in the low ceiling buzzed angrily and Slater blinked as he entered the room, squinting in the harsh glare. There were four desks on the far side of the counter, but Lisa Colchester was alone in the room, manning the big Motorola and flipping through a worn copy of *People* magazine.

Lisa was thirty, ten years younger than her boss, unmarried, and plain. She was short, had a face dotted with the scars of adolescent acne, a billowing chest out of scale with the rest of her body, and short, lackluster, mouse brown hair. But she'd scored at the top of her class for the academy entrance exams in Manchester, outshot anyone on the force (Slater included), and had a sunny, perpetually optimistic personality that made even the worst days seem tolerable.

She looked up from the magazine and smiled brightly as Slater came into the office. Then she stood up and came to the counter.

"Anything going on?" asked Slater, flipping through the log-book on the counter. As Chief of Police and County Sheriff, he could have legitimately kept regular nine-to-five hours, but instead he did a regular duty shift like everyone else. On Fridays that meant four to midnight.

"Nothing special," Lisa said. "Zeke is umping the Little League final at the park and Norm is cruising Frenchtown."

"What about Van Heusen?"

"At the Medical Center for his physical. It's in the log."

"Anyone in the tank?"

"Not yet. Too early."

"Okay," Slater said, nodding. "I'm going over to the Bo-Peep for coffee. I want everyone who's going to be on duty tonight in by five." He tapped the walkie-talkie clipped to his wide Sam Brown. "Buzz if you need me."

"Sure." Lisa looked at her watch. "You remember to take your shot?"

"I'll do it when I get back." He smiled. "Thanks for reminding me."

"Part of the service." Lisa grinned. "And I told Chang not to let you have any more of those sugar doughnuts, so don't even ask."

"You're a hard woman, Office Colchester."

"Bet your ass, Chief."

Jack, Jake, Slater, and occasionally Sheriff, but never Chief. Lisa was the only person he knew who used the title, and Slater found it mildly embarrassing, considering the minuscule size of his force. Smiling, he waved the woman away, then turned and left the office. He zipped up his jacket again, went out through the main doors and across the street to the Common. Pulling up the collar of his jacket against the chill, he jammed his hands into his pockets and headed for the Bo-Peep Grill on the far side of the square.

Police Chief Jack Montgomery Slater. But the title said nothing about the man. A week ago he'd turned forty, the event celebrated by a bizarre triple-layer cake, each layer a different flavor, baked by his daughter, Karen. Instead of a card, she'd rummaged through her old toys and come up with a Ken Doll and a Skipper, dressing the Ken in a makeshift policeman's uniform and binding the two dolls together at the wrists with a tiny pair of handcuffs made out of aluminum foil. She'd glued the two dolls to a wooden plaque from the Craft House on Main Street and inscribed it with a felt pen: *For Daddy. Yours Forever, Karen.*

He was touched that she'd gone to so much trouble, but he caught the underlying message. He'd made his choice returning to the Falls, and she was bound to it. At fifteen she was beginning to get the same wanderlust itch he'd had at that age, and almost overnight Jericho Falls had become a boring claustrophobic trap. Not a day went by without her mentioning the fact that they lived in a social and cultural backwater. What she didn't understand was that after a three-year stint as an MP in Vietnam, a soured marriage, the discovery that he had an incurable disease, and the responsibilities of being a single parent to a growing daughter, Jericho Falls—plain, simple, and uncomplicated—was exactly what he wanted. A safe, if boring, harbor for a battered old ship that had seen too much of the outside world and was beginning to show its age.

Slater reached the edge of the Common and crossed the street. Forty. Once it would have seemed ancient, but so far, breaking the four-oh barrier didn't seem to be having much of an effect on him. He made a little grunting sound and smiled to himself. He'd had his mid-life crisis a long time ago, herding diplomats aboard the helicopters landing on the embassy roof in Saigon.

He pushed open the door of the Bo-Peep and stepped inside, his nostrils instantly bewitched by the hot-sweet smell of the french fries that had made Chang's greasy spoon famous. The restaurant was long and narrow, squeezed onto the edge of the Murray Theater property, and the large window fronting the Common was permanently obscured by a haze of steam. Normally, the stools along the counter and the dozen booths against the opposite wall would have been packed with kids at this time of day. But with Halloween only a few hours away, the place was empty except for Chang, reading a copy of the *Leader Post* at his old-fashioned crank-operated cash register, and Bodo Bimm, hunched over a cup of coffee at the far end of the counter.

Slater dropped into the booth nearest the door, and without being asked, Chang brought him a large mug of coffee. The Bo-Peep's owner wiped his hands on the long, stained apron he wore and sat down on the other side of the table. He fished around under his apron, brought out a match, and pulled the stump of a Camel from behind one ear. He lit up and sighed, leaning against the backrest of the bench seat.

"Damn, but it's been a long day!" sighed the short, balding man. The accent was pure New Hampshire without a trace of Chinese. Chang was a hometown boy and the restaurant had been in his family for half a century.

"Busy?" asked Slater, looking over the rim of his mug.

"Inspectors," answered Chang, sighing again. "State Health, Frank Rifkind playing at being a fireman, and some fool from Manchester making sure that the new wiring on the deep fryers was up to standard."

"How'd you make out?" asked Slater. Chang was renowned in the county as being a chronic complainer about government intrusion into what he referred to as "the entrepreneurial spirit that made this country what it is today." Given the slightest encouragement, he'd launch into any one of a score of different tirades about free enterprise. Slater, like everyone else in Jericho Falls, had heard all of them at least once.

"I made out fine," answered Chang. "No roaches; Frank couldn't find so much as an oily rag; and the guy from Manchester called the wiring 'solid professional work.' "

"Didn't you do the wiring yourself?"

"Of course I did it myself!" snorted Chang. "I've forgotten more about deep fryers than Colonel Sanders ever knew. It's just another example of the state prying into the affairs of the individual citizen."

Slater sensed a lecture coming and did his best to change the subject quickly. "All set for tonight?" he asked.

"Umm." Chang nodded. "Paulette Doyle and her swarm were in this morning about the coffee arrangements for the town hall party. They seemed a little upset when I wasn't willing to donate free cream and sugar, as though getting the coffee and the plastic cups weren't enough. Amazing. It wasn't even noon and you could smell the Binaca from across the room.''

"She was drunk?"

"Let's just say all the wrinkles had been smoothed out," answered Chang delicately. Slater tried not to laugh. He took another sip of coffee instead.

"Being married to Dave Doyle isn't the easiest role in life," he offered after a moment.

"True enough," Chang said with a nod.

At thirty-five Dave Doyle had his finger in just about every pie in town. He was chairman of the Junior Chamber of Commerce, junior partner at Frame, Doyle and Van Heusen, local organizer for State Senator Barrett O'Neill, the town's most famous native son, sat on the Town Council, and was a school board trustee. On top of that he was also the personal counsel for Luther Coyle, which gave him more clout than all his other positions combined. On the other side of it, there was also a rumor going around that Dave was neglecting his marital duties and that Paulette had turned into a bit of a roundheel on the tennis courts in Old Creek Park during the summer.

"I think I'm about ready to eat," Slater said finally. He didn't want to get into a gossip session with Chang about Paulette Doyle's morals.

"Poached eggs, whole wheat toast, dry, no fries." Chang slid sideways out of the booth and stood up.

"Is that a suggestion or an order?"

"It's what the menu sheet Dr. Payne gave me *says* you should have," the Chinese cook said firmly. Rembrandt "Payne's the name and Pain's the game" Payne was the white-haired, iron-jawed head of the Jericho Falls Medical Center, and he'd been Jack Slater's doctor since childhood. When Payne discovered that Slater had been diagnosed as a diabetic, his reaction had been swift and deadly: feed the police chief of Jericho Falls anything not on his diet and feel the wrath of Rembrandt Payne. An under-the-table sugar doughnut or a clandestine order of Chang's french fries could result in anything from the Bo-Peep's failing health inspections to a nasty letter from old man Bell at the Savings and Loan. And Chang knew it.

"Okay." Slater knew better than to argue. And it was for his own good, after all. "But let's have the yolks firm this time. I'm tired of soggy toast."

"Coming up."

Twenty minutes later, meal finished, Jack Slater headed back to the police station. All three of the green-and-white cruisers were lined up neatly in their reserved slots beside his own un-marked car. He looked at his watch. It was 5:05 and twilight was setting in.

The swing shift, working from five until one in the morning, was composed of three men: Norm Lombard, working a double shift for the overtime, now that his wife was expecting; Charlie Hill, the rookie; and Tom Dorchester, the senior of the three. They were all waiting for Slater in the outer office, sitting at their desks, drinking sludge from the Mr. Coffee, and teasing Lisa Colchester, who was still at the radio. Seeing her boss enter the room, she raised her eyebrows and got up, slipping on the uni-form jacket hanging over the back of her chair.

"Thank God!" she groaned. "These guys were driving me nuts." She waited until Slater lifted the hinged pass-through in the counter and entered the office, then she squeezed through the opening. "I'll be at home if anything comes up," she offered, turning back at the door.

"No date for the Halloween party?" asked Dorchester, his wide, strawberry-cheeked face splitting into a mocking grin. He had his feet up on his desk, a cup of coffee balanced precariously on his mounded beer belly.

"Kiss mine, 'cause I sure as hell won't kiss yours," said Lisa. She threw him a quick finger and went out, slamming the door behind her.

"Why don't you leave her alone?" asked Slater, frowning at the heavyset deputy. "You're no prize yourself, Tom."

"I didn't mean nothing." Dorchester looked up at his boss innocently, the small, pale blue eyes cold and hard. Dorchester was a good ten years older than Slater and resented the younger man's appointment, a position he felt he deserved by seniority. Dorchester wasn't quite an alcoholic, but he didn't miss by much, and half the town knew it. On top of his drinking problem, he was also a bully, and Slater knew that one of these days he'd have to pull the plug on him, one way or the other.

"Just leave her alone, all right?" Slater sat down at the radio desk and swiveled the chair around to face his men. "All of you read the duty sheet?"

The three men nodded. Dorchester looked bored, Charlie Hill looked eager, and Norm Lombard looked his usual serious self. Slater and Lombard were almost the same age, and the two men were reasonably good friends. Norm's wife Lois had been playing matchmaker almost from the time Slater returned to the Falls, and she was responsible for introducing him to every eligible spinster in town.

"How come Norm is on radio duty again?" asked Dorchester. "He sits on his butt all night while we do the rounds."

"At least he'll stay awake," answered Slater. He cleared his throat. "Okay, down to business. As Tom mentioned, Norm will be on radio duty until end of shift at one o'clock. Six to nine I want Tom in Frenchtown. Charlie, you cruise River Park and the Hill. That leaves me downtown. I'm going to have to make some kind of appearance at Stark Hall during the party, so that makes sense." He eyed Dorchester. "And let's not be stupid about this. It's Halloween. Soaping windows, firecrackers, and kids drinking a bit too much beer isn't grounds for arrest."

"So where do we draw the line?" said the older cop.

"Common sense," answered Slater. "Soaping a storefront or a car isn't vandalism; lighting fires and trashing headstones in the cemetery rates. Most of all, I want you both to keep an eye on the little kids. Zeke handed out a few hundred of those reflective stickers they sent up from Highways, so there shouldn't be much trouble."

"You got me doing 115 and Old River Road from nine on," said Dorchester.

"That's right. You have a problem with that?"

Dorchester shrugged. "No. I just don't see the point. No one's going to be on the highway that late, and ever since they ran the Interstate around, you could plant corn on Old River Road."

"Maybe," Slater said, "but Zeke noticed some kids dragging out there a few nights ago. It's worth checking out."

"Probably those freaks from the Mill," grunted Dorchester, lighting a cigarette.

"I doubt it, Tom," said Norm Lombard. "Those people are into windmills and bicycles, not glaspack pipes and hot rods. More likely Vince Wrigley's gang."

"Always ready to knock the Frenchtowners," said Dorchester. "And kiss every ass on the Hill." Dorchester was the son of a Frenchtown granite cutter who'd worked in the old Notch Quarry to the west of town; in his books, anyone raised east of the Common was by definition a pansy. Lombard's dad, long dead now, had been an accountant in the County Treasurer's Office. Lombard, used to dealing with Dorchester's small-mindedness, chose to ignore the snipe and turned his attention to Slater.

"What about fire calls?" he asked. The Jericho Falls Fire Department was volunteer and depended on the Police Department to relay alarms. In the event of a fire, the person manning the radio pulled a wall switch that set off the old air-raid siren mounted in the clock tower of Stark Hall. By letting out a variety of coded blasts on the siren, the radio man signaled the seriousness of the fire.

"Kirby Jones will be on the truck. Most everyone else will be at the party until midnight. Give it one toot and then get the address out on the radio."

"Okay."

"Anything else?" asked Slater. Charlie Hill's hand shot up.

"If I'm cruising the Hill, that means the Medical Center, right?"

"That's right," said Slater. "They're on light staff because of the party," he added, anticipating the young policeman's follow-up. "If there's some real emergency, call it in to Norm." He looked from man to man and then stood up. He could feel the first flushed symptoms of his fluctuating blood-sugar levels, and he gritted his teeth. Diabetes was a disease that didn't let you forget, and his shot was now long overdue. "Okay, gentlemen, that's it. Back here at one, and I'll try to have some of the food from the party brought over." Charlie Hill and Tom Dorchester stood up and moved out of the office while Norm Lombard sat down at the radio desk, slipping the old-fashioned headset around his neck.

"You okay, Jack?" he asked, looking up with a frown. Slater nodded, feeling the sweat beading out on his forehead. It was crazy, trying to ignore it, trying to beat it, when his kit was only a few feet away, behind the closed door of his office. But sometimes, just for a few minutes, it was worth it, trying to pretend that he was normal.

"Sure, Norm," he answered, putting on a smile he didn't feel. "I'm fine and dandy. The streets are crawling with bogeymen, and later on tonight we'll be attacked by the hounds of hell. Another boring night in Jericho Falls."

Arnie Redenbacher sat in the Bretton Woods Donut King and dunked his second, day-old cruller into his third cup of coffee. It was too hot in the brightly lit restaurant, and he was sweating. Outside the big plate-glass window that looked across New Hampshire 302, night had fallen, and he could no longer see the looming hulk of Mt. Washington. Glancing at his watch, he saw that it was almost seven. Another few minutes and he could get moving. Good thing too; another cruller in this hothouse and he'd puke. His stomach had been acting up lately, and he'd been plagued by almost constant acid indigestion the whole day.

Arnie was fifty-eight years old, ugly as a crushed beer can, forty pounds overweight, and mindless. If it hadn't been for the Korean War, he probably would have become a petty criminal of some kind, but his stint in the army had given him the single skill that had supported him ever since.

Arnie was a driver. He'd chauffeured generals through war zones in rattletrap jeeps and foreign correspondents through the red-light districts of Seoul. He'd driven a cab in Manchester, run American cigarettes into Quebec, and hauled milk trucks from one end of New Hampshire to the other.

And he hated it. Arnie Redenbacher's idea of heaven was a place without any form of wheeled conveyance. But considering his past, he knew he was probably going to be consigned to some sort of Interstate hell, gridlocked into an eternal lineup at a toll-booth where no one ever had the right change.

He frowned at the sludge at the bottom of his cup. Somewhere in the dim recesses of his brain he knew that things could have been worse. The work was steady, and he wasn't smart enough to be bored; the money was good enough to let him keep a pretty decent apartment, and doing the once-a-month trip to Bretton Woods gave him enough extra to pay for booze and the occasional run at one of Manchester's professional ladies.

He knew the trip was a special one, but in two years he'd never once questioned or even really thought much about the special procedures and precautions. It was precisely this absence of imagination, curiosity, and basic intelligence that made him perfect for the job. He took his orders directly from Mr. Simington, his dispatcher, and he followed those orders to the letter.

The pattern never varied. On the last day of each month he took the same dark green, unmarked Econoline from the Brown Avenue Yard and drove to Bretton Woods, following Interstate 93 up through Concord and into the mountains. Ten miles out of Franconia, he turned onto U.S. 3, usually arriving in the little resort town sometime in the late afternoon. It didn't matter when, as long as he got there before 5:00. He parked the van in a lot on Main Street, locked up, and then took in a movie. Under no circumstances was he to return to the van until 7:15.

Leaving the parking lot, he would drive through Bretton Woods, past the cog railway that went up Mt. Washington, turn onto U.S. 302, and head south toward Hart's Location and Notchland. At no time was he allowed to return to the Interstate, even though it meant taking the long way through the mountains. Below Notchland, he left U.S. 302 and began making his way east, south, and then west, following a complex route of local highways that took him steadily toward Jericho Falls.

The route had been designed to take him through the fewest number of communities, along highways with statistically low levels of traffic. There was a governor on the engine of the Econoline that prevented him from exceeding fifty-five miles per hour, and a bulky device like a taxi meter had been mounted below the dash. The device had more in common with an airplane flight recorder, but the single visible dial was marked in miles and elapsed time, so Arnie knew it was some kind of odometer.

Other than piloting the van from the Bretton Woods parking lot to Jericho Falls, Arnie Redenbacher's only other job was to press a large blue button fitted onto the odometer at thirty-minute intervals, timed from the moment he left the parking lot. To ensure that Arnie did this, a buzzer sounded every half hour. He was also required to press the button if he stopped for fuel, to relieve himself, or if he had mechanical difficulties.

Reaching Jericho Falls, Arnie took the van along Old River Road, then hooked across the Jericho River, briefly following 115A along the Strip to Airport Road on the far side of town. From there he turned south again, driving past Drake's Farm to the small, single-runway airport, where he would park the truck in front of the small, blockhouse office of Coyle Air Services. Entering the offices, he gave his keys to whoever was there, poured himself a cup of coffee, and sat down to wait. Exactly thirty minutes later, the man with his keys would return and Arnie was free to go. Arnie had been making the run for almost two years, and he knew every mile by heart.

Once, after stopping in a gas station to use the toilet, Arnie Redenbacher had been seized by a vague urge to know what it was he was taking from Bretton Woods to the Jericho Falls Airport. He'd tried all the keys on his ring, but none of them had fitted the heavy-duty locks fitted onto the rear and side doors of the truck.

There was a steel panel behind the driver's compartment, sealing the cargo section, and without using a crowbar or a cutting torch there was no way he was going to get in. The relatively limited security precautions were enough to dampen his enthusiasm, and he never thought about it again. If the company wanted to keep the cargo secret, that was their business and none of his.

At 7:08 P.M. on Friday, October 31, Arnie Redenbacher left the Donut King and began walking back to the parking lot, trying to swallow the hot-sick burning in his throat. He stopped and bought a roll of antacid tablets in a drugstore and continued on. At 7:17, he reached the van, unlocked it, and climbed into the cab. He started the engine, pressed the blue button on the odometer box, and began the ninty-seven-mile trip to Jericho Falls. By the time he reached the little town of Hart's Location, barely ten miles out of Bretton Woods, he'd already consumed the entire roll of antacids.

"Fucking lousy coffee," he grumbled, one large hand rubbing his chest.

It was to be his epitaph.

CHAPTER TWO

9:00 P.M.

Jack Slater cruised slowly down Main Street, his peripheral vision picking up each dim-lit storefront and alleyway, his mind wandering easily as he did his rounds. There hadn't been a store break-in for six months, and no one had tried to rob the Jericho Falls Savings and Loan since Marcel LaFramboise, a latter-day Clyde Barrow from Trois Pistoles, Quebec, made an attempt in 1954. LaFramboise had chickened out at the last minute and was caught on Old River Road after slamming his stolen car into a telephone pole.

Crime in Jericho Falls was usually more personal: Dermit Culligan drinking too much and slapping his wife around again; Bob Hartley complaining about Harriet Newcomb's poodle shitting on his lawn; Ralph Beavis calling up from the Slumber-King out on the Strip, reporting some salesman who'd beat him out of a night in one of his rooms.

Slater paused briefly at the bottom of the street, then he turned west onto Overlook. Kids had strung up a large and vaguely obscene banner across the doors of the Episcopal Church, but Slater decided to leave it up for a while. He drove on, skirting the lower edge of the Common, turning up Sherbourne Street and moving north along the border of Frenchtown. He lit a cigarette, dragging the smoke deeply into his lungs, then frowned. Maybe Karen was right; when you got right down to it, not much ever happened in Jericho Falls.

He rolled down the window, letting in a blast of cool night air, and caught a faint whiff of woodsmoke. People were using their fireplaces and woodstoves—a sure sign that winter wasn't too far off. He felt a tug of sentiment. That smell, and the fluttering rustle of the last leaves, always took him back to his childhood, and it made him sad that Karen couldn't have the same good feelings about the town. But times had changed, even if he hadn't. Karen lived in a world underscored by rock videos and the six-o'clock news, and at fifteen she was bewilderingly sophisticated.

Slater shrugged off the thought. Bringing up a teenage girl alone was hard enough without brooding about it. He swung onto Quebec Street, rolling past the high school. He spotted a blur of movement out of the corner of his eye and slowed, but it was only a gaggle of kids cutting across the playing field, accompanied by a parent. Stopping the car beside the baseball diamond, he leaned back against the seat and finished his cigarette. So far there hadn't been any problems, and the radio had been silent except for the regular half-hour check calls. He glanced at his watch, peering at the glowing white figures on the dial. Twenty minutes more and he could head over to the library and pick up Jenny.

He smiled, thinking about her. Trust him to complicate things by getting involved with Jennifer Hale. It was bad enough that she was ten years younger than he was, but on top of that, she was also Karen's homeroom teacher. They'd tried to keep things quiet at first, but, like everything else in the Falls, love affairs didn't remain secret for long. Karen considered the relationship to be the worst kind of treachery, while everyone else in the town was laying bets on when the date was going to be set.

"Horse twaddle," muttered the sheriff, crushing the remains of his cigarette into the ashtray. It had been a long time since he'd felt good about being with a woman, and if Karen didn't like it, that was her tough luck. If his daughter thought being forty meant hanging up his spurs, then she had another think coming. Rolling up the window again, Slater eased the shift into drive and let the car make its own way along the tree-lined park. It was pitch dark now, a sickle moon appearing now and again through the low scudding clouds. A perfect night for ghosties and goblins.

He considered turning on his flashers and letting go with the whooping siren hidden under the hood, but he stopped himself. Forty-year-old police chiefs could just barely get away with dating thirty-year-old teachers, but scaring hell out of the townspeople was going too far, even on Halloween. He turned down Brewer Street, moving past the rows of small frame houses, and began making his way back to the Common.

The usually gloomy attic of the Jericho Falls Public Library was brilliantly lit by half a dozen photofloods on tripods, all of them aimed at a large trestle table in the center of the slope-roofed, dark-raftered room. Piles of dusty ledgers were stacked beneath the low eaves, and there were cobwebs in the corners that dated back to Harry Truman.

Jennifer Hale adjusted the focus on the Nikon and took a shot of Sparrow as he bent over the huge model laid out on the felt-covered attic table. She advanced the film and took another exposure, concentrating on the man's hands. They were large, like the rest of his body, the fingers thick, the nails cracked and horny. A workingman's hands, but moving with a surgeon's deftness as he gently fitted a tiny window into place on the wall of one of the buildings.

"You're supposed to be taking pictures of the model, not me," said the big man, looking up for a moment. The face was like something out of a *Life* magazine spread from the sixties. William McKenzie Hawke, better known as Sparrow to friend and foe alike, was the perfect hippy, still keeping the faith with past-shoulder-length hair, a bushy lumberjack beard, and a faded headband. An aging hippy, Jenny amended. The ginger beard was streaked with gray, the hair on his head was thinning, and the lines and wrinkles on his deeply tanned face were a visible calendar of the passing years.

"It's important to document the model maker as well as the model," she said.

"I really doubt the Smithsonian is going to care," he snorted, placing another window on the main building.

"I just think you're shy. You should be proud of what you've done."

"Umm."

The model was the culmination of a project that Sparrow and his companions at the Mill Co-op had been working on for almost a decade. During the sixties, the area around Jericho Falls had attracted its fair share of back-to-the-land types, but it had taken Sparrow, out-of-work helicopter gunship pilot and sometime carpenter, to bring them all together. Resplendent in full-dress Marine whites, he approached the town council and somehow managed to convince them to lease him the derelict mill property for a dollar a year. The only codicil was that he had to bring the main mill building up to fire and electrical standards within twelve months. Sparrow, aided by more than a score of local craftspeople, had managed it in six months, and after that first meeting, he'd never worn his uniform again.

Sparrow established the Jericho Falls Craft Cooperative as a non-profit corporation with full tax-deductible charitable status; within five years, the Coolis Mill Co-op had become the largest arts and craft center in Northern New Hampshire. The two upper floors of the mill were subdivided and rented out as work and living areas for local artisans, while the main floor was turned into a backwoods version of a shopping mall, complete with health food store, day-care center, holistic health clinic, do-it-yourself bookstore, and a plant shop. A couple of young architects specializing in retrofitting old buildings had moved in, the New Hampshire Tourist Authority had set up shop, and eventually a disillusioned chartered accountant who'd moved up from Boston for his nerves created the Spinners and Weavers Credit Union, which was beginning to give the somewhat less than imaginative Savings and Loan a literal run for its money.

Even Luther Coyle, who'd been against the co-op at the outset, grudgingly admitted that it was an unqualified success. So much so, in fact, that for the last year he'd been quietly seeing what he could do to break the lifetime lease Sparrow and his people had on the property.

With the co-op firmly established, Sparrow had begun to work on his own project. Once upon a time, before lysergic acid, C grades, and the Vietnam War got in the way, Bill Hawke had dreamed of becoming an archaeologist, but not one who dug up the remains of long-dead civilizations in other lands. Bill Hawke was going to be a truly American archaeologist, poking into the dusty corners of his own country's history. The leasing of the Mill Co-op gave him the opportunity he'd always wanted.

He began by reading everything he could about Jericho Falls, haunting the basement of the town hall, poring over records that hadn't been consulted in more than half a century. His research took him back to the establishment of the town in the late 1700s by the Drake family, who built the first mill at Fourth Chute, a tiny village consisting of half a dozen houses, a blacksmith's forge, and an inn called the Eagle.

After researching for more than a year, Sparrow became an authority on early mill construction, and during one winter he built an eighth-scale model of an undershot wheel. Sam Quarrel at the *Leader Post* did a story on the wheel, and eventually someone from *National Geographic* came around. And, as Sam was so fond of saying, the rest was history. *Geographic* ran a photo story, the Smithsonian got into the act, and six months later Sparrow had funding for a full-scale excavation at the original site of the mill. Over the next four summers the mill, carding house, and the remains of the Eagle were uncovered, along with a wealth of early American artifacts, all of it brought about by the enthusiasm of a "bunch of longhairs."

Using the information he'd gathered, Sparrow had begun work on a model of the first Jericho Falls, complete with an operating mill, and now it was almost complete. After a few finishing touches and Jennifer's photographic record, the model was going to be disassembled and sent to the Smithsonian.

"I guess that just about does it," said Sparrow. He stood up, eyeing his creation. He reached into the front pocket of his overalls, pulled out a battered Sherlock Holmes–style pipe, and lit it with a kitchen match. A familiar, pungent odor filled the large attic room of the library, and Jenny wrinkled her nose.

"What kind of tobacco is that?" she asked.

"Pinch of this, pinch of that." Sparrow grinned, taking a deep draw and holding it down. He exhaled noisily and plucked the pipe out of his mouth. "Want some?"

"No thanks. Jack'll be here in a few minutes. High school teachers aren't supposed to do that kind of thing. Especially when they're going out with the sheriff."

"Jack's a good head," said Sparrow. "It's just a bit of homegrown. Nothing serious."

"That's not the point."

"Guess you're right," Sparrow said with a nod. He tamped down the bowl and slid the pipe back into his overalls. He smiled at Jenny. Tall, ash blond, with a master's degree in history and a teaching certificate to boot, but she'd never once condescended to him about his qualifications to lead the Mill project. Helpful hints once in a while, especially about proper documentation, but no more. Jack was a lucky man.

"How are you two getting along?" he asked. "Any more flack from Karen?" Jack Slater's daughter had worked on the dig during the summer, and Sparrow had gotten to know her quite well. Smart, pretty, and stubborn. A tough combination.

"She plays the little angel in class, but every now and again I get these hot looks from her. She doesn't approve. She's petrified that Jack's going to propose and I'll be her stepmother as well as her homeroom teacher."

"Any chance of that?"

"What? Jack proposing?" Jenny shrugged. "I don't know. I haven't given it much thought, really." She and Karen's father had been seeing each other for almost a year, but it was only in the past few months that things had started getting serious. For serious read sexual, she thought. She would have jumped into the police chief's bed after the second date, but he hadn't made a move. In the end, she'd enticed him with oysters in white wine sauce, half a bottle of Jack Daniel's, and a few well-placed spritzes of Chanel.

The result had surpassed her wildest dreams. Jack Slater was a kind, considerate, and very, very proficient bedmate. A dozen years of lackluster lovemaking went by the board. She might not wind up marrying him, but Jack had set a new industry standard as far as she was concerned. In Jack Slater's bed, Quality was Job One.

"Like the cliché-maker said, you better strike while the iron is hot, lady," Sparrow offered. He leaned down and adjusted the covered bridge that spanned the poured acrylic model of the Jericho River.

"What's that supposed to mean?"

"Nothing much." Sparrow shrugged, stepping back and squinting down at the model again. "But I can read the signs."

"What signs?"

"Bit of an itch. I've got it myself now that this is all over." He waved a large hand over the model. "Xenia calls."

"What's a Xenia?"

"Xenia, Ohio. My hometown," explained the big man. He raked at his beard with his thick, splayed fingers. "Kind of like the Falls, only bigger. I've had a dozen New Hampshire winters ma'am, and I think the next one's going to be my last.''

"We'll miss you," Jenny said, meaning it. Sparrow was exactly the kind of man she'd always wanted as a brother.

"Some will." Sparrow nodded. "Some won't. Luther Coyle's been nosing around, sniffing money. And the Mill people have always been . . . a little bit apart from the other people in the Falls.''

"Oh, come on now," Jenny scoffed. "This isn't 1968. You've been accepted here.''

"Sure," drawled Sparrow. "Like the Jews in Warsaw."

"You're imagining things," Jenny said, shaking her head.

"Maybe. But it's as good an excuse as any other."

"So you'll go home?"

"For a while. Maybe cut my hair and become a businessman, develop a chain of doper's cafés. 'Seeds and Stems,' what do you think?'' There was a twinkle in his eye.

"I think you're pulling my leg," Jenny answered, "and I still don't know what it has to do with Jack. Jericho Falls is where he was born.''

"And he's got a daughter who's hot to see if the moon is made of green cheese."

"So let her find out on her own," Jenny said. "Another few years and she'll be away at university.''

"Maybe. But Karen is Jack's excuse, just like me telling myself I could never really be a part of the community here. He and Karen are peas in a pod, Jenny, that's why they fight so much. They both need challenges, and neither one is getting them here. Crime in Jericho Falls is not leaving a big enough tip for Chang at the Bo-Peep.''

"He doesn't have to be a cop for the rest of his life."

"Sure he does, if he stays in Jericho Falls," said Sparrow. "What else is he going to do? Run for mayor against Luther Coyle and his Normal Majority?''

"That's not such a bad idea."

"Give me a break, lady. The day Jack Slater turns into a politician, I'll take up golf and start drinking cocktails with little umbrellas in them.''

They heard the sound of footsteps on the stairs behind them

and turned to see who had made the long trip up to the attic. Jack appeared, uniform cap in hand and his battered old bomber jacket unzipped. Belle MacCracken, the eighty-six-year-old librarian, turned on the heat at the first sign of cold weather, and during the fall and winter the library was uncomfortably hot for anyone under the age of seventy.

"Thought I might catch the two of you in the act," Slater said with a grin, crossing the attic to the table. "You and Paul Bunyan here spend so much time together that I'm beginning to wonder."

Jenny smiled. Jack was the least jealous man she'd ever met, unlike her ex-husband, and the last year had been a joy. She looked fondly at him, still mildly surprised that they were together. The loden green uniform suited his dark features and curly black hair, but she still hadn't been able to get him to give up the jacket. It dated back to his days in the service and you could still make out his name stenciled over the right breast pocket. Karen had roughly sewn Jericho Falls Police Department crests on both shoulders, but the jacket still looked like something from a Salvation Army thrift store.

"Is that an illegal substance I smell?" asked Jack, sniffing in Sparrow's direction. The big man grinned broadly.

"Hell no," he said. "Just my after-shave."

"You haven't shaved since 1964," Slater said. His expression changed. "If Luther or any of his friends on the Hill knew you were smoking pot, we'd all be in a lot of trouble, you know. The Co-op would be finished."

"The Mill's clean, Jack, you know that," said Sparrow. "I'm not a complete idiot."

"Neither is Luther," said Jack. "So be careful."

"Point taken. I'll be cool."

Slater looked down at the model, obviously impressed. Topologically as well as technically correct, it showed every dip and hollow in the terrain. Drake's Farm was there, complete with the swimming hole, and so were all four of the whitewater cascades along the winding course of the Jericho River. The top edge of the model showed the darkly wooded hills north of the present town, and modern buildings were painted plain white, indicating growth over the years. Sparrow, long-haired and rough-hewn, had created a masterpiece.

"Town's come a long way in a hundred and fifty years," Slater commented.

"Population of ninety-six in 1830," Sparrow said. "And most of those were itinerant workers from downstate. The Drake family owned all the land from Notch Road to Mountain Creek and from the river to the hills."

"And Zachariah Coolis bought the mill site for six dollars," put in Jenny.

"Luther Coyle's patron saint, I'll bet," laughed Slater.

"Not a chance," Sparrow said. "Old Zachariah was an early abolitionist, one of the first mill owners to stop making 'Negro cloth,' even though it was really profitable. He also took good care of his workers. Even had a pension plan for them, and a doctor. Doesn't sound like Luther's type at all. Zachariah Coolis wanted to build a community, Luther wants to own one."

"I think you're being a bit hard on him," Slater said. "Luther may not have the sweetest personality in town, but he's done a lot of good for the Falls. This place was on its last legs before he convinced them to build the Medical Center here."

"And how did he manage to do that? I was here when that whole scam went down. Luther's got Dave Doyle in his back pocket, and Dave is an old school friend of Barrett O'Neill. You know as well as I do that the Medical Center was slated for Plymouth, but all of a sudden it comes here. Dave Doyle gets a pat on the back, and all of a sudden Luther's got a lock on things. He has the ambulance business, the air ambulance business, Coyle Cleaners does all the linen, Coyle Construction puts up the building, and Coyle Business Systems furnishes the place, then leases them all their office equipment, while Coyle Maintenance cleans up the mess. Real pork-barrel politics."

"That's how it works in a small town," Jenny said.

"It stinks."

"If you don't like it, go talk to Sam Quarrel at the *Leader Post*. Write an editorial," Slater suggested. Sparrow let out a long, rumbling laugh.

"Are you serious?" he said after a moment. "Who do you think owns the building the *Post* is in, and who do you think owns a 40 percent share in the *Leader Post Press?* Sam's not about to cut his own throat."

"Why are we standing around in an old attic talking politics?"

Jenny interrupted. She stepped forward and put her arm through Slater's. "There's a party going on, remember?" She turned to Sparrow. "Coming?"

"Uh-uh," he answered, shaking his head. "Too uptown for me. I'm going to stick around here for a while and finish up. The kids at the Mill are having a bash. Maybe I'll drop in there."

"Tom Dorchester's cruising the other side of the river tonight," Slater warned. "Anything to worry about?"

"Not unless late corn and bobbing for apples has been made a crime. But thanks for the word."

"No problem," Slater said, smiling at the big man. He and Jenny turned away and went down the stairs, leaving Sparrow alone in the attic. The bearded man looked down at the model and shook his head. The cornfields around Drake's Farm had been replaced by the paved streets and run-down houses of Frenchtown; the meadows on the far side of Mountain Creek sprouted the split-level houses of the Hill; and the Fourth Chute bridge was a steel arch span, not timber and cedar shingle.

"Things change," Sparrow whispered. "Nothing stays the same forever."

Karen Slater lay in semidarkness, watching as Billy Coyle's hand rummaged around underneath her sweater like some kind of small burrowing animal. She shifted slightly on the couch, giving him more room, noting that her bra was now crammed up around her right shoulder. There was a small popping sound as Billy's other hand undid the clasp of her jeans and a few seconds later she felt his cool fingers drifting over the soft patch of her pubic hair. She tensed for a second and then relaxed as the fingers dropped lower into the warm dampness between her legs. She closed her eyes, willing the sensation to come the way it did when she touched herself, but Billy was being too rough, poking instead of stroking, as though his hand were involved in some kind of race against time.

She moved again, eyes still closed, and Billy pulled up her sweater, his mouth coming down on the nipple of her right breast. That was better, and it was something she couldn't do herself. She wove her own fingers into Billy's hair, bringing his head down firmly, and opened her eyes. Billy moved to the other side of her chest and she saw her watch: 9:30. The Frasers would be home from the party any minute.

"My turn," she whispered into Billy's ear. She rolled slightly, moving herself to the outside of the couch, and then sat up, straddling the young man beneath her. She reached down, feeling the taut stretch of his denim-covered groin, and smiled to herself. It wouldn't take long at all.

She eased back until she was lying between his legs, then she deftly undid Billy's jeans and carefully pulled down the zipper. He shuddered slightly, and she smiled again, running her tongue over the nickel-plated braces covering her teeth. Cold steel for Billy. Hooking down his Jockeys, she freed the young man's rigid organ, almost laughing as it sprung up toward his belly, the swollen tip gleaming like a polished crabapple. She took a breath, then slipped it into her mouth, gripping the shaft lightly with one hand. Billy jerked, and she felt his thighs tighten under her elbows. She let her tongue dart into the small hole, tasting the first salt tang, and then she began to move her mouth up and down in a gentle rhythm, speeding up as she felt Billy's hips start to move.

It was all over in less than a minute. She swallowed it this time, since there was nothing to clean up with close at hand. Billy let out a single, low-pitched groan, and then he relaxed. Karen sat up between his legs and cleared her throat, trying to get the clotted feeling out of her tonsils. She wondered if the great Miss Jennifer Hale swallowed it. Or did it at all, for that matter. Probably not.

"Feel better?" Karen asked as Billy's eyes fluttered open.

"You make it sound as though I was sick or something."

"I didn't mean it that way."

"What about you?" asked Billy, pushing himself up and snapping his jeans closed.

"It was nice. I like being close, even if we can't go all the way."

"I'm sorry about not getting the safes."

"Don't worry about it." Karen shrugged, then reached up under her sweater and shifted her bra into place again, doing up the front clasp. "It's not the end of the world."

"It makes me feel like such a teenager," he grumbled. Karen laughed, sitting back against the couch and flipping her hair into place.

"You *are* a teenager. I told you, don't worry about it." She looked down, located her shoes, and slid her feet into them. "I just thought of something," she said, frowning. "That time we did it, when my dad was out of town. How long ago was that?"

"A couple of weeks ago. Just before we had that environmental studies quiz. Why?"

"Because I should be getting my period."

"Today? How can you be so sure?" There was a trace of nervousness in the young man's face, and Karen saw something she'd never seen before—an arrogant, hard set to Billy's jaw that reminded her of his father.

"I'm not exactly sure. But I usually feel something a few days beforehand, and there's nothing."

"Nerves," said Billy. He stood up and zipped his fly with a quick movement. She could still feel him, like raw egg in the back of her throat, and he was ready to run.

"Sure. Nerves." She nodded.

"Look, I better get out of here before the Frasers get back. See you at Marty's?"

"Okay." The last place she wanted to go was Martin Doyle's place on the Hill. She wanted to go home and check her diary and the special calendar she'd drawn up in it.

Billy leaned over and kissed her on the cheek. "Love ya, kid," he whispered. He squeezed her shoulder and then walked out of the room. A few seconds later, she heard the front door of the house close.

"Love you too, Billy," she muttered.

Shortly after being drafted, and six months before finding his niche in the Seoul motor pool, Arnie Redenbacher was given an intelligence test. Arnie scored ninety-nine, putting him in that most dangerous of categories, low average. He was smart enough to lose out on the various benefits available for people who could be classified as retarded, but he was too stupid to understand just how dumb he really was. Even so, by the time Arnie reached South Tamworth at the base of the Ossipee Mountains, he knew he was sick. He was sweating buckets, his acid indigestion had turned into a killing case of heartburn and every now and again his vision was blurring.

Anyone with an IQ ten points higher would have gone looking

for a doctor, or at the very least pulled off to the side of the road, but Arnie kept right on going. A doctor would cost money, and stopping the van or deviating from his regular route might cost him his job. Without a job he'd have no money for booze and broads—a simple equation built on the kind of logic that usually keeps the Arnie Redenbachers of the world out of positions of power. In this case, the logic was fatally flawed.

Gritting his teeth and swabbing the perspiration out of his eyes with a wadded-up Kleenex, Arnie piloted the van through the I-93 underpass, skirted Plymouth on the 3A bypass, and pushed north on 118, heading for Rumney Depot and Jericho Falls, the dark mass of the White Mountain National Forest half a mile away to his right. Fighting the growing pain, Arnie concentrated on the tunnel of light thrown by his headlights, forcing his arms to adjust the wheel, keeping the hypnotic ribbon of the dotted line on his left, blinking painfully and cursing every time another vehicle swept glaringly by, going in the opposite direction.

At 9:40, his numbed brain working on automatic, Arnie swung off 118 onto 115A, Old River Road, leading into Jericho Falls. He could feel the thunder of his own heart pounding in his ears now, and every few seconds a lancing pain would shoot up his left arm and into his shoulder. His legs felt like lead, and he had no sensation of his foot on the accelerator, but the governor on the engine kept him from going over fifty-five. It was getting hard to swallow now, and the blurred vision was constant, all classic symptoms of an impending heart attack. But Arnie was too stupid to realize that he was already dead, a demi-corpse at the wheel of a three-ton coffin speeding through the Halloween night.

At exactly 9:45, Arnie's body decided that the game had gone on long enough. A tiny blood vessel, shaped like a milkweed pod and swollen like a kid's balloon filled with water, exploded in the middle of Arnie Redenbacher's brain. For a split second Arnie was confused, wondering how someone had managed to let off a hand grenade in his head, and then he dropped dead. The van kept on going for another hundred yards, slowing down slightly as Arnie's foot came off the gas, and then the dead man slumped sideways, one arm hooked into the wheel, dragging it around. The van went off the road, hammered into the ditch, and then curved back up onto the road. It veered, spun, and then slid into the opposite ditch, the right-side panel slamming hard into the trunk of a gnarled elm. The engine coughed once and then died, just like Arnie. Fifteen minutes later Tom Dorchester appeared on the scene, called the accident in, and then climbed out of his car to investigate. QQ9 was about to claim its first victim.

CHAPTER THREE

9:30 P.M

Tom Dorchester climbed out of the cruiser and hitched his belt up over the broad swell of his belly. He was pissed off, and the wreck in the ditch, ticking quietly as it cooled, wasn't helping any. He'd intended to take a fast run down to the 118 bypass, finish off the six-pack he had in the trunk, and then catch a quick nap. Rousting the fags at the Mill and coming up empty-handed had put him in a bad mood, and the last thing he needed was some asshole who'd fallen asleep at the wheel and driven off the road. Dealing with the van would take him at least an hour, and Slater was a killer for filling out reports. The night was shot to hell.

The big, slab-faced man approached the wreck carefully, his thick, rubbery nose testing the air for the slightest trace of gasoline fumes. There was nothing. Cool night air, a trace of leaf mold from the thick screen of trees on both sides of the road. It was quiet except for the dull throb of the cruiser's idling engine and the distant whisper of the river. Dark too, the moon and stars hidden by low, ragged clouds.

He unhooked the heavy flashlight from his belt, switched it on, and swung the beam around. From the looks of things, the driver had gone from one ditch to the other, decreasing his speed before he slammed into the tree. The stupid shit-eater was probably still alive.

Dorchester moved forward, still cautious, his boots crunching on the gravel shoulder. One of the van's headlights had smashed, and the other had popped half out of its socket, pointing up into

34

the night like a single unblinking eye, light fading as the battery died.

He swore under his breath and eased his bulk down into the ditch, moving toward the driver's side of the van. He poked the flashlight in through the shattered window. The driver was slumped across the seat, motionless. Twenty years a cop removed any doubt. The poor fucker was dead, you could always tell. They looked like bundles of dirty laundry.

Dorchester frowned, swinging the flashlight beam across the tilted passenger compartment. No blood anywhere, and what was the weird box under the dash? He reached his other arm in through the window, grunting as he groped for the ignition. He turned the key and the dimming eye of the headlight vanished.

The policeman stepped back and swept the outside of the van with his flashlight. No markings at all. The side door had sprung, but it was squeezed tight by a stump. Except for that and a few dents and scratches, there wasn't too much damage. He knew he should have been checking the driver out more carefully, but he was more interested in the truck. Normal procedure said that any vehicle involved in a fatal accident had to be impounded. Since there was no real auto pound in the Falls, that meant taking it to the Beavis Gas Bar and Garage on the Strip. Dorchester knew three or four guys with vans who might be able to use parts.

He went around to the rear of the truck and checked the license plate: New Hampshire commercial. The dealer decal said Mooney's GM, Manchester. The policeman's frown deepened. Unmarked, commercial, heading northwest on a secondary highway a long way from home and late on a Friday night. It smelled. Cigarette runner on his way to the border? That'd sure be a prize. He could unload fifty or a hundred cartons through his connections without any trouble, and with the guy at the wheel dead, who was going to tell?

He aimed the light at the rear doors. They were solid, but that was no sweat. He clambered up out of the ditch and went back to the cruiser. He popped the trunk, found the tire iron, and went back to the van. Checking his watch, he swore again. It was going to be tight. He'd called the accident in five minutes ago and Lombard would be right on the ball. The tow truck would be here in quarter of an hour, tops.

Dorchester slid down into the ditch again, hooked the flashlight

back onto his belt, and got down to work. He slid the chisel end
of the tire iron in between the doors, jammed one foot against the
bumper, and put all his weight onto it. There was a snapping
sound, and the lock let go. He almost fell, but he regained his
balance and took out the flashlight again. Breathing hard, he
grabbed one of the doors and pulled, swinging it open, the ruptured lock mechanism grinding. Hanging on to the door for le-
verage, he hauled himself up into the body of the van.

The stiff up front hadn't been jacking cigarettes, Dorchester
saw that right off. The van was empty except for three medium-
sized containers that looked like the kind of ice chests you took
on a picnic. Well, the driver hadn't been going on any picnics in
the middle of the night, either. Hunching down, the big man
shifted forward.

Lined up in a row about two feet back from the bulkhead
separating the body from the passenger compartment, the chests
were fitted into custom-built wells in the floor of the van and
strapped in with rubber. Someone had gone to a lot of trouble.
Squatting down, Dorchester examined the chests carefully. Plastic, or plastic-coated, and unmarked, just like the van. All three
were fitted with heavy-duty hasps and padlocks, and each of the
locks was threaded through with a wire and lead seal. Open the
lock and you broke the seal. He checked the seals. Nothing official, just a string of letters and numbers.

Dorchester sat back on his heels, thinking hard. Smart money
said leave well enough alone. Cigarettes would have been quick
and easy, but this was something else again. On the other hand,
you didn't go to all this trouble for nothing, which meant that
whatever the chests contained was probably valuable.

"Ah, what the fuck." The guy was dead, the van was a wreck,
and no one was going to complain if it got wrecked a little more.
Using the tire iron again, Dorchester ripped the hasp and lock off
the middle chest, then pried back the lid. He put down the tire
iron and poked the beam of the flashlight inside.

"Huh?"

The stupid bastard had been hauling thermos bottles. Big ones
made out of stainless steel. There were eight of them in the chest,
each one fitted into a hole in a slab of foam rubber. He slid one
up out of its nest and looked at it. Nothing to say what was inside,
just another string of numbers, like on the lead seals.

He stuck the flashlight under his arm and tugged at the top of the bottle, unscrewing it. Inside the bottle there was another insert of foam rubber and what appeared to be a second metal container, about the size of an old-fashioned seven-ounce Coke bottle. Dorchester made a small sound of annoyance. It was like those Ukrainian dolls that kept on getting smaller. He slid the smaller flask out and looked at it. Another string of numbers and a thin seam in the metal about a third of the way down. Putting the two pieces of the big container on the floor of the van, he wrapped his hands around the smaller flask and twisted. It opened easily, revealing its contents. There, nestled snugly in a bed of ordinary cotton wool, was an egg. Grade A Large by the look of it.

"Christ on a fucking crutch!" snorted Dorchester, disgusted. All that effort for a goddamn egg. Using two fingers, he picked the egg up from its bed of cotton. The guy up front was a lunatic, running around the countryside with crates of eggs all bundled up like they were the fucking Crown Jewels of England. Furious, the policeman threw the fragile orb against the inside wall of the van. The shell broke wetly and a gluey mixture of yolk and white splattered everywhere. Dorchester wrinkled his nose and then sneezed hard. On top of everything else, it smelled like the things were rotten.

"Shit!" Sneezing again, Dorchester backed out of the van, eyes watering at the foul odor. What a goddamn joke! Not only was the night screwed beyond redemption, but now his uniform smelled of rotten egg. He dropped down to the ground and slammed the door shut. His eyes were still watering from the stink, and his nose was running. He wiped it on the sleeve of his jacket and backed away from the van.

Grumbling, trying to wipe away the thin stream of snot coming from his nostrils, Dorchester went back to the cruiser, climbed in and lit one of his little cigars, trying to banish the smell he'd inadvertently brought on himself. He called in to Lombard again, requesting an ambulance as well as the tow truck. Lombard started asking questions about the driver's condition, but Dorchester snapped the radio off angrily. He sneezed again and sat back against his seat. The meat wagon boys from the Medical Center could handle it from here on, because he sure as hell wasn't going near the van again. He sneezed a third time and sniffed, trying to suck the watery mucus back into his nose.

"Christ! What a fucking night!"

The interior of Stark Hall was filled to overflowing, two-thirds of the occupants in costume and the rest in their Sunday best. An apple-bobbing contest was going on in one corner of the big, high-ceilinged room; another group was dancing to Alf Wannamaker's Allstate Insurance Trio; and a trailing line of partygoers was winding past the stage, loading up paper plates from the buffet.

Paulette Doyle and the other Auxiliary ladies had outdone themselves with the decorations and lighting. The big overhead chandeliers had been turned off, and dozens of orange plastic Chinese lanterns threw an appropriately jaundiced glow over everyone at the party. Orange and black crepe paper had been festooned from the upper gallery rails; the walls were plastered with construction paper witches, ghosts, and jack-o'-lanterns; and every one of the tables scattered around the room had its own Styrofoam and toothpick centerpiece. With variations, it was exactly the same kind of decoration that Paulette and the "girls" created for Easter, the Fourth of July, the August Heritage Days Festival, and Christmas.

The noise level was about the same too: two decibels below chaos, the oozing, stumbling strains of the Allstate Trio trying to squeeze "String of Pearls" out of a snare, a tenor sax, and an electric organ, mixing with laughter and too-loud conversation greased by the gigantic bowl of pink-champagne punch donated by Luther Coyle on behalf of the town council. The pink was food coloring, the champagne was carbonated white-wine spritzer, and the punch came from three gallons of the base alcohol Fern Addison used in place of vodka for his mixed drinks at the Empire Hotel bar.

"This kind of thing gives me a headache," said Jack Slater. He and Jenny had found a table nearly hidden under the jutting overhang created by the upper gallery of the hall, out of the way of the milling crowd. He stared at the Styrofoam ball witch in the middle of the small card table and ignored the plastic tumbler of punch between his hands.

"How can you have a headache? You haven't had anything to drink," said Jenny.

"I should be at work."

"You should be trying to have fun," Jenny chided. "How about dancing?"

"Forget it." He reached below the table and found her hand. "And, anyway, I can think of much better things we could do together."

"Later. Right now you're making an appearance as the Jericho Falls police chief. By rights, we should be mingling."

"Luther can mingle for both of us."

Standing just in front of the buffet lineup, Luther Coyle was posed like a sovereign receiving homage from all his subjects. Fifty-seven years old, his once-blond hair gone nicotine white, Luther was dressed in a three-piece suit complete with fob and chain across an affluent belly. Like a lot of men gone to fat in middle age, Luther's face was still thin, at odds with the rest of his body. The eyes were large and deep-set enough for his brows to cast shadows, his nose thin, matching the narrow line of his mouth. Every time someone approached to shake his hand, the mouth would snap into a quick efficient smile, cutting off after a few seconds as though the man were trying to conserve his good humor.

"He looks like something out of *Citizen Kane,*" Jenny said.

"He's playing the part well enough," agreed Slater. "He stands in the middle of the room until all the attention is on him, and then he goes into his humble routine. That's how he got to be mayor."

"How did he get rich?" Jenny asked. "Is Sparrow right about him?" Jenny had only been in the Falls for three years; Slater had grown up with Luther playing Godfather.

"He was born rich. A little rich, anyway. His father was an accountant for the mill and dabbled in real estate. When the mill closed down, Luther's old man held paper on half the houses in Frenchtown. Luther just took it from there. He's not so bad, really. There are ten thousand Luther Coyles in this country, and towns like the Falls would be dead without them. A shrewd son of a bitch, but he's got the best interests of the town at the root of it all."

"Utter nonsense," said a gruff voice. Both Slater and Jenny looked up, surprised. Rembrandt Payne, director of the Medical Center, eased his bulk down into one of the folding chairs at their table. He was an impressive figure: 280 pounds of beef wrapped up in a tweed suit from a 1940 Sears Roebuck catalogue and topped by a jowled, leonine head, complete with a bushy ruff of pure white hair. "I heard every word of that, young man, and it is hyperbole, all of it."

"Hi, Doc. Enjoying yourself?" Slater smiled fondly at the old man. Rembrandt Payne had been everyone's doctor in the Falls for half a century, and he held no favorites. He'd make a house call to a Frenchtown rooming house as easily as to one of the big houses on the Hill.

"Quit trying to change the subject, lad," Payne snapped. "You're whitewashing Luther. Tantamount to saying that Bengal Plague is no worse than a head cold."

"Bengal Plague?" asked Jenny.

"Cholera," Payne explained.

"You've never treated a case of cholera in your life!" laughed Slater. "You're old, Doc, but you're not ancient."

"Treated an outbreak of cholera at the mill in 1932. Fellow named Singh. Jumped ship in Boston and found his way up here. Could have been bad."

"That's fascinating," Jenny said.

"That's bullshit," Slater said, smiling broadly.

"And so is saying that Luther Coyle has the best interests of the town at heart," snorted the doctor. "He's a slick, avaricious little snot, just like his father before him. If I hadn't press-ganged young Doyle and the other members of the council into making me head of the Center, you'd have seen meters in the operating rooms. He's still angry about my establishing an outpatient clinic for the old folks in the area. Medicaid cases aren't profitable, you see."

"You're just angry that he won the election," Slater said, amused.

"He only beat me by two hundred votes. And I still think there should have been a recount."

"Well, at least you were the sentimental favorite," Slater said.

"Crapple," muttered the old man, settling even more deeply into the chair. "Taught me a lesson, though. No good having your finger on the pulse of the town when Luther has his on its testicles, if you'll pardon the expression, Miss Hale." The doctor frowned at the glass of punch in front of Slater. "You're not actually drinking that concoction are you?"

"No."

"Good. Play hell with your blood sugar." Payne shot Jenny a corkscrew glance from beneath his outrageously bushy eyebrows. "You're watching his diet for him?"

"He watches himself pretty well, but I keep an eye on him," she said with a smile. The old man was genuinely concerned. "He still cheats a bit with Chang's french fries."

"Umm," Payne grunted. "I'll have to speak with the little heathen tomorrow." He stroked his own tweedy belly thoughtfully. "God knows, though, he can do things with a potato I never imagined. Even smelling the damned things can harden your arteries." He paused, squinting over Jenny Hale's shoulder toward the back of the hall. "I do believe trouble's on the way, Sheriff Slater, if the expression on Norman's face means anything."

Slater turned in his chair, frowning. "What the hell is he doing here? He's supposed to be on the radio."

Norm Lombard threaded his way between the tables, tight-lipped and obviously anxious. He reached the table, breathing hard.

"Sorry to bother you, Sheriff, but we've got a problem," he said quietly.

"Bad enough for you to leave the station?"

The policeman nodded, and Slater tensed at once. Norm Lombard was the last person in the world to overstate a case.

"What is it?"

"Dorchester called in an accident about twenty-five minutes ago. A van had gone off the road. About three miles out of town on Old River Road."

"Go on."

"I radioed Bert at the Gas Bar and told him to get out the tow truck. About six or seven minutes later Dorchester radioed that the driver of the van was dead and that I should get an ambulance out there as well."

"It was a single-vehicle thing? Nobody else involved?"

"Dorchester didn't say. I think it was just the van, though. Anyway, I called the Medical Center, and they sent out an ambulance. I just got off the radio with their driver. They found the van, and Dorchester was right. He was dead. Trouble is, so was Tom."

"What!"

"That's right. Sitting in his car."

"Heart attack," put in Rembrandt Payne. "Tom Dorchester was walking on thin ice with that weight and the booze he was taking in."

"Maybe," Lombard said. "But I don't think so. The ambulance driver said there was blood everywhere. Weird thing is, they couldn't find any wound."

"What's happening now?" asked Slater.

"Corky White is bringing the van to the Gas Bar, the ambulance is bringing the driver and Tom to the Medical Center. Corky said he'd make a second trip and come back for the cruiser."

"Okay. I saw Zeke Torrance and Randy Van Heusen around here somewhere. Find them, get them back into uniform. And phone Lisa. I want her back on the radio."

"What about me?"

"Get the kit and head out to the scene. Tell Corky to leave the cruiser where it is for now."

"What about you?"

"I'm going to the Center to see Dorchester and the driver of the van. Doc?"

"Certainly, lad." The old man nodded. Payne was listed on the AMA rolls as a general practitioner, but he'd been doing autopsies for Kancamagus County for thirty years.

Slater looked over at Jenny. "Sorry to break this up, but—"

"Forget it," she said. "I can find my own way home. Will I see you?"

"Later. I promise."

"Okay. I'm sorry about Tom Dorchester."

"Yeah," Slater said, rising from his chair. "So am I." He turned to Norm Lombard again. "One more thing. Tell Corky to seal the van tight. I don't want anyone but him touching it. Got that?"

"Sure."

"Good. Come on, Doc, we've got work to do." He walked away from the table quickly, Rembrandt Payne following. Norm Lombard tipped his cap to Jenny and then went looking for the two off-duty policemen, leaving her alone at the table.

Neither she nor any of the others noticed that on the far side of the hall, Luther Coyle was watching them curiously. As Slater and Payne disappeared, the dark-eyed man turned and whispered quietly to one of his aides. After shaking a few more hands, Luther excused himself politely, and then he too disappeared. Alf Wannamaker and the other two members of the Allstate Trio finally wound up "String of Pearls," and without a pause they segued into a ballroom version of "Feelings." No one in the room paid them the slightest attention. The Halloween party at Stark Hall continued unabated.

The Hill, once the upland pastures of Drake's Farm, was made up of ten sloping blocks between Van Epp Street to the south and Pineglade Drive and Old Creek Park to the north. Its western boundary was the narrow, willow-lined course of Mountain Creek, while the eastern boundary was formed by the grounds of the Medical Center and the town limits, where Van Epp Street became New Hampshire Highway 107. Beyond Old Creek Park there was nothing but the first dark spines of the White Mountain foothills, while below the arbitrary line of Van Epp, the Hill became the somewhat less prestigious neighborhood of River Park.

River Park had been an established community in Jericho Falls since the late 1800s, but the Hill was almost entirely a creation of Luther Coyle. His father had purchased the land in the twenties as a potential garbage dump site, but the closing of the Coolis Mill in the mid-thirties had effectively stopped growth in the town.

During the late sixties, as New Hampshire's no-income-tax system became more attractive to light industry, several small but affluent firms, all involved in electronic development, moved to the area, settling in a small industrial park along Notch Road on the eastern edge of town. Overnight, the Hill dump site became valuable, and Luther began building custom homes for the influx of high-rolling executives. The area, formally called Crestview Heights, was cut with streets, each named after a different tree. A piece of land was set aside at the creek end of Van Epp Street for tennis courts, and another larger area to the east was reserved for a school. The school had never been built, but the land was eventually used for the Medical Center. From the beginning, the Hill had been enormously profitable for Luther, and by the mid-seventies, a house on Aspenfall, Larchwood, Sprucehaven, or Willowtree was the mark of someone who had arrived, no matter how much the mortgage payments strained the new arrival's budget. Luther's town house, a huge, out-of-scale split-level with an indoor pool backing onto the meadows of Old Creek Park, was the largest and highest on the Hill. Dave Doyle's house, three doors down on Pineglade Drive, was almost as large, although not quite as elevated, which was only fitting, considering their relative positions.

"Of course, there aren't any pines at all."

"Pardon?" said Karen Slater, turning away from the big, plate-glass French doors and the leaf-strewn surface of Marty Doyle's pool.

"There aren't any pines on Pineglade Drive. It's almost all spruces, and there's no glade, either."

Bentley Carver Bingham was standing just behind her in the darkened Doyle living room. Below her feet, Karen could hear the steady thumping bass and syncopated caterwauling of one of Marty's Iron Maiden albums. As usual, Bentley was involved in one of his well-known semiconversations. Bentley would start a train of thought somewhere deep in that dome-shaped head of his, develop it, and then out of the blue he'd begin talking. Bentley Carver Bingham—commonly known as B.C. Bingham, Bug, or Shrimp—was shorter than average, had his clothes chosen for him by his mother from the preteen rack at Woolworth's, and wore glasses and lace-up Savage shoes. Not surprisingly, he was the class nerd, even though everyone wanted to crib his notes, especially in math and science. Nerd or not, B.C. was also the class brain.

"What are you talking about, Bentley?"

"I was just thinking about the street names on the Hill. None of them fit. There aren't any larch, beech, or butternuts within fifty miles of the Falls. And did you ever notice they don't have anything called a street? Drives, Crescents, Lanes, and Avenues, but no Streets."

"You're weird, Bentley."

"Yeah. That's what everyone says, even my parents. It comes from having no identifiable peer group to relate to. I skipped two grades, so I'm younger than everyone else, and the kids my own age are still playing with Tonka trucks. I think maybe there's a hormone imbalance, too. Thirteen years old and no sign of puberty anywhere."

"Is there something you wanted, Bentley?" she asked. "I came up here to be by myself."

"What? Oh, yeah. Billy sent me to look for you."

"Why didn't he come himself?" Karen asked.

"He and some of the E. A. Coolis Heroes Society are hatching a plan to make Halloween memorable this year."

"Really."

"Something to do with Bodo and the Gas Bar. Marty's got some leftover fireworks his old man saved from the Fourth of July, and Wally Corcoran is going to dress up like the Headless Horseman."

"Billy's in on this?"

"He's the only one with his own car. The getaway vehicle."

"Shit."

"Yeah, that about sums it up."

Karen took a long breath and let it out slowly. All in all, it had been a pretty lousy day. Billy and his friends taunting poor old Bodo was the last straw. She'd go home, make herself a gigantic bowl of popcorn, and watch Jamie Lee Curtis getting attacked by what's-his-name with the butcher knife.

"You go tell Billy and the others you couldn't find me," she said. Downstairs, the music had changed. Bruce Springsteen. She could feel the floor vibrating. They were dancing. Give it twenty minutes and they'd be into something slower and then every available corner of the rec room would be taken over by kids necking.

"If you go downstairs to get your jacket they'll see you," Bentley said.

"You're right." She frowned. The last thing she wanted now was a confrontation with Billy. The words *I'm pregnant* went on and off in her mind like a neon sign.

"You go out the front door, and I'll get it for you," Bentley offered. "I'll meet you outside."

"Thanks, B.C.; you're a lifesaver," she said, relieved. The boy shrugged.

"I was thinking of leaving myself." He flushed so rapidly that Karen could almost feel the heat of his blush on her face. "Maybe we could walk together. It's on the way for me."

"Sure," Karen said, putting on her best smile. "That would be nice."

Walking down the hill along Aspenfall Drive, the two young people could see most of Jericho Falls laid out below them. Lights still twinkled in Frenchtown, its dark center marking the large, rectangular park containing the high school and Jericho Junior. Beyond it, the Strip blinked on and off, and even farther south they could see the winding line of the Jericho River. It was past ten now, and the streets were empty. Halloween was almost over for another year.

"Pretty," Bentley commented. He was walking close enough to Karen so that his arm brushed hers every few seconds, and she could feel him desperately wanting to hold her hand. She kept them both deep in the pockets of her ski jacket. She was angry with Billy, but holding hands with B.C. Bingham was taking it too far.

"Cold," she replied. The wind rustling through the trees was coming out of the dark north, from the sea of shadowed mountains behind them, and she shivered. The thought of a tiny alien life growing molecule by molecule in that secret place below her belly was more frightening than anything she'd ever thought about, and for the first time in her life she had a real understanding of what the word *lonely* meant.

" 'Turn up the lights, I don't want to go home in the dark.' "

"What?"

"O. Henry's dying words," B.C. explained. "It was a joke."

"You really are weird, Bug," Karen laughed, but he had made her feel better.

"I wish you wouldn't call me that," he answered. "Bug, Shrimp—all those names."

"B.C.?"

"Not even that."

"Bentley Carver?"

"No, the real ones are even worse. How about something more suitable, like, uh, Stud, or Mr. Macho?"

"You're kidding!" Karen giggled. She looked down at Bentley, suddenly realizing what he'd been doing. "You're trying to cheer me up, aren't you?"

"The thought crossed my mind. You know what they say, 'laugh and the . . .' "

" 'World laughs with you,' " she completed.

"I bet you don't know the rest of it."

"I didn't know there was any more."

The short young man stopped on the sidewalk and struck a theatrical pose, one hand tucked into the breast of his child-sized duffel coat.

" 'Laugh, and the world laughs with you,' " he decried. ' "Weep, and you weep alone. For the sad old earth must borrow its mirth, but has trouble enough of its own.' " Karen laughed and applauded while Bentley took a deep bow. "Ella Wheeler Wilcox," he went on. "From *Solitude,* a collection of verse."

"How much time do you spend reading?" Karen asked as they started walking down the hill again.

"Not as much as you think." He grinned, the glow from a streetlight glinting on his glasses. "I've got a really good book of quotations. Some people read the Bible, I memorize quotations. One a night. Good for study habits."

"Have you got one for how shitty it is living in a place like the Falls?"

They reached Van Epp Street and crossed the line into River Park. Karen's house was at the foot of Dixon, almost on the river. Bentley lived a little farther east, somewhere along Parmenter. The trees in River Park were older, turning the streets into long dark tunnels, and unlike the Hill, there were no lights. As they headed down Old Creek Lane, Bentley was almost invisible beside her. In the distance Karen could hear the wobbling siren of one of the Medical Center ambulances. Someone, at least, was having a worse Halloween than she was.

"George Bernard Shaw," Bentley said, his voice coming to her out of the darkness. " 'Home is the girl's prison and the woman's workhouse.' "

"Not bad."

They reached Karen's corner and stopped together on the sidewalk. The wind had died and the last echoing wail of the ambulance had vanished. In its wake there was a deep, eroding silence, waiting like some unknown beast in the night, an instant away from its killing leap. Above them, the overhanging branches of the trees blotted out any view of the sky. It was ridiculous, but suddenly Karen wanted Bentley to walk all the way home with her, to see her safe to the door of her own warm house.

"Well, I guess this is where we part company," Bentley said. He stood nervously, hands in the pockets of his coat.

"Thanks for walking home with me."

"No problem," Bentley said, his face a slightly darker blob a few feet in front of her. He cleared his throat. "One last quote."

"Sure."

"It's from Shakespeare. *A Midsummer Night's Dream.*"

"Okay." The wind was rising again, the leaves above them rattling like old bones.

" 'Things base and vile, holding no quantity, love can transpose to form and dignity. Love looks not with the eyes, but with the mind, and therefore is wing'd Cupid painted blind.' "

There was an awkward silence, and then, completely spontaneously, Karen leaned forward slightly and kissed Bentley Carver Bingham, her lips barely touching his. He jumped back as though someone had stuck a hot coal in his mouth.

"You're weird, Macho Man," Karen said, "but you're sweet."

"Uh, right. Well, I guess I'll see you at school on Monday."

"Okay."

"Good night." He lifted one hand, and then he was gone, racing down Parmenter Street as though the hounds of hell were nipping at his heels. Karen watched him for a moment and then began walking the last block to her house.

"My God!" she whispered, not quite believing what she'd done, and still not sure why she'd done it. "I just kissed B.C. Bingham!" But the fear seemed to have receded, at least a little bit, and for the moment life didn't seem quite so bad.

A few moments later she reached the front door of the little Victorian cottage-house her father had inherited when his parents died. She found the key under the doormat and let herself in, shutting the door on the night behind her.

CHAPTER FOUR

10:15 P.M.

The Jericho Falls Medical Center was an ultramodern, three-story hospital facility on a nine-acre parcel of land just beyond Crestview Heights at the eastern edge of town. Built in 1980, it had 170 beds, a children's ward, and two excellent surgical suites.

Like most rural medical centers, the majority of its clientele were emergency accident cases, and almost half of the main floor was given over to an extensive emergency ward. Cases requiring more complex care were usually airlifted out to hospitals in Manchester and even Boston, but the Center also had a well-equipped intensive-care unit close to the third-floor operating rooms. The Center was computerized, and its three labs and radiology department could do highly sophisticated work-ups.

From the beginning, Rembrandt Payne had complained that the Center was an overstatement, but since it was almost entirely state-funded, there weren't too many complaints. There were eleven doctors on staff or associated with the Center, thirty-eight full-time nurses, half that many part-time, a nine-man maintenance department, and a score of other employees. In addition, the Center was a major source of secondary revenue for Jericho Falls, since the facility was serviced almost entirely by local businesses, a number of them owned by Luther Coyle, either directly or through one of his holding companies. As far as the town, the state, and Luther were concerned, the Jericho Falls Medical Center was a gleaming steel-and-glass showpiece.

One of the least-talked-about aspects of the showpiece, and the aspect old Doc Payne had fought hardest for, was the pathology department. Its inclusion had been dismissed as both unattractive and unnecessary during the early planning stages, but the old man had stuck to his guns. Without a modern pathology department, there would be no Rembrandt Payne as director, and even Luther Coyle respected Payne's influence, both in Jericho Falls and well beyond. The old man had argued that pathology was a necessary part of quality medical care, and in the end he'd had his way.

The truth of it was that a pathology department at the Center finally made it possible for the county to have its own medical examiner, a position Payne ran for and won by acclamation. Since medical examiner was a state-certified title, it allowed him to monitor the functioning of the Center outside the control of the Center's board of directors, most of whom were in Luther Coyle's hip pocket. On top of that, Doc Payne got a free car out of the deal, even though everyone in town called it the Meat Wagon.

Like pathology departments the world over, the morgue at the Jericho Falls Medical Center was located in the basement. It had a plain, unmarked entrance well away from the brightly lit main reception–emergency entrance, and few of the Center's clients even knew the morgue existed.

Jack Slater drove into the staff parking lot of the Medical Center right behind the Meat Wagon, and then he wordlessly followed Rembrandt Payne down the narrow flight of steps leading to the basement entrance. Doc Payne took a large ring of keys from the pocket of his voluminous car-coat, found the right one, and opened the door.

The various rooms, wards, and corridors of the upper floors had been designed and painted on the basis of an expensive study done by a research psychologist specializing in institutions. The basement had received no such attention. The passageways from the side door to the pathology department were narrow, with overhead pipes and conduits stenciled in black, red, or yellow; the walls were raw concrete, still showing the swirling woodgrain of the retaining forms.

Skirting the boiler room, the central elevator core, the linen storage and laundry, they finally reached a pair of swinging doors and went through them. Slater's nose was immediately assaulted by the stinging-sweet and unmistakable stink of formaldehyde. Unbidden, the image of a mangled, half-dissected cat from his high school biology class leaped into his mind. He swallowed hard and kept on the doctor's heels.

The morgue shared space with the blood bank, since they both required refrigeration. To the left of the swinging doors was the blood storage room and the cadaver vaults, to the right was the pathology lab. Payne turned right and headed through another set of swinging doors.

Reuben Wilson, Doc Payne's longtime assistant when he was in private practice in the Falls and now diener, or morgue assistant, was puttering around the long, brightly lit room, assembling the tools of the medical examiner's trade. There were three examination tables, arranged in a row in the middle of the room. Two held sheet-draped bodies. Each table had a matching sink against the wall, and the tables themselves were fitted with blood gutters and a spigot pointing to a drain in the highly polished and spotlessly clean floor.

"How are we doing tonight, Reuben?" asked Payne as he swept into the room. He stripped off his coat, replaced it with a long meat-cutter's smock, and tossed another one to Slater. Slater hung his jacket on a hook beside the doors and slipped on the protective cotton gown.

"Doin' okay, Dr. Rembrandt." The morgue assistant was black, a good ten or fifteen years older than the doctor, and spoke with the lilting accent of central Maine.

"The subjects ready?"

"Uh-huh," said the black man. He rolled an instrument cart in between tables one and two, then pulled down both the recording microphone and the plug for the bone saw. He plugged in the gleaming, stainless-steel saw, then tested the microphone foot pedal on the floor. "You got the Doe on table one and Officer Dorchester on two." His voice was matter-of-fact and emotionless.

"Which do you suggest I begin with?" asked Payne, smiling at his longtime companion.

"The Doe," Reuben said. "Thought you might like to kind of ease into things, umm?"

"Personal effects?" asked the doctor.

"On the desk." Reuben nodded his head toward the office desk against the far wall, jammed in between the blood analyzer and a portable X-ray unit on casters. There was a computer terminal on the desk, and the old man had stacked the personal effects of the van driver and Tom Dorchester in front of the keyboard. Slater, glad for an excuse to move away from the draped tables, went to the desk and began going through the assembled contents of the two men's pockets. He sorted out Dorchester's effects and picked up the van driver's wallet. Payne stripped the sheet off the figure on table one.

"His name was Redenbacher," Slater said, checking the man's license.

"Like the popcorn," Doc Payne said. He took a pair of surgical scissors off the wheeled cart and began slicing through the fabric of Arnie Redenbacher's trousers. He cut through one leg and then the other, joining the cuts at the crotch. Immediately following Arnie's death, he had soiled himself, and the rank odor of fecal matter was beginning to overpower the formaldehyde. Reuben shuffled arthritically across the room to a wall switch and turned on the big overhead vent fans. Returning to the table, he took away the front half of the dead man's pants while the doctor began working on the jacket and shirt.

"First name Arnold, middle name Saxon," Slater read out loud, still standing by the desk. "Lived on South Main Street in Manchester. Employee's card from someplace called Speedmaster Transit on Daniel Webster Highway."

Doc Payne stared down at the naked man on the table. He reached out and gently palpated the neck and then the arms. "No rigor yet, and he's still within five degrees of normal. I'd say Mr. Redenbacher's been dead for under two hours." He peeled back the eyelids and took a closer look. "Eyes are hemorrhaged and bulging. Coronary or maybe a massive stroke. Could be both. He's sclerotic, too. A boozer. Raspberry marks on the cheeks."

Slater looked up from the wallet just in time to watch as Doc Payne picked up a large dissecting scalpel and ran it down Arnie Redenbacher's chest from throat to pubic bone. He made the cut a second time, slicing deeper, and blood began to ooze out over the man's graying, waxy skin. Horrified but fascinated, Slater continued to watch. Working confidently, the big knife held like a conductor's baton, Doc Payne sliced down through the flabby chest muscles, then flipped them back over Arnie's uncaring face. From where he stood, Slater could see the thick, yellow layers of fat around the stomach cavity, and the liquid coils of the man's intestines, lying in short loops.

Payne dropped the knife back onto the tray and picked up a pair of bone cutters. He hooked the lower, curved blade under Arnie's bottom rib and began to snip, crunching easily through the bone. He cut up to the breastbone, then pulled back the chest plate, exposing the heart and lungs. Picking up a smaller scalpel, he dissected the heart from its attachments to the vena cava and arteries, then picked it up in one hand. Arnie's corpse began to look like meat on a butcher's block, organs exposed and gleaming under the big reflecting pan lights, bone ends dark with ocher marrow, blood dripping freely down the runnels to the spigot. Slater could taste bile in the back of his throat, but he didn't look away.

"Look at that," Doc Payne said, poking at the excised lump of flesh. "Enlarged twice normal size, walls tissue-paper thin, and enough fat here for a barbecue. Mr. Redenbacher was definitely living on borrowed time." He tossed the heart back into the chest cavity and shook his head. "I'll take out the brain later and do some tissue sampling, but you can bet it was congestive heart failure."

"No foul play?" asked Slater, his mouth dry.

"Not a chance, lad." He flipped the chest plate back over the exposed heart and lungs, pulled down the curtain of muscle and skin temporarily shrouding the dead man's face, then picked up the big industrial stapler from the tray. Working efficiently, he hammered a dozen staples in a ragged line down the front of the body, then nodded to Reuben.

"You can take him to the cooler for now. I'll get around to him later in the week. Might have an interesting brain. Good bet you'd find all sorts of interesting things in there."

The old black attendant pulled a gurney up to the table, dropped a sheet over the corpse, and with Payne's help manhandled it onto the wheeled stretcher. Whistling tunelessly under his breath, Reuben pushed the gurney through the double doors and out into the hallway.

"You look a little pale, lad," Payne said, squinting at Slater. The sheriff shrugged.

"I'll be all right. Takes a bit of getting used to."

"Ready for Officer Dorchester?"

"Ready as I'll ever be."

Payne wheeled the instrument cart to the second autopsy table and pulled the sheet away from Tom Dorchester's body.

"My God!" whispered the doctor, stepping back.

"Jesus Christ!"

Neither the violence of the Vietnam War nor a lifetime of medical trauma had prepared either of them for what lay on the table.

The Jericho Falls Police Department regulation uniform consisted of a light blue shirt and light brown trousers. Tom Dorchester's uniform was stained a deep, terrible rust color. Thick ropes of drying blood and mucus ran from his nostrils, and huge gouts of the same hideous mixture had spilled out of his mouth and down his shirt. Trails of drying blood ran down out of both ears, and Slater saw that even the eyes had filled with blood, the liquid bursting out of the ruptured sockets. The policeman had either coughed or vomited much of the blood, spilling it down his front, but even that couldn't account for the sodden state of the man's clothes below the waist.

Hands trembling, Rembrandt Payne reached for the scissors on the tray and repeated the operation he'd performed on Arnie Redenbacher a few moments before. Cutting complete, he gingerly peeled back the clotted pieces of cloth, then sliced through Dorchester's underwear, revealing a monstrous, impossible erection. The man's penis had engorged with a huge amount of blood, eventually rupturing through the spongy tissue.

Slater winced as the doctor picked up a small scalpel and deftly sliced through the tautly stretched skin, slashing deeply down from just below the bulbous tip to the scrotal sac. A thick surge of semiliquid blood burst from the organ with enough force to spatter the doctor's gown, and the erection subsided slowly. The testicles too had swollen to three or four times normal size and had taken on a deep purple coloration.

With the trousers and underwear removed, it was also possible to see that the man had hemorrhaged rectally as well, feces, blood, and more of the jellylike mucus running down both legs and finally soaking into his heavy socks and steel-capped shoes.

"Jesus!" whispered Slater, his own bowels turning to water. "Look at his hands!"

Swallowing, a tic starting up on his jowled cheek, Rembrandt

Payne lifted Tom Dorchester's large, limp hand. At the base of each hair there was a single, drying drop of blood, and the same was true of each pore. Using the dissecting knife, the doctor slashed through Dorchester's jacket and shirt, exposing the arm. Each hair follicle and pore was dark with blood. It looked as though the policeman had been beaten with a sledgehammer over every square inch of skin.

"He's exsanguinated," Payne said, appalled.

"What the hell does that mean?"

"He bled out," croaked the doctor. "Mouth, nose, ears, eyes, anus, genitals, pores. Every blood vessel in his body must have burst. My God!"

"Someone did that to him?"

"No. No, that's impossible," the old doctor muttered. "There's no other damage, no trauma at all. He just . . . bled to death. All at once."

"How?"

"I don't know. I've never heard of anything like this before in my life."

"Jesus, Doc, there's got to be some kind of answer."

"There is," Payne said, regaining a little of his composure. "I just don't know what it is." He picked up a large magnifying glass from the tray and bent over Dorchester's hideously mottled corpse. It was all Slater could do to keep from throwing up on the spot. The doctor began going over Dorchester's skin.

"Anything?"

"The palms of his hands have some little pustules on them, like burns, or a rash of some kind." He moved the glass up to the dead man's head, paying particular attention to the ears and nose. He stood up, shaking his head. He put down the magnifying glass; then, using both hands, he tapped at the chest.

"What?" Slater asked.

"Odd. The majority of the bleeding is associated with mucosa. Snot to you, lad. And the lungs are terribly congested, full of fluid." He pointed to the slack-jawed mouth. "He was trying to cough it up as he died." Payne took a long-handled spoon and a small specimen bottle off the instrument tray and dug into Dorchester's open mouth, scooping up a sample of the jellied red-green discharge. Slater looked away, gagging. "Did you speak to him today?" asked the doctor.

"Before he went on duty. Five o'clock," Slater said, trying not to look. Payne capped the specimen bottle and put it on the tray.

"Was he coughing, sneezing, anything like that?"

"No, not that I can recall, why?"

"Because even without the bleeding he would have died. He would have choked to death—drowned in all of this."

"That's crazy!" Slater said. "He wasn't sick."

"He got sick, lad. Terribly sick, in four hours or so."

"Is that possible?"

"Not to my knowledge."

"Then what happened?"

"God knows, lad," Payne murmured, looking down at the obscenity on the table. "I'll have to run a number of tests, and even then I doubt we'll have an answer."

"Guess," Slater insisted. "Give me something to go on."

"Poison," Payne answered, his voice flat. "Between the last time you saw him and approximately 9:00 P.M., he came in contact with some sort of poison. The bleeding suggests a massive interference with his clotting factors, leading to a systemic hemorrhage, something like an induced hemophilia. The rash and the mucus indicate some sort of respiratory allergy. And it wasn't like a virus, either. From the looks of him, there was very little time between contact and death. No more than a few minutes."

"That's incredible."

"Indeed it is." Payne nodded. "Incredible and unlike anything in my experience."

"The van," Slater said. "It has to have something to do with the van, the one Redenbacher was driving."

"Possibly. But the man on table one died of heart failure, not poisoning. How do you explain that?"

"I don't. But that van is sitting on Ralph Beavis's lot at the Gas Bar. If it was carrying some kind of poisonous substance . . ."

"I suggest you find out," Payne said. "Soon."

"What about us?" asked Slater. He began unbuttoning his smock. "The ambulance attendants, Reuben. We've all come in contact with him."

"It's a little late to think about that," Payne said dryly. "And it would seem that whatever killed Officer Dorchester is no longer lethal. If his body was capable of causing us harm, it would have become apparent by now, I think.''

"Okay," Slater said, stripping off the smock. "I'll go and check the van out."

"Exercise a great deal of caution. We can get in touch with the owners of the van tomorrow. Until then, I suggest you do no more than make sure it is secure."

"What about Tom?"

"I'll run what tests I can immediately. We should have some results in the morning."

"All right," Slater said. He went to the coatrack and picked up his jacket. "Keep me advised."

"Of course." Slater headed for the doors. "Jack?" called Rembrandt Payne. The sheriff paused and turned.

"Yes?"

"I don't think you should mention this to anyone. Not yet, anyway. There's no sense in alarming people."

Slater took a last look at what was left of Tom Dorchester. It was like something out of a horror movie, and he knew that his first sight of the bloody, oozing corpse would haunt him for the rest of his life.

"Yeah," he said. "I see what you mean."

Bodo Bimm leaned against the counter of the Gas Bar office and leafed slowly through the pages of an old Silver Surfer comic someone had left behind in the gas station a year ago. It was one of his prized possessions, and when he wasn't actually looking at it, he kept the dog-eared magazine rolled up in a pocket of his coveralls. He couldn't read, but after almost twelve months he was beginning to get a bit of the story in his head. One thing he did know, the Silver Surfer was alone in the world, and sometimes he cried. Bodo knew how he felt.

Like now. He was alone, and he didn't like it much. It was better in the afternoon or the early evening. Townies would drop in, say hello to Mr. Beavis, and get some gas. Bert and Corky, the mechanics, would be around too, finishing up, and sometimes one or the other of them would buy him a bag of chips or a Pepsi from the machine outside. That was nice.

But Bert had gone and Corky hadn't stayed long after bringing in the van with the Gas Bar tow truck. He'd given Bodo enough money for a Pepsi, but he'd finished that off a long time ago. Now he wouldn't have anything to drink but water until morning, and he didn't dare take any chips from the rack, no matter how hungry he got. He'd done it once and Mr. Beavis had yelled at him, and there was nothing worse than that.

Bodo yawned and looked up from the comic. Through the smudged window of the office he could see out to the pump island and across the highway to T.J.'s Restaurant. Bodo couldn't tell time, but he knew it was pretty late because there were only two or three cars in front of the low, ranch-style eating place. He'd know when midnight came because that was when Mr. Kartosian turned out the lights and went home. According to Ralph Beavis, Mr. Kartosian was a foreigner, but Bodo wasn't quite sure what that meant, except that Ralph Beavis frowned when he said it. It was the same kind of frown he used when he called Bodo a fuckin-re-tard, which was at least a dozen times a day.

Pretty soon now Bodo would be able to go into the toilet on the other side of the counter in the corner of the office. He'd shit, and then he'd sit on the john and play with himself until he felt better. He did it every night, but he never told anyone about it. When he'd done that, he'd look at the Silver Surfer comic again, then go to sleep in the big wooden swivel chair Mr. Beavis sat in when he used the old crank adding machine.

There wasn't much business at the Gas Bar during the night, but it was enough for Ralph Beavis to stay open. He'd already cleared the till and taken the money to the Slumber-King next door. There was a trip-bell across the front of the Gas Bar lot, and it would wake Bodo up if someone pulled in. Most of the late-night traffic was from truckers, and they all knew Bodo. They'd get a fill-up and pay, either giving him the correct amount or filling out their own credit card slips.

Mr. Beavis had kept Bodo working nights at the Gas Bar for almost six years, and after a long time checking the gas-pump levels every morning and comparing them with the previous night, the gas station/motel owner had grudgingly come to the conclusion that most people were pretty honest and that Bodo was just too stupid to steal.

Bodo yawned again. Stealing from Mr. Beavis had never crossed his mind. Mr. Beavis paid his room and board at Mrs. McQuire's rooming house on Concord Street in Frenchtown and gave him pocket money besides, three dollars every morning, like clockwork. Since his meals were included in the money Mr. Beavis paid Mrs. McQuire, he could spend the money on anything he wanted. For Bodo, it was the best of all possible worlds, and he wasn't about to destroy things by stealing.

Bodo smiled and rubbed one large, grease-stained hand across his thinning hair. "Time for a trim," he said out loud, pleased with the way the words sounded. "Time for a trim."

Tomorrow, he'd spend his three dollars at Willard's, and for a whole day he'd smell of Wildroot and talcum powder. He loved the mixture of the two scents, and he had his hair cut every week. It was as much a part of his routine as his before-work cup of free coffee at the Bo-Peep or masturbating after his late-night defecation.

In the blink of an eye, the big revolving sign out beyond the pump island went out and Bodo froze, his heart suddenly beating hard. A split second later, the interior lights in the station went out as well, and Bodo was left in complete darkness. He began making a frightened, mewling sound. More than anything in the world, he hated being in the dark.

"Bodo!" It was a harsh whisper, metallic, and it seemed to be coming from close by.

"Who'sat?"

"Ichabod, Bodo. Ichabod Crane!" The voice seemed even closer now. The Silver Surfer comic dropped from Bodo's fingers. He could feel wetness running down the leg of his coveralls, but he paid no attention. Myopically, he squinted through the grime-coated window of the station, sensing movement outside.

"I don' know no Ich—Ichabod." He groaned. It was like the dreams he sometimes had. Dreams of darkness, filled with voices he could never identify. He heard a faint creaking sound, like someone pulling open a rusty car door, and then there was silence. He began to breath rapidly, hyperventilating.

"Somebody there?" he called out.

Silence.

"Mr. Beavis? Gawd, Mr. Beavis, come and help me!"

More creaking sounds out front and something like muffled laughter. Then the voice again, only a few feet away. In the garage?

"He's dead, Bodo!" The awful voice. Bodo tried to yell, but

no sound came. He wanted to run, but it was as though his legs had turned to stone. "He's dead, Bodo! *I cut off his fucking head!*"

There was a tremendous burst of light and a roaring explosion. No more than a yard to his left, standing in the open doorway leading to the garage, loomed a huge figure, at least seven feet tall, dressed in a long black cape, headless above the neck. Blood had dripped down the front of the cape, blood too red to be real.

The figure raised its blind hand. A series of half a dozen fire-balls exploded outside, and in the glaring light Bodo saw what the hand was holding, and he screamed. Blood oozing from the stump of a neck, the dark figure's long leather fingers curled in its hair, it was a severed head, eyes rolled back, black tongue protruding: it was Mr. Beavis. Bodo screamed.

"What the fucking hell is going on!" The voice entered Bo-do's numbed brain as he continued to scream, and he recognized it as belonging to Ralph Beavis. By some sort of terrible ventriloquism, the severed head was speaking, making it sound as though the voice was coming from far away. There was another explosion, much brighter than the first two, and a huge, *whoof*ing *thump*. Suddenly, it was daylight, but Bodo wasn't looking anymore. He stood, still frozen, eyes squeezed tightly shut, his screams lost in the uproar. The headless figure turned, stumbled, then dropped the head as it backed out through the door.

A chrome-steel guided missile howled through the front window of the station and slammed into the rear wall. The air was suddenly full of flying glass, but Bodo was saved from serious injury as the concussion of the explosion blew him backward off his feet. Idiotically, the raw smell of burning gasoline was over-shadowed by the stink of rotten eggs.

Outside, half a dozen running figures were outlined in the flames belching up from the damaged van parked beside the tow truck. The figures ran toward the rear of the station, making for the narrow path that led to the back of the Gas Bar property and then meandered through the Drake's Farm woodlot.

Another figure, dressed in pajamas and a threadbare terry-cloth bathrobe, appeared, silhouetted by the roaring flames. Cursing at the top of his lungs, bathrobe flapping around his ankles, Ralph Beavis scuttled across the asphalt, doglegging around the burning van. He ran into the station, slamming open the door.

"Bodo! You fucking retard! Where the hell are you?" he roared. But Bodo didn't hear him. Bodo was behind the counter, on his hands and knees, hands clapped over his ears, the sound of his own screams drowning out everything else.

Jack Slater arrived at the Beavis Gas Bar no more than three minutes ahead of the first truck from the Jericho Falls VFD. By that time all six of the boys involved in the Halloween prank had vanished, and Bodo Bimm was still screaming. It took a five-man team almost twenty-five minutes to put out the fire that had consumed the van, and when they were finished, there was very little of it left above the axles.

Slater discovered a gruesome Halloween mask fitted over a Styrofoam wig dummy lying on the floor of the Gas Bar office and several pieces of shiny metal lying in the shards of broken glass from the window.

Since no one at the scene appeared to be ill or bleeding mysteriously, he cast up a grateful prayer and assumed that if there had been some sort of toxic material in the van, it had been totally consumed by the fire. The prank, dangerous as it was, had been providential, and Tom Dorchester's death had been a freak accident, not to be repeated.

He was wrong.

PART TWO

BLACK ROLLER
Saturday, November 1

Upon notification of BLACK ROLLER status, the unit will endeavor to provide complete aerial and ground reconnaissance as authorized by sub-unit commanders. It is of particular importance that the unit commander be provided with a control sample as early as possible. Strict visual and electronic surveillance will go into effect as soon as the unit is on site. Once a full *cordon sanitaire* has been established, the unit will remain at BLACK ROLLER status until otherwise notified by the unit commander.

—Lt. Col. James H. Wright
 Commander, Special Unit 7
 AMCCOM
 Rock Island Arsenal
 Rock Island, Illinois
 Section 2, Number 1, Page 26
 BM-31-210

CHAPTER FIVE

7:15 A.M.

Josh Robinson woke up, yawned, and pulled the thick quilt up around his nose. The loft was drafty at best, and at this time of the year it was actually cold. Down at the end of the roughly constructed hatch-cover bed, Scoobie the Terrible Terrier sneezed and shifted around, growling sleepily. The boy peeled the quilt back slightly and used one hand to push the thick, red-brown hair out of his eyes.

"Hey, Scoob," Josh whispered. On the other side of the partition he could hear snores. The high-pitched whistle was his mother, the deeper chain saw was probably Terry Morgan or Sandy Shaw. It was hard to tell which, since his mother spent just about equal time with both men.

Josh yawned again. No point putting it off. He was wide-awake now, and Scoobie was stirring some more. Like any other eleven-year-old, Josh couldn't conceive of anyone wanting to stay in bed after waking up. He was bored within five minutes.

Taking a deep breath, he threw back the quilt and jumped out of bed. The thick, yellow-pine floorboards were the original ones laid when the mill was built, and they were polished smooth by more than a century of use. They were also freezing. Organic. No wall-to-wall carpeting here, and no heat except for wood stoves and whatever you could pump out of the ancient boiler in what had once been the picking house. Abnormal, just like everything else in his life.

Every day he left the mill, crossed over the bridge, and walked half a mile to school, and every day, at least once, he wished he could be like the other kids in his class. Warren LaCroix, his best friend at school, had a father who sold insurance and a mother who worked at Woolworth's. His own mother made big abstract wall hangings on her loom, and he didn't have a father at all, since you couldn't count Terry Morgan or Sandy Shaw.

Josh picked through the pile of clothes he'd left on the floor and started dressing. Not only couldn't you count Terry or Sandy, you couldn't even talk about them. He was no brain, but he knew mothers on the north side of the bridge didn't have two men to sleep with. Josh wasn't absolutely sure, but he thought his mother might have had both together in her bed one night.

More than once his mother had explained it all by saying that the people who lived and worked at the Mill were different. The implication was that the Mill people were somehow better than the townies, but no one ever came right out and said it. Different, abnormal—it didn't matter what word you used. As far as Josh was concerned, it was all a crock.

He squeezed into his jeans, threw on a long-sleeved T-shirt, and added one of his big bulky sweaters for good measure. He sat down on the bed and began pulling on a pair of thick socks. There'd be frost on the ground. Scoobie the Sock-Sucker made a play for one of them, but it was halfhearted. The grinning, dust-colored wirehair wanted out, and soon. Sighing, Josh reached for his boots and put them on, pulling the laces tight.

When you got right down to it, the townies weren't much better than the people at the Mill. Whether they know it or not, eleven-year-olds are well acquainted with social order, and Josh Robinson was no exception. He saw it every day, in his own class.

There were three kinds of kids in Jericho Falls: Hill kids, River Park kids, and Frenchtowners. Hillers, Parkies, and Frogs. Hillers tended to be snobs and talked about the new cars their fathers just bought; Parkies were okay, but all they talked about was television and rock and roll; and the Frogs were poor and tried to beat the shit out of you at every opportunity. There were lots of variations on the basic theme: Hillers embarrassed by the money they had, Parkies wanting to be Hillers, Frogs pretending to be Parkies, especially if they lived on Gowan or Overlook, streets close to the creek . . . the combinations were endless.

And the Mill kids, about twenty sprinkled through all the grades from one up through high school, were different again. Sons and daughters of old-guard hippies and freaks, children of recent soft-tech converts, the hybrid progeny of both. Even the Mill had its own order, its own hierarchy.

"Anilingus," Josh muttered to no one in particular. It was a good word, especially when you knew what it meant. He'd picked it up from Lionel Clemmens down on the second floor.

Now, Lionel was *really* different. Lionel's father, Garth Clemmens, the manager of the health food store on the main floor level, was gay. He and Lionel lived with Scott Honeywell, and Scott had once lived with Shayna Cappodocci. Shayna, Josh's mother's best friend, was now eight months pregnant with Scott Honeywell's child. Lionel thought it was pretty sick, and Josh tended to agree. Still, it was better than being a Frog.

Dressed, Josh tiptoed out around the partition, Scoobie on his heels. He glanced in at the area his mother used as a bedroom. The man in the bed with her was Sandy Shaw; you could tell by the huge mass of red-blond hair bushing up off the pillow.

Sandy was a writer, and since he also had a degree in Business Administration from Cornell, he acted as the Mill bookkeeper, making sure that none of the artisans in the sprawling building got into too much trouble with the IRS. Josh wasn't quite sure what it was that Sandy wrote, but according to his mother, nothing had been published.

Josh made his way quietly past the bedroom area and went into the loft's main room, a combination kitchen, work area, living room. Early morning sun poured in through the five deeply inset windows in the thick stone walls, throwing weak bars of light across the floor. His mother's loom stood silently at the far end of the high-ceilinged space, the kitchen butted up against the bedroom partition, and the rest of it was living room. The bathroom, shared by the other five tenants on the fourth floor, was down the center corridor.

He grabbed an apple off the handmade kitchen table, then scooped a handful of health-food kibble out of the burlap bag beside the fifties vintage refrigerator. He let Scoobie eat out of his hand, then they headed for the door. Josh scooted the dog out into the corridor and followed, easing the door shut behind them.

His bladder was sending urgent signals, but instead of heading for the big lavatory that had once served the sixty or more workers tending the mill's rattling jennies and mules, he turned in the opposite direction and went down the winding, cast-iron stairs. It was always better to have the first whiz of the morning outside. Abnormal maybe, but better.

"Is pissing outside abnormal or just different? See page two." His voice echoed in the confined space of the stairwell. Below him, Scoobie's high-flag tail disappeared around the next turn. "Abominably abnormal anilingus!" he boomed.

The stairwell was built into a tower at one end of the building, matched by a similar one at the opposite end, which contained the toilets. There were two doors at the base, one leading into the main floor, the other an exit to the outside. Reaching the bottom, Josh put his weight on the modern crash-bar and stepped outside.

A few seconds later, he was enjoying a long, glorious pee, making puff balls with his breath and watching Scoobie leap around in the icy air. It was Saturday, the sky was a perfect, cloudless blue, and any thoughts the boy had about structural sociology vanished.

He zipped up, pulled the apple out of his pocket and followed Scoobie as the dog raced out across the frost-covered field. A round-trip to the quarry and back would take about an hour. Plenty of time to have a proper breakfast before his nine o'clock guitar lesson.

Munching on the apple, Josh reached the edge of the field fifty yards behind his dog and crossed Mill Road, making for the base of Quarry Hill. The ground on the far side began to slope gently upward, scrub brush and small stands of pine clinging to the rocky soil. A few minutes later, he reached the old railroad tracks and turned west, Scoobie still well in the lead, mincing from one overgrown tie to the next, wispy tail high in the air.

The track, unused since the close of the quarry almost thirty-five years before, was a spur off the main Chesapeake and Ohio line that ran farther south. Back then there had actually been a small station just the other side of the river, a couple of miles from town, but now it was used as an office by the people who ran the little dirt-strip airport.

Scoobie stopped for a moment, head rising to the breeze, then turned away from the tracks and headed upslope again. The dog was moving more urgently now, obviously working a scent. Josh turned off the tracks and followed him, occasionally catching sight of his pet moving rapidly through the trees. The boy tossed the core of his apple away and swore under his breath. The last time Scoobie had gone chasing rabbits, he'd wound up with a snoutful of porcupine quills. Good dog but no brains, as his friend Sparrow often commented.

Now there, thought Josh, was a guy who'd make a terrific father. For Josh, Sparrow Hawke was something of an idol: smart, tough, strong, and fair. He'd watched his mother hitting on Sparrow a couple of times, but nothing ever came of it. As far as Josh, his mother, and anyone else at the Mill knew, the Bird Man was a monk.

The trees thinned out, opening into a broad, upland meadow. Standing at the edge of the woods, Josh let out a piercing whistle and Scoobie stopped cold. They were way off course for the quarry, and Josh was getting hungry. The whistle didn't hold the dog for long: his nose went down to the ground, and he began to edge forward. Even from a hundred feet away, Josh could hear the dog's low, insistent growling. Definitely a rabbit.

"Scoobie! Stay!" called Josh, and this time the dog obeyed, sitting back on his haunches. It was then that Josh noticed it. There, low on the dog's flank, was a tiny, brilliant dot of color. Green. Even as the boy watched, the spot moved, edging across the dog's belly and along its back. Josh frowned, peering around the clearing. The spot of color was like the reflection from a watch crystal or a pair of binoculars, only brighter, and that strange, brilliant green.

"Scoobie?"

The light crept up the animal's throat, magically changing color as it reached the head. Bright green to bloodred, the light intensifying as it stopped just below the ear. Josh had never seen anything like it in his life.

"Scoobie!" he commanded. "Here, boy!"

The dog began to turn, but the light moved with him. Scoobie took two hesitant steps toward his master and then, without any warning and without a sound, the terrier's head exploded, blood, brains, and bone splinters blossoming silently into the air.

"Scoobie!" Josh began to run even before the decapitated body of the dog folded toward the ground, blood still fountaining from the ragged stump of the neck. The head itself had vanished, vaporized in an instant.

Heart in his throat and tears streaming, Josh ran toward the dog. He blinked, horrified, as he noticed a green spot on the shoulder of his sweater. It changed to red as it centered on his chest, and he had sense enough to swerve. The light flickered down to his leg, instantly changing to green, and Josh veered again, this time in the opposite direction. Unseen, the green light caught his back as he ran for the trees, inching up his spine like some terrible crawling insect.

Ten feet from the edge of the clearing, the light reached the nape of his neck, flickered, then flashed to red. Josh experienced a single instant of terrible pain and all sensation vanished. There was an avalanche of roaring, all-consuming blackness, and then Joshua Robinson's world came to an end.

For Rembrandt Payne, his fourth-floor corner office at the Jericho Falls Medical Center was an island of culture in an otherwise sterile environment. A floor-to-ceiling oak bookcase covered one wall, filled with medical books and journals and his pride and joy, a complete hardcover set of every Nero Wolfe book ever written by Rex Stout.

An ornate Kazak rug was spread in front of his big partners desk, and a large, pedestal globe stood in the corner closest to his custom-made office chair. There were two chairs for visitors on the other side of the desk, both leather, one red and the other yellow.

The decor was the old doctor's private joke, since it was a perfect match for the office described in the Wolfe books, right down to a framed print of a waterfall hanging on the partition wall screening off his private washroom. The only anomaly was the state-of-the-art IBM XT computer on his desk, linking him directly to the Center's own network, and by telephone modem, to medical databases all over North America.

Payne sat slumped in his oversized chair, hands folded across his impressive belly, thumbs twiddling. He watched the amber screen of the computer, lips pursed as Tom Dorchester's vital statistics slowly scrolled past. The doctor had been at work since returning to the hospital almost three hours before, but he was still no further along.

His first thought was that the policeman had been poisoned, and on that assumption he'd used the modem and accessed MED-TEXT, the central database covering all recent medical journals and the active files of the American Medical Association. MED-TEXT had led him to TOXINT, a secondary database devoted to poisons, and finding no help there, he crossed the country electronically to DISCON, feeding into the mainframe files of the Centers for Disease Control in Atlanta, Georgia. So far, he'd flipped through everything from DIC, Diffuse Intravascular Coagulation, to Korean Hemorrhagic Fever, but nothing fit. It was as though Dorchester's killer had mimed the symptoms of three or four poisons, a couple of viruses, and even a plague or two.

It was confounding. His function as medical examiner, as described by law, was to establish "manner, cause, and circumstance" leading to death. Cause and circumstance were relatively easy, at least on the surface. Dorchester had bled to death, probably in a matter of minutes, and he had done so seated in his police cruiser, parked on a dark stretch of Old River Road. Manner was something else again.

So far, Dr. Payne had ruled out virtually any known toxin, but suppose the van had been carrying some new, unknown poison? Jack Slater had called late last night, telling him that the van had been destroyed during a Halloween prank at the Gas Bar, and the sheriff was obviously relieved that whatever had been in the van had been destroyed. But what if the unknown element that killed Dorchester hadn't been in the van at all?

After Slater had left the Center, Payne had worked on Dorchester until the small hours of the morning, doing a careful autopsy. He'd prepared tissue samples from several major organs, including the heart and brain, as well as samples of body fluids. All of them had been sent to the Center labs for study, but so far, Payne had only the most basic blood scan information to go on.

Sitting forward, the old man tapped the appropriate codes on the XT keyboard. The screen cleared, then filled again, displaying the preliminary findings from the big Hewlett-Packard Gas Chromatograph.

TEST	NORMAL	SAMPLE
Hematocrit	40–60	8
Bun	10–20	40
pH	7.4	3.2
SGOT	40	126
Sed	9	36
Amylase	70–200	730

Rembrandt Payne shook his head. If the blood had been taken from a living human, it would have been conclusive proof that the person was dead. No one could live with a pH that low and a hematocrit showing an almost total lack of living red blood cells. Both the SGOT and the sedimentation rate indicated massive tissue damage. Tissue damage so widespread Dorchester had died of it in the blink of an eye. It was impossible, but it had happened.

The telephone beside the terminal beeped loudly, and Payne picked it up, scowling.

"What?"

"Simms down in the lab, Dr. Payne. I've finished the tissue samples you wanted."

"And?"

"You're not going to believe it."

"Don't be coy, man! I've had less than five hours of sleep. Get to the point!"

"Yes, sir. I centrifuged the blood sample as you requested, and I've digitized the results. Are you on line at the moment?"

"Yes."

"Uh, then hit WW57Y and it should come up." Payne tapped in the code and the screen cleared again. There was a brief pause, then it filled, this time with a digitized diagram of Tom Dorchester's centrifuged blood, broken down into its component parts.

"Good Lord!" Payne whispered, staring at the screen.

"Yes, sir," Simms said. "That's what I said. It sure explains that low pH though, and the SGOT."

The screen showed three lines of cells: granulocytes, lymphocytes, and monocytes, all white cells involved in bodily defense; red cells, the main factor in human blood; and the much smaller platelets, the vital clotting agents. Instead of the cells being well formed and complete, they were all cytolic. Each one had been ruptured.

"There's no mistake about this?" Payne asked, still staring at the screen. "You didn't use the wrong preparation fluid?"

"No, sir. And it's the same for all the other tissue samples. They're all hypotonic, almost completely salt free, and that's what caused the cytolysis. The cells all filled with water, then ruptured."

"I'm familiar with the term," Payne said dryly. "Any evidence of toxins, some sort of chemical agent?"

"No, sir. But there was an anomaly, especially in that mucus specimen you drew off. It's in the other samples too, but not as extensively."

"Go on."

"Staphylococcus aureus—at least, that's what it looks like. And lots of it."

"You've made cultures?"

"Of course, Doctor."

"Get a slide up to me," Payne ordered. "Stat."

"Right away."

Payne hung up the phone and glanced at the screen showing Dorchester's ruptured cells. Staph aureus was the bacteria responsible for Toxic Shock Syndrome, blood toxemia, and pneumonia. It was also the bacteria responsible for pimples and, next to E. Coli, one of the most common found in and on the human body. The chance of Dorchester's overabundant supply of Staph aureus being the cause of his death was slim, but the bacteria was blood-associated, and that was at least a start.

Rembrandt Payne stared down at his hands, examining the clean, lightly tanned skin and the freshly trimmed nails. Under a microscope, those same hands would be crawling with any number of Staph and other bacteria. A handshake, a peck on the cheek, even normal conversation could pass the bacteria from one person to another. It happened all the time.

He looked at the ruined cells on the screen again, and suddenly he was afraid. If the Staph bacteria was somehow related to the policeman's death, the people of Jericho Falls were in deep, deep trouble.

The distant echo of a ringing telephone disturbed Jack Slater's sleep, but it was the combined odor of frying bacon and fresh-brewed coffee that kept him awake. After dealing with the van incident at the Gas Bar, he'd stopped off at Jenny's apartment on Main Street, and he hadn't made it back to his own bed until almost four in the morning.

He rolled over and gingerly cranked open one eye. The uncaring moon-face of the Big Ben alarm said 9:45. He opened the other eye, wincing in the bright sunlight that poured in through the big bay window overlooking the river. His father had designed the house around that view more than fifty years ago, long before the idea of a night-shift son ever occurred to him.

The lure of the smells wafting up to him from the kitchen was impossible to ignore. He sat up, groaning, blessing, and cursing his young daughter simultaneously. Blessing her for the coffee and the bacon, cursing her for cooking them at such an ungodly hour. He couldn't really blame her, though; she had no idea how late he'd come in. Or did she? Culinary sabotage of his affair with Jenny?

He threw back the down-filled comforter and reached out to the chair where he'd hung his clothes last night. Yawning, he pulled on socks and his uniform pants, then stumbled to the closet on the other side of the room and picked out a clean shirt. Leaving it unbuttoned, he headed for the bathroom, running an exploratory tongue over his teeth. Cigarettes and white wine. A morning taste sensation.

"Morning," he said, coming into the kitchen a few minutes later. Standing in front of the stove, Karen looked back over her shoulder.

"You look awful." She grinned. "Late night?"

"Late enough," he answered, yawning. She was dressed in skintight jeans, a black-and-white ski sweater, and a pair of shapeless, bright pink slippers that were the only evidence of a short-lived knitting class she'd attended the year before. He sat down at the pine kitchen table. "What about you?" he asked. She shrugged, her back still to him.

"It was a stupid party," she said. "I came home early."

"Fight with Billy?" Slater guessed. He knew his daughter well enough to realize that she was upset.

Karen transferred a spatula of scrambled eggs onto a plate, added several strips of bacon, and poured a mug of black coffee from the pot on the back element of the stove. She brought the plate and mug to her father, then sat down across from him.

"No fight with Billy," she said. "I just left early."

"I don't like you wandering around alone at night," he said, digging into the eggs.

"Don't be medieval. I'm fifteen. I wasn't wandering, and I wasn't alone. I came home with B.C."

"B.C. Bingham?" asked Slater. He took a sip of the aromatic coffee and sighed contentedly. "I thought he was the class nerd, or whatever you call them these days."

"He is the class nerd," said Karen. "Also a dweeb and a geek. But he's nice. And smart, too."

"Good." Slater nodded. "Change will do you good."

"I'm not going out with him, Daddy! Billy was being an assho— Billy was being really stupid, and B.C. was leaving at the same time, that's all.''

"What was Billy doing that was so stupid?"

"I don't want to talk about it," she said, her features darkening. "What about you? How was the party at Stark Hall?"

"Predictable," he answered. "There was a traffic accident out on the Old River Road, though. Tom Dorchester was killed." There was no sense in giving her the gruesome details.

"Oh." Karen knew Dorchester to see him, but that was all. "That's too bad."

"Yeah," Slater said, the events of the previous night coming back. He didn't want to go into the details with Karen. "Who was that on the phone a few minutes ago?" he asked, changing the subject.

"Billy," she said. She stood up, took her father's near-empty mug, and refilled it from the pot.

"What did he want?"

"He wanted to know why I'd left the party without him. He asked me to meet him at the Bo-Peep."

"Are you going?"

"Maybe. I haven't decided yet." More tension. There really was something wrong between them. Lovers' quarrel? Or was it more than that? Something clicked in Slater's mind, and he frowned. "Did Billy's being stupid have anything to do with a Halloween prank?" He watched as his daughter stiffened.

"No," she said. "Why?"

"Because some kids played a bad joke on Bodo Bimm over at the Gas Bar last night. They torched a van that was on the lot and scared the poor guy half to death. They had to give him a shot and take him to the Medical Center. Ralph Beavis figures they did about five hundred dollars damage to the Gas Bar, not to mention the van."

"What makes you think Billy was involved?" Karen asked.

"Sol Kartosian, the man who runs T.J.'s Restaurant on the Strip, says he spotted a blue Camaro burning rubber out of the Kentucky Fried Chicken parking lot next door about two minutes after the van blew up," said Slater. "That's the kind of car Billy drives, isn't it?"

"That's circumstantial," Karen said defensively. "He doesn't have the only Camaro in town."

"We'll see," Slater said. "But you can tell him from me that I'm not going to let this go and that he can't hide behind his father if I connect him to what went on last night."

"You just don't like me going out with Luther Coyle's son," Karen snapped. "I don't tell you who to go out with . . . or whatever it is you do."

"That doesn't have anything to do with it," Slater said evenly, trying to keep his temper in the face of the obvious insult. He put his knife and fork down and looked across the table at his daughter. "I'm talking police business. Whoever was involved in that prank caused a lot of damage, not to mention the effect it had on Bodo. Who, by the way, has exactly the same rights as anyone else in this town."

"I've got to get going," Karen said abruptly. She stood up.

"I don't know where I'll be most of the day," Slater said. "If you need me, I'll be on the beeper. You know the number."

"I won't need you." Karen turned on her heel and slammed out through the kitchen door. Slater slumped back in his chair, rubbing one hand across his stubbled jaw. The large, sunlit kitchen was silent except for the muted bubbling of the coffepot and the hum of the refrigerator.

"Shit," he whispered. He stood up, taking his coffee mug with him, and made his way through the archway into the living room. Like the master bedroom, it faced the river rushing by less than a hundred feet away, partially screened by a stand of birch.

Beyond the river, he could see the dense cedar forest that stood between the water and Old River Road, where Tom Dorchester had died, and farther still, he could see the sun-washed ridges of Quarry Hill. It was a beautiful day, and he couldn't have been in a worse mood if World War III had just started.

"Shit," he said again. Behind him, the telephone rang. He turned and dropped down onto the couch, picking the receiver up from its place on the end table. "Slater," he said crisply.

"Jack. Rembrandt Payne. I'm at the Center. You'd better get up here right away. I think we've got a problem."

"What kind of problem?"

"A bad one. Very bad."

CHAPTER SIX

10:30 A.M.

Sparrow moved slowly along the overgrown railroad right-of-way, looking for signs of Josh Robinson's passage. So far, he'd picked up a trail of crushed grass and an apple core, the white flesh only just beginning to turn brown. It looked as though the boy was headed for the quarry, which tied in with what his mother had said.

Jill Robinson hadn't quite been hysterical when she banged on the door of the refurbished carding house behind the Mill, but she'd been close. Josh was over an hour late for his guitar lesson with Lenny Freed, the Mill's resident musician, and Sparrow knew how obsessive the kid was about learning the instrument. He'd never try to duck out of his lesson, so if he was late, it meant something was wrong.

According to Jill, her son usually took his dog out around seven o'clock and often went to the quarry. The main pit there was over a hundred feet deep and half filled with water, a worried parent's nightmare. Josh was a good swimmer, but at this time of year the water would be freezing cold, and the sides of the hole were fifty-foot cliffs. He might be able to keep afloat for a while, but the cold would eventually kill him.

Sparrow had told her not to worry; Josh was a smart kid and a reasonably careful one. The most likely explanation for his being late was the dog. Everyone at the Mill knew what a scatterbrain Scoobie was, and it would be just like the crazy wirehair to take off after a rabbit or a squirrel and then get himself lost along the scrub-covered ridges of Quarry Hill. That raised problems of its own, though—hypothermia in particular—and, according to Jill, her son had probably gone out dressed in nothing but jeans and a sweater. Sparrow offered to go out and have a look for the boy.

The ex-pilot spotted a double swath of bent grass that veered off to the left. The narrow path would be the dog, the wider one beside it would be Josh. Sparrow nodded to himself—so far, so good. He followed the trail up into the trees. It was a lot warmer than when he'd set out from the Mill, and that was good, too. The warmer it became, the less chance there was of Josh's getting into real trouble.

Sparrow moved steadily onward, the trail easily visible. A few minutes later, he reached the upland meadow and paused, senses tingling. There was a faint something in the air making the hairs on the back of his neck rise. Frowning, disturbed by a sensation he'd almost forgotten, he opened up the leather case clipped to his belt and took out a compact pair of rubber-jacketed binoculars, one of the few mementos he had of his time in Vietnam. He scanned the clearing, not quite sure what he was looking for.

Using the glasses, he picked up the bent-grass trails. The narrower line moved to the middle of the meadow, then widened into a slightly darker circular patch. The second pathway, Josh's trail, went halfway to the middle, then veered abruptly. From there, it zigzagged for thirty or forty feet, ending in another, larger path of disturbance. From there, the trail seemed to move west into the trees on the far side of the clearing.

Sparrow took the binoculars away from his eyes, still frowning as he tried to reconstruct events. Scoobie runs into the center of the clearing, then stops. Josh follows the dog, but halfway there he veers away—running, from the looks of it. A boy playing tag with his dog? Maybe. Or maybe something else. That sixth sense was nagging again, and for the first time in over fifteen years, he wanted to feel the comforting weight of a sidearm on his hip.

Following Scoobie's track, Sparrow cautiously moved out into the clearing. He reached the disturbance in the center of the meadow and stopped cold. Squatting, he reached out and touched a large irregular stain smeared on the grass. He looked at his fingers and swallowed, his mouth dry: blood. A foot away, a small patch of light-colored fur was clinging to a bit of scrub. He raised his fingers to his nose and sniffed: copper. Quick death. If the fur was any indication, the blood was Scoobie's. Someone had shot Josh Robinson's dog. But where was the dog now, and where was Josh?

Sparrow stood up, a deep-rooted anger rising within him and a bitter, harsh taste filling the back of his throat. There was no possible reason for shooting the terrier. Quarry Hill was county land and off limits for hunting, even if there had been something among the rocks and scrub to hunt. Fear for the boy began to mix with his anger. It would take an unfeeling bastard to shoot a boy's dog, but what kind of person shot a dog and then removed the carcass?

He crossed the meadow quickly, heading for the other disturbed area. He reached it and paused, looking for more blood. Nothing, just a flattened area of grass four or five feet long and three wide. From it, the trail led west. Sparrow followed it to the edge of the trees and then beyond.

The tingling feeling at the base of his neck started up again, and he paused, thirty or forty feet into the trees. The trail he was on had widened, and from the looks of it, the path was a regularly used route for small animals. He stood silent, listening, his eyes slitted. Something was nagging in the recesses of his mind. Intuition? Memory? 'Nam, that was certain. And then he saw it and froze, horrified.

A dull-metal line of wire, almost invisible under the carpet of rotting leaves and cedar boughs. It ran left to right less than a yard in front of his boots. Another step and he would have hit it. Sparrow slowly dropped down onto his knees, peering into the dappled shadows beside the trail. It took a moment, but he eventually spotted it, a tiny crown of bare metal fitted with a small eyebolt. The taut wire ran through the eye, then turned at a forty-five-degree angle, connecting to an anchor pin embedded in the loose soil a foot or so to one side.

Almost two decades had gone by, but he still remembered. The device was an M16A1 BAM, sometimes referred to as a Thumper or a Jumping Jack Flash. The three-letter acronym stood for bounding antipersonnel mine. Trip the wire and the mine went off, the smaller primary charge pushing the mine three or four feet into the air, the second, much larger charge sending out a deadly hail of shredded steel for ninety feet in every direction. Anything from the chest up was turned into hamburger. The device was standard U.S. Army issue, and thousands of them had been planted along the jungle trails of Vietnam.

The disarming procedure for the mine was simple enough, but Sparrow wasn't about to play hero. He could also have stepped over the wire and continued on, but the chances were good that whoever had laid the BAM had also salted other, less visible traps along the path. The message was plain: follow me and die. It was time to go for help. He stood up carefully and began to back down the path. A moment later, heart hammering painfully in his chest, Sparrow regained the clearing and started to run.

"What am I supposed to be looking at?" asked Jack Slater, gazing at the projected image on the television monitor. He and Rembrandt Payne were standing in the Medical Center blood lab. They were alone, Payne having told Simms to take a coffee break. The image on the screen showed a static view of jumbled, rod-shaped organisms, stained a livid blue.

"This is a standard comparison slide of a common bacteria called Staphylococcus aureas," Payne said.

"As in Staph infection?"

Payne nodded. "Sometimes. The bacteria that causes Staph infections is a variant. So is gonorrhea."

"You're telling me Dorchester had the clap?"

"Not that I know of," Payne said. He fiddled with the controls on the microscope console beside the television monitor and the screen split. The S. aureas shifted to the left; the right side was taken up by a new image.

"They look the same," Slater said. "Except the slide on the left is green."

"Different stain," Payne said. "Look closely."

"The slide on the right has some small blobs . . . reddish. And the rod shapes are thick at the ends and narrower in the middle."

"Very good." He nodded. "The slide on the right is a sample taken from Tom Dorchester's spleen, or what was left of it. The bacteria looks like S. aureas, but it's different. The small blobs, as you call them, seem to be some kind of parasitic bacteria that feeds on the larger host, and the difference in shape is due to the fact that these bacteria are reproducing."

"So?"

Payne played with the console controls again, and the split

images faded. They were replaced by what looked like a wriggling mass of worms. Even as he watched, the mass became denser.

"The same bacteria growing on a chocolate agar solution," Payne said. "These are alive." He worked the console again and the image vanished. "The next view is of a petri dish filled with Ringer's solution. Glucose-based and pH adjusted to suit the human body. Keep watching." Slater kept his eyes on the screen, and Payne moved away. He bent over a Plexiglas glove box in the corner of the room. The box was used to prepare slides in a controlled environment and was fitted with its own microscope lens tied into the video system. "First a small sample of the bacteria from Dorchester."

Watching the screen, Slater suddenly saw a dark object in the upper left-hand corner. The Ringer's solution rippled as the bacteria were introduced via syringe. A small cluster of the wormlike bacteria began to swim over the screen.

"Now a drop of blood," Payne said, still hunched over the glove box. The magnified end of a syringe appeared again, and a scarlet puddle appeared on the screen. The bacteria, which had been swimming aimlessly, suddenly began to move rapidly, swimming toward the blood. Almost instantly, the bacteria spread around the perimeter of the blood sample like an encircling army. For a moment, nothing happened. Then the circle of bacteria seemed to darken, expanding and thickening. By the time Payne reached Slater's side, they had doubled in number. The blood sample appeared to swell and then a split second later the entire screen turned bright red.

"What was that?" Slater asked. "It looked like a bomb went off."

"That was Tom Dorchester dying."

"The bacteria eats blood?"

"No, nothing quite that simple. It absorbs salt."

"That doesn't sound so bad."

"It might not be under normal circumstances," Payne answered. He got up and went to the lab computer station on the far side of the room. He tore off a long strip of paper from the printer and returned to the television monitor. "It's a question of speed," he continued, looking at the printout. "The bacteria works incredibly fast. It converges on the blood cells, leaches the salts, and the cell immediately goes into cytolysis. It ruptures. Every blood cell in Officer Dorchester's body burst within a period I've extrapolated out to about ninety seconds. Maybe two minutes.''

"Christ!''

Payne handed the printout to Slater. "I did the same experiment you just saw about an hour ago and had the computer digitize the results. Right-hand number is the elapsed time. X are bacteria, Y are blood cells.''

```
00:001
              xxxxxxx                    yyyyy
             xxxxxxxxxx                  yyyyyyy
             xxxxxxxxx                   yyyyyy
             xxxxxxxx                    yyyy
              xxxxx                      yy
               xxx


00:012

                    xxxxxxx
                   xyyyyyyx
                   xxyyyyyxx
                  xxxyyyyxxx
                   xxxyyxxx
                    xxxxx


00:032

                    xxxxxxx
                    xxxxxx
                   xxxxxxxx
                  xxxxxxxxx
            xxxxxxxxxxxxxxxxxx
             xxxxxxxxxxxxxx
                xxxxxxxx
```

00:172

```
xxxxxxxxxxxxxxxxxxxxxxxxxxxxxxxxxxxxxxxxxxxxxxx
xxxxxxxxxxxxxxxxxxxxxxxxxxxxxxxxxxxxxxxxxxxxxxxxxxx
xxxxxxxxxxxxQQQQQQxxxxxxxxxxxxxxxxxxxxxxxxxxxxxxxxx
xxxxxxxxxxxxxxxxxQQQQQQQxxxxxxxxxxxxxxxxxxxxxxxxxx
xxxxxxxxxxxxxxxxxxxxxxxxQQQQQxxxxxxxxxxxxxxxxxxxxx
xxxxxxxxxxxxxxxxxxxxxxxxxxxQQQQxxxxxxxxxxxxxxxxxxx
xxxxxxxxxxxxxxxxxxxxxxxxxxxxxxxxxxxxxxxxxxxxxxxxxxx
xxxxxxxxxxxxxxxxxxxxxxxxxxxxxxx
```

01:00

```
QQQQQQQQQQQQQQQQQQQQQQQQQQQQQQQQQQQQ
QQQQQQQQQQQQQQQQQQQQQQQQQQQQQQQQQQQQQQQ
QQQQQQQQQQQQQQQQQQQQQQQQQQQQQQQQQQQQQQQ
QQQQQQQQQQQQQQQQQQQQQQQQQQQQQQQQQQQQQQQ
QQQQQQQQQQQQQQQQQQQQQQQQQQQQQQQQQQQQQQQ
QQQQQQQQQQQQQQQQQQQQQQQQQQQQQQQQQQQQQ
QQQQQQQQQQQQQQQQQQQQQQQQQQQQ
```

"X are the bacteria, and Y are the blood cells. What's Q?" asked Slater.

"Q appears in the field within seventeen seconds, like a nucleus to the bacterial culture as a whole. Within sixty seconds, the culture has completely shifted. The original bacteria have reproduced and formed endospores."

"You've got me, Doc. What's an endospore?"

"A latent bacteria. Like a peanut in a shell. It means the bacteria is virtually indestructible in its new form. The endospore usually forms in an environment that would otherwise be incapable of supporting the bacteria. It's really quite brilliant. The original bacteria kills the host, and having done so, it mutates into an endosporic state until the spores are triggered back into an active phase."

"How long can it stay in the spore state?"

"They've found endosporic bacteria in the gastrointestinal tracts of Egyptian mummies and in the bellies of mammoths fast-frozen in Siberia. They can last a long time."

"Harmful?"

"I don't know," Payne said. "That's what I'm worried about. The new form could be completely benign. On the other hand, it could be wildly toxic. I do know that the bacteria reproduces at an incredible rate and there's no antigen for it. It masks itself as S. aureas, and that's how the body reads it. The only trouble is the S. aureas antigens in the body have no effect on it. This is something completely new.''

"How do you find out if the mutant bacteria is harmful? Tests on rats and that kind of thing?''

"Humans.''

"Isn't that a bit risky?'' Slater asked. The doctor shrugged his massive shoulders.

"We don't have any choice in the matter,'' the big man answered. "The bacteria is aerobic, transferred through the respiratory system and mucous membranes. You and I were breathing the stuff in by the lungful last night. So was everyone else who came in contact with Dorchester's body or the car he was driving. You and I have passed it on to everyone we've been in contact with since we were infected, and they in turn have passed it on to everyone they've been in contact with. The infection rate for this kind of thing is geometrical, and this is a small town. Give it twelve hours, and everyone in Jericho Falls will have it.''

"What do we do?'' asked Slater, suddenly feeling nauseous at the thought of the unknown bacteria breeding within him.

"To start with, I think fervent prayer would be in order,'' Rembrandt Payne said.

"Come on, Doctor. I'm serious. You're talking about an epidemic.''

"I am serious.'' Payne shrugged. "And you're right, it is an epidemic. The trouble is, we have very little information to go on. Where the bacteria came from, for instance.''

"The van,'' Slater hazarded.

"Perhaps. But where did the van come from? The driver shows no sign of the bacteria at all.''

"I can call the courier company he was working for. There has to be a waybill somewhere.''

"It's Saturday,'' Payne said. "And even if you could find the waybill, I seriously doubt that it would tell you anything.''

"Why not?''

"Because of the bacteria itself,'' he said, his voice dark. "I told you, it's like nothing I've ever seen before, and there's nothing even close to it on file at the Centers for Disease Control in Atlanta, that much I know.''

"What are you saying?''

"I think the bacteria is man-made,'' Payne answered. "I think someone has taken S. aureas and fiddled around with it on a molecular level, creating a recombinant.''

"That's insane!''

"That's your opinion. The federal government disagrees.''

"You're talking about some kind of bacteriological warfare thing,'' Slater said.

"That's right. Nixon banned chemical and bacteriological stockpiling for offensive purposes, but the law doesn't say anything about research for supposedly defensive purposes. A nice big loophole for the military and the companies they contract with to crawl through. I've spent the last two hours thinking about this, lad, and it's the only thing that makes any sense, no matter how farfetched.''

"That still doesn't tell me where the van was coming from and what it was doing outside Jericho Falls.''

"They opened up a Science Park in Plymouth a little over three years ago, quite close to the University Campus. There's a company there called Genetrix. It may well have come from there. And perhaps the van was just passing through.''

"I don't buy that,'' Slater said, shaking his head. "If the van was passing through, why use Old River Road? Why not use the bypass? No. God only knows why, but that van was coming to Jericho Falls.''

"It doesn't really matter at this point,'' Payne said. "You said it yourself: we're faced with an epidemic, and we don't even know what the disease is and what effect it could have on the population. As medical examiner, I have to call in the State Health Department. You'll have to deal with the townspeople.''

"Wonderful. I'll call a meeting at Stark Hall and tell everyone we're in the middle of an epidemic, but I don't have the slightest idea what that epidemic is and what can be done about it.''

"I don't think you have to do that. Not yet, anyway. Let me talk to the State Health people, and then we'll take it from there.''

There was a long silence. Jack Slater looked down at the computer printout in his hands, biting his lip.

"What about us, Doc? You, me, the ambulance driver, Corky White? How are we going to know if we're sick?"

"That's impossible to say. I've already taken a blood sample from myself, and I'll get one from you before you leave. If something triggers the spores in our systems . . ." He let it dangle.

"Then we die like Dorchester?"

"It's possible." The old man nodded. "If the new bacteria acts like the original. I can't say, not yet."

"I feel like I've got a knife at my throat."

"We all do," Payne said. "The entire town."

Karen Slater made her way slowly up and down the aisles of Havelock's Pharmacy, well aware that Mildred Havelock was watching her every move in the big convex mirror mounted at the rear of the long, narrow drugstore. Old Man Havelock's pinch-faced, beady-eyed wife thought everyone was a shoplifter, and not even the sheriff's daughter was exempted.

For the third time in five minutes of browsing, she found herself in front of the feminine hygiene section, discreetly placed at the rear of the store. Camouflaged by half a dozen shelves of napkins, panty liners, tampons, and douches was a tiny display of do-it-yourself pregnancy tests: Confidelle, Prognosticon, Novesse. All the names sounded like cheap perfumes.

She picked up one of the kits. Confidelle. It promised results in one hour. She could find out yes or no in sixty minutes, just by laying out eleven dollars. She put the box back on the shelf. Buying a pregnancy test was one worse than Billy trying to buy a three-pack of Trojans. Mrs. Havelock, every artificially colored strand of her scouring-pad perm in place, would raise one eyebrow, run it through the cash register, and in thirty seconds she'd be on the telephone to the whole town.

She'd consulted her diary the previous night, confirming her suspicions. As of right now, she was six days late. For most girls her age, six days wouldn't be a lot, but Karen had been supremely regular right from her first period. Six days was a death knell.

"Hi, Karen! Anything I can help you with?"

She almost fainted, then got a grip on herself and turned around. It was Bentley Carver Bingham again, this time in a long white apron, and carrying a broom.

"Jesus, B.C.," she moaned. "You almost gave me heart failure!"

"Sorry. I saw you there, and I just thought I'd say hello."

"Hi, Bentley." Karen tried to put on her best smile. "How come you're here, anyway?"

"Derek's got the flu, so I'm filling in for Mr. Havelock. General dogsbody, learning the pharmaceutical business from the ground up." He lifted the broom and mimed a brief thrust and parry. "Literally. But it's four dollars an hour."

"Good." She wondered if B.C. had seen her looking at the Confidelle box, but then realized she had nothing to worry about. He was doing his best to not even look at the display of napkins.

"Shopping?" asked B.C.

"Not really. I'm supposed to meet Billy at the Bo-Peep."

"Then how come you're here and not there?" asked the boy.

"Don't be nosy."

"Sorry." There was a long pause, and then Bentley frowned. "Have you noticed anything weird this morning?"

"Just you."

"No, really. About seven o'clock a plane flew over, no more than a couple of hundred feet up."

"Jericho Falls does have an airport, B.C. It was probably one of Mr. Coyle's."

"No it wasn't," said B.C., shaking his head. "AirMedic has two red-and-white Comanches. Coyle Air Transport flies black-and-gold Citations. This was an army plane. A small one."

"So what?"

"It came back about twenty minutes later, made another pass. The second time I noticed, it had a big bulge under it. Not the same color as the rest of the plane."

"You're imagining things, B.C."

"I'm not imagining the phones."

"Now what are you talking about?" Karen said, exasperated. She had more important things to think about than the Bug's fantasies.

"Old Man Havelock put a call in to some big wholesaler he deals with in Manchester, and he couldn't get through. He tried about three or four times, but nothing worked, so he called the operator. She said they were having trouble with their long-distance switching system."

"So?"

"It's an example of what they call mosaic thinking," B.C. replied, leaning on his broom. "Most people think in straight lines; you know, one thought leading to another—that's linear. In mosaic thinking, you put together ideas that don't seem to fit and make them work. I put the airplane and the telephone screw-up together."

"What did you come up with?"

"There's a Russian spy in the Falls and the army is trying to find him, using a sophisticated camera system on the plane. They've cut off the long-distance calls so he can't call his friends for help."

"I'll see you later, Bentley. Good luck with your mosaic or whatever it is." Karen turned and headed for the front of the store.

"He doesn't really care for you, Karen. Not really." She stopped and looked back over her shoulder. Bentley was watching her, still leaning on the broom, eyes solemn behind his glasses.

"What are you talking about?"

"Billy Coyle. He only cares about you because you make him look good. Like his car and his clothes."

"Why don't you mind your own business," Karen said.

"Yeah, that's what everyone says." He nodded glumly.

Karen walked angrily to the front door, ignoring Mildred Havelock's icy stare. She slammed out of the drugstore and turned up the street, heading for the Bo-Peep and her meeting with Billy.

He was waiting for her as she came in the door of Chang's place, sitting in their favorite booth at the very back of the restaurant. She frowned when she saw that Marty Doyle was with him. The Hardy Boys, Doyle and Coyle. Except for the fact that they lived almost next door to each other on the Hill, Karen couldn't see why they got along, unless you believed that opposites attracted. Marty was the same height as Billy, but he was a good sixty pounds heavier, most of the weight on his gut. His hair was dark, and even at seventeen it was beginning to thin. He had a small, girlish mouth, a forehead full of zits, and he used too much Old Spice to cover up the fact that he didn't take enough baths.

Karen slipped into the seat across from the two boys and shrugged out of her jacket. She grimaced as Marty's eyes flickered over her breasts. She wished she'd worn a sweater instead of the U of H sweatshirt she'd borrowed from her father's laundry hamper.

"Karen." Marty nodded, the small mouth bending into a reasonable facsimile of a smile.

"Hi, Marty."

Billy reached out and took her hand. She let him hold it for a second and then pulled it away, tucking it into her lap. She'd eaten a full breakfast, but the rich aroma wafting up from Chang's deep fryers was almost enough to make her swoon.

"I'm sorry about last night," Billy said, smiling across the table at her.

"There's nothing to be sorry about. I just didn't want to go out and make a fool of myself." She frowned. "Or set fire to a van and scare Bodo out of his wits."

"He doesn't have any wits to get scared out of," Marty grunted. "And who says we had anything to do with that van getting torched, anyway?"

"I do," the young woman said coldly. "And I think it was pretty goddamn stupid."

"Relax, Karen, no one got hurt," Billy said.

"Tell that to Bodo. They took him away in an ambulance and had to sedate him. He's still in the Med Center."

"Look—" Billy began.

"You have any proof we were involved?" asked Marty Doyle, his lip curling. Chang appeared and slid a tall foaming chocolate milkshake in front of the overweight teenager. "I mean, were there any witnesses, Karen?" he added after Chang had gone. He slid the straw into his mouth and sucked at the shake, watching Karen over the rim of the glass.

"Yes, Marty, as a matter of fact there was a witness. Mr. Kartosian at T.J.'s Restaurant. He saw a blue Camaro peeling out of the Kentucky Fried."

"My car?" Billy said, worried.

"He saw a blue Camaro," said Marty Doyle, shrugging. "So what?"

"My father knows what kind of car Billy drives."

"It was just a joke," Billy said weakly. Beside him, Marty Doyle had suddenly broken out in a sweat. He made a small choking noise, lifting his mouth away from the milkshake straw.

"Martin?" Karen said, staring at him. She blinked. The pimples on the fat boy's forehead seemed to have burst, thin trickles of blood mixing with the sweat now pouring off him. "What's the matter?"

"I—" He made another choking sound, then coughed heavily. A thick splash of blood and mucus spurted out of his mouth, and thin streams of scarlet began to pour from his nostrils. Karen screamed, lurching back as the spray from his bloody vomit sprayed across her jacket and sweatshirt.

"Holy shit!" Billy yelled, pulling away. Marty Doyle swayed, trying to pull himself out of the booth. The exposed skin on his arms, neck, and face began to blacken as thousands of blood vessels and capillaries burst underneath his skin. His eyes began to bulge, showing nothing but bloodshot white. Karen, her eyes glued to the bloody sight, was still screaming, backed into a corner of the booth. Heads had turned, and the other customers in the Bo-Peep were beginning to yell now, too. Chang, back to his deep fryers, was standing transfixed, watching as Marty Doyle finally made it to his feet.

The boy stood between the counter and the booths, his entire face now a mask of blood, more fluid seeping through the fabric of his shirt, a huge stain darkening the front of his jeans. A terrible odor began to rise, and then Marty coughed again, the sound no more than a wet gurgle. He lifted his bloody hands weakly, cupping them over his mouth, catching only a tiny fraction of the thick, stringy fluid drooling over his chin. Blood was running freely from his ears, and a viscous, dark red pool was forming between his legs. Marty's hands fluttered up to his head, weakly trying to stop the terrible pain as the blood pressure within his skull climbed over 350. His back arched as his brain finally hemorrhaged out, and he slid to the floor, then slumped face first into the hideous, reeking puddle of his own body fluids and excretions. QQ9, after its all too brief hibernation, had been reborn.

CHAPTER SEVEN

11:45 A.M.

Jack Slater and Jenny Hale were waiting anxiously in the kitchen of the sheriff's River Park house when Rembrandt Payne lumbered down the stairs and entered the room.

"How is she?" asked Slater.

Payne dropped heavily into one of the antique ladder-back chairs.

"Well enough physically. She's in shock. I gave her something to make her sleep. She'll be out until this evening, but someone should stay with her in case she wakes up."

"I will," Jenny offered.

"What about Billy Coyle?"

"Luther insisted I admit him to the Center," Payne said. "He's the same as Karen. Shock. Seeing the Doyle boy die like that was traumatic. Chang has closed the restaurant, and the story's going around like wildfire."

"Christ, that's all we need," Slater muttered. "As if things weren't bad enough already."

"Jack said something about an epidemic," Jenny said, looking at Payne. "Does that mean we're going to have more deaths like Marty?" The apprehension in her voice was obvious.

"I don't know," said the old doctor, shaking his head wearily. "I won't know until I autopsy the lad. It's possible."

"Did you talk to the State Health people?" Slater asked.

"I tried," Payne said. "Apparently, the long-distance circuits aren't functioning. The computer lines are down as well. I can't get any databases except the Center mainframe."

"We can drive up to Rumney," Slater said. "You can call from there."

"You go. I've got enough on my plate here. Tell them what's happened, and make sure they get an epidemiological team up here as fast as possible."

"All right." The sheriff turned to Jenny. "It'll take me about an hour, round-trip. Get on the phone to Norm Lombard. He's holding the fort down at the station. I want an emergency meeting of the town council. We can do without Dave Doyle under the circumstances, but I want everyone else there." He pushed away from the table and stood up. "You're sure Karen will be okay?" he asked Payne.

The old man nodded. "She'll be fine."

There was a clattering roar from outside the house as a battered fifties pickup truck pulled into the driveway. A few seconds later, a door slammed heavily and Sparrow Hawke appeared at the side door of the house. Slater let him in.

"I heard about what happened at the Bo-Peep," said the tall, long-haired man. "Is Karen okay?"

"Fine," said the doctor. "There was no need for you—"

"I didn't come up here to see about Karen," interrupted Sparrow. "I came about Josh Robinson?" Slater asked.

"Who is Josh Robinson."

"Grade seven boy," supplied Jenny. "His mother is a weaver."

"That's right." Sparrow nodded. "He's missing."

"How long ago?" asked Slater.

"This morning, around seven-thirty or eight."

"It's only noon," Slater replied, annoyed. "He hasn't been gone long enough to qualify as missing."

"Maybe not. But I went looking for him. He had a habit of taking his dog for a run up to the old quarry. It looks as though someone shot the dog and took Josh."

"*What?*" Slater frowned.

"That's not all. I kept on looking for him, and I almost tripped over an antipersonnel mine someone had laid. You know what a Jumping Jack Flash is, Sheriff?"

"A bounding mine," Slater said, brows creased. "Used in 'Nam a lot."

"Right in one."

"That's insane," Slater said.

"Perhaps not," commented Rembrandt Payne. Slater turned and looked at him.

"What's that supposed to mean?" he asked.

"Nothing." The doctor shrugged. "But I suggest that you leave for Rumney as quickly as possible." The white-haired man was staring at the kitchen ceiling, lips pursed thoughtfully.

"You're going to Rumney?" Sparrow asked.

"That's right. The long-distance lines are out."

"I want to go with you," the old hippy said quickly.

"Why?"

"I've got a bad feeling, that's all."

"Okay," Slater said after a short pause. "I guess I could use the company." He turned to Jenny. "Take care of Karen, and call Norm."

"Consider it done," she said, trying to smile.

"I'll be at the Medical Center," Payne said. "Get in touch with me as soon as you get back."

"Will do." Slater bent down and gave Jenny a brief kiss, then turned away, following Sparrow out through the kitchen door.

Rembrandt Payne assumed, incorrectly, that Martin Doyle had died as a result of the bacteria's emergence from its endosporic phase. In fact, Martin Doyle's death was caused by a primary contact with the original bacteria, the infection occurring shortly after the young man's ill-fated imitation of the Headless Horseman the previous night.

The explosion of the van's gas tank destroyed most of the containers carrying the bacterial cultures, but two of the thermoslike vessels survived. One was blown through the hedge of head-high cedar separating the Gas Bar from the Slumber-King Motel, where it landed close to the rear wall of the building.

The second container was responsible for shattering the front window of the Gas Bar office, disintegrating against the lip of the counter. Unlike Tom Dorchester, Martin Doyle, protected by his costume, had received a very small dose of the bacteria.

The low dosage only served as a stay of execution, however, and slightly less than twelve hours after his initial contact with the bacteria, he died in the Bo-Peep Grill, bleeding into the remains of the double-chocolate milkshake that was his last meal on this earth.

During those hours between infection and death, Martin Doyle passed on a secondary form of the bacteria to Billy Coyle, the four others who had taken part in the Gas Bar prank, both his parents, David and Paulette Doyle, Estelle LaCroix, the Doyle family's cleaning lady, George Sawchuck at Sawchuck's Variety Store on Main Street, where Martin had stopped to purchase a Baby Ruth Bar prior to visiting the Bo-Peep, three other customers who happened to be in Sawchuck's at the time, and seven others in the Bo-Peep, including Chang.

Billy Coyle and the other four boys involved in the prank had also passed the infection on and so had the six people who had come into direct contact with Tom Dorchester's corpse and the police cruiser he died in.

By noon, supported by a base of twenty-seven primary cases, 729 people in Jericho Falls had received a secondary infection, each one of those cases in turn becoming virulently infectious. Another twelve hours, and with almost no exceptions, the entire population of Jericho Falls would be carrying the endosporic mutation of QQ9, Q Variant One, or more simply, QV1.

Unlike its violently dramatic parent, the first symptoms of QV1 were rather ordinary. Headache, mild nausea, excessive and painful urination, and a general run-down feeling. By late morning on November 1, dozens of Jericho Falls residents were having these symptoms, but none thought them serious enough to require medical attention. By noon, the number of people had increased dramatically, and those infected earliest were struck by two new symptoms: an arthriticlike aching in the joints, accompanied by rising temperature.

Had there been an epidemiologist on site, and had these early symptoms been reported, the first "cluster phenomena" would almost certainly have been spotted. The symptoms were most strongly evident in people between the ages of sixteen and forty-five, the figures spiking in a limited range between the ages of nineteen and twenty-six, without sexual discrimination. Virtually no one under the age of twelve or over sixty showed any initial effects. There were other clinical exceptions, but these did not become evident for some time.

Shortly after noon, the first extreme cases began trickling in to the emergency room of the Jericho Falls Medical Center. Most of these were fever related, with temperatures as high as 108°F. Male patients complained of painfully swollen lymph nodes and a feeling of extreme thirst, while a number of the female patients reported spontaneous and abnormal menstruation as well as lymph pain and dehydration.

By 12:20 P.M., a few minutes before Rembrandt Payne returned to the hospital, the trickle of patients had become a flood and Dr. Sheldon Brewster and Head Nurse Betty Van Heusen decided to call in all available staff to deal with the situation. Brewster, recently graduated from Boston Medical, was convinced that they were in the midst of an early flu onslaught, but Betty Van Heusen wasn't so sure. She'd never seen a flu that made women menstruate, and she'd never seen an outbreak of any disease that came on so quickly. There were six doctors on Brewster's emergency call list, and twenty-one nurses on Betty Van Heusen's. Of those staff contacted, only two of the doctors and eleven nurses were in any shape to respond. At 12:22, Officer Randy Van Heusen, Betty Van Heusen's husband, called the hospital and advised them that Corky White had been discovered in his home in Frenchtown. He had bled to death in his own bed.

"Quiet," Sparrow Hawke commented as he and Jack Slater drove down the Strip, heading for 115A. "Half the stores along here aren't even open."

"I noticed," Slater said, seated behind the wheel of the unmarked car. Normally, Saturday morning traffic on the Strip was heavy, the parking lots filled with cars. Today, there was almost nothing. Slater glanced at the fuel gauge on the dashboard. He was running close to empty. "I'm going to get some gas." Reaching Ralph Beavis's Gas Bar, Slater turned off the road, guiding the car up to the pumps. Directly in front of them was the blackened ruin of the van. Slater felt his stomach knot.

"Doesn't look like there's anybody around," Sparrow said. Slater looked out through the side window of the car. The front window of the Gas Bar office had been blocked off with a large, dirt-smeared sheet of plywood. Both the service bay doors were closed, and there were no lights on.

"Ralph has to be around here somewhere," Slater said. He

climbed out of the cruiser and walked across to the office. Peering in through the grimy glass in the door, he could see that the interior was dark and empty. He tried the door handle. Locked. Slater went back to the car.

"Nobody home?" Sparrow asked.

"Maybe he's at the motel."

"You go look for him; I'll fill up the tank," Sparrow suggested, climbing out of the cruiser. "The pumps aren't locked."

"I noticed." He turned around and walked over the Gas Bar lot to the Slumber-King. It wasn't like Ralph at all, leaving the pumps wide open when he wasn't around. He checked his watch: past noon. The Gas Bar was supposed to be open twenty-four hours a day. Bodo was at the Medical Center, but where was Ralph, and where were Bert and Corky, the mechanics?

Slater went through the opening in the hedge that led to the covered walk around the motel office. There was only one car on the lot, at the far end. Reasonable enough for this time of year. He made his way to the office entrance and pulled open the outer screen-and-glass combination. He rapped on the inner door and waited.

Nothing. He could see lights inside, but it appeared that Ralph wasn't in the motel office, either. Frowning, he tried the handle of the inner door. Locked up tight. He knocked again and waited, but there was still no answer. He shrugged and let the outer door close on its spring. Beavis was probably down at Charlie Rice's Insurance Agency on the Common, trying to collect on the broken window from last night.

He went back to the cruiser, arriving just as Sparrow was hooking the nozzle back onto the pump. "No Ralph?" asked the long-haired man.

"No Ralph," Slater said, slipping in behind the wheel again. Sparrow got in on the passenger side.

"Sixteen bucks on the dial," Sparrow commented. "And no one to collect it. Maybe Ralph got religion or something."

"I'll pay him later." He turned on the ignition and rolled back onto the Strip. A few moments later, they reached the 115A intersection. To the right, Notch Road led north into the mountains, cutting in behind the long steep-sided shape of Frenchman's Ridge. To the left was the two-lane blacktop of Airport Road, a straight line heading due south with Drake's Farm on one side and Coppertop Hill on the other. Half a mile down the highway, the hills closed in at the neck of Jericho Falls Valley. Slater drove through the intersection, heading west.

Sparrow pulled a crumpled package of Luckies out of the breast pocket of his denim jacket. "Want one?" he asked, gesturing with the package. Slater nodded. Sparrow tipped two cigarettes out of the pack, lit them both with a wooden match, and handed one across to Slater. "You think you might let me in on what's going on?"

"Your guess is as good as mine."

"Bullshit. You didn't even twitch when I told you Josh Robinson had disappeared, and that's not the kind of thing you take lightly. Not to mention the fact that someone out there is planting land mines."

"You heard about how Marty Doyle died?"

"Yeah. What was he, a hemophiliac or something?"

"No. The same thing happened to Tom Dorchester last night."

"Dorchester's dead? Jesus!"

"Doc Payne thinks we're in the middle of some kind of epidemic. According to him, it's incredibly infectious. I've been exposed to it, and so has he. You too for that matter."

"You mean we're going to go like Dorchester and the Doyle kid?"

"I don't know. I don't think so. Doc says the original bacteria has mutated into some kind of spore."

"When I got back to the Mill after trying to find Josh, Annie in the health food store said about half a dozen people had gone to the Medical Center."

"Bleeding?" asked Slater, turning his head sharply to look at Sparrow.

"Uh-uh. More like flu. Temperature, aching. You think there might be a connection?"

"I don't know. That's why I'm making the trip to Rumney. Doc Payne wants an epidemiologist up here as fast as possible."

"I'm still freaking out about that Jack Flash." Sparrow took a long drag on his cigarette, then ground out the butt in the dashboard ashtray.

"Maybe you imagined it," Slater offered, pulling the wheel over slightly as they climbed up out of the valley and turned south. The cedar-covered slopes of the White Mountain foothills rose steeply on either side while behind them, Jericho Falls had vanished from sight around the curve.

"I was never into acid. A bit of weed now and again, no more than that. I saw what I saw, Sheriff. Someone offed Josh's dog and took the boy. I'm sure of it."

"Where would anyone get a bounding mine?" Slater asked skeptically. "You don't pick them up in the local Seven-Eleven."

"I know. That's been bugging me too. Holy shit!"

Jack Slater stood on the brake pedal and the cruiser slowed to a screeching stop. Fifty feet in front of them a large, high-sided stake truck had spread itself across the narrow highway. The red-and-white cab was tilted on its side, while the body was canted steeply in the opposite direction. The side of the body facing them was a splintered ruin, and the two men in the police car could see the torn and ravaged corpses of at least a hundred chickens littered across the blacktop. There were feathers everywhere.

"That's Corney Drake's truck," Slater said. He pushed open the door of the cruiser and got out, unbuttoning the flap on his holster. Sparrow got out on the other side, and they walked cautiously toward the overturned truck. Corney Drake owned the last seventy-five acres of Drake's Farm. With the steady encroachment of the town, Drake's Farm had turned away from cash crops, and ever since Jack Slater could remember, Cornelius Drake had raised broiler chickens, selling some locally, but shipping most of them to the big processing plant just across the state line in Montpelier, Vermont.

Slater picked up a faint odor of gasoline and carefully stubbed out his cigarette before going any closer. They picked their way through the gruesome litter around the truck, Slater climbing up to inspect the cab while Sparrow checked the back of the truck.

"What about Corney?" Sparrow asked. Slater boosted himself up and looked into the cab. The windshield was shattered, and the door was pocked with dozens of neat punctures. There was blood on the seat back, and the upholstery had been torn open. Slater dropped down to the ground and joined Sparrow.

"Corney's not in the cab. It's been shot up."

"So has the body," Sparrow said, pointing. The side of the truck was stitched with scores of half-dollar holes that went from left to right and top to bottom. There was an immense gaping wound low and to the rear, the splintered edges scorched and dark. Inside the four-foot-wide hole, Sparrow and Slater could see spattered remnants of more chickens, burst chunks of gore, and thousands of feathers glued to the blood-covered walls. "Looks like someone used a heavy machine gun and a T.O.W.," said Sparrow, one hand reaching out to touch the edge of the large hole.

"I don't understand any of this," Slater said, a frightened note in his voice. "Why in God's name would anyone want to blow up Corney Drake's truck?"

"Who'd want to kill Josh Robinson's dog?" Sparrow asked coldly. "But it's got to be the same people. Now do you think I was having an acid flash up there on Quarry Hill?"

"It just doesn't make any sense."

Beside him, Sparrow stiffened, his head cocked to one side: "Quiet!"

"What?"

"Listen, damn it!"

A rhythmic clattering began to fill the air, like the muted punch of a jackhammer. The noise level increased quickly, seeming to come from the west. Slater felt Sparrow's strong hand gripping him by the arm, pulling hard.

"What is it?"

"Into the ditch!" commanded Sparrow, dragging Slater away from the truck. "Under cover, now!"

Slater let the big, long-haired man pull him to the side of the road. Sparrow dropped down into the shallow ditch beside the gravel shoulder, jerking Slater with him.

"Into the trees!" Sparrow hissed. "Quick!"

The two men crawled rapidly up the other side of the embankment and rolled into the low cedar scrub. The clattering became a stupendous roar, edged with the high-pitched whine of a turbine.

"Keep down!" Sparrow insisted. Slater tucked his head low and looked back toward the road. An instant later the source of the pounding noise revealed itself. A helicopter slid around the opposite hillside, bulbous, stubby missile racks attached to its landing skids and a drooping proboscislike appendage dangling under its shark nose. Bizarrely, the helicopter was painted a bril-

liant, shining white, and there were large red crosses painted on
the fuselage and belly.

"A Huey Cobra," Sparrow whispered, staring bug-eyed at the
machine as it swooped down over the highway. "With a fucking
chain gun and T.O.W. rails!"

"But—"

Slater's words were drowned out by the cataclysmic thunder
of the 30mm cannon in the helicopter's nose. Asphalt flew in all
directions as the shells slammed into the road, carving a path
toward the sheriff's car. The insectlike aircraft seemed to hesitate
for a split second, and then there was an ear-splitting, sledgehammer detonation as the wire-guided missiles slung on the landing
gear went off. The helicopter was briefly hidden by a huge ball
of smoke as the missiles skittered away, and then it reappeared
as the spinning rotors blew the smoke toward the ground.

The missiles reached their target, one striking the front of the
car while the second sheared through the windshield. There was
a heartbeat pause, then the car vanished in a blazing fireball. The
helicopter hung suspended over the remains of Cornelius Drake's
truck for a fraction of a second and then seemed to stand on its
tail. It jerked upward as though pulled by invisible strings, did a
neck-snapping turn, and then nosed down at full speed, turbines
screaming as it swept back around the side of the hill and vanished as suddenly as it had appeared.

"My God! What happened?" Slater asked, staring dazedly at
the furiously burning wreckage of the police car.

"We just survived a firefight," Sparrow said. "Come on,
we've got to get out of here. Back to town." He took a quick
look up the highway and then stood, pulling Slater up by the
elbow.

"Who *were* they?" Slater asked, his voice numb.

"The bad guys." Sparrow slid down into the ditch and then
climbed up onto the shoulder. "Come on, Sheriff. We've got to
get the hell away from here before they send somebody out to do
a body count."

By 1:30 P.M., the town of Jericho Falls was held tightly in the
grip of a dark and frightening malaise. Initially, it had been ru-
mored that Martin Doyle had died as a result of food poisoning
contracted at the Bo-Peep, but it soon became obvious that this

was not the case. The flulike sickness was everywhere and played no favorites. The stores and other business establishments that had opened on Saturday morning were closed by noon, either because of a lack of business or because there was no staff capable of working.

Townspeople well enough to be interested in news of what was going on discovered that WKLC, the local radio station, was not broadcasting at all, and the telephone lines to the radio station, the police, and the city council offices were constantly busy. All citizens-band radio frequencies were inoperative due to a steadily pulsing static signal, and Lisa Colchester was unable to raise the state police offices in Rumney, Plymouth, or Canaan. She was also unable to reach Jack Slater in his cruiser. As deputy chief in Jack Slater's absence, Norm Lombard sent Randy Van Heusen to the airport, hoping that the VHF radio there would be able to raise a signal. When Van Heusen didn't report back after almost an hour, Lombard sent out Zeke Torrance to look for him, and Torrance too disappeared. Lombard and Lisa Colchester thus became the only active members of the Jericho Falls Police Department, since Charlie Hill had reported in sick earlier that day. Except for one or two of the older men, the Jericho Falls VFD had been put out of commission by the sickness, but fortunately there were no fires reported during the morning or afternoon.

Sam Quarrel, editor of the Jericho Falls *Leader Post,* remained in his office, but by noon he realized that for the first time in almost seventy-two years there would be no weekly edition. None of his people had showed up for work, and the page proofs remained on the makeup tables untouched. Spurred by anger as much as by his journalistic instincts, Quarrel began nosing around, trying to find out just what was going on, but most people were too ill or too distressed by the situation to talk to him. Returning to the *Leader Post* offices in the Stewart Block on Constitution Common, the elderly editor noticed for the first time that his three teletype machines were silent, even though there was obviously plenty of electrical current to run them.

Sitting down at the "send" station, he composed a brief test message and tried to put it on the AP wire, but nothing happened.

He tried again with UPI and the Hearst Wire, but the result was the same. The last method of communication between the town and the outside world was inoperative. Jericho Falls was completely isolated.

CHAPTER EIGHT

2:45 P.M.

The two men moved as quickly as they could through the heavy undergrowth, keeping close to the clear, narrow stream that bisected the high-walled valley. Sparrow was in the lead, his eyes scanning the way ahead, while Slater followed, his police special gripped tightly in his right hand. There was no discernible trail, and the going was slow.

"If we keep on going up the Notch, it's going to take us at least another hour," the sheriff said, keeping his voice low. "Christ! I haven't been up here since I was a Boy Scout." He shivered, even though his bomber jacket was zipped tightly to the neck. The air was cold and the brittle, icy silence seemed to magnify every sound.

"Let's take a break," Sparrow said, pausing. They squatted down in the light shelter of a Volkswagen-sized boulder a yard or so from the stream. Even resting, the long-haired ex-pilot kept watch, his head turning now and again to check the sides of the valley. "Didn't you once tell me you were in 'Nam?" Sparrow asked after a moment. "You don't seem too comfortable in the woods."

"I was an MP in Saigon. We busted hookers and made sure the black market didn't get out of hand. I was never into jungle tactics."

"Learn," Sparrow said, grinning.

"I still don't see why we just didn't go back along the road."

"They would have picked us up in five minutes. If we keep to the bush, we'll avoid any GSR they've got set up."

"What makes you think they're using Ground Surveillance Radar?" Slater asked as they pushed on up the tree-choked defile.

"That Cobra didn't find us by accident. They've got observers posted, and they saw us coming. I remember exercises like this in Happy Valley and Bong Son. Observers to forward positions with GSR, call in the Killer Teams, and then bring on the gunships. It's a classic encirclement operation. Except this time we're the guys in the black pajamas. I get the feeling Jericho Falls is about to be sanitized."

"That's crazy."

"Sure. So was 'Nam, but that didn't make it any less real."

"This is New Hampshire, not South Vietnam."

"Same problem. If Doc is right, then somebody made a big mistake. One of their nasty bugs got loose, and they've got to get it back, any way they can, or at least contain it until they figure out what to do with us."

"Goddamnit, we need help, not helicopter gunships. Why don't they send in doctors?"

"Maybe they know more about the bug than we do," Slater said ominously. "Maybe it's too late for doctors."

"Then why the red cross on a white helicopter?"

"Protective coloration," Sparrow said. "The Falls was put off the beaten track when the 115 bypass was built. Block 115A, Old River Road, and Notch Road into the mountains, and you isolate the town. A squad at each end to tell people the army is conducting war games in the area, and no one's the wiser."

"Quarantine," Slater said. "But they can't keep it up forever."

"I know. That's what I'm worried about." He stood up, brushing pine needles off his jeans.

"How much farther do you think?" Slater asked.

"The stream winds around Beacon Hill. We keep going up for another mile or so until we reach Notch Ridge. From there we can get down to the road west of Frenchtown."

"You saw a mine up by the quarry. What about the Ridge?"

"Maybe, but I doubt it. They knew someone would come looking for Josh eventually, so they dropped the mine. That trail leads down to the old railway bridge. They just didn't want anyone following. They might have an observer posted, though."

"What do we do then?" Slater asked.

"Kill him."

"Then I guess I should make you a deputy."

Rembrandt Payne shifted uncomfortably in his chair and grimaced, his eyes fixed on the computer screen. Outside his office, he knew that the small hospital was in chaos, but his value in the Emergency Ward was outweighed by the work he was doing trying to make some sense out of the plague that had descended on Jericho Falls.

The Medical Center was now beyond capacity, with cots set up in the halls. For the past hour they had been turning all but the most serious cases away. There was very little the steadily decreasing staff at the Center could do anyway, except prescribe aspirin and cold packs as a way of lowering the higher fevers.

The old doctor cursed, one hand massaging his billowing stomach. He'd barely eaten a thing all day, and the overabundant gastric juices in his stomach were giving him a frightful case of gas. He tapped at the keyboard, scrolling back and forth through the limited case information he had, trying to search out some clue.

So far, he had discovered only one meaningful fact: the secondary infection seemed to ignore young children and older adults, the reverse of any type of flu he'd ever seen. On the other hand, the comparison was irrelevant since influenza was a virus, not a bacterial infection, and Redenbacher's Syndrome (as he'd named it) was definitely microbial in origin.

Payne shook his head wearily. What was the point? If the original biological toxin had been produced as a CBW weapon, it was highly unlikely that a rural medical center and its septuagenarian director were going to find any quick cure.

And quickness was the name of the game now. Billy Coyle and some of the other adolescent patients admitted with the disease were running desperately high temperatures, and even with intravenous drips and cold packs to prevent, or at least slow down, dehydration, they were in serious trouble. Sandra, Mildred Watchorn's seventeen-year-old, was close to renal failure, and without immediate attention, she'd be dead by nightfall.

"Hell and damnation!" he muttered. It would be at least another half hour before the results of the latest culture samples were ready. In the meantime, he decided on another tack with the computer. He sat forward, tapped the ESCAPE key, and the screen cleared, taking him back to the Medical Center's mainframe database directory.

He scrolled through the subheadings and then called up the admissions code for those now in the hospital with symptoms of Redenbacher's Syndrome, cross-indexed against patients who had been admitted prior to the outbreak of the sickness. Fortunately, admissions had been light prior to the outbreak, and the list was a short one. There had been twelve patients in the center on Halloween night. Those who now showed signs of Redenbacher's Syndrome appeared in boldface.

ADM/JFMC. . . . . .OCT 31/NOV 1

NAME	DOB	PREDIAG	ATTPHYS
ALLINGHAM W.	3/11/22	GALL	SEYMOUR
AMERY L.	5/5/49	ORTH	BLAINE
BIMM B.	N/A	SHOCK	PAYNE
COWPER E.	2/7/54	OBGYN	MCNIVEN
DAVIDSON S.	4/5/59	OBGYN	MCNIVEN
GLADSTONE E.	3/2/14	CARD/S/ICU	SEYMOUR
HUGHES M.	9/4/48	HERNIA	SEYMOUR/ LEWIS
JOHANNSEN P.	4/7/51	RESP	KEENE
LASSITTER V.	3/10/70	ORTH	BLAIN
MORIN T.	5/8/65	OBGYN	BREWSTER
SLOANE K.	8/5/48	CARD	SEYMOUR
VAN EPP T.	5/26/49	OBGYN	BREWSTER

Payne leaned back in his chair, gazing at the screen. Now *that* was interesting. Of the twelve patients listed, five had contracted Redenbacher's Syndrome, all of them within the suspected age parameters, three male and two female. But of the remaining seven patients listed, five were still within the limits, but none had contracted the disease. Of those five, four were pregnant, which was just about the normal ratio for this time of year. So what did old people, young people, and pregnant women have in common that made them immune to Redenbacher's?

There were two anomalies to consider: Jack Slater, who should have shown signs of the disease long ago, and Bodo Bimm. As far as Payne knew, Bodo had no real medical record, so for the moment he ignored him, turning his attention to Jack instead. The obvious thought was the lad's diabetes. If pregnancy was a factor in immunization, why not diabetes mellitus?

He cleared the screen again, returning to the directory, then zigzagged his way through the records until he had a list of out-patients who'd been given repeat insulin prescriptions. Since the list included everyone in the county who'd ever come to the Center, it took him a fair amount of time to trim it down to those diabetes patients who actually lived in Jericho Falls. There were forty-seven of them, and of those, all except three were well outside the age parameters of Redenbacher's Syndrome. Not surprising, since, for the most part, diabetes was a sickness associated with old age. He took those three names, Jack Slater's included, and cross-indexed them over admissions made to the hospital that day. None of the names appeared. He nodded to himself. It wasn't absolute proof by any means, but it looked as though diabetes sufferers were immune to the toxin.

"But why?" he whispered, staring at the silent screen. Medically, old age and youth had no more in common than pregnancy and diabetes, yet all four situations gave immunity. In terms of epidemiology, there were five basic forms an immunity could take: acquired immunity, brought about by a previous exposure; active immunity, a resistance developed in response to an antigen; natural immunity; passive immunity, such as that conferred by a mother to her child; and a specific immunity brought about by a vaccine.

In the case of Redenbacher's Syndrome, none of these could possibly apply. The Syndrome had been brought about by a recombinant bacteria, which ruled out previous exposure, the natural development of antigens, a vaccine, and natural immunity, such as human resistance to canine distemper. Passive immunity was ruled out as well, since it was the pregnant mothers who appeared to be immune, not their unborn children.

Yet there had to be an answer, some linking factor. Payne dumped out of the database and then pulled himself up out of the big chair behind his desk. Howard Simms, the lab technician in the hematology lab, had gone home an hour before, complaining of fever and nausea. If the blood tests Payne had done held any information, Payne knew he'd have to check the results himself. He pulled out the old-fashioned pocket watch from his vest and flipped it open: 3:00. In an hour, he was supposed to be at the city council meeting at Stark Hall. He sighed wearily. They'd want answers, and he had none to give. He shambled heavily out of his office and headed down to the blood lab.

Jenny Hale sat in the slowly darkening kitchen of Jack Slater's house, sipping at yet another cup of coffee. Almost four hours had gone by since Jack and Sparrow left, and the silence was beginning to get to her. No ringing telephone, no talk of upcoming events, no visitors, not even TV or radio—she'd tried both. It was spooky.

She picked up one of the magazines she'd found and leafed through it briefly. A newsmagazine, full of bright snappy stories and color photographs to show you what was happening around the world. She tossed the magazine back onto the table. She didn't give a damn about the rest of the world, she wanted to know what was happening right here and right now.

Where the hell was Jack? Rumney was no more than twenty or thirty miles away, and two hours was more than enough to make the round trip, yet he and Sparrow had been gone twice that long. She picked up her mug of lukewarm coffee, then almost dropped it at the sound of someone hammering on the door.

She got up quickly and crossed the kitchen in three steps. As she pulled open the door, her sudden expectations vanished. It wasn't Jack, it was the half-pint figure of B.C. Bingham, one of her best students, but one with the irritating habit of sometimes correcting her blackboard English. The worst of it was that he was always right.

"Hello, Bentley. What are you doing here?"

"Uh, hi, Miss Hale. I came to visit with Karen, if that's okay," he said. What God had given B.C. Bingham in the way of brains, he'd balanced by making him a foot shorter than the rest of the kids in his class and by giving him thick glasses and a dress sense that made her wonder if the kid weren't color blind. Today, it was a robin's egg blue quilted ski jacket, a lime green sweater, and light brown corduroy pants.

"Karen is in bed. I'm afraid—"

"I know," B.C. said with a nod. "I was working at Have-lock's when it happened. I thought she might like some cheering up." He lifted a crumpled brown paper bag. "I got her a present."

"It's a nice thought, Bentley, but—" Somehow the boy managed to get by her.

"I won't stay long," he said.

"Okay. You can peek in, but if she's still asleep you'll have to go, understand?"

"Of course," B.C. said. He stripped off his jacket and hung it over one of the kitchen chairs. "How come you're not sick?" he asked, looking at his teacher appraisingly.

"What do you mean?" Jenny asked, sitting down at the table again.

"This flu thing. Just about everyone in town has it. Both my mom and dad are in bed. They tried going to the hospital, but the waiting room was all filled up."

"Flu?"

"Aches, pains, high fever, uh, diarrhea, that kind of thing."

"I feel fine," Jenny said, frowning.

"Oh, well, that's good," B.C. said with a nod. "I guess I'd better go and look in on Karen."

"Top of the stairs on your right," instructed Jenny. "And remember what I said."

"Sure, absolutely," Bentley answered, clutching the paper bag. He gave her a quick, utterly insincere smile and bolted from the room.

He found Karen's room and gently opened the door a crack. The bed was in the far corner, backed by a bookcase built into the headboard. The curtains were drawn, and Karen was nothing but a featureless lump, curled up on her side, a heavy, blue-and-white quilt pulled up to her chin. Bentley stepped into the room on tiptoe and closed the door behind him.

"Karen?" he whispered. She moved slightly under the covers but didn't answer. Bentley swallowed and looked around nervously: plain pine chest of drawers, white enameled shelves filled with stuffed animals and dolls, old-fashioned rag rug on the floor, and a giant poster of Mick Jagger and David Bowie, lip to lip and microphone to microphone. Bentley approached the bed and took a deep breath. Maybe puberty wasn't so far off after all, because he was starting to tingle all over and his stomach was in a knot.

"Karen," he whispered again.

"Uh?" She rolled over. There was a crease across one side of her face, her eyes were puffy, and her hair was a mess. It didn't matter at all. If anything, the tingling became more intense.

"Karen? It's me, Bentley Carver Bingham."

"Wha— Oh shit. B.C." Karen groaned, her lips parting gummily. She drew herself up onto the pillow, absently checking to make sure that the buttons of her flannel nightgown were done up. They were. "What do you want?" she asked, squinting at him in the half-light. "What time is it?"

"Close to four o'clock. Uh, I heard what happened."

"I don't want to talk about it," Karen answered stiffly. Bentley could see her lower lip quivering as the horrible memory came back. He sat down on the edge of the bed without thinking and put his hand on her shoulder.

"I'm sorry," he whispered softly, and then, incredibly, she was in his arms, her face tucked into his neck, the sweet-smelling mass of her hair brushing his face. He could tell she was crying, and he patted her gently on the back.

"Oh God, it was awful!"

"I know," he whispered, his hands moving back and forth. "I know, but it's okay now."

"Blood . . . everywhere, he just turned into blood . . ."

"Shhh," he murmured, comforting her, and feeling like an utter bastard. She'd gone through hell and all he could think about was the fact that her breasts felt incredible pressed against his chest. He put his hands on her shoulders and gently pushed her back down onto the pillow. "You take it easy now," he instructed, relieved that she wasn't so close. "I brought you something." He opened the paper bag, reached in, and pulled out a small stuffed animal.

"It's a rat," said Karen, not believing it. The creature was gray, with tiny black glass eyes, the glint painted in by some anonymous assembly-line artist in Hong Kong. It had two bucked fangs and acetate whiskers. Somehow, the overall effect was almost charming. "It's adorable!" said Karen, brightening as he handed her the animal. Bentley took off his glasses and examined the lenses.

"I thought Ramon might be a good name," he said. "He looks sort of Spanish."

"Ramon," Karen repeated. She was smiling. Bentley put his glasses back on and cleared his throat.

"I wanted to talk to you," he said slowly. "I've been checking things out. I didn't think anyone else would believe me."

"Checking what out?" asked Karen, sitting up, Ramon in her lap.

"You remember in Havelock's, I told you about the airplane and the telephones being out?"

"I remember."

"There's more to it now. Everything in town is closed. It's this flu thing."

"What flu thing?"

"I think it started just after . . . what happened in the Bo-Peep. People started getting sick all of a sudden. I took my bike over to the Medical Center: it's crazy over there. Something really strange is going on, Karen. It's like watching an old 'Twilight Zone' show, except this is real."

"What does my dad think?" she asked. "Have you talked to him?"

"No. Miss Hale's downstairs; I think she was kind of baby-sitting you while you were asleep. I saw your dad and that long-haired guy from the Mill driving out of town a long time ago. I guess they're not back yet."

"Miss Hale is here, in this house?" asked Karen, unable to keep the annoyance out of her voice. Bentley nodded, biting his lip.

"Yes, and she looks nervous. Very nervous."

"I don't want her here," Karen said angrily. "I don't want her doing anything for me. I'm getting up." She threw back the covers, but Bentley lunged forward and pushed them back.

"No!" he hissed, looking back over her shoulder. "She'll kill me. Just stay in bed until your dad gets back."

"Bentley, what is going on?" Karen insisted.

"I don't know," muttered the boy. "I wanted to tell someone, but they'd think I was crazy. Who's going to believe a thirteen-year-old dwarf?"

"Tell what?" she demanded.

"About one-thirty, Old Man Havelock got a call. I think it

was from the Medical Center. He and the old lady got very uptight. They wouldn't say a thing except that they were closing for the day and I should go home. Which I did. That's when I found out my parents were sick. I got scared, so I took my father's binoculars and went back into town. I went up the tower in Stark Hall.''

"And?"

"You're going to think I'm out of my mind," he moaned.

"No I'm not. What did you see?"

"Martians, Venusians—whatever you want to call them."

"Oh, come on!" laughed Karen. "You've been reading too much science fiction."

"Marty Doyle puking up all eight pints onto the floor of the Bo-Peep wasn't science fiction," the boy said, appalled by the brutality of what he'd just said. Karen blanched. "I'm sorry, but this is getting to me," he added in a rush. "The phones don't work; everybody's getting sick. All the *Leader Post* boxes are empty. I asked around a bit, too. Mr. Sawchuck didn't get his regular bread delivery today, and the TV and radio don't work. I even tried that shortwave kit I built this summer. Nothing. Not even static, just this long cycling drone."

"Is this some kind of joke, B.C.?" Karen asked. "I mean, is this some weird thing you're doing to try and cheer me up? Because if it is, I don't think it's very funny."

"I don't think it's funny, either. And it's no joke. I wish it were."

"But what does all this have to do with Martians? I mean, really, B.C."

"I saw them," he said, his voice dull. "Through the binoculars. Way up Quarry Hill on the other side of the river. Two of them. They had these space suits on with helmets. It was hard to see them at first because the suits were camouflaged."

"And what were these camouflaged Martians doing?"

"Sitting. They had some kind of little radar dish on a tripod. It was swinging back and forth. Like they were doing guard duty."

"Martians on guard duty."

"I guess it does sound kind of stupid."

"Just a little," Karen said gently. "Maybe you just imagined it, B.C."

"Maybe." He didn't sound convinced. "But I just wanted to
. . . I don't know. Warn you, I guess."

"Thanks."

"Uh, I brought you something else, too," the young boy said.
He reached into the paper bag again and handed a black cardboard
box to Karen. The name Confidelle was written across the box in
white flowing script. Karen's eyes widened when she saw what
it was.

"Bentley—"

"I'm sorry if I did wrong," he said quickly, holding up a
defensive hand. "I mean, you were pretty obvious about it in
the drugstore, so I swiped it on the way out. I figured you
couldn't have bought it without all sorts of rumors spreading
around town."

"Thanks," she said quietly, looking at the box, color rising to
her cheeks.

"You're worried about being . . ." He gestured toward the
box. She nodded.

"Pregnant."

"Billy?" he asked bluntly. Karen looked sharply at the dimin-
utive boy perched on the edge of her bed.

"I don't think that's any of your business."

"Sorry." There was a pause. "He's in the Medical Center, in
case you wanted to know. He freaked out just like you did. Luther
called an ambulance. When I biked up to the Center, I asked
about him. They said he had the flu, but that's all. They didn't
say anything about Marty."

"This sickness, it's really that bad?" Karen asked.

"Worse," said B.C. "It's like those pictures of the Black
Death in the Middle Ages, except nobody's dead yet, not that I
know of."

"Except Marty," Karen said, her fingers tightening around the
stuffed animal on her lap.

"Yeah," said Bentley Carver Bingham. "Except Marty."

"See anything?" asked Jack Slater, prone on the cold, stony
ground beside Sparrow. The bigger man shook his head, the small
field glasses scanning the land below them. The sun was slowly
dropping at their backs, the tall pines around them on the high
ridge throwing long, concealing shadows. They'd reached the

summit of Notch Hill almost half an hour before, but Sparrow had insisted on waiting before they continued. Below them, the slopes of the tree-blanketed hill swept down to the toe of Jericho Valley, and even without the binoculars, Slater could make out the town, no more than three miles away.

At the base of the hill, Notch Road cut north into the White Mountains, and beyond it Slater could see the faint pall of smoke that was a permanent, light brown signpost marking the town's fifty-five-acre dump site. The dump was screened from the town by a dense forest of second-growth cedar, and still farther east was Riverview Park, the municipally operated non-denominational cemetery that stood somberly on the edge of Frenchtown.

"How do we go from here?" Slater asked. Sparrow put the glasses down, but kept his eyes to the east.

"A couple of years back, I used to come up here bow-hunting. As far as I can recall, there are two trails. One follows the top of the ridge south back to the highway, and the other goes straight down from here through the trees. Comes out on Notch Road right in front of the dump."

"That sounds like the fastest," Slater said. "Dwayne might not be in the shack, but we could get in and use the telephone. Norm or one of the others could come and pick us up."

"Smarter to use the garbage truck if it's there. If these people do have forward observation posts, they might get upset seeing a cop car coming up Notch Road."

"We haven't seen a sign of anyone," Slater replied. "Maybe we're making too much of all this."

"You're dreaming, Sheriff. Someone's put a clamp on the Falls, no one in or out. Just because we haven't seen anyone doesn't mean they're not around."

"I guess you're right. It's just hard to believe. One minute everything's boring and normal, the next . . .''

"That's how it goes." Sparrow shrugged, picking up the glasses again. "I had a friend, a pilot like me. He always wore his lucky T-shirt: 'Life is a Bitch and then You Die,' in Day-Glo pink on black. He did two tours. Mang Yang Pass, Pleiku, Ia Drang, the Rifle Range, Bong Son, all of it. Never a scratch, never a bad bird, nothing. When he got out, he treated himself to a holiday in the Caribbean. Club Med. He was there about three hours when the taxi he was in got into an accident. Killed him. You never know.''

"You really know how to cheer a guy up, Mr. Hawke.''

"Glad I could help." He put down the glasses again. "Nothing, not even a branch moving.''

"So it's clear?''

"Maybe. Only one way to find out. Just keep low for a little while, until we're off the horizon line.'' He stood up in a crouch and began to move downward to the trees. Slater followed closely. A moment later, they reached the tree line and Sparrow picked up the trail. It was wide and obviously well used, by both man and animals, and there was ample evidence of both. Within a hundred yards, Slater had seen deer droppings, a crushed and empty Michelob can, and a broken, moss-covered rack of white-tail horns, nearly hidden among the dense sprays of fern lining the edge of the path.

The light had turned the forest a dozen shades of green and gold, and the air was tart and fresh with the scent of cold, wet earth and pine needles. If it hadn't been for their present circumstances, Slater thought, the walk down the mountain would have been quite pleasant.

If the figure hadn't shifted slightly an instant before they stepped into the clearing, Sparrow Hawke and Jack Slater might have blundered right into him. Instead, spotting the movement, Sparrow brought up his arm across his companion's chest, stopping him in his tracks. The long-haired man eased back a few feet, taking Slater with him. Pausing, he brought his mouth up to the sheriff's ear and spoke quickly, his voice less than a whisper:

"On the far side of the clearing, sitting on a rock ledge. Wearing some kind of space-age outfit with a helmet. The camouflage is almost perfect. He's got a mid-range GSR unit on a tripod in front of him." Slater nodded without speaking, watching as Sparrow slid to the ground and began unlacing his hiking boots. With the boots off, he squirmed around, and suddenly there was an evil-looking survival knife in his hand, the blade a good two inches longer than the legal maximum. Slater dropped down to the ground.

"What are you going to do?" he asked.

"Take him out. He's sitting right across the trail.''

"Why don't we try to capture him?" the sheriff asked.

"How?"

"I've got this." He held up the police special.

"You've got that and he's got the biggest fucking sniper rifle I've ever seen in my life across his lap. This is no 'bang-bang you're dead' game, Jack. This is for real."

"All right. What do you want me to do?"

"Don't fire off that pistol, that's the most important thing. You'd hear it for miles. I'm going to try to get around to his blind side, get close enough to use this." He held up the knife. "When you see me make my move, step out where he can see you, wave your arms—anything to distract him."

"What if he spots you first?"

"Then run like hell." Sparrow stood up, gave Slater a quick smile, then slid into the shadows on the edge of the path. The sheriff watched him melt into the trees and then slithered forward on his belly until he reached the edge of the clearing.

It took him a moment, but he finally managed to pick out Sparrow's target. Space-age was hardly a description for what the man was wearing. He sat on a small rock outcropping, the camouflage so perfect that he was almost invisible. Slater had never seen anything like it. The battle dress consisted of an oversized helmet with a flat-fronted, polarized face plate attached to a one-piece quilted jumpsuit by a flexible collar. From what Slater could see, the gauntlets and boots were built into the suit.

The observer was sitting obliquely, and the sheriff could see a coiled rubber cable and hose snaking from the helmet to a large, rectangular backpack slung across the man's shoulders. The weapon in his lap was fitted with a large, awkward-looking scope sight, and a second cable led from the sight to the backpack.

Bizarre though it was, Slater could see the purpose of the suit immediately—a totally self-contained unit, like a spacesuit worn by astronauts, providing the wearer with a sealed, filtered environment. It was the logical extrapolation of the old-fashioned gas mask and a perfect defense against virtually any kind of chemical or biological offensive.

Slater swallowed hard, his mouth ash-dry. The suit confirmed Rembrandt Payne's suspicions. High tech or not, no one would be wearing it unless he feared a serious infection by a chemical or biological agent of some kind. Sparrow was right: these people were deadly serious.

He sneezed.

"Oh Christ!" he whispered, sniffing. The observer's helmeted head snapped around and he strode up, making some sort of adjustment to the scope sight. Slater wriggled backward, but it was too late; the man had seen him.

"UP!" The voice was harsh and electronic, amplified through the helmet somehow. Slater did as he was told, rising up out of the bracken. He walked out into the clearing, and the helmeted man swung the sniper rifle up.

The sheriff watched as a tiny, bright green dot of light raced across the small, rocky path of ground, changing to red as it climbed his legs, finally settling onto his chest. Slater had read about things like that; a laser-operated "fire and forget" system. All you had to do was put the dot of light on your target and press the trigger—100 percent accuracy every time. He stood silently, every muscle in his body quivering. Unless Sparrow suddenly came out of the woodwork, he was as good as dead.

"COME FORWARD." Again the mechanical voice. "DROP YOUR WEAPON." Slater realized he was still gripping the .38. He dropped it instantly. There was no way of telling the helmeted man's reaction behind the black plastic visor, but Slater was sure that the small aiming dot on his chest wavered slightly. It occurred to him that the man in the suit might be just about as nervous as he was.

"My name is Slater," he said, his voice croaking slightly. "I'm a police officer." He gently pulled back the side of his jacket to show the large steel-and-black-enamel badge pinned to his shirt.

Sparrow came up out of the bush so quickly Slater almost missed it. He took three quick steps and then brought the knife down in a blur, first cutting through the cable connecting the helmet to the backpack, then turning and jamming the long wide blade through the collar.

Sparrow rolled away to the left, and the man crumpled to the ground, the dot of light fading. Pausing just long enough to pick up his pistol, Slater rushed across the twenty yards separating them. Sparrow, already on his feet, kicked the rifle out of the man's hands, then knelt down beside him, peering at the collar, now slick with blood. He drew the knife out carefully, then pulled the tang on the zipper closure. He rolled the figure onto its side, then peeled off the helmet.

The face under the visor belonged to a man in his twenties. He was blond, a faint hint of stubble on his cheeks and upper lip. The eyes were blue and wide open.

"I'm going to get my boots," Sparrow said quietly. He stood up and walked away. Slater took a deep breath and let it out, reminding himself that the young man in the suit had been aiming a high-powered rifle at his heart. He began checking out the suit and eventually found the various tabs and zippers that had made it into a sealed, single unit. He managed to open the upper section and peeled it back. Beneath the lightweight fabric, he could feel moving plates of some hard substance. As well as being protection against CBW, the suit was also some kind of body armor. Sparrow came back and squatted down beside Slater.

"Find anything?"

"Not yet." Beneath the twenty-first-century suit of armor, the young man was dressed in plain, dark green fatigues. No unit markings, no rank insignia, nothing.

"The camo is spray-painted on," Sparrow said, examining the helmet. "Custom job, depending on the terrain. Jesus! These people thought of everything."

"I can't find any I.D.," said Slater. He'd managed to roll the body over, unzipping the trouser section. Sparrow had the rifle in his hands. He looked up and nodded.

"I didn't think you'd find any. He must have belonged to some special group. Maybe those Ninth Infantry hi-tech guys from Ft. Lewis. Quick and dirty, with all sorts of super-duper ordnance. The rifle is some kind of far-out Armalite." He threw it to one side. "Shit, man! This is like a bad dream. I thought I was through with all this."

"You didn't have any choice," Slater said, standing up. "I'm witness to that. You said it yourself, these guys are for real."

"That doesn't make him any less dead."

Slater walked out to the edge of the little rock plateau. Another half mile and they'd be down to the North Road. He turned and looked back the way they'd come. The shadows were even longer now. He went across to where Sparrow was standing, looking down at the young face of the man he'd killed. He touched his companion gently on the sleeve.

"Come on. We've got to get going."

"Sure," he said, his voice flat and emotionless. "We've got to get going." And together the two men walked away from the body, heading down the trail again in the gathering dusk.

CHAPTER NINE

4:30 P.M.

The town council chamber was on the second floor of Stark Hall, its tall, multipaned windows looking out onto Constitution Common. The heavy, plum-colored velvet curtains had been drawn, and the long rectangular room was lit by three ornate chandeliers which hung over the big, felt-covered conference table. The side walls of the room were fitted with dark oak floor-to-ceiling bookcases filled with leather-bound volumes of bylaws and minutes of council meetings going back more than a century, and the wall opposite the windows was hung with portraits of previous mayors and prominent councilmen. The floor was made of the same oak as the bookcases, pegged and highly polished by decades of wear.

The full council was made up of twelve men and women, not including the mayor, but there were only seven people seated in the deep, green leather and brass tack armchairs set around the table, and only three of them were actually members. Normally, there would have been water glasses, jugs, and notepads at each place, but Tom Barnett, the town clerk, had been too ill to attend the meeting.

At the head of the table, Luther Coyle, dressed formally in a pinstripe suit and white shirt, lifted the old cherry-wood gavel and brought it down on the small block of polished New Hampshire granite in front of him.

"I think it's about time we called this meeting to order," he said stiffly, his sharp, hooded eyes looking around the table. "Sheriff Slater asked for this emergency session, but it appears that he is not going to grace us with his presence."

"He went to Rumney for help," Rembrandt Payne said, seated at the far end of the table. "He should be here any minute."

"Let's hope so," murmured Coyle. He glanced down at a neatly piled sheaf of foolscap paper in front of him, then looked up at the people gathered around the table. He folded his hands on the papers, his narrow-lipped mouth set in a tight frown.

He was flanked on either side by two of his business managers, Gabe Turcott and Frank Ludder. The men looked more like well-dressed thugs than businessmen, which wasn't far from the truth. Turcott ran Brightway Finance, a Coyle-owned finance company, and Ludder was the head of Coyle Property Management, the company that handled most of the low-end rental properties in Frenchtown.

"In Mr. Barnett's absence, I have asked Mr. Ludder to take the minutes," Coyle said. "The record will show that in addition to myself, Mr. Ludder, and Mr. Turcott, this meeting was attended by Loretta Simms, PTA and School Board, and Dwayne Kennaway, Public Works. Also present are Dr. Rembrandt Payne, director of the Jericho Falls Medical Center and county medical examiner, and Norman Lombard, deputy sheriff." Coyle glanced briefly at Frank Ludder, who was scribbling away to his left, then turned his attention to the table.

"It appears that we have something of a crisis on our hands," continued the mayor. "According to Dr. Payne, we are undergoing an epidemic of a flulike illness that seems to have blanketed the entire town overnight. In addition, we have suffered some sort of communications failure. Long-distance telephone service, television, and radio are all out. An unfortunate coincidence."

"It's not a coincidence at all," Payne said from the far end of the table. "And you know it, Luther."

"You're out of order, Doctor. And might I remind you that you are here in a completely advisory position, nothing more."

"To hell with rules of order! God's teeth, man! Out of four thousand people in this town, half of them are seriously ill. A disease has been let loose, and from what I'm given to understand by Norman here, we've been put under some sort of violent quarantine by God knows what branch of the military. We have to do something!"

"Speculation," Coyle said. "There are no facts to back up

your statements. And wild supposition can do nothing but cause panic."

"I've talked to several people," said Dwayne Kennaway, the Public Works councilman. He was a short, bald man in his late fifties, his face weathered by years working outside. His company, K-Way Sanitation Services, maintained the town dump, operated a fleet of half a dozen garbage trucks, and installed septic tanks. "There hasn't been a delivery made anywhere in town since yesterday. Corney Drake left with a truckload of broilers this morning, and no one has seen him since."

"I sent two cars to the airport to see if they could use the high-frequency radio out there," offered Norm Lombard. "Neither one has come back."

"More speculation," Coyle said. "And the radio at the airport is out just like everything else. My man out there says it's probably due to sunspots."

"You've talked to the airport?" Lombard asked, surprised.

Coyle gave the policeman a long look. "Certainly. Why do you think I'd lie?"

"I think we should be worrying more about this flu epidemic," put in Loretta Simms. A onetime principal of Earl Coolis High School, Loretta Simms was a reed-slim, iron-haired woman in her sixties.

"It's not influenza," Payne said. "It's a secondary infection brought about by exposure to a mutated bacteria. It seems to affect people between the ages of fourteen and fifty-five, men and women. For some reason, pregnant women don't get it, and neither do diabetics. By my estimation, at least two-thirds of the citizens of this town who fall within that age group have contracted the disease to a greater or lesser extent."

"How many have died?" asked Luther Coyle.

"None. At least, not as a result of the secondary infection. There have been three deaths from the initial exposure."

"I just spoke with the hospital," Coyle said. "They tell me that Billy's temperature is falling quickly. A number of others at the Medical Center have already been released. It would appear that your 'epidemic' is of the twenty-four-hour variety."

"I don't jump to medical conclusions. And I don't think you should, either."

"Nevertheless, Doctor, it doesn't seem logical that, right or wrong, the government would produce a bacteria with such fleeting results."

The door to the council chamber swung open and Jack Slater appeared, Sparrow Hawke behind him. The sheriff went to the far end of the table and sat down beside the large figure of Rembrandt Payne. Sparrow took the next chair, seating himself between Slater and Norm Lombard.

"You decided to join us after all," Coyle said. "Might I ask what Mr. Hawke is doing in this chamber? I don't recall his election to the town council."

"Mr. Hawke is now a deputy on the Jericho Falls Police Force. I asked him to be here."

"Perhaps the two of you should have changed your clothes before coming." The long trek had left both men covered in dirt, and there was a definite sour odor clinging to both of them.

"We had to requisition one of Dwayne's garbage trucks," Slater answered, glancing at Kennaway. "We didn't have much choice."

"Dr. Payne informs us that you were on your way to Rumney. What happened to your police vehicle?"

"It was blown to shit," Sparrow said.

"I beg your pardon?" Coyle said, obviously startled by the news.

"We were attacked out on 115A," Slater said. "Someone had demolished Corney Drake's truck. With Corney in it, from the looks of things."

"My God!" whispered Loretta Simms.

"We came back up the Notch," continued the sheriff. "We ran into one of the people blockading the town."

"Really?" Coyle said skeptically. "What did he tell you?"

"He didn't tell us anything," Slater answered coldly. "He tried to kill us. Sparrow got to him first."

"You killed him?"

"That's right." Sparrow nodded, his features rigid.

"He was with the military?" Dr. Payne asked.

"I think so," Slater said, turning to the heavyset man. "He had on some kind of suit to guard against infection, but there was no I.D. on him."

"This is incredible!" Coyle said, stunned.

"That's one word for it," Slater said. "The point is, Luther, I'm declaring a state of emergency in Jericho Falls. Martial law."

"You can't do that, Slater! You're an elected official of this town. You'll follow the dictates of this council."

"Go fuck yourself, Luther." Loretta Simms paled at the word, and for a moment it looked as though she were going to faint. "In accordance with the Defense Civil Preparedness Agency manual guidelines, I'm taking over all governmental powers within Jericho Falls. That's EO11490, in case you want to look it up." He unbuttoned his holster and laid the .38 caliber revolver on the felt. "I can requisition matériel, weapons, food, and anything else I want. I'm also empowered to deputize people like Mr. Hawke."

"This is insanity!" Luther Coyle said.

"Good lad!" whispered Rembrandt Payne. "Now perhaps we'll get somewhere."

"As of now, the town council is dissolved," continued the sheriff. "You take orders from me, Norm Lombard, or Sparrow here. Failure to obey will result in immediate incarceration . . . or worse."

"Dr. Payne thinks that Jericho Falls has been placed under some sort of quarantine," Luther Coyle said, his voice brittle. "You seem to have supplied firsthand evidence of this. Under the circumstances, I suggest that we try and contact the people responsible and find out what they want. After all, Sheriff, this is a civilized country."

"Not anymore," Slater said harshly. "Remember what it says on your license plate, Luther. 'Live Free or Die.' The time has come to test that out." He picked up his revolver, slid it back into the holster, and walked out of the room. The council meeting was over.

"Luther Coyle is a pompous ass," Rembrandt Payne grunted, settling cautiously into a chair in the outer office of the Jericho Falls Police Station.

"He didn't see Corney's truck," Sparrow said, pouring himself a mug of coffee.

"Or the kid in the space suit," added Slater.

"Good Lord! You're both defending him!" wheezed Payne.

"No we're not," drawled Sparrow, sipping at his coffee. "There's just no sense bad-mouthing him, that's all."

Norm Lombard came into the office, shaking his head.

"It's like a ghost town out there," he said. "Everything on the Common is shut tight, and so is Main. I didn't bother going out onto the Strip." He dropped down into a battered armchair. "God knows what'll happen if we have any kind of crime."

"There won't be any looting or anything of that nature," Payne predicted. "Everyone is much too sick."

"Was Luther right about the people at the Medical Center getting better?" Slater asked.

"To a degree," said the doctor, shrugging his huge shoulders. "I just called in, and it seems that some of the early admissions are being released."

"Then it's over?" Norm Lombard asked.

"I doubt it," Sparrow said cautiously. "The whole town has been cut off. They wouldn't do that for a twenty-four-hour flu."

"It occurs to me that 'they,' whoever they are, might not know what sort of agent was released from Mr. Redenbacher's van."

"Worst-case scenario." Sparrow nodded. "Full-scale preventative measures until they find out what they're dealing with."

"Makes sense," Slater said. "Maybe that's why they abducted the boy from the Mill. Maybe they needed someone to run tests on."

"Hardly the most scientific way of going about things," grunted Payne.

"So what do we do now?" asked Norm Lombard. "We're down to a three-man force, and that includes Mr. Hawke here. Do we just sit and wait?"

"No," Slater said firmly. "I don't think so. Like Luther said, that might be the civilized thing to do, maybe even the smart thing to do when you get right down to it. But it stinks. All of it stinks. The kid, the dog, Corney, and the way that chopper came down on us." He turned to Sparrow. "What did they call those squads in 'Nam, the Special Forces types?"

"Hunter-Killer."

"Right. Hunter-Killer, that's the attitude I've seen. If they were worried about the general population, they would have come in with Medevac units, doctors, the whole shot. Instead, they've cut us off, quarantined us. Why?"

"Because they don't want the news to get out that the armed forces of the United States have been developing bacteriological warfare compounds and toting them across the countryside without a fare-thee-well!" Payne said angrily.

"Can you imagine what the press would do?" Sparrow said. "They'd have a field day."

"We've had three horrible deaths so far," Payne added. "That's murder. Not to mention hundreds of people falling terribly ill. Field day hardly describes it, Mr. Hawke."

"Well, they can't keep it a secret forever," Norm Lombard said.

"Really?" Slater returned, his voice hard. "What about Sparrow's worst-case scenario?" The sheriff ran a hand through his hair nervously. "Christ! What if they've got a whole bunch of guys out there like the one we ran into, and they don't have the slightest idea what to do next? They might have had a contingency plan for something like this happening, but now they've got the real thing to handle."

"So they wait," Sparrow said. "Just like us. Watch the universe unfold and all that Karma shit."

"I'm serious," Slater said.

"So am I. Maybe that's the plan. They quarantine the town, cut it off from the rest of the world, and then wait and see what happens."

"Presumably, we are the sheep in this scenario," said Payne, shifting in his chair. "Or perhaps Thanksgiving turkey would be a more appropriate analogy."

"I don't intend to sit around waiting for the axe to fall," Slater said angrily. He stood up and began pacing back and forth between the radio desk and the coffee machine.

"What choice do we have?" said Norm Lombard.

"Lots," Slater said, stopping in midstride. "The first thing we need is some men. Enough to cover the main access routes into town."

"Roadblocks?" Sparrow said.

"An early-warning system. Flare gun at each post. If those people out there make a move, at least we'll know about it."

"Gaudet's Hardware carries flare guns," said Lombard.

"Get them," Slater instructed, "and clear out all the firearms you can find. Ammunition as well. When you've done that, start rounding up all the able-bodied men you can find."

"I'll give him a hand," Sparrow offered. "What about transportation?"

"Four-wheel drives," answered Slater, pacing again. "Requisition what we need. The bigger the better, none of that Japanese crap like Todd Bell uses for his fishing trips."

"Okay, then what?" asked Lombard.

"It's just past five," said the sheriff, checking his watch. "Meet back here at midnight. I want you to get at least a dozen men for tonight. We can beef things up later. I want lookouts on Van Epp just past the Medical Center, someone on the roof of the Mill with a pair of binoculars, and another post out at Airport Road and the highway. Two men at each post. That should do for now."

"Good enough." Sparrow nodded as he and Norm Lombard got up and went out through the counter pass-through.

"It's shaping up like the last stand at the Alamo," Payne said as the two men left the police station and headed into the gathering dusk.

"Sure," Slater said. "I'll be Davy Crockett. Just give me a coonskin cap. Sparrow can play Jim Bowie."

"Much as I hate to admit it, Luther has a point. Perhaps it would be better to try and make contact with these people."

"I'm willing," Slater said, pouring himself a mug of coffee. "But they can be the ones who come forward waving a white flag. So far, they've been shooting first and not asking questions at all."

"I appreciate that. And I also appreciate the fact that you've been through a very trying period. I suggest you go home and rest. Miss Hale must be quite concerned. And there is Karen to consider as well."

"What about you?"

"I shall return to the Medical Center. Luther seems to think the worst is behind us, concerning the epidemic. I'm not so sure."

"Neither am I," Slater muttered. "Somehow, I think our troubles might be just beginning."

They lay in the dark room, covers pushed down to the end of the bed, their naked bodies lit by the pale glow of the rising moon. Jack Slater stared up at the ceiling, hands cupped behind his head, while Jenny curled into his shoulder, one hand playing gently with the soft mat of curling hair on his chest.

"I'm sorry," he said.

"Don't be. It happens."

"I've got too much on my mind." He sighed. "It feels as though everything is going crazy. It's all out of control, and I don't have any way to stop it."

"You're not responsible for what's happened." She let her hand drift down over the corded muscles of his stomach.

"I'm supposed to represent the law. That's my job—to serve and protect the people of Jericho Falls. Now, all of a sudden, there is no law, the rules are all changed, and I don't know what to do. Up there in the hills with Sparrow, I realized just how impotent I was." He laughed quietly. "Good choice of words," he added.

Jenny leaned forward and nipped him on the chest. "Stop it," she demanded.

"It's true. There I was, the sheriff, macho-man chief of police, the man with the gun, and it's Sparrow, a burnt-out old hippy, who comes to *my* rescue. I felt like a complete fool."

"I think the word now is *dweeb*," said Jenny. "According to Karen and her friends, anyway."

"How is Karen? I looked in on her; she seemed to be sleeping."

"She's okay. I took her up some dinner just before you got back. She seems to have come through it all pretty well. One of her classmates came over and that seemed to cheer her up, but she treated me like I had bad breath. God! How can a fifteen-year-old kid make you feel like dirt?"

"She's jealous," Slater said. He reached out blindly and found his cigarettes on the bedside table. He lit one and took a long drag.

"Jealous of me?" asked Jenny. "Why?"

"Because you're sleeping with her daddy, or trying to, anyway. It probably offends her sense of what a parent should be, not to mention how her teacher should act. I'm sure it's all Freudian."

"I hope she grows out of it."

"I hope she has the chance to," Slater said, fear and worry in his voice.

"You really think it's that bad?"

"Yes. They killed Corney Drake, I'm sure of it. And they kidnapped the Robinson boy."

"But what are they going to do?" said Jenny. "There are four thousand people in this town. They can't kill all of us."

"Why not?" Slater asked baldly. "I think Doc Payne is right. They lost that bug of theirs, and they'll do anything to get it back, or cover up the fact that it ever existed."

"You can't just make Jericho Falls disappear," Jenny countered. Slater lifted his shoulders and took another drag on the cigarette.

"You can't do it easily," he agreed. "Maybe that's why they haven't made any real moves yet." He brushed a hand across his eyes. "Jesus, I'm exhausted," he said quietly.

"You really have to go out later tonight?" asked Jenny.

"I'm afraid so."

"Then sleep now. I'll wake you up when it's time to go."

Slater turned his head on the pillow. Her shoulder-length hair was tousled from their earlier attempt at lovemaking, and the spill of faint light coming in through the big window had turned it the color of beaten silver. Her eyes were full of concern, her wide, full mouth turned down in a worried frown.

"I can't sleep." He smiled. "Not with you lying there without a stitch on."

"I could get dressed," she offered.

"No, don't do that," he whispered, rolling over and reaching for her.

Across the narrow hall, Karen Slater sat up in bed, hands over her ears to block out the rising sounds of passion coming from her father's bedroom. She wasn't quite sure which was worse: the embarrassment of knowing what her father was doing, or the anger she felt toward the woman he was doing it with. Having her in the house at all was like an invasion of privacy; having her in her father's bed was an outrage.

Hands still over her ears, she slipped out from under the quilt and pushed her feet into the wool slippers beside the bed. She shuffled over to the window and looked out. Her room faced the street, the roof of the front porch a couple of feet below the windowsill. It would be easy enough to climb out onto the roof, then climb down the gnarled old elm that shaded the front yard.

At first she'd thought Bentley's idea was stupid, but she was beginning to find it more and more appealing. According to the instructions in the Confidelle box, you were supposed to put a sample of urine into the little test tube and then wait for an hour. If a whitish ring precipitated out of the solution after that time, you were pregnant. No ring and you were okay.

There was no way she could leave the test tube and its little plastic stand anywhere in the house, and Bentley had suggested using the washroom at the Crestview Heights Tennis Club in Old Creek Park. His father was the club manager, and he could easily get the key. He'd offered to meet her in the park at eleven and let her in to use the facilities, and she'd eventually agreed.

Karen turned away from the window and tiptoed back to the bed. She peered at the luminous dial of the alarm clock on her night table. It was almost ten. She took her hands away from her ears and forced herself to listen. From the sounds of things, they'd be at it for a little while longer. Moving quickly, she began to unbutton her long flannel nightgown. If she hurried, she could be out the window and gone before they were done.

"Please, God!" she whispered, pulling a sweater over her head and then struggling into her jeans. "No little white ring!"

Jenny Hale had set the bedside alarm for 11:30, but it was a different sound that yanked Jack Slater out of his too brief sleep. He knew he'd been having some kind of terrible dream, because he was drenched in sweat. He rolled away from the sleeping figure of Jenny and groped for the telephone, squinting blearily at the clock: 11:03. He dragged the receiver from its cradle before it could ring again, then sank back down onto the pillow.

"Yeah."

"Sheriff Slater?"

"S'right."

"Jack Slater?"

"Yes. Who is this?"

"My name is Wright, Sheriff Slater." The voice seemed distant and faintly blurred by some kind of electronic hiss. "Colonel

James H. Wright. I believe we have things to discuss." Slater came wide awake and sat up, heart pounding.

"Are you the sons of—"

"Please, Sheriff, just listen. I want you to be on Constitution Common at exactly midnight. Furthermore, I want you to be unarmed. Any interference by you or any of your people will be dealt with severely, do I make myself clear?"

"Yes, but—"

"You have one hour, Sheriff. Be there." The line went dead in Slater's ear. He hung up the phone and leaned back against the headboard of the bed. It looked as though the bad guys were finally making their move. Beside him, Jenny was still sleeping, one clenched fist dragging the sheet up around her throat as usual. That's what was so frightening, the normalcy of it all. It was as though the town of Jericho Falls had been locked inside some sort of soundproof enclosure, forced to live out its nightmare alone while the rest of the world went about its normal business.

Slater had never suffered from claustrophobia before, but now it seemed as though the walls were crushing in around him. He let his head fall back and stared up at the dark ceiling, trying not to give in to the panic beating a tattoo inside his chest. Every nerve in his body said "Run," but in this particular nightmare there was nowhere to go.

"Hang on," he whispered softly to himself. "Hang on."

CHAPTER TEN

11:30 P.M.

Night has always been a time of fear, a place where unseen terrors lurk and frightening creatures pace with impunity. Man's first conscious thought must have been a quaking horror of the infinite hours after the setting of the sun, and even now, after a million years, he still huddles around the light, waiting for dawn to come, telling himself that there is nothing to fear and not believing it. Night makes frightened, superstitious children of us all, no matter how artfully we deny it; except for the sunrise, there is no fire bright enough to dispel that nameless dread.

That night, even the most insensitive observer would have seen at once that there was something terribly wrong about the town of Jericho Falls. Every door was barred, every curtain drawn, every shutter closed. Except for the streetlamps, there was no visible light, and nothing moved along the empty sidewalks and the streets.

Although the flulike epidemic seemed to be fading, rumors about the disappearance of Josh Robinson and Corney Drake had spread as widely as the illness, and everyone in town had heard about what happened to Martin Doyle at the Bo-Peep. Somewhere, a silent curfew bell had tolled, and everyone was heeding its warning. Almost everyone.

The Crestview Heights Tennis Club was one of Luther Coyle's few mistakes. A sprawling contemporary ranch-style mansion on three and a half acres of land above Van Epp and bordering Mountain Creek, the property had been custom-designed for the president of a computer manufacturing company who was considering relocating in Jericho Falls. The president of the company was an avowed tennis enthusiast, and Luther had built the house and the adjoining clay courts to sweeten the relocation deal.

In the end, the computer company went bankrupt during the microchip wars of the early eighties and the deal had fallen through, leaving Luther with a 4,200-square-foot house and two tennis courts, with no buyer. Rather than admit defeat, Coyle stripped the interior of the house, put in a parking lot, and hired himself an aging tennis pro from the Palm Beach circuit. He added six asphalt courts, refitted the house as a restaurant-bar and sports shop, and the Crestview Heights Tennis Club was born. The area was zoned against any sort of commercial operation, but Mayor Coyle had no trouble getting the bylaws amended and ramming through a liquor permit approval. Residents of Crestview Heights paid an enormous membership fee, townies paid a day rate, and Coyle Industries had another money-making business on its hands.

Within six months, the club, managed by B.C. Bingham's father, was doing land-office business, serving midmorning drinks to bored housewives and overpriced business lunches to their husbands. After a year and several near scandals, the bar, coyly called the Broken Racket, had been just as coyly nicknamed the Broken Marriage.

Trudging up the hill along Willowtree Lane, Karen Slater reached the pillared entrance to the club grounds just after eleven-thirty. At the top of the winding gravel drive, she could see the dark, swept-wing shape of the clubhouse, while off to the left she could make out the high-fenced court area. Beyond the courts and screened by a long, drooping line of weeping willows was Mountain Creek, a narrow, ice-cold stream that twisted back into the looming foothills and provided the dividing line between the town and the residential areas of the Hill and River Park.

Karen paused at the gate, peering up at the house. There was no sign of B.C. anywhere. She shivered, beginning to regret her late-night journey. It was cold, pitch black, and spooky. Except for her own breathing, there wasn't a sound, and every house on her way up to the club had been dark. No blue glow of TV sets tuned to the Carson show or the late-night news, nobody out walking dogs, no cars. Nothing. Jericho Falls was a ghost town, like B.C. had said, a rerun of one of those old "Twilight Zone" episodes.

"Hi."

"Jesus!" Karen whirled around as B.C. stepped out from behind one of the tall, stone pillars. "I really wish you wouldn't do things like that, B.C."

"Sorry," the boy said. "I didn't mean to scare you."

"Did you get it?" asked Karen.

B.C. nodded. He dug into the pocket of his windbreaker and pulled out a jangling ring of keys.

"Mom and Dad were still feeling sick. They've been asleep for hours. It was easy."

"Good. Let's get it over with." Of all the people to share a secret like this with, B.C. Bingham was the last one she'd have imagined.

"How long will it take?" the boy asked as they headed up the drive toward the clubhouse.

"An hour," Karen answered briefly. "Is that a problem?"

"No," said B.C., shaking his head. "There's no night watchman or anything. Just the burglar alarm."

"What burglar alarm?" She had a terrible vision of her father pulling up to the club, siren wailing, and finding her with the testing kit.

"Relax. I found all the instructions in my father's den. You open the door and then use another key to turn off the alarm system. You've got sixty seconds before anything happens."

"You better be right, Bentley," she warned. "Anyone finds out about this, and you're dead meat."

"I told you," he soothed. "Relax."

They continued up the drive, their feet crunching softly on the gravel. Reaching the flagstone walk leading to the main door of the club, B.C. brought out the ring of keys and sorted through them. He found the right key, slid it into the lock of the big, carved-wood front door, and pushed it open. Karen waited while the short young man disappeared into the dark interior of the club. Nervous, she looked back the way they'd come, half expecting the sound of the burglar alarm to split the night at any moment.

"Got it," B.C. said, reappearing in the doorway. "Time to spare." He ushered Karen into the large, slate-floored foyer, then closed the door behind her, locking it carefully.

"I can't see anything."

"No problem," B.C. answered. He brought a small flashlight out of his windbreaker and snapped it on. The foyer, cathedral-ceilinged, was hexagonal. Directly in front of them and down three wide steps was the bar, screened by a boxed row of artificial shrubbery. To the right was the tennis shop, while the left wing of the building contained the restaurant. A spiral staircase set to one side led up to the private dining rooms and offices on the second floor. B.C. swung the flashlight beam toward the stairs. "There's a private bathroom in my father's office upstairs, or you can use the one in the restaurant," he offered.

"The restaurant," she whispered, not liking the idea of possibly being trapped on the second floor.

"You can talk normally," B.C. laughed, leading the way across the foyer to the restaurant entrance. "There's nobody here except us."

"I feel like a criminal," she muttered.

" 'Behold, I come as a thief in the night,' " B.C. quoted. "The Bible: Revelations."

"You don't say." The restaurant at the Crestview Heights Tennis Club took up what had once been the west wing of the house. There were a score of round tables, each covered with crisp white linen, a brass-and-teak bar with glasses hanging down from overhead racks, and a dais with a baby grand at the far end of the room. A row of windows to the left looked out onto the court area, while the right-hand side gave a view of the creek and the mountains beyond. Predictably, the restaurant was called the Wimbledon Grill, and all the drinks and entrées had tennis-style names. A Goolagong was the Wimbledon version of a whiskey sour, the Jimmy Connors was steak and lobster, and the McEnroe Ace was a tequila sunrise. Exotic coffees and desserts were listed on the menu under the general heading of The Final Volley.

"Where's the bathroom?" Karen asked.

"Just to the right of the bar," B.C. said, pointing with the flashlight. "I'll wait for you here."

"I wasn't going to ask you to come along."

B.C. flushed and sat down at one of the tables. Karen crossed the room, bringing the test kit out from under her ski jacket. Five minutes later, she was back. She dropped into a chair across from B.C.

"All done?" he asked. She nodded.

"No problems?"

"I can pee into a test tube along with the best of them," she answered. "Now all we have to do is hang around here for an hour and wait for the bad news."

"Maybe you're not . . ." began the boy.

"Pregnant, B.C. Your ears won't fall off if you say it out loud."

"I didn't—"

"Look," she broke in. "Let's get it all out right now. Billy was the only one, and it wasn't that often, and it wasn't that good. If I am pregnant, I don't know if I'll want to get an abortion or not, no I don't feel ashamed, and yes I feel like a complete idiot.

"I'm also very scared, okay? You got me the test kit, and I'm grateful, but that doesn't make us best friends or anything. Understand?"

"I understand," B.C. said. He looked down at the tablecloth, running his thumbnail over the starched white fabric. "I just wanted you to know that I cared, that's all. And I'd like to help . . . if you want me to."

Karen looked across the table. Even in the dim light coming through the windows she could see B.C.'s narrow, serious face. His hair grew in half a dozen different directions, he wore thick glasses about five years out of date, dressed like a *total* dweeb, and sweated when he got nervous. On the other hand, he hadn't given her any lectures, made any jokes, or tried to capitalize on her problem. And right now, he was the only friend she had.

"I'm sorry, Bentley," she said softly. "This has got me pretty badly rattled."

The large, empty restaurant was suddenly lit up brilliantly as the beams from a pair of headlights swung across the room. The two young people ducked involuntarily. They could hear the muffled sound of tires on gravel and then the muted growling of a car engine.

"I thought you checked the alarm!" Karen hissed angrily.

"I did!" He got up quickly and ran across to the windows, keeping his head down. The lights disappeared, and a few seconds later Karen heard the sound of a car door being shut. B.C. crouched by the window for a moment and then raced back to the table. He grabbed Karen's hand and pulled her toward the bar.

"Come on! We've got to hide. Behind the bar!"

"Who is it?" Karen asked, her heart beginning to pound. B.C. dragged her down behind the protective barrier of the bar.

"Billy's father!"

"Luther? What's he doing here at this time of night?"

"I don't know," Bentley said. "But he's coming inside!"

Rembrandt Payne sat at a corner table in the Medical Center cafeteria, flipping through an accordion-fold sequence of computer printouts and ignoring the leathery remains of the plate of pork chops in gravy on the table in front of him. From time to time, he took small sips from his water glass. Except for the girl at the cash register and a weary-looking nurse hunched over a cup of coffee, he was alone.

Between noon and 10:00 P.M., almost eight hundred Jericho Falls residents had been admitted to the hospital with symptoms of Redenbacher's Syndrome. Seven hundred and forty had been released. Statistically, it looked as though almost everyone in town had contracted the disease, but very few exhibited any symptoms that appeared dangerous.

It looked as though Luther Coyle had been right—Redenbacher's was a short-lived, fairly innocuous flu variant. Unlike flu though, it seemed to hit hardest among people between adolescence and middle age: Billy Coyle, Luther's son, still showed a temperature, and Sandra Watchorn was on dialysis.

Which didn't make the slightest bit of sense. Jack Slater was sure that Jericho Falls had been put into some sort of quarantine by the army, and they were willing to kill to keep that quarantine intact. The eventual repercussions of closing off the town and murdering Corney Drake would be enormous, so why take such risks for a disease that had a barely perceptible fatality rate?

"Utterly absurd," the old doctor murmured. Weapons were meant to kill, and as far as he could see, Redenbacher's Syndrome barely qualified as an incapacitating agent. He was missing something, and he knew it. A movement on the far side of the cafeteria caught his eye, and he looked up. It was Howard Simms, the lab technician.

Slim, pale, and vaguely effeminate, the man always appeared to be a bit on the anemic side, but tonight he looked like a bit player in a vampire movie. Even from fifty feet away, the old man could see the sheen of sweat on the technician's face, and as the man made his way across the room, he actually staggered. He slumped down into one of the formed plastic chairs on the other side of the doctor's table, and Payne laid his computer report aside.

"What are you doing back here? You went home sick."

"I'm feeling a bit better," Simms answered. He dug a package of cigarettes out of the pocket of his lab coat and lit one. Payne noticed that the man's hand was shaking as he brought the cigarette up to his mouth.

"You're still running a fever."

"It spiked at a hundred and three. It's down two degrees."

"You should be in bed," grunted the doctor. "In fact, I insist on it, young man. We don't need any false heroics."

"I figured it out." He gestured toward the doctor's water glass. "You mind?"

"No."

Simms picked up the glass and drained it in a single long swallow.

"I figured out what the endospores are. Thought you'd like to know."

"Really?" Payne asked, arching one bushy eyebrow.

"I'm allergy prone," the technician explained weakly. "You name it, I get it. Hay fever, asthma when I was a kid, cats, dogs, leaf mold. It's one of the reasons I went into lab work. Nice clean environment."

"Go on."

"I went home around six. Felt like hell. Fever, the runs, stomach pains. Just like everyone else. I went to bed and woke up about nine. The fever had dropped, and the gut pain was gone, so I decided to make some soup for myself. Keep the fluid levels up." Simms paused again and took another sip of water, obviously far from well.

"Yes," Payne prompted quietly.

"Ten minutes later this started showing up." The lab technician carefully rolled back the sleeve of his lab coat, revealing a large, gauze dressing on his lower arm. Fingers shaking slightly, he peeled back the dressing and revealed a large, purple welt, raised almost a quarter of an inch from the surrounding skin. The edges of the hideous-looking boil were oozing clear fluid.

"Good Lord."

Simms extended the arm, and the old doctor bent forward to examine the large pustule. He reached into the pocket of his jacket, removed an orange stick, and prodded the infected area. The pustule was firm, almost leathery. He sat back in his chair. The lesion looked extraordinarily like an anthrax sore, but he wasn't about to tell Simms that.

"There's another one on my chest and a third on my left thigh," the technician went on. "They appeared within fifteen minutes of eating. It was tomato soup, Campbell's."

"You're allergic to tomatoes?"

"Mildly. Nothing like this, though. I put dressings on all three sores and came down here. I took a swab of the fluid leaking out of the wound on my chest and checked it out."

"And?"

"It was swarming with the endospores from the bacteria you were running all those tests on. Some of them were breaking down, and I could see whole colonies of antibodies swimming around."

"You're saying that the endospores are actually antigens?" murmured Payne.

"It looks that way."

"Interesting." It was more than interesting, it was the thing he'd overlooked. The Redenbacher bacteria was undergoing a second-phase mutation, a common enough occurrence, but to mutate from an ordinary bacteria to an antigen changed everything. Almost everyone was allergic to something, and if Simms's massive boils were a mild reaction to his allergy to tomato soup, what about people with chronic allergies like hay fever? Redenbacher's bacteria as a weapon was finally beginning to make sense. "I think I'd like to run some further tests," Payne finally said.

"Way ahead of you." The lab technician grinned weakly. "I've already done fifteen agar samples. I swiped a test kit from Dr. Kreuger's office." Kreuger was an allergist who lived in Manchester and came to the Center one day a week.

"Good lad." He peered at Simms thoughtfully. "Sure you're up to this?"

"I think so. You seem pretty concerned, so I figure it's important, right?"

"I think it may well be a matter of life and death." He stood up. "I'm going back up to my office. Let me know when you have some results."

Karen Slater huddled behind the bar and wondered how long it would be before she wet her pants. B.C., a few inches away, was peering out around the side of the waist-high barrier, keeping his head low.

"What's he doing?" Karen asked.

"I don't know. I can't see anything. I think he went upstairs."

"What's up there?"

"My dad's office and some meeting rooms. I don't get it."

"I have to go to the bathroom."

"Hold it. We can't make a move until he's gone."

"What's he doing here at this time of night?" Karen asked.

"That's what I'd like to know," B.C. said. Karen felt him tense.

"What's the matter?"

"Listen." In the distance, Karen could hear a faint mechanical sound. At first she thought it was Luther operating some kind of machine, like a typewriter or a copier, but eventually she realized that it was coming from outside.

"What is it?" she whispered. Her bladder felt like it was going to explode.

"A helicopter," B.C. answered. The sound grew louder. It was coming out of the north. B.C. heard footsteps and gripped Karen's arm. "Luther's coming," he whispered.

Crouching behind the bar, they waited, nerves wire-taut. The footsteps grew louder, hard-rubber heels clicking on the tile floor. There was a scraping sound only a few inches away, and Karen squeezed her eyes shut. He was sitting down at the bar. There was a clinking noise, and Karen realized that Luther was pouring himself a drink. Another minute more and she *knew* she was going to wet herself.

The noise of the helicopter had blanked out every other sound, and opening her eyes fractionally, Karen saw a sweeping bar of light cross the ceiling. Luther stood up, the chair scraping again. From what Karen could tell, the helicopter was landing in the parking lot of the club. She managed to stop thinking about her bladder, her curiosity aroused. There was no doubt that the helicopter was landing outside, and she was equally sure Luther Coyle had come to the club to meet it. But why?

Karen cautiously unfurled from her crouch and turned slightly, rising on the balls of her feet. B.C. tugged at her arm but she shook him off. She moved upward, inch by inch. Directly above her on the bar was a tray full of glasses. If she was careful, she could use them as a screen and still be able to see.

Luther was standing on the far side of the restaurant, his back to the bar as he looked out the big windows facing north. Peeping between the brandy snifters on the tray, Karen could see the blinking landing lights of the helicopter as it sank slowly to the ground. She'd somehow expected the craft to be painted in army camouflage, but instead it was a gleaming white. It was also a lot bigger than she'd expected, not like the buzzing, insectlike machines she was used to seeing on television.

A floodlight mounted on the side of the craft snapped on, bathing the inside of the restaurant in a searing light. Karen ducked, and Luther Coyle must have sensed something, because he half turned, looking back over his shoulder. Karen froze, and a second later, Luther turned back to the window. The floodlight went off, and Karen blinked, any night vision she'd had gone instantly. Squinting, she was vaguely aware of a sliding panel opening on the side of the helicopter and a figure stepping out.

Karen blinked again. The passenger from the helicopter was like something out of a science-fiction movie, clothed from head to toe in a shining, metallic suit, the face and head obscured by a dark-visored helmet. As the figure moved away from the helicopter and approached the club, Karen saw a small light on either side of the helmet come on. There was a web-belt around the figure's waist, slung with a holster and a battery pack. The suited man was also carrying a stubby, shotgunlike weapon in one hand, a thin cable snaking back from the butt of the weapon to a large, rectangular backpack. Strapped to the man's other wrist was a large pocket calculator-style keypad, also connected by a cable to the backpack. The gauntleted hand below the keypad held a large, plastic-wrapped package.

Karen swallowed hard, watching as the man moved out of sight. The gleaming figure was the personification of death, and for the first time she fully understood that she and B.C. were in terrible danger. If either Luther or the sinister figure from the helicopter found them hiding behind the bar, Karen knew that their lives would be forfeit. She stood, frozen in her half crouch, partially hidden behind the tray of glasses, unable to move a muscle.

Above the throbbing noise of the idling helicopter rotors, she could hear heavy footsteps as Luther moved away from the window. Shifting her head slightly, Karen saw the man in the shining suit walk into the room, the twin beams of his helmet's lamps swinging coldly across the empty tables. For the first time, Karen saw that there were three saucerlike indentations in the helmet, one where the ears would be and a pair set into the forehead. Just below the dark visor, looking like a hideous parody of an open mouth, was a fourth indentation.

Luther and the man in the suit met in the center of the restaurant. The mayor of Jericho Falls extended his hand, but the man in the suit ignored it. He spoke, and from the artificial amplification and electronic timbre, Karen realized that the indentation below the visor was some sort of speaker.

"MR. COYLE?"

"That's right." Luther, usually the quintessence of businesslike coolness, was obviously nervous. His voice was shaking.

"WE'VE GONE AS FAR AS WE CAN AT THIS POINT," said the electronic voice. "WE'LL NEED YOUR COOPERATION IF WE INTEND TO PROCEED."

"I understand," said Luther.

"PUT THIS ON. THEN WE CAN GO." He handed Luther the package. The mayor opened it up, revealing a one-piece bodysuit made out of some sort of silvery metallic fabric. He put it on while the helmeted figure watched. The suit was complete with padded feet, loose gloves, and a balaclava-style headpiece. The headpiece had a clear, flexible face plate and a pair of disc-shaped filters. The whole thing was sealed by a single zipper that went from crotch to neck. When Luther was completely covered, the helmeted figure stepped forward and helped seal the headpiece to the neck with a long Velcro strip and a row of snap closures.

"THE FILTERS ARE COMPLETELY SAFE," explained the man in the helmet, stepping back. "YOU'LL BE ABLE TO BREATHE NORMALLY, BUT IF YOU WANT TO SPEAK YOU'LL HAVE TO RAISE YOUR VOICE." Luther nodded without speaking. The helmeted man turned back toward the door and then paused, head cocking slightly as though he were listening to something. He turned around quickly, sliding the shotgun into a sleeve built into the chest of his suit. He lifted his other arm and tapped at the buttons on the wrist keypad. He waited silently for a moment, his visored face a blank. Still hidden behind the bar, Karen held her breath and tried desperately to will herself smaller. The man in the suit moved his head, the twin beams swinging slowly around the room, sweeping across the wall behind the bar, barely a foot over her head. He nodded to himself, apparently satisfied, then motioned to Luther Coyle.

"FOLLOW ME."

Luther nodded, the metallic fabric of the loose-fitting suit rustling softly. The man in the helmet moved away, with the bizarrely dressed mayor close behind him. They left the restaurant and went into the foyer. A moment later, Karen heard the sound of the front door slamming shut. She sagged against the bar, letting out a long sigh.

"They're gone," she whispered. B.C. stood up.

"Jesus! Look at that!" he said, staring goggle-eyed at the helicopter outside the window. "A Sikorsky Blackhawk."

"It came for Luther," Karen said. "Look." Through the window they could see the mayor and the helmeted man climbing into the waiting machine. The engine noise began to increase, the big rotors beginning to whirl faster and faster.

"That's Luther?" B.C. asked.

"None other. The one with the helmet made him put on the suit."

B.C. made a clucking noise. "If Luther's going off with him, that means he's involved in this whole thing. We're going to have to tell your dad about this. Right now." The power plant had spooled up to full takeoff speed now, the main rotors a shivering blur.

"How am I supposed to explain being here in the middle of the night?" Karen said. "With you?"

"That doesn't matter now," B.C. said. "This is more important."

"To you maybe," said Karen, "but I've—"

The two men came out of nowhere, suddenly appearing in the restaurant doorway. They were wearing suits like the man who'd come on the helicopter, but while his was shining silver, theirs were colored in mottled blues and grays. The men both carried short-barreled weapons that looked like overweight flare guns.

They fired at the same instant, almost invisible threads of wire unreeling toward Karen and B.C. Karen felt a brief stinging sensation just below her breasts, and she jerked back. She had just enough time to see the small projectile strike B.C. in the chest before the high voltage charge from the Taser slammed through her body. The two young people were thrown back against the rear wall of the bar and then dropped to the floor, unconscious.

The suited men shut off the current, snapped the thin wires leading toward the bar, and went to collect Karen and B.C. They loaded the two unconscious teenagers into heavy-gauge, zippered body bags, lugged them outside, and loaded them onto the helicopter. The suited men stood back, waved the machine off, and the whine of the rotors increased. The craft lifted, and then, tilting slightly, it began to climb, rising quickly as it headed north toward the mountains.

Unnoticed, the Confidelle test kit stood mutely on the windowsill of the restaurant ladies' room, a perfect ring of white slowly forming at the bottom of the test tube.

PART THREE

KHAMSIN
Sunday, November 2

Upon notification by the Unit Commander and after not less than a twelve-hour period from prior escalation, BLACK ROLLER may be escalated to KHAMSIN status. This escalation requires a second control subject from the target population. It should be noted that escalation to KHAMSIN status is irrevocable, even by Executive Order, and there can be no stand-down. General briefings regarding KHAMSIN may be found in the sub-unit commanders' manuals. Specific briefings on KHAMSIN/SPRING RAIN will be given by the Unit Commander. In the event that KHAMSIN/SPRING RAIN should prove ineffective, a further escalation may be necessary. Such escalation shall be at the discretion of the Unit Commander only.

—Lt. Col James. H. Wright
Commander, Special Unit 7
AMCCOM
Rock Island Arsenal
Rock Island, Illinois
Section 3, Number 1,
Page 82
BM-31-210

CHAPTER ELEVEN

12:05 A.M.

The flight of four, pure white, teardrop-shaped helicopters raced over Jericho Falls at treetop height from north, east, south, and west. The tiny Hughes Defenders took up positions at the corners of Constitution Common, hanging forty feet in the air, their noise-suppressed turbines giving off a dull, muted whine. Each of the helicopters was fitted with a belly-mounted searchlight, the powerful beams playing hotly over the Common in a random pattern. The machines were also equipped with an auxiliary, strut-mounted chain gun and four Hellfire air-to-ground missiles on pods slung under the main rotors.

Jack Slater stood on the steps of the police station, one hand shading his eyes as he looked up at the helicopters. Sparrow stood beside him, hands jammed into the pockets of his faded jean-jacket. Neither man was armed. Slater, the zipper of his battered flight jacket pulled up under his chin against the cold, shivered and tried to keep his teeth from chattering. He could taste the bite of winter in the air and wondered if he was going to live long enough to see it come.

"Nice show," said Sparrow, frowning as he glanced up at the pale, insectlike machines. "I think we're supposed to be impressed."

"I am," Slater answered. "Those little bugs could take out the whole downtown in about thirty seconds."

"And this Colonel Wright you talked to wants us to know it."
Slater glanced at his watch: 12:05. "He's late."

"Psych-out time. The son of a bitch wants a little edge."

"He's got four of them," Slater said dryly, looking up at the

151

helicopters. For Slater, growing up, helicopters had meant the "Whirlybirds" TV show and funny-looking machines with fat pontoons and bubble cabins. The Vietnam War had changed all that forever. Helicopters were the fire-breathing dragons of a new age, armor-plated mythical beasts bringing down death from above.

And the four Defenders were just the devil's outriders. In the dark distance to the south and west there was a new sound, a deep-throated stuttering roar that soon drowned out the whispering chatter of the small, one-eyed machines. The roar turned into rolling thunder, echoing up from the ground, and a few seconds later the source of the violent banshee wail finally showed itself.

Snow white, its seventy-foot-long fuselage bathed in the light of the Defenders' searchlights, the huge Sikorsky Super Stallion appeared above the Common, the stunning downdraft created by the seven eighty-foot rotors tearing the last leaves from the trees around the square and creating a blinding storm of dust and litter.

It hovered over the Common for a long minute as the lights from the four outrider ships pointed out a clear landing spot to one side of the bandstand, then it settled slowly to the ground, the heavy shock absorbers of the tripod undercarriage taking the twenty-ton weight of the giant machine. Once fully down, the sound of the three big G.E. turbines began to fade, and as the rotors slowed, the cargo loading ramp under the tail dropped down.

"The bastard must be from Hollywood!" Sparrow said, shouting into Slater's ear. The sheriff nodded, keeping his eyes on the ramp. Sparrow was right; it was like something out of *Close Encounters.*

A single figure appeared, walking slowly down the ramp, and the science-fiction analogy grew stronger. The man was wearing a suit and helmet like the spotter they'd run into on the Notch, except that this time the suit was a glittering reflective silver. Other than a holstered sidearm, the figure carried no weapons.

The man reached the end of the ramp and stepped down onto the ground. He ducked under the tail and took a few steps, moving out from under the massive rotors, drooping slightly now as they slowed to a stop. Slater stood where he was for a moment before he realized that forcing the man to come to him would be a foolish show of bravado, especially considering the firepower of the still hovering Defenders. He walked down the station steps and crossed the street to the Common, Sparrow trailing slightly behind him.

Slater reached the grass at the edge of the large, rectangular park and stopped. Halfway was far enough. He stared at the suited man standing fifty feet away, face hidden by the blank, expressionless mask of the dark visor. The man remained where he was for a moment, then walked forward, stopping again a few feet away from Slater and his long-haired companion.

"SHERIFF SLATER?" The voice was coming from a small, circular speaker built into the helmet, just below the visor.

"That's right."

"WHO IS THE MAN WITH YOU?"

"His name is Hawke. He's a deputy."

"I SEE."

"You're the man I spoke to on the telephone?"

"YES. LT. COLONEL WRIGHT."

"From what army?" Sparrow asked, unable to keep the anger out of his voice.

"THE UNITED STATES ARMY, MR. HAWKE."

"When did the U.S. Army start blowing away its own people and kidnapping kids?" answered Sparrow. "Not to mention killing dogs."

"IT WAS NECESSARY UNDER THE CIRCUMSTANCES," answered the suited man.

"Right."

"Can it, Sparrow," Slater ordered sharply. "This isn't going to get us anywhere." He turned back to Wright. "I think your actions do require some kind of explanation."

"CERTAINLY," answered Wright, the helmet nodding. "IT'S QUITE SIMPLE, ALTHOUGH UNFORTUNATE. YOUR TOWN IS UNDER QUARANTINE."

"Why?"

"PLEASE, SHERIFF SLATER. NO GAMES. YOU ARE AWARE OF THE SITUATION. A GOVERNMENT VEHICLE WAS INVOLVED IN AN ACCIDENT HERE. THE VEHICLE WAS THEN INVOLVED IN A HALLOWEEN PRANK. IT CONTAINED A HIGHLY VIRULENT ORGANISM BEING TRANSHIPPED TO OUR LABORATORY AT FT. DETRICK. THAT ORGANISM HAS SINCE CAUSED SEVERAL DEATHS AND HAS RE-

SULTED IN WIDESPREAD ILLNESS HERE. MY JOB IS TO STOP ANY FURTHER SPREADING OF THE INFECTION.''

"The head of our Medical Center here says the 'organism,' as you call it, is a recombinant bacteriological warfare germ."

"HE'S WRONG," answered the colonel. "THE ORGANISM WAS DEVELOPED AS A COUNTERMEASURE TO A SOVIET CBW THREAT WE KNOW EXISTS IN EUROPE. THE CULTURES ACCIDENTALLY DISSEMINATED HERE WERE THE BASIS FOR RESEARCH INTO AN ANTIDOTE.''

"Horseshit," said Sparrow under his breath. Wright ignored the comment.

"THE CULTURE CONTAINED A WEAKENED VARIANT STRAIN," Wright continued. "FROM WHAT I GATHER, THERE HAVE BEEN SEVERAL DEATHS, BUT THE LARGEST PROBLEM HAS BEEN A WIDESPREAD FLU. NOTHING VERY TERRIBLE. AN INCONVENIENCE.''

"Tell that to Corney Drake," Sparrow said. "And what about Josh Robinson?''

"Look," Slater broke in, "why don't you tell us what you want? You've cut off our communications and blockaded the town. If this bug is so weak, what's the problem?"

"THINK FOR A MOMENT," Wright said. "YOU ARE AWARE THAT THE ORGANISM IS EXTREMELY CONTAGIOUS. WEAK OR NOT, LETTING IT GO BEYOND THE TOWN LIMITS OF JERICHO FALLS WOULD BE LIKE SETTING OFF AN ASIAN FLU EPIDEMIC. STATISTICALLY, IT WOULD RESULT IN THE DEATHS OF ALMOST SIXTY THOUSAND PEOPLE IN THE CONTINENTAL UNITED STATES, AND PERHAPS TEN TIMES THAT MANY WORLDWIDE. WE'RE TRYING TO STOP THAT.''

"By putting us under quarantine," Slater said.

"AS A PRELIMINARY STEP.''

"What's next?" Slater asked.

"EVACUATION, I'M AFRAID.''

"You've got to be kidding! You're talking about almost four thousand people!''

"SHERIFF SLATER, PLEASE. THE STORM WARNING CONTINGENCY PLAN HAS BEEN IN PLACE FOR THE BETTER PART OF A DECADE. IT WAS INEVITABLE SOMETHING LIKE THIS WOULD HAPPEN EVENTUALLY. THE PROCEDURES ARE QUITE CLEAR.''

"Really?" Slater said. "Too bad no one told me anything about them.''

"SHERIFF, PLEASE DON'T MAKE A DIFFICULT SITUATION EVEN

WORSE. AS I TOLD YOU, THE PROCEDURES ARE QUITE CLEAR. ONE WAY OR ANOTHER, THIS TOWN IS GOING TO BE EVACUATED. EITHER WE GET YOUR COOPERATION, OR WE DO IT THE HARD WAY." The man's head barely moved, but Slater knew he was talking about the gunships still hovering over the Common.

"I don't like being threatened."

"IT'S NO THREAT, SHERIFF. IT'S FACT. I GIVE THE WORD AND YOU'RE ALL DEAD MEN. BELIEVE ME."

"I get the picture." Slater lifted his right arm stiffly, the fist clenched. "Let's hope you get it, too. I drop my arm and you get a 30-30 slug in the neck. It's the weakest point of your little Darth Vader outfit, as far as we can tell. We've got a dozen people in buildings scattered around the Common. Deputy Hawke here used to be a chopper pilot in Vietnam. He tells me a bullet in the tail rotor can do wonderful things. So back off, Colonel. This isn't some little village in Nicaragua you're doing a number on."

"THIS IS VERY FOOLISH OF YOU."

"Probably. But I want some time to think this out. Call it a truce if you want."

"WE DON'T HAVE MUCH TIME, SHERIFF, THAT'S THE POINT."

"Noon. Call me."

"I'M NOT SURE I CAN ACCOMMODATE YOU, SHERIFF."

"Make up your mind. My arm's getting tired."

"PERHAPS I SHOULD CALL YOUR BLUFF," said Wright. "MAYBE THERE ARE NO MEN AT ALL."

"Sparrow?" said Slater. The bearded man nodded and waved his left arm. There was a brief pause and then a two-inch chunk of dirt flew into the air six inches from the Colonel's foot. "Dickie Morgan," the sheriff said calmly. "He works at Gaudet's Hardware and Sporting Goods. He takes his work very seriously. What you might call an avid sportsman. Good enough bluff, Colonel Wright?"

"NOON," said the man in the suit. To give him credit, he hadn't moved an inch when the shot went off. "THE CALL WILL COME TO YOUR OFFICE." He turned and walked slowly back to the waiting helicopter. He walked up the ramp, and it hissed slowly closed behind him. A few seconds later, the main rotors began to move, the triple turbines firing up. Slater and Sparrow shut their eyes against the whirling cloud of dust and leaves, the roaring of the engines and the scream of the rotors pounding into their ears. They stood their ground as the huge machine lifted ponderously off the grass, gaining height before it swung away toward the river. The four Defenders lagged slightly, the beams of their searchlights tilting up to wash over the buildings around the Common. Then they were gone, forming a head-to-tail formation, following the big Sikorsky south.

"What do you think?" Sparrow asked, turning to watch the buzzing flight of helicopters disappear into the darkness.

"I think we bought a little bit of time and made an enemy. A dangerous one."

Driving the Meat Wagon south on Gowan Street, Payne ducked involuntarily as the thundering flight of helicopters roared directly over his head. He slowed the station wagon and peered out through the windshield, watching as the ghostly formation swung over Mill Park and followed the dark ribbon of the Jericho River, moving south.

The helicopters had obviously come from the Common, and for a moment Payne considered turning around to investigate. Instead, he increased his speed and continued along the darkened street, heading for the Strip and Frenchtown. The call he'd taken at the Medical Center a quarter of an hour before took precedence over his curiosity.

He drove west along the Strip past the Slumber-King, then turned north on Morin, easing his way along the narrow street. The houses here were small frame bungalows and row houses, most of them built during the boom years just after World War I. Some of them were owned by their occupants, but most were rentals, handled by Luther Coyle and his various nasty little enterprises.

The old man scowled, large muscular hands gripping the steering wheel tightly. If you were old, poor, or unemployed, you lived on these streets, and that meant your day-to-day life was ruled by Luther. You paid your rent to him, and if you couldn't make the payments, you borrowed from his finance companies. One way or the other, he controlled you. The man's title of mayor was merely icing on the cake. You could have elected Dennis Chang to the position, and Luther still would have had a stranglehold on the town.

The doctor threaded his way through the maze of back streets and finally pulled up in front of a small, cottagelike house on South Beacon. He turned off the ignition and sat for a moment. The house was much like its neighbors, but instead of old tires and garbage in the pocket handkerchief front yard, 38 South Beacon had shrubs and flowers. The story-and-a-half structure was painted white, the trim done in a pleasant dark green, and it was obvious that the person who lived there took pride in the house. The fat man opened the car door and slid out from behind the wheel, thoughts of Luther Coyle fading as better memories rose in his mind.

Rembrandt Payne had known Rebecca Hardy almost his whole life, and for all that time he'd loved her. His father had been the town's first real resident doctor and both Rebecca's parents had worked for him, Steven Hardy as handyman, Mrs. Hardy as cook and housekeeper. When Rembrandt's father died, he willed the Hardys the house on South Beacon.

Rembrandt had tried to keep their economic differences from coming between them, but inevitably the social and financial gulf had its effect. Rembrandt went to university in Boston, while Becky had to struggle just to get her normal-school certificate from Manchester.

Eventually, Rebecca became a teacher at the run-down little Catholic school in Frenchtown, but by then it was too late. The passage of time and the events of the world took their toll, and even after returning to the Falls to take up his father's practice, Rembrandt could never find the passion that had once burned between them.

He and Rebecca met occasionally at gatherings of one kind or another, and sometimes, looking at each other from across a room, he was sure he saw the old spark there, but nothing ever came of it. Neither married, neither had children, and neither one of them forgot the other; they maintained a distant, cautious friendship of a sort, and after more than half a century, the relationship had become comfortable for both of them.

He hadn't hesitated when she called him at the Medical Center. She was ill and she needed help: he picked up his bag and left, pausing just long enough to drop in on Simms in the lab and tell him he was going out on a call.

He opened the waist-high gate in the picket fence and went up the short walk to Rebecca's front porch. The two-seat glider was still there, and so was the trellis. The old boards took his weight, creaking as he crossed the porch and opened the front door.

The narrow foyer was dark. He closed the door behind him and went along the gloomy passage to the main hall. The house was small, with two rooms and a kitchen on the main floor and two small bedrooms under the sloping eaves. At the rear of the house, beyond the kitchen, was another yard, only slightly bigger than the one in front.

The hall was lit by a pair of small sconces set into the wall. By their dim light, the old man could see the faded, pale blue wallpaper and the thin, well-worn carpet underfoot. He went up the narrow stairs slowly. Weight and age had ruined his knees years ago, and now he only climbed stairs when it was absolutely necessary. He reached the top of the stairs and paused to catch his breath, realizing then, that in all the years he'd known Becky Hardy, he'd never once set foot in her bedroom.

The wooden door directly in front of him was open, soft light spilling out to light the peak-roofed landing. He knocked on the doorframe softly and heard Becky's soft voice telling him to come in.

The small room was plainly furnished with a bed, a dressing table, and a simple desk set under the window. There was a standing wardrobe in one corner of the room, and the polished wood floor was covered by a large oval rug, its deep green worn through in the middle from decades of traffic.

Becky lay in the bed, coverlet drawn up around her shoulders. Her hair, once jet black and thick as dark molasses, was thinner now and almost totally gray, spread out like a fan over the piled pillows behind her head. Her face was pale and lined, and there were dull, bruised shadows under her blue-green eyes. She drew one hand out from under the covers and extended it, smiling weakly. Payne lowered himself carefully onto the edge of the bed and took the hand in his own. It was warm, but dry and brittle, like an autumn leaf.

"Hello, Rebecca," he said softly.

"Hello yourself, Dr. Payne," she answered. "I'm terribly sorry to have you out so late, but I felt it was important." Even after all these years he could still hear a trace of her father's Irish in her voice.

"You weren't very clear on the telephone."

"No."

"So what's the problem?" he asked gently. By a long-standing, unspoken consent, Payne had never acted as her physician, and he felt a little ill at ease in the role.

"I understand that almost the entire town is down with some sort of flu."

"It was." Payne nodded. "It seems to be passing." There was no point in going into any details. Better to soften things.

She wouldn't have it. "Don't fib to me, you old goat," she chastised. "I've had half a dozen people in here today telling me all about it. From the sound of things, it's not normal, is it? It's no ordinary illness."

"No," Payne admitted. "There's been an accident, I think. A bug that got away from the people who were working on it."

"I see. In that case, I was right to call you."

"The illness doesn't seem to have much effect on older people. I'm surprised you caught it."

"It's no little bit of influenza that I'm concerned with," she said.

"Then what is it?"

She squeezed his hand. "I don't want to prejudice your thoughts by saying anything. I'd like you to examine me."

"I'm not sure that I—"

"Oh, come now, Rembrandt," she laughed. "Sixty years ago you invested a great deal of time and energy convincing me to take off my clothes, and now I'm asking you to do so. You didn't succeed then, so take your victory now." Her eyes twinkled, and to his horror, Payne realized that he was blushing.

"I don't think that will be necessary, Rebecca."

"I do," she said firmly. "Examine me. I think it may be important."

"If you insist."

"I insist."

The doctor reached forward and gently turned back the coverlet. As he did so, the elderly woman gathered the fabric of her nightdress and pulled it up to her breasts. Instantly, Payne was aware of a strong, sickly sweet odor. His eyes widened as he looked down at the woman's body.

The flesh of her chest, abdomen, and pelvis was a mass of

large ulcers, edges elevated, the craterlike centers exuding a dark, foul-smelling secretion. The skin around the ulcers was dry and scaled, like ezcema, and the remaining flesh was covered with small raised papules, like tiny grapes, swollen and dark.

"My God, Rebecca!" whispered Payne. "How long have you had this condition?"

"That's what I found so extraordinary," the woman answered calmly, her eyes avoiding the ruin of her lower body. "Yesterday there was nothing except a few patches of dry skin, slightly itchy. The ulcers appeared this morning. By noon I was covered in them. I can't say positively, but I think I have them on my back as well."

"Why didn't you come to the Center, call for an ambulance?"

"I didn't see the point," she said, shrugging her thin shoulders. "According to the neighbors, the Center was filled to overflowing, and the ulcers aren't painful. I find the odor somewhat offensive, though. It also occurred to me that I might be infectious."

Rembrandt Payne continued to stare at the hideously deformed skin. At first glance it looked as though she'd been repeatedly burned with the hot end of a cigar. He'd never seen anything like it in his career or read about anything close to it in the medical literature.

"Is it cancer?" asked Rebecca. Payne shook his head.

"No. There's no cancer in the world that develops that fast. At a guess, I'd say it's some kind of fungoid. Mycosis sarcomata."

"You're an appalling liar, Rembrandt. I taught in a Catholic school for almost forty-five years. Mycosis sarcomata is nothing but a Latin description of my symptoms. What I want from you is an opinion."

"Yes?"

"Is this . . . thing I have in any way connected to the sickness everyone seems to have come down with?"

"I have no idea."

"Could it be a result of a drug interaction?"

"It's doubtful." He looked at Rebecca curiously. "Why? What kind of medication have you been using?"

"Aspirin for my arthritis and some pills Dr. Blaine prescribed."

"What kind of pills?" asked Payne.

"Some sort of therapy for weak bones and also my . . . hot flashes."

"Where are they?"

"In the night table."

Payne leaned forward and opened the drawer of the small table beside the bed. He took out a plastic pill bottle and examined the label: Estropan.

"These are hormone pills," he said.

"That's right."

"How long have you been taking them?"

"Quite some time. Several years. Dr. Blaine called the condition 'senile vaginitis.' They seem to have done me some good."

"No problem like this before?"

"Never."

"All right." He drew up the coverlet and then slipped the pill bottle into the pocket of his jacket. "I'm going to take these with me, just in case." He stood up. "Did you try to get in touch with Dr. Blaine?"

"Of course," she said. "He didn't answer his telephone. I waited for quite some time before I called you. I didn't want to be any bother."

"Don't be ridiculous," Payne said, putting on his best smile. "It gave me an excuse to come and see you."

"You don't need excuses, Rembrandt. You never did."

"Yes, well. Are you sure there's no pain?"

"None."

"All right. We'll leave things as they are for the moment. I'll call on you again tomorrow to see how things are coming along. It may just be a passing anomaly. If it persists, I'll want you to come in to the Center."

"Of course." She lifted her hand again and the old man took it, looking down at her. The distance between them seemed to vanish for an instant, and he had a brief urge to lean down and kiss her. He resisted the feeling. She was a patient, and if he was right, she'd just given him the key to his problem, or part of it, anyway. He had to get back to the Center.

"Call me if you need anything, Rebecca."

"I will."

"Good night, then." He squeezed her hand gently, not wanting to leave and feeling as though he was deserting her by doing so. She shook her head against the pillow and made a little clucking noise with her tongue.

"Don't be silly, Rembrandt," she said quietly, as though reading his mind. "I'm sure I'll be quite all right. Get along with your business now." She pulled her hand away from his and made a little sweeping gesture. "Get along," she repeated. He nodded silently and left the room.

A few moments later he was out on the dark street again, one hand in his pocket, clutching the little pill bottle Blaine had prescribed. He maneuvered his bulk into the Meat Wagon, started the engine, and glanced at the upper window of the house. Now he knew what the victims of Redenbacher's Syndrome had in common, he was sure of it.

"God bless you, Becky," he whispered into the darkness, and then he drove away.

Bodo Bimm sat under Mill Bridge and stared blankly down at the frothing water of the Fourth Chute. The steep slope of dirt and dried grass underneath the single stone arch was littered with beer cans, bits of cast-off clothing, and the rotting detritus of a hundred teenage gatherings, but it was safe and it was secret. Not like the Medical Center, with its bright lights and echoing corridors, and not like Mrs. McQuire's on Concord Street.

He'd gone there right after leaving the Medical Center, but he hadn't stayed very long. All the boarders were sick, and Mrs. McQuire was the worst of all. He'd peeked into her room, once the front parlor of the house, and the smell had driven him off. It smelled of dead things, and when he whispered her name, she'd groaned but she'd said no words. He'd gone to the bathroom there, and it was even worse than the toilet at the Gas Bar. Foul, the toilet unflushed, the rust-spotted porcelain sink spattered with crusting vomit. He went to his room, changed out of the hospital pajamas, and then he left.

At first he'd thought about going to the Gas Bar, but that meant returning to the fear, and he couldn't do that. The Gas Bar was the headless thing and the fire. He walked through the dark streets of the town instead, eventually reaching the Common.

And that was almost as frightening as the Gas Bar. It was all dark, and when he went past the Bo-Peep, he saw that the big front window was smashed, the open part roughly covered with a flattened cardboard box and held on with masking tape. Something bad was happening. Except for the Gas Bar and Mrs. McQuire's, the only safe place he knew was his hiding place under the bridge.

For a time it had been his home, the only place he could avoid being seen when he first arrived in Jericho Falls. He couldn't remember much before that, except for scattered images, most of them dark and unhappy. He'd slept beneath the bridge during the daylight hours and gone foraging for food at night. One summer night, coming back from a raiding expedition through the town's garbage pails and the back alleys behind the Common, he'd returned to find his nest occupied.

Two young people, a girl and a boy in their late teens, had spread a blanket and were making love. He'd crept as close as he dared, the sound of the rushing water tumbling over the old millrace covering his movements. Watching, he'd marveled at the sight of the boy's thrusting motions and the young girl's soft, animal cries.

The boy's thing had seemed huge, glistening wetly as it appeared and disappeared magically between the girl's legs, and it seemed incredible that the soft, dark cleft could spread so wide and take him so deeply. Best of all were the last few moments when the boy, his mouth suckling hard on the girl's breast, had plunged totally within her, his buttocks clenched hard, his legs thrashing, tangled in the blue jeans around his ankles. The girl's head had lashed back and forth against the blanket, the white wool of her sweater bunched around her neck, her hands clutching at the boy's blond, curly hair. Finally, they had come apart, exhausted. The memory still excited him and had been the source of his own masturbatory fantasies for a long time.

But he couldn't think about that now. There was no time. He had to do something about the panic twisting in his belly like some coiling worm, chewing at his insides. Bad things were happening, and he wanted to run, to leave Jericho Falls. But the thought of leaving was almost as frightening as staying where he was. From day to day, the enclosing wall of mountains around the valley had given him a sense of security. He knew the boundaries, could see them, and that was comforting. To leave meant going beyond and nights spent in unfamiliar darkness.

"Trout in there," he whispered to himself, looking down at the icy black water. "Lots of trout in there." But saying the old words didn't make him feel any better. The old words didn't work anymore. There were new ones.

"Topsy-turvy," he said. "Town's gone topsy-turvy."

He didn't like the new words at all.

CHAPTER TWELVE

6:10 A.M.

Bentley Carver Bingham awoke by stages, each stage more revealing and more painful than the last. At first, unconsciousness was a dark, safe womb, a velvet nest at the bottom of an invisible well, sounds and sensation coming to him only dimly. Eventually, though, the well became a claustrophobic coffin, and he was overjoyed when vision returned, even if a splitting headache and a burning pain in his chest came along with it.

A bed—crisp sheets and a blanket binding him with military precision. The ceiling over his head was white, plastic and lit from behind. It was also quite low. Humming electrical sounds; a faint ticking, like a metronome, all of it wrapped in a faint vibration he could feel throughout his body. At first, he thought he was moving, but the sensation was too regular. An airplane? What was he doing on an airplane?

No. A hospital bed, but not the Medical Center. He'd been there when he had his appendix out. The Medical Center rooms had pale blue walls, and they weren't lit like this at all. Definitely a hospital, though. The room smelled like a doctor—too clean to be real and overlaid with a faint aroma of soap and Cepacol mouthwash. But if he wasn't in the Medical Center, where was he?

He sat up, realizing dimly that he was dressed only in a short hospital gown of some kind. He put a hand up to his chest and touched gingerly. A dull pain like a bruise, but nothing serious. Nothing like the belly-deep tugging of surgery. He blinked and swallowed hard, his eyes going in and out of focus. He took a deep breath, and the vertigo receded.

"Relax," he muttered under his breath. "We're looking for

165

logic here." Everything was fuzzy. No glasses. He panicked for a moment and then looked around. The wire rims were folded neatly a few feet away on the bare enameled surface of a metal nightstand. He reached for them and felt the pull of something at his wrist. Handcuffs?

I.V. Grunting with the effort, he rolled over onto his side, grabbed his glasses, and put them on, sighing with relief as the world came back into its proper perspective. He blinked, held up his wrist, and examined it. There was more than a simple intravenous line. There was also a thin plastic wire that appeared from under the two-inch square of bandage and disappeared somewhere behind him. He squirmed around, following the tube and the wire. They led to a large metal box screwed onto the wall. Some kind of electronic device, dotted with dials, switches, and a stacked series of colored video displays. Every time he moved, the squiggling colored graphs twitched. Squinting, he read off the labels.

"Respiration, Pulse, EEG, B-Tox, Temp." Easy enough to figure out. The other switches were more difficult. "Rec. ERA, MSA, StatCall." He was beginning to think more clearly as the last trailing effects of the Taser shock dissipated; with clarity, came a growing fear.

The last thing he remembered was the two suited men in the Broken Racket, but it was obvious that he'd been taken to some sort of medical facility, where he was now under observation. His wristwatch had been taken, but somehow he knew that he hadn't been unconscious for all that long, a few hours at most, so wherever he was wasn't far from Jericho Falls. He turned around and let his head fall back against the pillow. Right now, the wheres and whens weren't important, it was the whys.

B.C. took a deep breath, let it out slowly. He closed his eyes against the bright glare of the plastic panels overhead and tried to put things together. Somehow, the man who'd been talking to Luther had known that he and Karen were in the restaurant and had ordered them taken. The best reason for their capture was the simple fact that they now knew Luther Coyle was involved in whatever was going on in the Falls.

Traitor. Benedict Arnold, and they were the only witnesses. But if that was true, why all the medical paraphernalia? You didn't put witnesses in the hospital, you put them under lock and key.

B.C. opened his eyes again and sat up. Maybe it amounted to the same thing. He looked around the room. Ten by twelve at most. Bed, bedside table, the electronic junk, and two doors. One set into the far wall, the other a hatchway with a central lock-wheel, like something you might find on a submarine. Up in the far corner, perched on a metal bracket, was a small video camera, a bright red light over the lens showing that it was in operation. He was being watched, and probably listened to as well. He swallowed, his mouth dry. The machines behind his head and the camera would have alerted his captors that he was conscious again, and they'd probably be along to check on him fairly soon.

He swung his legs out over the side of the bed, his growing fear turning to outright panic. This wasn't some crazy TV show, this kind of thing didn't happen to kids like him. He wanted to go home. Right now.

"Baby!" he whispered, almost spitting out the word. But it was true. He wanted to go home. He wanted his mother and father. Young enough to want his parents in a time of crisis, he was also smart enough to know that it wasn't likely to happen. Jericho Falls had dropped into some hideous sort of nightmare time warp involving Luther Coyle, and he and Karen were the only two people aware of his complicity.

He sat slumped on the edge of the bed and picked at the bandage on his wrist, slowly peeling it back to reveal a dark, irregular bruise. The shiny upper end of the intravenous needle protruded slightly from the middle of the discolored patch, while beside it was the dime-sized head of a tiny electrode held in place by a strip of tape. B.C. bit his lip. He wasn't going to get anywhere hooked up to the machines behind the bed.

With his thumb and forefinger, he gripped the intravenous needle, took a deep breath, and pulled. It slid out of his vein easily, a small dot of bright red blood oozing up. One down, one to go. He hooked his thumbnail under the electrode and peeled it off. Free. He turned his head. The monitor graphs had all dropped to nothing. If anyone was keeping track, they'd realize that he'd disconnected himself. Too late to think about that now.

He slipped off the bed, weaving slightly, the fingers of one hand clutching at the bedclothes for support. He waited until the spell of dizziness passed and then tiptoed toward the hatchway door. The lock-wheel was stiff and even with both hands he couldn't budge it. Either he was too weak to open the doorway, or it was secured from outside. He went to the second, smaller door and turned the knob. It opened easily.

He stepped into a room identical to his own. Karen Slater, her naked rear end poking out of a hospital gown much too short for her long-legged figure, was examining the monitor panel behind her bed. She too had taken out the intravenous tube and the electrode. Hearing B.C. come into the room, she whirled around, one hand grasping the tape closure on the back of the gown. B.C. blushed furiously.

"Sorry," he said. "I guess I should have knocked." Karen's response took him completely by surprise. She ran across the room and threw herself into B.C.'s arms, pressing her cheek into his neck.

"Oh God!" she whispered. "I'm so glad to see you, B.C." For the second time in twenty-four hours his glands asserted themselves, and this time there was nothing between them except two thin layers of cotton. B.C. wanted to sink through the floor with embarrassment, but Karen didn't pay any attention at all. In fact, she pressed herself even closer. "I thought you were dead!" she moaned. "I thought I was all alone." B.C. concentrated, and the unwelcome erection subsided.

"It's okay," he soothed. "We're going to be okay." He put one hand against her back and nudged her toward the bed. They sat down together, Karen still gripping his arm.

"What happened to us?" she asked.

"I think it's called a Taser," B.C. answered. "High-voltage shock. I've seen ads for them in magazines."

"This is all crazy. Why would anybody want to do that to us?"

"We saw Mr. Coyle. He's involved in this whole thing," B.C. said.

"What whole thing?"

"I don't know. But it has something to do with the military. This is some kind of medical facility they've set up."

"It's more like a jail."

"Quarantine," B.C. said. He poked his chin toward the oval hatchway on the other wall. "That's some kind of air lock. They've got cameras on us, and I bet they can hear everything we're saying, too."

"They're going to kill us, aren't they?" Karen said dully. B.C. looked around the cell-like room, biting his lip and trying to keep back the tears filling his eyes. He'd never been so frightened in his life.

"No," he said quietly, trying to keep his voice from trembling. "They're not going to kill us. I mean, this is Jericho Falls, New Hampshire, not Moscow."

There was a hissing sound from the direction of the hatchway door and the two young people looked up apprehensively, watching as the lock-wheel began to move. The hatch opened outward, and a moment later two people stepped into the room. They were dressed identically in light blue, loose-fitting suits, their heads covered by clear plastic hoods. Each suit was fitted with a thin yellow tube, coiled like a telephone cord. The tubing trailed behind them, disappearing back through the open hatch. The suits seemed to be inflated, the yellow tubes pumping in a constant flow of air. The lead figure carried a bright blue plastic case that looked like a space-age doctor's bag, while the man in the rear was holding a short-barreled weapon of some kind. The rear figure took up a position to one side of the hatchway, while the other approached the two teenagers on the bed.

"I see both of you are up," said the lead figure, the voice pleasant and only slightly muffled by the suit. Through the plastic, Karen and B.C. saw that the figure was female. Young, no more than twenty-five or so, with dark brown hair cut just above the shoulders.

"Why are we here?" asked B.C.

"Tests," the woman said. She put the case down on the bed and snapped it open, revealing an array of instruments and small bottles, each one tucked into a foam-lined niche.

"What if we don't want the tests?" said B.C.

"Then my companion will be forced to shoot you with that tranquilizer pistol he's carrying," the woman replied, smiling. "You'd wake up in a couple of hours with a splitting headache." She took two small bottles out of the case and broke open a plastic package containing a pair of large syringes.

"Can you tell us where we are, please?" Karen asked. The woman smiled and shook her head.

"I'm afraid not, dear. That's classified."

"Then this is some sort of army installation?" B.C. prodded.

"That's classified, too. But you're quite safe. There's nothing at all to worry about." The woman took a packet of needles out of the case and deftly began screwing them into the syringe barrels. B.C. noticed that her hands were covered by tight-fitting surgical gloves attached to the wrists of the suit.

"Are you a doctor, or is that classified, too?" B.C. asked dryly.

"I'm a doctor," answered the woman. She approached B.C., one of the hypodermics in her gloved hand. "Now please, no more questions. I have work to do." She pushed up the sleeve of the young man's gown, found a vein in the elbow, and swiftly plunged in the needle. She pulled back the plunger, and B.C. swallowed, watching the barrel fill with dark red blood. When she was finished taking the sample, the woman emptied the hypo into one of the small bottles, poking the needle through the rubber top. Then, taking another hypodermic, she repeated the sampling with Karen. Blood testing complete, she put the bottles and the used syringes back in the case and snapped it closed.

"That's it?" B.C. asked.

"That's it," answered the doctor, smiling again.

"Can I ask a question?"

"Of course." She nodded, the air-filled headpiece bobbing up and down.

"Do we get fed?"

"In about an hour."

"There's no toilet," Karen said.

"Bedpans in the side tables. The big one is for bowel movements, the small one is for urine. I'd like samples as soon as possible, actually."

"Gross," Karen said, wrinkling her nose. Bentley forced himself to keep a straight face. If he started laughing, he knew he might not be able to stop. Panic was still only one step away.

"Uh, when do we get . . . interrogated?" he asked as the woman picked up the case.

"I'm not sure I understand what you mean," she said. He could see her frowning behind the facepiece.

"You're being pretty good, making it seem like this is all really normal, but you're not wearing that suit for nothing, and we weren't brought here so you could take blood samples."

"Or dig around in our shit," Karen added, anger burning in her voice.

"As far as I know, nobody wants to ask you any questions. My instructions were to take blood samples and make other medical tests. That's all."

"So you're just following orders, is that it?" Karen said.

"You could put it that way if you wanted. Now I've really got to be going. You'll be brought a meal in about an hour, and I'll be back to do some more tests later on." She turned and retreated through the hatchway, the yellow tubing coiling up behind her. When she was through the opening, the man with the pistol followed, stepping backward, his eyes never leaving them. The hatch closed and the lock-wheel turned again.

"What was that all about?" asked Karen when they were gone.

"Just what she said." B.C. shrugged. "Tests. The suits were airtight. Whatever it is we've got, they're afraid of it."

"But neither one of us got the flu bug."

"Maybe that's why they're interested," Bentley said thoughtfully, his eyes on the hatchway. "Maybe we don't fit the pattern."

Rembrandt Payne drove the Meat Wagon through the silent streets of the town as the sun crept slowly up behind the forbidding screen of hills to the east. Dawn cast a cold light on the dark houses of River Park, and the skeletal trees along the banks of Mountain Creek looked like huge gnarled arms pushing up out of the hard soil, twisted fingers clutching at the ice blue sky. There was a skin of hoarfrost on the grass of Constitution Common and the director of the Jericho Falls Medical Center shivered, even though the station wagon's heater was on full blast.

"Old bones," he muttered to himself as he pulled into a parking space in front of the police station. He climbed out of the car, locked it, and went up the steps. The front office was empty, and there was no one at the radio, which was surprising, but Payne finally found the sheriff in his office, telephone to his ear. As the old man entered the room, Slater dropped the telephone back into its cradle and leaned back in his chair. He looked worn-out, dark circles under his eyes, a shadow of bristle smudged across his jaw and chin.

"Morning, Doc. You're up early."

"You look as though you haven't slept at all," commented the heavyset man, lowering himself into the wooden armchair across from Slater.

"I haven't. I've spent all night trying to figure out how to get us all out of this mess."

"I understand you met with our adversaries last night."

"How did you know that?"

"Miss Hale informed me when I called your house. Presumably, the meeting was something less than cordial."

"You might say that," Slater grunted, yawning. He picked up a mug from the desk, glanced into it and grimaced. He took a swallow of cold coffee and sat back in the chair. "You were right. The man was a bird colonel, dressed in some kind of space suit. He came in on a big Blackhawk helicopter with four gunships for outriders. Very impressive. According to him, we have to evacuate the town."

"I see." Payne nodded. "Did he have any explanation for the outbreak of illness?"

"He said it was a weakened strain of a flu bug. Nothing really bad, but it has to be contained."

"Did you believe him?"

"No."

"Good. He was lying. The Redenbacher bacteria has nothing to do with influenza. I found that out last night."

"What is it?" asked Slater, dropping forward in his chair.

"An allergen. The first indicator came from one of my lab technicians, the second from a dear friend I visited on a house call. Redenbacher's is an allergen that triggers profound and widespread cancers of several different types. So far, they seem to be epidermal."

"Skin cancer?"

"Put simply, yes. I'm afraid it may get worse, however."

"Jesus!"

"Indeed. The bacteria was released less than seventy-two hours ago, and I have seen evidence of fully formed sarcomas."

"An allergy that causes cancer?"

"No, not exactly. The bacteria is nothing more than a ground for the formation and rapid growth of the disease. The cancers are triggered by something else. Moreover, I have discovered the parameters of the target population. As far as I can tell, most of the victims are chosen on the basis of hormonal function.''

''I don't understand.''

''It makes sense if you look at it from the military's point of view.''

''What the hell is that supposed to mean, Doc?'' Slater asked irritably. He reached out and pulled a cigarette out of the pack on his desk. He lit it and let out a hacking cough.

''The Redenbacher bacteria is a weapon; weapons have targets. In this case, the target is a population cross section; specifically able-bodied men and women between the ages of fourteen or fifteen up to roughly fifty in the case of women and sixty in men. The approximate level of military usefulness. The disease was created to hit the target nation's military age population.''

''I fall into the age group,'' Slater interrupted, ''and I was directly exposed to the bacteria.''

''There are several exceptions I've noticed so far. There may be more, but I'm limited by both time and resources. It seems that people with diabetes are immune to the disease, although I have no idea why. So are pregnant women, presumably because of their high levels of HCG, human chorionic gonadotropin, a natural immunosuppressive, as well as placental lactogen, alpha-fetoprotein, and uromodulin. Prepubescent children and the aged are unaffected because they have low levels of sex hormones.''

''What about Karen? Or Jenny, for that matter?'' Slater asked, worried. ''Will they develop cancer?''

''I'm not sure.'' Payne shrugged. ''Neither Karen or Miss Hale seems to have contracted the influenza phase, so perhaps they fall into another immune category I haven't been able to discover. Presumably, neither one of them is pregnant.''

''Not that I know of,'' Slater said. He stubbed out his cigarette. ''Shit! What in God's name are we going to do now?''

''What did this colonel say?''

''He said that the entire population would have to be evacuated until the flu had been isolated. He made it sound like they had some kind of vaccine.''

''Balderdash. There is no antidote for cancer.''

''How long will it take to get really bad?''

The old doctor lifted his massive shoulders again. ''Impossible to say until we know what actually triggers the bacteria. In the case of Simms, my lab technician, it was almost immediate. The same for Rebecca Hardy. In other people it may take longer. Simms is strongly allergic anyway, which may have made him more susceptible. In the case of organ cancers, it would take much longer for the disease to make itself known.''

"This is a nightmare," Slater said, shaking his head. "I've already got my entire squad off sick, except for Sparrow. Except for a bunch of old men from the Volunteer Fire Department, we're up the creek.''

"Old men have their uses," Payne said, smiling crookedly. "And speaking of Mr. Hawke, where is he?''

"Scouting the territory. Trying to find out where these people have got themselves based. This man, Colonel Wright, gave me until noon to come to some kind of decision. The implication was pretty obvious—do what he wants or he blows us away. Sparrow figured that forewarned was forearmed, not that I think knowing where they are will do us any good, since I have no way of getting at them anyway.'' He glanced at his watch. "It's seven now, hardly enough time to mount a counteroffensive.''

The office door burst open and Jenny Hale appeared, hair flying, a frightened expression on her face. She had obviously dressed quickly, pulling on jeans and one of Slater's sweatshirts.

"Karen's gone!" she said, breathing hard, standing in the open doorway. "I looked in on her, and she's gone!''

"Calm down," Slater said. He got up and went to her, putting one arm around her shoulders. He guided her to the straight chair next to Doc Payne and then sat down behind his desk. "Explain," he said. "Slowly.''

"Dr. Payne called me about half an hour ago. He wanted to speak to you, so I told him you were down at the station. I couldn't get back to sleep and went down to the kitchen to make some tea. While it was steeping, I went back up to look in on Karen, and she was gone. I think she went out through her window, the way you told me she sometimes does.''

"Maybe she just got up early and went for a walk," Slater suggested, although he didn't believe it.

"At six in the morning? And why go out through the window? No, I think she's been gone a lot longer than that, and I think B.C. Bingham has something to do with it, too.''

"Why?''

"He was the only person to visit her yesterday, and he walked her home from the party Halloween night."

"Pretty circumstantial."

"I realize that. I called B.C.'s parents before I came down here. They both have the flu. Mrs. Bingham appears to be getting better; Mr. Bingham isn't doing so well."

"We were talking about Karen and B.C."

"I realize that. Anyway, Mrs. Bingham went to check on Bentley. He wasn't there, either. They're both missing."

"I hardly think *missing* is the right word."

Jenny looked startled, then angry. "We're talking about your daughter, not some runaway!" she said. "My God, Jack! Quit being a policeman for five minutes!"

"You don't have to lecture me on my responsibilities as a parent, Jen. But I know Karen. She's stubborn and smart. And if she's with B.C., she's not alone. She'll be okay. Probably be back home by lunchtime."

"I hope you're right," Jenny said coldly. She gave Slater a long, searching look. "I'll be waiting back at the house if you want me." She turned on her heel and left the station. Slater waited until he heard the glass doors swing shut, then he slumped back in his chair.

"You handled that extremely well," Payne murmured. "From the expression on your face, I'd say you were quite concerned about Karen's whereabouts."

"Of course I am!" snapped the sheriff. He pushed his chair back angrily and stood up. "The stupid child has gone wandering off, and I've got a whole town under siege. Jesus!" He slammed the open drawer of one of his filing cabinets shut, then turned back to Payne. "So tell me, Doc, what should I do? Go looking for my wayward daughter, or do my job?"

"I think you should get some sleep. Or you won't be able to do either. I also think that your calming little speech to Miss Hale is probably quite close to the truth. No doubt Karen will turn up safe and sound in the next few hours. I've tended the needs of Jericho Falls adolescents for almost half a century, and the only thing I've learned about them in all that time is that they seem to act like aliens from another planet. Bizarre behavior is the norm."

"You give pretty good calming speeches yourself, Doc. I hope you're right." He went back to his desk and sat down, drumming his fingers on the wooden arms of the chair. Frowning, he glanced at his watch again. "Almost seven-thirty," he said aloud. "Sparrow went out two hours ago. I hope to hell he hasn't gone missing, too."

Dressed in battle fatigues he hadn't worn in over fifteen years and moving through the predawn darkness, it had taken Hawke a full hour to get from Mill Bridge to the edge of the Drake's Farm woodlot. The trees, some of them almost two hundred years old, formed a dense wall of foliage that roughly followed the winding course of the Jericho River. By staying right at the river's edge, he was fairly sure that any ground radar would miss him, but even so, he moved with care, pausing every few minutes to listen. The bird colonel in the funny suit was no fool and there was a good chance he'd have set up some kind of perimeter patrols.

Hawke's objective had been Slater's idea, and Hawke agreed. Everything pointed to the fact that the bacteria accidentally released in the town had been on its way to Jericho Falls in the first place. Except for the Medical Center, the only other logical place it might have been going to was the little municipal airport just beyond the southern town line. It also made sense strategically.

Assuming something on the order of company strength, the colonel's men would have been airlifted, probably using Herkeybirds from the Military Air Transport wing at Pease Air Force Base in Portsmouth. The Hercules was capable of landing on the fifteen-hundred-foot runway and coming in low from the south, so they wouldn't have attracted any attention from the town. Isolated, built on open ground, the airport was the obvious place to establish a staging base.

The Jericho Falls Municipal Airport, one of Luther Coyle's better ideas for the town's economic diversification, was located on a roughly triangular piece of land bordered by the hilly, wooded edge of Drake's Farm, the north-south Airport Road, and the old Baltimore and Ohio railway line running east to west.

Coming to the edge of the woodlot, Sparrow was within two hundred yards of the end of the single runway, but getting to the small terminal building, invisible in the darkness, meant crossing an open field. It was almost certain that the fence line would be patrolled at regular intervals, and if there were radar posts set up, this was where they'd be. Sparrow, armed with only a hunting crossbow and a sheath knife, wasn't about to test the hypothesis. This was reconnaissance, not attack. He decided to follow the riverbank down to the railway bridge, keeping under cover.

The second phase of his journey took another forty minutes and by the time he reached the stone abutment of the old single-track steel bridge that crossed the quickly flowing river, dawn was creeping up over the dark, scarred hump of Quarry Hill, the trees on its summit a black etching against the lightening sky. Between the river and the road was a thinning screen of trees, and beyond the road, the airport itself. Dropping down to the cold, musty earth, Sparrow began to crawl forward. Five minutes later, he'd reached the edge of the trees, and the road was directly ahead. He quietly removed a small pair of binoculars from the pouch on his belt and took a look.

There was no perimeter fence along the property, only a shallow drainage ditch. Normally, all he would have expected to see was the narrow dirt road leading to the one-and-half-story terminal building, the two prefab, corrugated-steel buildings housing the AirMedic and Coyle Air Transport twin Comanches, and the old service hangar, which was really only an oversized barn. Instead, to the left of the terminal and no more than fifty yards from the drainage ditch, he saw a dozen small Hughes Defenders grouped on the cracked, concrete hardstand, their rotors drooping, Plexiglas bubbles wet with dew.

Surrounding the waiting birds was a low, concertina, barbed-wire fence and he spotted two guards, both dressed in fancy suits like he'd seen the day before, but colored a startling, brilliant red. A third, red-suited guard paced back and forth in front of the service road leading to the terminal. In the distance, partially screened by the terminal, Sparrow thought he could make out a row of bivouac tents. The oddest thing was a line of at least nine giant Whyte, Mack, and Bulldog transport trucks ranged beside the terminal, all minus their trailers. Sparrow frowned and put down the glasses. He was going to have to get closer. He sank back into the trees and stood up. Unlimbering the crossbow from its sling across his back, he cranked it back, loaded a short, lethal bolt, and engaged the safety. Carrying the weapon at port arms, he made his way along a faint rabbit trail through the trees, working his way through the woods until he was a good five hundred yards from the airport entrance road. Bent low, he came out of the protective screen of trees and crossed the road at a dead run, then rolled into the drainage ditch and came up again, scrambling for the limited cover offered by the shrub-covered hillock that stood behind the terminal building. He buried his face in the earth, feeling his heart pounding, and waited: nothing. No one had seen him.

He counted slowly to one hundred before moving again. He rolled over, pushing the crossbow in front of him until he reached the crest of the little hill. Lifting his head, he looked down on the rear of the concrete-block terminal building. It was an impressive sight.

A hundred yards to the right of the line of trucks beside the terminal was another concertina-wire perimeter. Within the compound formed by the barbed-wire enclosure was a large, flat-roofed structure comprised of two windowless, square wings joined by a long narrow rectangle. Bizarrely, the outer wall facing him was inscribed with writing in twelve-foot-high letters:

RADIO SHACK

The front wall of the wing to the right of the adjoining rectangle carried a different message:

MAYFLOWER

Astounded, Sparrow dug out his binoculars and took a closer look at the building. Then he understood. The building was up on wheels, twelve to a side. The building wasn't a building at all; it was a prefabricated structure made up of the trailers that went with the big trucks parked beside the terminal. Playing the binoculars back and forth, he slowly figured out how it had been done. Each wing was made up of four tractor trailers formed into a square. Panels within the containers were slid out top and bottom, thereby roofing and flooring the enclosure. Another trailer formed the corridor that joined the two squares together, forming a complex a hundred feet long and forty feet wide. An entire military field headquarters in kit form, camouflaged in the liveries of major American corporations.

It was brilliant. The trucks, nine of them, could travel without hindrance, day and night, and no one would pay the slightest attention. Strung out in a convoy a couple of miles long they would look like a random collection of trucks heading in the same general direction.

Scanning the area beside the strange building, Sparrow noticed a trunk of cables leading to another wheeled container, this one connected to its tractor: a generator truck, supplying juice to the main complex. A narrow, rutted road led from the terminal to the front of the barbed-wire complex, and peering through the binoculars, Sparrow could see two guards at the entrance. Beyond that, lined up at an angle on the tarmac in front of the little terminal building, were four gigantic Blackhawk helicopters, six Huey gunships ranged in line abreast behind them. All of the helicopters were white, just like the ones he'd seen last night.

Turning the binoculars to the left, he counted fifty two-man tents, ten of the new Jeepster fast-attack vehicles he'd heard about, each mounted with a pair of fifty-calibre machine guns, two armored cars, a Deuce, and a half radio truck. In all he counted close to thirty men on guard duty, each dressed in one of the red space suits. Other than the guards, there seemed to be very little going on, but the big aluminum doors of both hangars were closed and posted with guards.

Sparrow slithered back into the low brush and tucked the binoculars away again. He'd seen enough. There was a small army waiting on the outskirts of town, with more than enough firepower to make good on the lieutenant colonel's threat. The long-haired ex-chopper pilot took a deep breath and exhaled slowly, his breath misting in the cold, early morning air. Time to report back to Slater. Sparrow shook his head. The sheriff wasn't going to like this at all.

CHAPTER THIRTEEN

10:00 A.M.

By 8:30 on the morning of November 2, the skies over Jericho Falls and the surrounding valleys were overcast, and by 9:00, it had begun to snow, the steady fall accompanied by rising winds. By 10:00, the early winter storm had turned into a full-scale blizzard.

Normally, the Volunteer Fire Department would have responded quickly, using the town's two big plows and half a dozen smaller vehicles to clear the snow from the main thoroughfares, but that day the snow lay where it fell, the wind pushing it into drifts that soon blocked the Strip, Old River Road, and the roads leading out of the valley. Within twenty minutes, the grass on Constitution Common was confectioner's sugar white, the bandstand covered in a pristine, gleaming coat like the central decoration on a wedding cake.

With the snow came an eerie dampening of sound, and along the empty streets and alleys the only thing to be heard was the relentless moaning of the wind. The only movement other than the whirling fall of snow was the dark, winding band of the river, frothing angrily as it went through the race at Mill Bridge, then turning south and following its ancient course toward the sea.

"The snow's a godsend," Sparrow said, turning away from the dusty window in the attic of the Jericho Falls Library. "Ceiling is maybe two hundred feet, and visibility is fifty yards at most. They won't be lifting choppers in this kind of weather. Looks like it's going to keep up for a while, too." The big, bearded man was still dressed in his fatigues, the heavy combat boots echoing on the old wood floor as he came back to the model table.

"It won't stop our friend Colonel Wright for long," Slater said, looking down at the scale model of the town. "I had a C.O. like him in Saigon. Everything by the book, and no excuses. According to what you saw out at the airport, he's got everything he needs to wipe us right off the map."

"Maybe." Sparrow slumped down into an old straight chair beside the table. For the first time, Slater saw how tired the man was. There were dark raccoon circles under his eyes, and he seemed to have shrunk inside his clothes.

"You feeling okay?" asked the sheriff.

Sparrow shrugged. "Well enough, all things considered. A little tired, and I'd be lying if I said I wasn't scared shitless by all this."

"Me, too." He lit a cigarette and tossed the package to Sparrow. "The question is, what are we going to do about it?"

"Like you said, Wright could take us out just about anytime he wants, but he hasn't. Why?" asked Sparrow, lighting up a cigarette.

"Maybe he's waiting for orders."

"I doubt it. He said it himself, this is a contingency plan that's been in place for a long time."

"So?"

"He's following procedure, like your C.O. in 'Nam. One step at a time. By the book. He said he'd call you by noon. He wants to evacuate. Give him any trouble and he'll escalate to the next step in the rule book. Mind like a Swiss watch, and just about the same amount of imagination."

"Perhaps," Slater said, peering gloomily down at the model. "But I think there's more to it than that."

"Like what?"

"Like the fact that none of it makes any sense. Why evacuate? What point does it serve? And once they've evacuated, what then?"

"They clean up. Find the source of the bug and eradicate it. Then everyone moves back."

"You don't believe that any more than I do," Slater said.

"No, but that's what we're supposed to believe."

"The cover story."

"Exactly. But what's the real scoop?" Sparrow asked.

"Try this on," Slater said thoughtfully. "They have an accident with a lethal bacteria. We know they're set up for just that kind of thing happening. Your little trip out to the airport proves that. They isolate the town completely, no radio, no long-distance telephone, no traffic in or out. Call that phase one. That's where we are right now."

"What's phase two?"

"Doc mentioned something called a 'life table.' It's a term epidemiologists use, like an actuarial table in an insurance company. You take a sample of the population and from that sample you can figure out the progression of illness over a period of time, mortality rate, that sort of thing."

"Wright's evacuation?"

"I think so," the sheriff said, nodding. "He had your kid from the Mill taken, what's his name?"

"Josh Robinson."

"Right. He has Josh kidnapped as a test case, but now he wants a bigger group. Doc Payne calls it a 'cohort.' By studying the cohort, they can figure out what's going to happen to the town."

"And if it's bad news?"

"I'm not sure," Slater said. "Doc thinks this bug is really contagious. That means Wright would have to put the whole town in quarantine until they figure out how to deal with it or . . ."

"Or take out the whole town. Sanitize it."

"Yeah." Slater nodded wearily. "I'm afraid so."

"How could they get away with something like that?"

"They've gone this far. Why not the whole way? Arrange some kind of catastrophe, an accident, fire, God knows. They might even get away with some kind of epidemic, blame it on a bunch of terrorists."

"Surely someone would find out," Sparrow said.

"Maybe, but if someone did, who'd believe them? The U.S. Army goes in and wipes out a whole town in New Hampshire? That's a one-way ticket to a rubber room, my friend. And it doesn't really matter anyway, because we're not going to be around to see how it all comes out in the end."

"So what do we do?"

"Stall, at least for the moment," Slater said, looking at the big model of the town spread out on the table in front of him. "And be as cooperative as we can."

"And in the meantime?"

"Pull the wagons into a circle," answered the sheriff. "We need to get as many able-bodied people as we can, put together an inventory of weapons, figure out some sort of defensive strategy."

"What's the point?" Sparrow asked. "They could wipe us out almost anytime they wanted. They've got the firepower."

"Obviously, their plan doesn't call for wholesale slaughter. If they'd wanted to blow us all away, they would have done it already. No, it's like you said: Wright is following his plan, step by step. What we have to do is delay it for as long as possible."

"Why?"

"Because they're on a schedule," Slater explained. "Bet on it. If they really wanted to, they could simply starve us out, but they don't have the time."

"You mean someone would start getting suspicious?"

"Sure, eventually. The most likely thing is that they're covering the whole thing by telling people on the outside that there's some kind of war game or military exercise going on. Keep that story going for too long and you're bound to get a reporter or two sniffing around. Then the shit would really hit the fan."

"If we start playing French Resistance, people are going to get hurt," Sparrow cautioned. "Most heroes seem to wind up in body bags."

"Corney Drake wasn't trying to be a hero," Slater said coldly. "He was just trying to deliver a truckload of fucking chickens. You can bet your ass that any plan Wright and his space-suit goons have isn't going to be pleasant. We don't have any choice, Sparrow, believe me."

"I guess you're right," he said, shaking his head. "The world brought down to a license-plate motto, just like you told Luther."

"You got it," said Slater. " 'Live Free or Die.' "

By B.C.'s estimate, the move came about three hours after the visit by the uncommunicative doctor. Three orderlies, armed and wearing the same kind of loose, airtight suit, entered the quarantine rooms and gave B.C. and Karen back their clothes.

Dressed, they were given two sealed packages, each containing a lightweight metallic coverall suit that B.C. said was made of Mylar, just like the astronauts used. The suits, like the ones worn by their guards, were equipped with headpieces, but the ones worn by the two young people had only simple air filters rather than hoses. Before zipping on the hoodlike coverings, they were both blindfolded.

The actual transfer seemed to take no more than five or ten minutes, and the only thing B.C. knew for certain was that they had spent some part of that time outside. For a few minutes, the air coming through the filter was cold and fresh; instead of the smooth metal flooring of the quarantine chamber, the ground underfoot was rough and uneven. Finally, after a series of steps both up and down and the sound of doors opening and then closing, they were left alone again. Within a few moments, B.C. and Karen managed to work their way out of the headpieces and remove the blindfolds.

"I think we've come down in the world," B.C. said, looking around. They were in an utterly featureless room, twenty feet on a side and without windows. The ceiling was low, covered in acoustic tile and fitted with four inset fluorescent panels, the floor was cement, and three of the four walls were made of concrete block. The fourth wall, the only one with a door, was smooth and painted white. The paint job was rough, and every four feet or so the faint lines of drywall tape were clearly visible. There were stacks of dull green, folding army cots piled at the far end of the room. Opposite, there was a big industrial sink and a small toilet cubicle. Hood and blindfold removed, B.C. crossed the room and inspected the door. It was metal, painted a dark, utilitarian green, and fitted with an imposing Chubb lockset. He tried the handle, but the door was locked.

"No way out there," he said. He went to the far end of the room, dragged one of the cots down, and opened it near the center of the room. He and Karen sat down.

"I wonder why they moved us," Karen asked, looking around.

"Maybe they needed the rooms," B.C. quipped nervously.

"Get serious."

"I am." He shrugged. "Figure it out. They had us in quarantine, then ran those tests. A few hours later, we get moved out. The tests must have come out negative."

"Why do you say that?"

"That other place was sealed tight, air locks and everything—better than an isolation ward in a hospital. This looks like somebody's basement."

"And they're expecting more visitors by the look of it," Karen said, staring across the room at the stacks of folded cots. B.C. stood up and jammed his hands into the pockets of his jeans. Karen stayed where she was, arms folded across her chest.

"We've got to get out," the young boy said finally.

"What's the matter?"

"I don't know. Something. Like waiting for an axe to fall. That other place was bad enough, but this is creepy."

"We can't get out, B.C., you know that. Unless you can pick locks or something."

"Not one of my better skills. I was never much into shops."

"I bet Billy would know how," Karen said, regretting the words as soon as they were out of her mouth.

"Right." B.C. smiled, but Karen could see that he was hurt.

"Sorry. I shouldn't have said that."

"It's okay. You're probably right. Every teenage girl's dream: your basic macho hombre stud with a hot car and overactive glands. Great for scaring village idiots and knocking up his girlfriend. Sure, he'd have had you out of here in a minute."

"I said I was sorry," Karen snapped. "You don't have to be mean."

"I always act like a shit when I've been kidnapped. Gets on my nerves a bit, you know?"

"Well, at least you're not quoting anybody anymore."

"I hate quotations."

"You could have fooled me."

"No." B.C. grinned. "That's a quotation. 'I hate quotations': Ralph Waldo Emerson, the *Journals*."

"Oh, shut up. You're just trying to make me feel better."

"Like hell. I'm trying to make myself feel better. I'm scared, Karen."

"Me, too."

"So let's figure a way of getting out of here." B.C. went back to the door and tested it again.

"You tried that."

"I'm just trying to be logical. Four walls, no windows, and a locked door."

"Good one, B.C. You proved you're not blind."

"Quiet, I'm thinking." He took off his glasses, blew on them, and then polished the lenses with the bottom of his T-shirt. He put the glasses back on and began to whistle tunelessly, walking back and forth in front of the tall metal door. After a moment he stopped, went to the wall beside the door, and tapped gently with his knuckles.

"What?" asked Karen, her voice echoing slightly.

"Just being a little more logical," he muttered. "Four walls, three made out of concrete blocks, one out of plasterboard, and a locked door."

"I don't see the difference."

"Look at the concrete blocks, and the floor, and this wall, and the door. What do you see?"

"Just what you said."

"Nothing else?"

"It all looks pretty new, that's all."

"Right. New construction. I remember something my old man said. He was talking to one of the guys doing work on the club. Something about twenty-four-inch centers not being up to code, but who was going to see once you had the drywall up?"

"I don't know what you're talking about."

"Drywall."

"I thought we were trying to get out of here."

"Same thing. You know what drywall is?"

"Sure."

"An eighth-inch of plaster sandwiched between two layers of heavy paper."

"So what?"

"That's what this wall is made of," said B.C., tapping again. He stepped up to the wall and pressed both hands against it. It moved noticeably. He turned around and looked at Karen, eyes flashing behind his glasses. "What have you got in your pockets?"

Karen shrugged and dug into her jeans. She came up with some loose change, a stick of gum, and her house keys.

"Keys!" crowed B.C. He ran back to her and grabbed them out of her outstretched hand. She followed him back to the wall.

"Have you gone crazy?" she asked.

"Shhh!" He put his ear to the wall and began tapping again,

moving his knuckles fractionally with each tap. "Stud," he said triumphantly after a few seconds. He took Karen's front-door key and scratched a mark on the wall. Then he went back to his tapping. Two feet farther on, he stopped again and made another mark. "Twenty-four-inch centers," he gloated, looking at the marks on the wall.

He took the keys and scribed a long line joining the two scratches, then scored downward, and across again. It took him less than a minute to mark out a large square on the wall. He stared at his handiwork for a moment, nodded happily, and started again, going around the square several times, deepening the scratches into visible gouges as a faint mist of fine plaster sifted down over his sneakers.

"You really think this is going to work?" Karen asked, watching him.

"Sure." He handed Karen the keys and, without pausing, whirled on the ball of his left foot, swinging his right leg up, knee bent. In midturn he straightened his right leg with a quick snap, the foot as rigid as a ballet dancer on point. He struck directly in the middle of the square, and almost magically the section of drywall separated and sagged inward. B.C. finished the move, coming back easily onto his feet.

"Amazing," Karen said, staring at the gaping hole in the wall. "I didn't know you could do stuff like that."

"It's not hard, really. You just follow instructions, like a recipe. Concentration."

"It's still amazing."

"Let's see what we've got," he answered, trying to shrug off the compliment, but obviously pleased with himself. He reached into the hole and pulled out the drywall. Beyond it there was an empty space and the rear of another sheet of plasterboard. "Interesting," he said, stepping back. "We're not too far from home."

"How can you tell?" asked Karen.

"The two-by-four in there has got a Coyle Building Supply stamp on it," said B.C. "Old Luther strikes again."

"This is getting too weird," Karen said, shaking her head. "Every time I try to make sense out of things, it feels as though my brain is going to burn out."

"The more I think about it, the more scared I get," B.C.

replied. "I figure the best thing to do is just take one thing at a time."

"So what's next?"

"The other side of the wall."

It took ten minutes, but finally they had created a two-foot-square opening. B.C. went through first, with Karen close behind. They found themselves standing in a narrow corridor, dimly lit. There appeared to be a flight of stairs at the far end of the hall and a door directly across from them. It was heavily hinged and made of riveted steel painted white. The door was held closed by a large sliding bar.

"What's it going to be?" Karen whispered. "The door or the stairs?"

"Life's business being just the terrible choice," answered B.C.

"That's a quote, right?"

"Robert Browning. *The Ring and the Book*. I say the stairs."

"The door."

"Go ahead. Just make it quick," B.C. said nervously. Karen nodded and approached the door. They pulled up the bar and dragged the heavy slab of metal outward on its hinges. Instantly, they were met with a blast of freezing air. Karen peeked in and found herself staring at a wall of black. Stepping around her, B.C. felt for a light switch on the wall, found it, and flipped it up.

"Oh God no!" moaned Karen. She clapped her hands over her mouth and felt her stomach heave.

The room, small, low-ceilinged, and freezing cold, looked like a slaughterhouse, except here the carcasses were human. There were six bodies, each nestled in the stiff confines of an open body bag. The corpses were arranged on trestle tables lined up in the middle of the room, while the headless remains of Josh Robinson's terrier Scoobie hung from a meat hook that dangled from an overhead pipe. Opening the door to the refrigerated compartment had let in a flood of warmer air, and the room filled quickly with a hazy fog that swirled lazily over the frozen cadavers.

Karen stood where she was, eyes wide, hands still over her mouth, but B.C. tiptoed hesitantly forward, then walked along the line of tables. The bodies were frozen solid, open eyes opaque with frost, ice crystals in their hair, all of them butchered to some degree. Even so, the frightened boy was able to identify most of them.

Tom Dorchester, the cop, split open from crotch to throat like a side of beef.

Marty Doyle, the upper half of his skull sliced cleanly off just above the bridge of his nose, the remains of his brain a gray cake of ice, bloody tears frozen to his cheeks, trailing down from ruptured eyeballs.

Corky White in a tattered dressing gown, internal organs piled on his chest like flowers on a coffin, a look of terrible pain and disbelief freeze-dried onto his bloody face forever.

Corney Drake, most of his face torn away, his chest and belly a single gaping wound, splintered ribs sticking up from the frozen, twisted meat of his torso.

An unidentified man, fat and strawberry-cheeked, neatly opened up like a slit purse.

And, finally, a boy, maybe ten or eleven. B.C. didn't know his name, but he'd seen him playing in the schoolyard of the junior high. One of the Mill kids.

Somehow, the kid was the worst and B.C. stood over him, staring down. At first glance he might have been sleeping, but then you saw the long, puckered incision that ran from his throat down to the hairless groin, tidily repaired with an efficient cross-stitch.

His skin was smooth and faintly blue, like marble, the lips a pale pink. The only thing to mar his deathly beauty was a two-inch stump of plastic jutting out just below the navel, the open end of the tube crusted with blood. A drain of some kind. B.C. turned away, his fear overcome by a terrible loathing for the people responsible for what he was seeing.

He went back to Karen and spotted a pile of flattened boxes leaning against the wall beside the door. Stamped on the boxes was the familiar green CI monogram of Coyle Industries, and circling it in blue were the words "Coyle Air Transport."

"Come on," B.C. said. He pushed Karen back into the corridor and pushed the heavy door shut. He dropped the bar back into position and then leaned against the wall, breathing hard. Karen stood, shoulders slumped and shaking, hands over her face. B.C. put his hand on her back, rubbing softly, not sure what else to do.

"What's happening?" whispered Karen, still crying. "Please tell me what's happening."

"They're dead," B.C. said, swallowing. "They don't feel anything." He bit his lip, then moved his hand to Karen's shoulder, turning her around. "Look," he said, trying to sound firm, "we can't do anything for those people, but we can save ourselves. We can get away and tell your dad."

"How?"

"I know where we are."

"Where?" Karen said, hiccuping. She took her hands down from her face.

"The basement of the airport terminal. That . . . place is the cold storage room they use to keep perishable stuff fresh before they ship it out. Luther again."

"Are you sure?"

"Positive. We can get away. We can sneak out and get home."

"Home," Karen said. Her face was streaked with tears, her eyes vacant. Seeing the ravaged bodies in the cold storage room had been too much, and had come too soon after seeing Marty Doyle die so horribly in the booth at the Bo-Peep. She was in shock.

"That's right." B.C. nodded, furiously wiping away the tears forming in his own eyes. If he let himself give in to his fear and anger now, they'd never make it. "We'll go home," he said softly, desperately trying to make himself believe it.

"How?"

"I don't know yet. But I've got us this far and I'll God damn well get us the rest of the way."

"This weather is an outrage!" boomed Rembrandt Payne, storming into the outer office of the Jericho Falls Police Station. He shook snow from the lapels of his duffel coat and stomped his galoshes on the floor. Frowning, he stripped off the coat, tossed it over the counter, and went into the inner office, slamming back the hinged pass-through. Seated at the radio table, scribbling away in a notebook, Jack Slater looked up.

"Still bad?"

"Preposterous!" Payne grunted, dropping into a wooden armchair. "I barely made it here from the Center." He dragged an immense handkerchief from the breast pocket of his tweed jacket and delicately patted the top of his head with it. "Any news of Karen?"

The sheriff shook his head. "No. I've called the Binghams a couple of times, but neither one of them has shown up."

"Apparently none of your deputies has either," commented the doctor, looking around the empty room.

"They're all too sick. And we can't raise Van Heusen or Torrance. Sparrow's over at Stark Hall with Jenny taking an inventory of able-bodied types . . . and weapons."

"Good Lord!" whispered Payne. "We're fighting the American Revolution all over again."

"Maybe." Slater shrugged. "Good enough place to do it."

"Perhaps we should look for the Benedict Arnolds in our midst."

"What's that supposed to mean?"

"It would appear that there is a spy among us. A number of bodies have disappeared from the morgue."

"You're kidding!"

"Certainly not. Redenbacher, the Doyle boy, Corky White, and Dorchester, all gone. My diener, Reuben Wilson, has vanished."

"You think he was involved?"

"I doubt it. He has something of a problem with the bottle, but he's not the Burke-and-Hare type."

"Who?"

"Body snatchers, London, the Victorian era," Payne said irritably.

"Why would anyone want the bodies?"

"For the same reason I did. Tests to find out why they died."

"Someone in the Center?"

"Perhaps. Someone with access to it, anyway."

"Christ!" Slater said. "One more thing to think about."

"One assumes that whoever took the bodies was in league with the people who have us under siege. They're the only ones who'd have any interest."

"Tidying up loose ends," Slater said. He stood up, slipped on his jacket, and turned back to the doctor. "Come on," he said. "I've got a few minutes before Colonel Wright makes his call. I want to check and see how Sparrow and Jenny are doing."

The two men went out into the storm and crossed the Common on foot. The storm was in full swing and across the park Stark Hall was nothing but a ghostly blur. The wind had piled drifts up against the bandstand, and the only vehicles in front of the hall were Jeeps and other four-wheel drives. They climbed the steps and slipped gratefully inside, closing the big wooden doors behind them.

All the lights were burning in the main meeting room, and the decorations left over from the Halloween dance were at odds with the piles of weaponry on the stage. There were sixty or seventy people at tables scattered around the room, and glancing around, Slater saw that almost all of them were men and women in their sixties and seventies. Doc Payne saw several people he recognized and excused himself while Slater continued on toward the stage. Jenny Hale sat behind a table, while a few feet away Sparrow was taking an inventory of the guns.

"We've got two hundred and thirty-eight names," said Jenny, looking up as the sheriff clambered up onto the stage and approached her. She made a sweeping gesture with one hand. "These are the ones who showed up."

"Forty-odd shotguns, same number of deer rifles, and maybe thirty handguns," Sparrow said, crossing the stage to the table. "Ammunition for most of it."

"Have you heard anything about Karen?" Jenny asked. Slater shook his head.

"Not yet. She'll turn up."

"You don't sound too sure," she answered.

"I'm not. But there's nothing I can do about it right now, okay?"

"Okay." Her voice was quiet, but Slater could feel the tension coming off her in waves. He sighed. No matter how much he needed her support right now, there was no time to make it good between them; that would have to come later. If there was a later. He turned back to Sparrow.

"Did you bring the model down from the library like I asked?"

"Sure," the long-haired man said, jerking a thumb back over his shoulder. "It's over there."

The sheriff walked to the wings, where the big sectional model had been laid out on a trestle table. Sparrow helped him lift off the large drop cloth, then switched on a bank of photofloods at one end of the table. Jericho Falls, in minute detail, lay before them.

"Strategy and tactics," Slater said, clicking his tongue against his teeth. "If you were our bird colonel, how would you take over the town?"

"With or without the choppers?"

"For the moment, let's say without."

"He's got all his forces centralized down here." Sparrow took a pencil from behind his ear and pointed to the airport at the southwest edge of the model. "There's no way he's going to take his armor through Drake's Farm—too much bush. So that leaves him two other routes. He can go up Airport Road to 115A and Woodbank, then turn along the Strip or go north into Frenchtown. The other alternative is to take his stuff across the railway bridge, skirt Quarry Hill close to the river, and then come across the bridges at Gowan Street and the Mill."

"So?"

"The easy way is to go up Airport Road, but if he's expecting any kind of resistance, he'll try the back door."

"Agreed."

"So what's the plan?" Sparrow asked.

"If we have to take the son of a bitch on, I'd prefer to do it at the bridges," said the sheriff. "Bottleneck him for as long as we can."

"So we make life miserable for him at 115A and the Strip."

"Can we defend it?"

"Not for long," Sparrow said. "He's got too many options, and we don't have enough firepower."

"What about blocking the streets?" suggested Slater. "The snow is already going to give him trouble. We've got enough people here to plug every road off the Strip and leading into Frenchtown with cars. A traffic jam at the intersection. That forces him to send people out on foot."

"And we have snipers in the houses?"

"Right. Harass and fall back. Five'll get you ten, he'll try a sortie up along Airport Road, just to test the bathwater, you might say. If it looks nasty, he'll bring his main force up the other way; it's all open ground. By then, we should be ready for him. While I'm talking to the colonel, you take one of the four-by-fours outside and get up to Luther's place. I want every pound of explosive Coyle Construction has got and the name of someone who knows how to use it."

"Forget that," Sparrow said. "I can do demo work. You want the bridges wired?"

"As fast as possible." Slater looked down at the model again, then turned and peered at the waiting group of men in the hall. "I also want you to put these men into some kind of order. I want an armed squad moving out into Frenchtown right away. We're going to have to get as many people out of the area as possible. DuBois to Brewer and a couple of blocks back from the Strip."

"Done."

"Put someone in Drake's Farm, as well. They should be able to see the airport from the top floor. Any sign of movement and they fire off a flare, then clear out."

"Kurt Shroeder and a few others are bringing in snowmobiles later on," Sparrow said. "Someone with a Ski-doo could get from the farm back to here pretty quickly by cutting up around the pond."

"Fine. Since the radios don't work, let's make the hall home base. Put somebody with a pair of binoculars up in the tower to keep an eye out."

"One if by land, two if by sea?"

"Something like that."

The two men looked out over the pitifully small assortment of personnel at their disposal.

"It's not going to work, is it?" Sparrow said softly.

"No," replied Slater. "It's not. But it will buy us some time. And that's the other thing I wanted to talk to you about. If it gets really bad, I want to save as many people as I can. Kids, pregnant women, anyone who's well enough to walk. Put Jenny on it. I want warm clothes, food, and medical supplies taken to the high school. She can get on the phone, call as many as she can. And let's make it fast, the snow isn't going to last forever. Oh, and by the way, you'd better warn your friends at the Mill. They're going to be right in the line of fire."

"Do you know how crazy all of this is?" said Sparrow.

"Sure. It would make a great story for *Time:* 'The Defense of an American Town.' "

"It never should have happened," whispered Sparrow. "It's the kind of thing they always said *couldn't* happen."

"But it did," the sheriff answered bluntly. He looked at his watch. It was 11:55. "I've got to get going."

The call came in at noon precisely. Slater, still in his jacket, sat behind his desk and stared at the flashing light on the telephone, letting it ring three times before he picked it up.

"Yes?"

"Colonel Wright."

"Yes?"

"I have had reports concerning activity in the town. Presumably, this means you are gathering your forces together."

"That's your assumption."

"I hope it isn't true, Sheriff. Resistance would be both foolhardy and futile, you know that."

"I don't know anything anymore," Slater said wearily. "I know I'm being threatened by a member of my own country's armed forces; I know a lot of people in my town are very sick; and I know you're responsible for that too. As far as I'm concerned, Colonel, you're one of the four horsemen of the fucking Apocalypse. You let some kind of foul plague out of Pandora's box, and we're paying the price for your mistake. I don't like that, Colonel Wright. I don't like that very much at all."

"Frankly, I don't care what you like, Sheriff Slater, and I don't really care what names you call me. You're right about one thing, though. A mistake has been made. It's my job to rectify that mistake."

"At any price?"

"I'm doing my job, Sheriff, that's all."

"Just following orders, marching us all off to the showers?"

"Please." Wright's voice was pained. "I told you. The infection in Jericho Falls is extremely infectious. The townspeople will be removed by MATS Command at Pease Air Force Base to an isolation area. The town itself will be vetted for infectious sites while your people are undergoing treatment, and then they will be returned. It's complicated, expensive, and unfortunate, but that is the situation as it stands. Resist our evacuation procedures and people will get hurt. The responsibility will be yours, Sheriff; we have no intention of harming anyone."

"Hang on," Slater said, squeezing his eyes shut and pinching the bridge of his nose. "I'm going to put you on hold for a

second.'' Without waiting for a reply, he stabbed the hold button
on the phone and put the receiver down on the desk. He dug into
his jacket, took out his cigarettes, and lit one.

It sounded so reasonable over the telephone that he almost
believed it. Almost. Until he thought about Corney Drake and
the others. Until he remembered the four gunships hovering over
the Common, ready to turn his town into an inferno. Until he
remembered what Rembrandt Payne had said. He took another
deep drag of his cigarette and hit the hold button again.

''I think you're full of shit, Colonel. I also think you're worried because your time is running out. You're on a schedule, and
you're falling behind. You've cut us off pretty well, but eventually people are going to get suspicious, and you're going to be in
trouble.''

''Think what you want, Sheriff. According to my meteorological reports, the storm should end shortly after dark, approximately nine tonight. Evacuation procedures will begin at that time,
with or without your cooperation. By our calculations it should
take about ten to twelve hours.''

''I don't think so.''

''I do. Listen, Sheriff.'' There was a faint click, and then Slater heard another voice, two of them in fact.

''What happened to us?''

*''I don't know. But it has something to do with the military
quarantine. They've got cameras on us, and I bet they can hear
everything we're saying, too.''*

''They're going to kill us, aren't they?''

*''No. They're not going to kill us. I mean, this is Jericho Falls,
New Hampshire, not Moscow.''*

''Not a particularly good image, but it will do,'' Wright said
plainly. ''You recognize the voices?''

''Yes. My daughter and Bentley Carver Bingham.'' Slater let
out a long breath and slumped back in his chair, the hard edge of
his anger dissolving.

''Correct,'' Wright said. ''We picked them up last night. A
coincidence, but a fortunate one, at least for me.'' There was a
brief pause. ''Can I assume that this puts a different light on your
position?''

Slater closed his eyes again and his jaw hardened. The telephone receiver felt like an iron weight in his hand, and he felt a

clutching bolt of nausea cramping in the pit of his stomach. For a moment, he thought he was going to be sick, then he gritted his teeth and spoke.

"No, it doesn't put a different light on my position," he said, trying not to scream. "It just means that if you hurt Karen, hurt her in any way at all, you'll be a dead man, Colonel. You can count on that." Slater put the phone back in its cradle softly, then stared at it, a vein on his forehead pulsing visibly. He looked down and saw that his hands were shaking; he clasped them together under his chin.

He stayed like that for a long time, and then suddenly, teeth bared, he came screaming up out of the chair, tore the telephone from his desk and threw it across the room. It bounced off the filing cabinets, then spun, rattling across the floor and finally coming to rest beside the wastebasket.

Slater stood in the center of the room, hands clenched at his sides. Up until he'd heard the sound of his daughter's voice, he'd been able to maintain some kind of clinical calm, a cop doing the things that a cop did, even under exceptional circumstances. But this was different. The nightmare had come home, spreading its sour wings across his heart, razor teeth and talons tearing into his soul.

"Bastards," he said, his voice barely a rasping whisper. "Oh, you bastards . . . ."

CHAPTER FOURTEEN

"Someone's going to find us if we stay here much longer," Karen said anxiously. Climbing the stairs at the end of the basement corridor, she and B.C. had found themselves in a small alcove. A door with a tiny, high-set window led outside, while a second flight of steps led upward. The window looked out on a narrow stretch of snow-covered grass that lay between the terminal and the high fence surrounding the airfield. Through the blowing snow, B.C. could make out the dark stripe of Airport Road and the woodlot beyond.

"We can't go out there," the boy answered, dropping down off his tiptoes, away from the window. "For one thing, this door is wired. Push the crash-bar and you'd set off the fire alarm. There's also the guards to think about. They go by once every three minutes by my watch. We'd barely make it to the fence. On top of that, there's a blizzard going on. Even if we did get out, we'd probably die of hypothermia."

"You said we'd get home."

"We will," B.C. said. "I've just got to think."

He went back to the window and looked out again, watching as a red-suited guard plodded into view, left to right, a short-barreled, shotgun-type weapon at port arms. He dropped down from the window again, brows creased. The first man he'd seen at the tennis club had been wearing an identical suit, but in silver, while the two others who'd fired on them had been wearing suits in camouflage colors. It stood to reason that the colors denoted

198

rank, and/or function. Red for guards, camo for general infantry, silver for an officer.

"Well?"

"I think we try the stairs," B.C. answered. He led the way, going up slowly, listening after each step. They reached a second landing, another flight of stairs spiraling upward. B.C. checked the edge of the blank, enameled door on the landing, where, unlike below, there were no obvious alarm wires. He pushed the crash-bar tentatively, wincing. The door cracked open fractionally, but there was no alarm. He peeked out. A corridor, linoleum-tile floor, several doors on either side. The landing below was the main floor, making this the second. Offices? He opened the door wider and stepped into the hall, Karen right behind him.

The young man tried the first two doors, but both were locked. At the far end of the hall he could see another stairway, this one open, leading both down and up. The knob of the third door turned in his hand and he opened it, holding his breath, ready to run if the room beyond was occupied.

It wasn't. He pulled Karen into the room, gently closing the door behind him. If the coffee machine and the worn-looking couches against the walls were any indication, the room had once been a lounge of some kind. Now it had been transformed into a workshop. At least a score of suits like the ones they'd seen their guards wearing hung on racks, and a long, Formica-topped table had been set up in the middle of the room. There was a faint smell of burnt insulation in the air, and B.C. could see soldering irons, toolboxes, and an assortment of electronic test equipment littered across the table.

"Come on," he said quietly. "I think we just hit the jackpot." He bypassed the table and went to the racks of hanging suits. They came in a variety of different colors: blue, green, red, silver, and a neutral sand shade. On a window ledge close to one of the racks was a line of large spray cans, each a different color. B.C. nodded to himself. The can colors could make up any sort of camouflage scheme you wanted and were probably used on the sand-colored suits. Customized chameleons.

"Now what?" Karen asked.

"Find a suit that fits you and put it on," B.C. said. "Red is for guards, silver for officers, and I'll bet the blue is for technical specialists. That leaves the green and the sand-colored ones. Go for the green if you can. We don't want to stand out.''

"You really think this is going to work?" Karen asked skeptically, fingering the lightweight fabric of one of the outfits.

Bentley shrugged. "We don't have much choice," he said. "Maybe if we put on a good enough bluff we can walk right out of here. But we have to hurry."

Karen nodded and began going through the racks, trying to find a suit in her size. B.C. did the same.

Each suit was made up of four major components: helmet and backpack, joined together by a short, coiled cable; a one-piece coverall, complete with feet and heavy gauntlets; a sleeveless padded vest, built to carry the backpack; and high boots with rigid, armored soles.

Karen found a green suit that looked close to her size, and B.C. helped her into it, figuring out the confusing array of tabs, plugs, and closures as he went along, frightened that they would be caught, but fascinated at the same time. The suits were a complete environment, powered by the backpacks, heated, air-conditioned, and bulletproof.

After helping Karen, outfitting himself took much less time, even though the suit he'd chosen was at least two sizes too large. Dressed, helmets under their arms, the two young people headed for the door. Reaching it, B.C. put a finger to his lips and pulled the door open slightly. The passageway beyond was clear.

"We'd better put on the helmets now," he whispered. Karen nodded and slipped the dark-visored headgear on. B.C. zipped the neck tab and then put on his own. The room turned dark green and the only sound was his own breathing.

"I can't see anything," Karen said, her voice muffled. B.C. did up the closure on his helmet and made a turning gesture with one hand. Karen's helmet nodded and she turned her back to him. B.C. found a series of switches on the side panel of the backpack and moved them all to the ON position. Reaching around with one hand, he found he could do the same for himself. He hit the switches on his own backpack and suddenly the suit came to life.

"Jesus!" he whispered. A tiny, diffuse red light came on in front of his face and he could suddenly see with almost perfect clarity. From somewhere behind his ears, he could hear a faint whirring sound, and then he felt a gentle flow of slightly warm air on his face. Just above eye level, he could see a line of indicators, like the cockpit of an airplane:

```
S1 S2 S3 S4 S5 S6 T1 T2 T3 "AID"
S7 S8 S9          T4 T5 T6
```

There was no way of activating any of the indicators outside the suit, and lowering his eyes, B.C. couldn't see any tongue-operated commands. So how did it work? He looked back up at the indicators. The letter–number combinations were red, the word *AID* was in green. Feeling like an idiot, he said the word aloud, speaking as clearly as he could.

"Aid."

Directly in front of his face, the visor darkened again and an outline of the suit appeared on the plastic in bright yellow. It was a schematic diagram, arrows pointing to different parts of the suit. On the right-hand side of the visor, he could make out a list of glowing yellow commands. Bentley reached out blindly and tapped Karen on the shoulder. He leaned forward until he felt the visor of her helmet bump into him.

"It's all voice-activated," he said loudly. "Say the word *aid* and you'll get a menu, just like on the computers at school."

"Okay."

S1—THROAT MICROPHONE
S2—POSITION DATA
S3—AUDIO SENSORS
S4—INFRARED
S5—FLASH ID/BEACON
S6—COMMLINK HQ FREQ
S7—BATTERY
S8—BIOSENSOR
S9—CLEAR VISION
T1—WEAPON ON
T2—TARGET RANGE
T3—TARGET ACQUISITION
T4—HUNT/SEEK—RANDOM
T5—DATALINK/HQ
T6—SITUATION/POSITION—OVERALL

"S-One," B.C. said. He hoped that would turn on the throat microphone and he would be able to talk to Karen normally. The menu vanished and the visor became a watery green again. "Karen?"

"Hey, I can hear you!" Her voice, booming in his right ear.

"You don't have to yell," he answered, wincing. "Just talk in a normal tone of voice."

"What about all the other commands?" she asked.

"Forget them for now. And no talking once we get outside. The microphones probably work with any suit within range."

"Okay." There was a pause. "Are we really going to try just walking out of here?"

"What else can we do?" he answered. "Keep close and play it by ear. Okay?"

"Okay."

B.C. opened the door and stepped out into the corridor. It was still silent and empty. He walked toward the stairs at the far end of the hall, the boots dragging heavily. Except for that, the suit was remarkably light, the backpack weighing no more than ten or fifteen pounds, and he was quickly getting used to the slightly darkened vision through the flat-faced visor.

They went down the stairs to the main floor without meeting anyone, then turned and went through the main doors of the terminal building. Stepping outside, B.C. was aware of a sudden change in the sound of the suit's heating/cooling fans, but even though the air outside was obviously colder, he felt no change in temperature.

The small terminal building was located close to the main entrance of the airport, its main doors facing toward the snow-blown hardstand a hundred feet away. To the left, B.C. could make out a concertina-wire corral enclosing a fleet of small helicopters, the white shapes almost invisible in the sheeting glare of the snow. On the hardstand itself there were half a dozen much larger helicopters, two Blackhawks like the one that had come to the tennis club and four Huey Cobras. All six were tethered down against the gusting wind, and tarpaulins had been wrapped around the delicate rotor mechanisms.

Beyond the gunships, they could make out a row of parked trucks, at least a dozen small vehicles that looked like ultramodern Jeeps, snow drifted up against their fat, oversized tires. The

Jeepsters, each mounted with a .50 calibre machine gun, partially screened another concertina-wire enclosure, this one containing a windowless, dumbbell-shaped building and a bristling array of antennas, including a large, motor-driven satellite dish. Guards patrolled the two helicopter stations and the building compound; B.C. counted almost twenty.

"Stay with me," he said quietly. Beside him, Karen nodded. B.C. walked forward, following a fresh track that led around the hardstand and headed toward the building compound. There were two stationary guards in front of the open entrance to the compound, but B.C. kept well clear of them, tramping steadily through the accumulated snow as purposefully as he could, making for a clump of trees he'd spotted as they left the terminal. The guards, blank-faced behind their visors, paid no attention, and there were no hailing voices coming across on the helmet radio.

They reached the trees and kept moving until the small patch of cedar lay between them and the compound. Nestled at the base of a low, wooded hill that rose on their right, B.C. spotted a small outbuilding that looked as though it had been deserted for years.

"Hang on." He stopped, recalled the AID menu, and scanned his choices. "S-Two," he said, trying to think it out. An instant later the visor darkened slightly and a scattering of yellow lines grew magically before his eyes. The outbuilding was outlined, as well as the hill beyond, the areas in between logged with synthetically generated symbols provided by the backpack computer. B.C. saw that he was being shown a three-dimensional map of the terrain superimposed over the real thing. According to the map, the outbuilding was designated Secure/CM3356/*XW. Some sort of code grouping. The area immediately beyond the building, close to the runway, was designated Aud4/77/ident to proceed, and showed a line of yellow bull's-eyes running off into the distance. An audio-sensor security network. So much for following the fence down to the end of the runway. He cleared the screen again and took Karen by the arm.

"The building," he instructed. The helmet was making him claustrophobic and more than anything else in the world he wanted to tear it off and breath real air again, even if it was only for a minute or two. Karen nodded and they moved toward the dilapidated structure.

Once upon a time the building had been a fuel storage shed, and there was still a litter of rusted, empty fifty-gallon drums outside. The door was hanging off its hinges, but at least it provided a bit of cover. They reached it and B.C. stopped again. He recalled the position-data function and looked toward the hill. The contour lines showed up clearly, as well as several large rock outcroppings, but there didn't seem to be any security measures. According to his sense of direction, the hill was north. Somewhere on its far side was Drake's Farm and Jericho Falls. He nodded to himself. A few minutes of rest in the shed and they'd be on their way.

He dragged the door of the shed open and stepped inside, looking around carefully. The interior was gloomy and cluttered. There were piles of old fuel drums, bins crammed with long-forgotten airplane parts, and a moldering old sofa, bleeding its mildewed stuffing onto the oil-stained floor. B.C. worked at the tabs and zipper closures on the neckpiece and finally pulled the helmet off. Karen did the same and they stood in the low-ceilinged room, breathing in the crisp, cold air.

"Wonderful," Karen whispered gratefully, tossing her hair back and closing her eyes for a moment. "I felt like I was going to suffocate."

"Must be like being on a submarine." Even though it was freezing cold in the little shed, he felt flushed and hot. "But we better get used to it, we're going to have to keep the helmets on for a little while longer. Until we hit town anyway."

"You really think we're going to make it?" Karen asked, eyes shining.

B.C. shrugged, the fabric of the suit rustling. "We're doing all right so far, aren't we?"

"You bet." She took B.C.'s shoulders, leaned down slightly, and planted a long kiss, directly on his lips.

"You didn't have to do that," he said as she finally broke the embrace.

"I know." She grinned. "I wanted to, idiot." She kissed him again, and this time her mouth opened slightly, and he felt the sweet-wet taste of her mouth. "The fact is, Bentley, you look kind of sexy in that suit. Short, but sexy."

"Gee, thanks," B.C. said, arching one eyebrow skeptically. "We should be going."

"Helmets on?"

"Helmets on." He nodded. "I want to check that Commlink-HQ function. Maybe we can do a little eavesdropping, see what's going on." He helped her put the helmet back on, checked the backpack switches to make sure that everything was functioning, and then replaced his own helmet. "S-Six," he commanded.

"Commlink, this is Perimeter nine."

"Nine, go ahead."

"We've got a malfunction on Video alpha. Getting nulls all the time."

"What's your request, Nine?"

"A technician to Quadrant 4, that's about fifty yards down the fence."

"Five minutes, nine. Let me check the screen."

"Thank you, Commlink."

"Break Commlink. Urgent."

"Who's calling break?"

"Commlink, this is Security. We've got something here at the terminal building."

"Go ahead, Security. Attention the break, anyone on Commlink Frequency."

"We've got two missing here. Live bait. Looks like they're ex the main building."

"Shit. Sorry. Uh. Okay, Security. Let's have Idents in the compound. Call for a full alert. How'd they do it?"

"Cut through the wall it looks like. And we might have some of the armor missing."

"They're wearing armor?"

"Looks like it."

"God damn! Okay. Full ident. Let's flush them out as fast as we can. Reports everyone, on the double!"

B.C. didn't wait to hear any more. He cleared the radio and called up the throat microphone again.

"The shit's hit the fan."

"What?"

"They know we've escaped, and they know we're wearing the suits. We've got to get the hell out of here, and fast!"

Rembrandt Payne walked slowly down the central corridor of the Medical Center's main floor, hands jammed deeply into the pockets of his white lab coat. The massive, white-haired man kept his eyes to the floor as he plodded along, brooding and lost in thought. Somewhere a telephone rang unanswered, but the dimly heard, insistent ringing barely penetrated the old man's consciousness.

Almost 75 percent of the regular Sunday shift was missing from the Center, and as far as Payne knew, there were only two other doctors in the building. Not that it mattered. Doctors and nurses were only useful when they had people to treat and except for less than a score of extended-care patients, the beds were empty.

Of the nineteen people still residing at the Medical Center, Payne had diagnosed cancers of one kind or another in fifteen of them. The carcinomas ranged from simple melanomas of the skin, like Rebecca Hardy's, to a full-fledged case of malignant leukoplakia that had appeared in the male patient's mouth within less than twelve hours. There was no way to be courtroom-positive, but the old doctor was sure all of the cancers were a direct result of the Redenbacher bacteria.

Payne bypassed the elevators and followed the corridor past the lounge and the cafeteria, pausing in front of the open door leading to the children's ward. Sandra Watchorn had died earlier that morning, her kidneys finally failing, and the only occupant of the seven-bed room was Billy Coyle, Luther's son.

The doctor stood at the end of the boy's bed, looking down at the quiet, sleeping figure. Good-looking, intelligent, and probably doomed. At seventeen, his glands were pumping out a torrent of hormones, which in turn were triggering the mutated allergens. Put simply, Billy Coyle's burgeoning manhood was almost certainly going to kill him. At a guess, Payne thought that leukemia was the most likely. He unhooked the chart from the foot of the bed and scanned it briefly. As of the night before, his white blood cell count was massively high, and there was no reason to think it had gotten any better in the meantime. There was no way to check, with all the lab staff out of action, including Simms, but Billy had enough other symptoms to make the diagnosis a good bet. He'd been running a constant low fever, bruised darkly at the wrist where his I.V. drip had been inserted, and his spleen was enlarged. Next would come the mouth sores and then pneumonia. An average case of acute lymphocytic leukemia often took months or even years to run its course. Billy's was gaining strength by the hour.

Payne hooked the chart back onto the end of the bed and walked slowly out of the large, brightly painted room. Cases like Billy's were springing into horrible life all over Jericho Falls by now, and there was nothing anyone could do about it. He paused again, leaning against the corridor wall, and closed his eyes. Fatigue was taking its toll; if he didn't rest soon, he was going to be no use to anyone, and if Jack Slater and Hawke were serious about playing Bowie and Crockett at the Alamo, his services were probably going to be needed.

He pushed himself away from the wall and continued down the corridor to the main blood lab. He let himself into the small, narrow room and sank down onto a stool. It was a nightmare, a terrible, futile nightmare. By his calculations, roughly 40 percent of the people in Jericho Falls would be infected by the second-stage allergy and there was nothing he or anybody else could do about it. Two thousand people were going to die because a truck-driver named Arnold Redenbacher had chosen Jericho Falls as the place to have his fatal heart attack.

Rembrandt Payne lifted his large head, blinking away fatigue. In the relentless series of events since Halloween night, he'd forgotten all about Arnie Redenbacher; now as he slouched on the lab stool, it suddenly occurred to him that maybe the dead man's presence in town hadn't been accidental, at all. Jack Slater had commented on it at the time. What was the van doing on Old River Road so late at night? Where was it going?

Highway 115A eventually led to the New Hampshire–Vermont border, but even at that, it was a fairly obscure route. Old River Road led nowhere except Jericho Falls, and unless Redenbacher had lost his way, it meant that he'd been heading for the town. That was absurd, though. Who in Jericho Falls would have any use for the lethal cargo carried in the van?

Payne tried to come at it from another position, charting out events by scientific process. Based on the hypothesis that the Redenbacher bacteria had been developed at one of the new private labs around the Portland campus of the University of New Hampshire, why would the bacteria have been transshipped to Jericho

Falls? There were no labs here, no new biomedical facilities, nothing. Events had proven that the bacteria had been developed for military application, and as far as Payne knew, that meant Ft. Detrick in Maryland.

And then he had it. He slapped his palm against the Formica surface of the lab counter, smiling fiercely. He'd have to check on a map of the state to be absolutely sure, but if memory served, Jericho Falls was the closest municipal airport to Portland. If the bacteria was being developed in secret—and that was almost certainly the case—they wouldn't have used the airport in Portland on a regular basis, but no one would have noticed regular weekly, or even monthly, shipments out of Jericho Falls. Portland to Jericho Falls by van, late at night, and then a quiet, discreet shipment out to Maryland.

"Luther," the doctor whispered. It had to be Luther. Coyle Air Transport was the only scheduled service out of the airport. C.A.T. and AirMedic had put the old runway strip back on its feet just after the construction of the Medical Center.

The old man stared. It all fit together. Barrett O'Neill, the state senator, was directly responsible for placing the Medical Center in Jericho Falls, and O'Neill had been elected on Luther Coyle's money. O'Neill would also have known about the shipments from Portland and would have suggested Coyle Air Transport as the logical carrier to Maryland: old-fashioned politics, one hand washing the other, and the soap was cold, hard cash.

So Luther Coyle had known from the beginning. He'd known the potential danger of the shipments to the town, known what would happen in case of an accident, and he'd gone along with it. Payne nodded to himself. Worse than that, Luther Coyle had probably been the one who'd told the authorities about the destruction of the van. He'd placed the town in jeopardy and then played Judas.

Rembrandt Payne stood up, the lab stool crashing to the floor unnoticed behind him. He had a sudden, horrible vision of Rebecca Hardy's ulcerated flesh. Features twisted into a deadly, furious mask, the white-haired man pushed through the doors of the lab and headed down the corridor toward the main entrance to the Medical Center. His mind had emptied except for one red-hot coal of thought: somehow, Luther Coyle was going to pay for what he'd done.

* * *

By two o'clock that afternoon, the blizzard whirling over Jericho Falls showed no signs of abating. Of the seventy-eight people who'd shown up at Stark Hall to volunteer their services, thirty had been dispatched by Jack Slater to move as many people as possible out of the area immediately around the junction of the Strip and Airport Road. Another dozen men had been given the job of blocking the Strip with vehicles, and six men had been sent by snowmobile across the fields behind the Slumber-King to take up positions at Drake's Farm. Breaking into the yard of the Coyle Construction Company on the northwestern edge of town, Sparrow and four others had come up with detonators, fuse wire, and eighty pounds of high-quality DuPont explosives. The remaining volunteers had been deployed on the town side of both the Fourth Chute and Mill Bridges.

Both bridges across the Jericho River had been rigged with dynamite, with trailing wires leading back to lookout posts on Gowan and Whitehill Streets. Max Korman, a retired lineman for New Hampshire Telephone, had done some fiddling at the exchange office on Overlook Street, and direct lines from the bridge lookouts were connected to the bell tower on Stark Hall. If any activity was seen close to the bridges, both spans could be demolished within seconds. Jenny Hale, acting on Jack Slater's orders and with the help of more than a dozen women volunteers, was setting up the gym and classrooms of the high school as a shelter, stocking it with food, bedding, and other supplies taken from stores around the Common and on Main Street.

A steady stream of people still healthy enough to make it through the snow was making its way to the school, while at the same time several of Jenny's co-workers were using a plow equipped with four-by-fours to clear a route up Sherbourne Street to North Road. If worse came to worst, Slater had decided to get as many people as possible out of town, taking them along the old ski road into the mountains. It wasn't the greatest plan in the world, but it was the best he could come up with under the circumstances. Jericho Falls might not be safe from an attack, but at least they'd have a little bit of warning.

Grunting with the effort, Jack Slater and Sparrow Hawke manhandled the heavy rubber boat down the embankment beside Mill

Bridge. Both men were dressed in silver snowmobile suits liberated from Gaudet's Hardware on the Common, and in the sheeting snow they looked like heavily padded ghosts as they struggled with the bright yellow dinghy. Sparrow had a big Remington deer rifle slung over his back and the sheriff was armed with a .22 calibre assault rifle and his old MP's .45 calibre Browning automatic pistol. They finally brought the boat to the edge of the water and paused, their breath exploding in steaming billows of condensation.

"I still don't know what you're trying to prove," said Sparrow, breathing hard, frost-rime turning his beard and mustache white.

"You don't have to come along," Slater said, adjusting the pistol belt around his waist. A few feet away, the black water of the Jericho River looked like the coiling back of a gigantic snake. "I can do this alone just as easily."

"Bullshit. This whole thing is bullshit."

"Karen's not your daughter."

"You really think you're going to be able to get her out of that place?"

"I can try."

"They've got surveillance radar, sophisticated weaponry, and God knows what else," Sparrow said. "Not to mention their numbers. It's suicide."

"I don't want to talk about it anymore. That son of a bitch has kidnapped my daughter, and I'm going to get her back."

"Right. Or die trying."

"Maybe."

"Jesus!" muttered Sparrow. "Pretty soon we're going to have the 'A man's gotta do what a man's gotta do' speech. I thought I'd heard the last of that in 'Nam." He shook his head. Slater turned to face the big, long-haired man.

"I'm not a complete fool, Hawke. And I'm not going to commit suicide. I want to see the layout. If I think there's a chance, then I'll go in. If not, I'll stay back. This shit-heel little colonel has me cold, and he knows it. Any decisions I make from now on are going to be influenced by the fact that he's got Karen and B.C. Bingham. So far, Wright and his people have been setting the rules and we've been taking everything they've handed out. It's time for us to take the offensive. If you don't agree with me, that's fine. There's lots of things you could be doing back in town. It's up to you.''

"How long you figure it's going to take for us to get down to the airport in this rubber duck?'' Sparrow asked blandly.

Blinking snow out of his eyes, Slater eyed the bearded man, then smiled.

"It's about two and a half miles according to the map in my office. With all this snow, the current's going pretty fast. Ten, maybe fifteen minutes. We won't be doing much more than steering.''

"What about getting back?''

"I'm not sure. Depends on what goes down. We tie the boat to a tree and use it to get to the other bank. If we can make it to the old railway station, we can take the trail around Quarry Hill and get back here in an hour or so. That's why I brought the skis along.'' He gestured with his chin at the four pairs of cross-country skis, boots, and poles in the bottom of the boat.

"Then let's pray the snow keeps up,'' Sparrow said, staring up into the dark gray sky. "If they've got enough visibility to get choppers up, we'll be sitting ducks.''

"That's a risk we'll just have to take.'' He bent down, grabbed one of the rope pulls attached to the side of the rubber boat, and began dragging it toward the water. "You coming?''

"Yeah, I'm coming.'' Hawke sighed, moving around to the other side of the dinghy. "But don't ask me why.''

CHAPTER FIFTEEN

2:15 P.M.

Weighed down by the armored suits, it had taken Karen and B.C. the better part of an hour to circle around through the dense bush and finally reach the old railway bridge spanning the Jericho River half a mile below Drake's Farm. The snow, pushed by strong winds blowing down from the mountains, had swept into drifts that were sometimes almost waist-high, and by the time the two young people came within sight of the bridge, they were exhausted.

Screened by the snow-covered trunk of a fallen tree, they peered out at the black, rusted span a hundred yards away. The blinding snow made the far side of the bridge invisible, but they had a clear view of the near side abutment. As far as B.C. could see, it was deserted.

"No guards?" Karen asked, slouched down beside her friend.

"Doesn't look like it," B.C. answered. "Hang on." He called up the visor's infrared function, and the pale green view in front of his eyes instantly switched to a deep red. The obscuring curtain of snow vanished, and at the far end of the bridge, he could see a brightly glowing dot of white. The computer in his backpack was picking up the heating-unit aura from a suit on the other side of the river. As B.C. watched, the white dot moved slightly, heading to the west, then stopped, turned and came back to the east. "Shit."

"What?"

"There's a guard on the other end of the bridge, walking back and forth. As soon as we try and cross, he'll pick us off. If I can see him on infrared, he'd be able to see us."

"So what do we do?"

"I don't know. Let me think." Between the edge of the trees and the bridge there was an open space of about fifty feet and then a short climb up to the tracks. Not impossible, especially since the gravel right of way and the stone abutment itself would screen them from the far end of the bridge and the guard. But then there was three hundred feet of track to cross and nowhere to hide. Even without the infrared function, the guard would eventually see them as they came out of the snow.

"What about going back the way we came?" Karen asked. "Maybe we could make it through the bush up to Drake's Farm."

"Forget it," B.C. answered, keeping his eyes on the bridge. "We tried that before. The snow's too deep. Unless we get across the bridge and onto Old Mill Road, they're going to get us eventually."

"Then what about the catwalk?"

"What catwalk?"

"Haven't you ever gone swimming off the bridge?"

"No. My dad wouldn't let me, especially after Mark Pender dove off and cracked his head open on one of the caissons."

"Billy and I used to do it," Karen said. "Last summer. There's this catwalk under the tracks. You can get to it from either side; there's a ladder bolted to the concrete."

"It goes all the way across?"

"Yup."

B.C. looked at the bridge again, letting his eyes trace down through the ironwork below the tracks. He could just make out a narrow metal framework, almost hidden by the snow and the shadows under the bridge.

"Where does it come out?" he asked.

"On the pier at the other side," Karen explained. "You climb down another ladder and you're right on the riverbank. There's a whole bunch of bushes growing under the bridge, that's where Billy and I used to—" She stopped.

"Okay," B.C. said, not wanting to hear any more. "We'll give it a try. Once we get to the far side, we can keep down by the riverbank until we're out of range."

"Great," Karen said. "Let's go."

"Not yet." Rolling over, he reached out for her backpack. "I'm going to switch everything off," he explained. "We'll wait until we can feel it getting cold before we go on. We won't be able to talk to each other, but if we can bleed off enough heat the guard won't be able to see us coming. Once we're far enough away, we can turn everything back on."

"Okay," Karen agreed. "Let's just get on with it."

"Five minutes, then we go," B.C. instructed. He flipped the row of switches on her backpack, and then turned off his own suit. Cut off from each other, the heating coils in the suits slowly cooling, they waited. Karen hesitated for a moment and then moved a little closer to B.C., tucking her arm into his, saddened by the fact that the bulky suits denied closer contact.

She tried not to think about what had gone on since Friday night, concentrating on the feel of B.C.'s arm, while the small corner of her mind not numbed by panic and fear wondered at the changes that could happen to someone in such a short space of time.

A little less than forty-eight hours ago, she'd been Karen Slater, a teenager with braces who had Billy Coyle for a boyfriend and who wanted nothing more than to shake the dust of Jericho Falls from her feet. B.C. Bingham was a dweeb who wore glasses and sucked up to Mr. Brisbois in environmental studies, and her father was a dull, uninteresting guy with a stupid job that she always found a bit embarrassing. Life in the Falls was a bitch, sex was a false alarm, and the future looked as boring as the past.

And now the future had risen up with a vengeance. Billy had proven himself to be an insensitive little shit, B.C. had turned out to be something of a hero, and boring old Jericho Falls had become a deathtrap. Forty-eight hours, and now all she wanted was her own bed in her own house and the sound of her father's voice telling her to get her lazy buns out of the sack or she'd be late for school. She shivered, looking out at the whirling snow, and wondered if she'd ever have any of that again.

Bentley tapped her on the shoulder and stood up. The suits had cooled off enough and it was time to go. Following his lead and keeping her head down, she stumbled forward across the open ground between the trees and the high, gray bulk of the bridge abutment. It took less than thirty seconds to cover the distance, but by the time she joined B.C. against the towering slab of pitted concrete, she was panting for breath. With the suit turned off she was dragging air through the vent screens by herself and it was an effort. If they had to run any distance she was going to be in trouble.

Bentley started moving again, edging along the abutment until they were almost directly over the molasses-dark water. There was less than a yard between the abutment and the edge and even that slim margin of safety had been shortened by the snow. She glanced down at the roiling water thirty feet below and then recoiled, flattening herself against the abutment. What had seemed so easy with Billy that summer had become a nightmare.

B.C. tugged at her sleeve and she nodded, keeping her eyes focused dead ahead. She inched along the narrow ledge, the palms of both gloved hands against the concrete wall. A few moments later they stopped, and turning her head, she could see the rusted iron rungs of the ladder. She looked up and swallowed hard. Things were going from bad to worse. The catwalk was there all right, but it was a good forty feet up, almost lost in the maze of lacy ironwork beneath the bridge.

B.C. shuffled beyond the lowest rung of the ladder and motioned her forward. He took one of her hands, planted it on the rung and jerked his thumb upward. He wanted her to go first. She nodded, glad that the green tint of the visor screened her expression. If B.C. knew how scared she was right at that moment, he would have left her behind. With the suit heating unit off, the snow was no longer melting on the faceplate of the helmet and she took a moment to wipe away the accumulated slush with her free hand. Then she began to climb, planting one booted foot on the rung and hauling herself upward.

The forty-foot climb took her a lifetime, but less than three minutes after she'd begun, Karen reached the metal-grate platform at the top. Directly ahead of her, the narrow catwalk spun off into the distance, the far end invisible in the snow. There was only a single iron bar on either side for a handrail and the catwalk itself was made of the same grillwork as the tiny platform she was standing on. There wasn't going to be much between her and the dead-black water far below. She bit her lip hard, feeling the salt taste of her own blood. One slip was all it would take, and with the suit on, she'd be dragged down in seconds.

B.C. clambered up onto the platform, and Karen moved aside to give him room, both hands gripping the iron handrail. Bentley took a moment to peer out along the catwalk and then nodded.

He put one hand on Karen's shoulder and squeezed. Somewhere, he'd found a three-foot length of pipe and he held it ready in his free hand. He used it to point out over the river and gave her a gentle push. For the first time since childhood the words of the Lord's Prayer came into her mind, and whispering them under her breath, Karen Slater stepped out over the yawning abyss.

Leaving the Medical Center, Rembrandt Payne quickly saw that any attempt to use the Meat Wagon would be futile, so he decided to walk the half dozen blocks to Luther Coyle's house at the top of Pineglade Drive. Jamming his well-worn old deer-stalker down around his ears, he bent his head against the stinging bite of the snow and struggled off across the parking lot.

The streets were empty, and within five minutes, the old man knew that he'd foolishly put himself into a life-and-death situation. He was old, sedentary, and overweight, and that made him a prime candidate for a heart attack as he forced his way through the drifting snow. Almost as dangerous was the possibility of a fall. An accident now, even something as simple as a sprained ankle, could be fatal in this kind of weather. Reaching the top of Medical Center Way, he stopped to catch his breath and looked back over his shoulder. He'd come no more than two hundred yards, but he was utterly exhausted, and the Center was completely invisible behind him. Gritting his teeth as the chill wind bit through to the bone, he continued on.

As he turned onto Pineglade Drive, the blowing snow grew worse, whirling down through the gap between the Ridge and Hunter's Hill, then roaring over the parklike meadows on the near side of Mountain Creek. With his eyes closed to narrow slits, the old man forced himself to keep moving, his heart like a hot coal in his chest, his breath coming in short, ragged bursts.

By the time Rembrandt Payne reached the big Colonial mansion with its back to the creek, he knew that his own personal hell would consist of an endless journey through a wilderness of snow. He stopped at the twin brick pillars in front of the house and peered up at the massive, two-and-a-half-story structure. Carol, Luther's wife, had been dead for several years, and Luther and Billy lived in the mansion alone. Now Billy was in the Medical Center, close to death, and the house would be Luther's mausoleum. By sheer force of will, the doctor dragged himself forward

until he reached the tall, white-painted door. There was a bell
push set into the frame but he chose to use the big, brass-lion
knocker instead, hammering it against the strike-plate with all his
might. Leaning against the doorframe, he grasped the Zippo
lighter he'd found in the reception nurse's desk drawer. If Luther
wasn't home, he'd burn the house to the ground. He smashed the
door-knocker again, and a few moments later Luther Coyle opened
the door just enough to look out.

"Dr. Payne. What in God's name are you doing here?" The
mayor of Jericho Falls was dressed in a dark green sweatsuit, an
opened can of diet cola in one hand.

"I'm here to see you," answered the old man. He pushed
against the door and brushed past the startled mayor. Luther closed
the door, shutting out the furious blizzard while Payne, still
breathing hard, unbuttoned his heavy greatcoat, pulled off the
deerstalker, and dropped both onto an imitation Queen Anne chair
in the foyer. Glowering, the old man looked around. The expan-
sive entrance hall was floored with dull red quarry tile, furnished
out of an Ethan Allen catalogue, and lit by an immense chandelier
that hung like a bizarre, glittering stalactite from the nubbly,
white-stucco ceiling. Luther's idea of expensive good taste.

"A drink?" asked Luther. "You look frozen to the bone, Doctor."

"Scotch," Payne said. Luther led the way across the foyer to
the open double doors leading into a large study. He ushered the
old man to a large, leather-upholstered chair that stood in front
of a huge mahogany partners desk and then went to the bar. The
doctor glanced around the room.

Three out of four walls were covered with floor-to-ceiling
bookcases, most of which were filled with leather-bound volumes. The books seemed to be arranged in accordance with the
color of their spines and Payne suspected that Luther had purchased them by weight from a decorator.

The carpet on the floor was three-inch broadloom in a rich
medium green that matched the ceiling, and the overall effect was
an exercise in understated masculinity and power. It was the kind
of room a retired judge could write his memoirs in.

Luther brought Payne a large, heavy glass of amber-colored
scotch, then went around to the far side of the desk and settled

into his high-backed brown leather swivel chair, the can of cola placed neatly on the polished surface in front of him.

"You wanted to see me," Luther said.

Even in the sweatsuit, Luther maintained a sense of sharp-edged intelligence. Payne silently corrected himself. It wasn't intelligence, it was cunning. Luther Coyle was an aging, gray-haired fox with an instinct for survival.

"That's right."

"Why didn't you telephone?"

"I wanted to see you in person. I wanted to see the expression on your face." He took a long swallow of his drink and winced as the liquid burned down his throat and began to warm his stomach.

"That sounds vaguely threatening," Luther said, smiling thinly and leaning back in his chair.

"No. There's no threat. I can't do anything to you, Luther."

"Why would you want to?"

"Because you know what's been going on here. You've known right from the beginning."

"What exactly are you talking about, Doctor?"

"The van. The sickness. The deaths. Jericho Falls has been given a death sentence, Luther, and you're responsible."

"I don't know what on earth you're talking about."

"You had the contract to ship whatever it was in that van, didn't you? How long have you been bringing that filth through my town, Luther? How long have you been risking people's lives?"

"*Your* town, Dr. Payne? When were you elected mayor?" Luther's narrow face hardened, and the man's pale blue eyes suddenly looked as cold as the snow outside.

"I care about the people here," the old man answered. "That's more than you can say."

Luther sat forward, the fingers of one hand gently caressing the can on the desk in front of him. He shook his head.

"You surprise me, Doctor. I would have thought that a man your age would have learned something after all these years."

"I know what's right and what's wrong, Luther. I've learned that much."

"What about practicality?" Luther responded. "What about

that, old man? This town was dying, I brought it back to life. All you've ever done was get in the way of progress."

"It would appear that progress exacts a terrible price, then," said Payne. "It may cost you your son's life, in fact."

"Billy will be all right."

"Who told you that?" Payne shot back. He reached forward and slammed his half-finished drink onto the desk. "This Colonel Wright fellow I've been hearing about? That's very funny, Luther. You're willing to believe the word of a man who trades in biological warfare matériel?"

"You don't know what you're talking about, Doctor."

"I don't know all of it. But I know enough. The substance in that van was a recombinant bacteria that remutates in the host's bloodstream. It becomes a hideously virulent allergen that causes massive cancers of every possible type. So far, I haven't identified the triggering agent, but it affects anyone with adult levels of testosterone or estrogen in their systems."

"I fall into that category," Luther said blandly. "And I feel fine." He smiled again. "In fact, I just spent the last half hour working out on the Nautilus downstairs."

"I've been thinking about that." Payne nodded. "I suppose your Colonel Wright has told you that there's an antidote for the bacteria?"

"It will be administered after the evacuation," Luther said.

"Why evacuate at all, then?" said Payne. "Why not just in-oculate everyone right here?"

"You don't understand the security implications, Doctor. I'm afraid this is way above your head. The whole procedure is being done with the approval of the Governor's Office."

"Codswallop," Payne said. "The whole procedure is being done with the approval of Senator Barrett O'Neill, yourself, and whatever goon squad Colonel Wright belongs to. This is a cover-up that makes Watergate look like a child shoplifting candy."

"You're playing with the big boys now, Doctor," Luther returned, his voice dangerously soft. "And I told you, you're in way over your head."

"I can swim just fine thank you, Mayor Coyle," Payne said. "You're the one who's in trouble, I'm afraid. Because there *is* no antidote. So far, the only immune sector of the population I've discovered is people with diabetes, women who are pregnant, and Bodo Bimm.''

"I'm neither pregnant, diabetic, nor a cretin, Dr. Payne.''

"No. And I'll bet they've been giving you shots right from the start, haven't they?''

"Perhaps,'' Luther said noncommittally.

"HCG,'' said Payne. "They've been shooting you full of human chorionic gonadotropins. It's a hormone you find in pregnant women. No deleterious effects, but it won't do much good in the end. A delaying tactic at best, Luther, no matter what they told you.''

"You're bluffing, Doctor.''

"Really? You're neither female nor pregnant. Considering your contact with your son and various other people who've been infected, there is no doubt that the bacteria is already in your system. Eventually, it will reproduce enough to overwhelm the HCG dosage. You're going to die, Luther, just like a lot of other people in this town, and quite frankly, it gives me a great deal of pleasure telling you so.''

"Why is it that the weak always envy the strong?'' Coyle said, apparently unperturbed by the old man's warning. "I've spent the better part of my adult life trying to make Jericho Falls into a growing, vital community, and during that time you and people like you have done nothing but gainsay every effort I've made. You're a whiner, Dr. Payne. A whiner, a bleeding heart, and a dinosaur. Progress, growth, success—they all require risks of one kind or another. I've never been afraid of those risks.''

"Especially when it was other people's lives you were risking,'' answered Payne. "But I'm afraid this time the joke is on you, Luther. You were risking your own neck this time, and you failed. When I tell Jack Slater and the others about your involvement in all of this, they'll probably want to lynch you. And if they don't kill you, and the bacteria doesn't kill you, Colonel Wright certainly will. This is the Night of the Long Knives, Luther. There aren't going to be any witnesses left behind.'' The doctor rose painfully to his feet, picked up the glass from the desk, and drained it. "Thanks for the scotch.'' Luther reached down, opened a drawer on his side of the desk, and reached into it.

"Perhaps you're right,'' the mayor said, nodding. He drew out a heavy, dark-metal automatic pistol and pulled back the slide quickly. He pointed the weapon at Rembrandt Payne, aiming at the old man's chest. "Perhaps there shouldn't be any witnesses." With his free hand Luther reached out and picked up the telephone on his desk. "Sit down, Doctor," he said quietly. "You should rest a while longer before you go out into the cold again."

"Okay, what now?" Sparrow asked, flat in the snow on the edge of the trees. Snow was still falling but the wind had dropped and the lead-sheet sky was lightening. Beside him, Jack Slater peered through binoculars, training them on the length of high, chain-link fencing fifty yards away on the far side of Airport Road.

"We get some idea of the guard schedule, and then we move," replied the sheriff, his voice low. The two men had ridden the rubber raft down the fast-flowing river to the dense woodlot across from the airport, pulled it up on the sloping bank, then trudged carefully through the trees to the road. The downriver trip had been relatively easy, but both men knew the return journey would be much more difficult.

"There's about a three-minute break between the guards," whispered Sparrow. "And the visibility is improving. We're not going to have much time."

"I'm aware of that. Thirty seconds to cross the road and reach the fence. A minute to get through with the bolt-cutters and then another forty-five seconds to get behind that first row of helicopters. That leaves about forty-five seconds of margin."

"What if the fence is wired?"

"It's not," said the sheriff, shaking his head. "No insulators."

"Mines, booby traps? Remember that Jumping Jack Flash I found."

"We'll have to chance it." He stiffened, adjusting the focus on the small pair of binoculars. "There's the first guard," he whispered. "The second one should come by in about fifteen or twenty seconds. Get ready."

"I am ready. I'm also freezing to death."

The second red-suited guard appeared, turned, then disappeared into the hazy curtain of snow again. Without a word, the two men pulled themselves up from the snow and began to run, legs pumping hard as they crossed the dangerous open ground between the trees and the fence. Jack Slater took the lead, fumbling at his belt for the pair of heavy-duty bolt-cutters, doing a slow count in his head.

They reached the fence at the twenty-five mark and dropped to the ground. Wind shear had pushed up a three-foot-high, sharp-edged drift a yard or so from the fence and the sheriff prayed that the obstacle would screen them from the perimeter guards long enough to get through the fence. He worked as fast as he could, numbed hands working the bulky, long-handled cutters. He snipped through the fence link by link, working from the top down as Sparrow pulled the opening wider.

"A minute five," the long-haired man whispered harshly. "Enough." They were twenty seconds ahead of schedule. Slater dropped the bolt-cutters into the snow and slithered through the opening. Sparrow followed, taking time to pull the peeled section of fence roughly back into position. By the time Sparrow was done, Slater was already halfway across the open field. The ex-pilot began to run, half-crouched, the deer rifle ready in his clenched hands, heart sledgehammering in his chest. He reached Slater, hidden behind the screening bulk of the first helicopter in the line, and dropped down into the snow again. Holding their breath, the two men waited, eyes fixed on the almost invisible hole in the fence. Thirty seconds later the first of the two guards reappeared, and then the second. They paused, turned, and resumed their patterns. Neither of them appeared to have noticed the hole in the fence.

"Made it," Sparrow said, breathing out slowly.

"For now," Slater said, watching as the guards faded away. "They could just as easily pick up the hole on the next pass."

"Are you always this pessimistic?"

"Comes with the job," Slater answered. He peeked out across the hardstand from below the tethered chopper. The terminal building was two hundred feet west and beyond it he could just see the line of long-haul truck cabs Sparrow had mentioned. The prefab compound made up of the truck trailers would be just beyond them, cordoned off by concertina wire.

"I know it's a bit late in the day," Sparrow whispered, "but are you still open for suggestions?"

"Like what?"

"Like a better plan for getting out of here. It took us a good ten minutes to make it up from the river to the edge of the trees, and with the kids it'll take even longer to get back. They'll be all over us.''

''I'm listening.''

''Why don't we fly out?'' said Sparrow, looking up at the riveted flank of the helicopter they were crouching behind. It was a UH-60 Blackhawk armed with a twin-barreled cannon and an octet of Hellfire antitank missiles. Like all the vehicles they'd seen, it was painted white.

''Are you crazy?'' asked Slater.

''Obviously,'' Sparrow answered. ''I wouldn't be here if I wasn't.''

''What about the weather?''

''Risky, but I'm willing to chance it. She's a big enough bird to handle any gusting.''

''Can you fly it?''

''Sure. Cut the tethers, heat up the coil, and she'll be ready to go when we need her.'' He grinned at Slater. ''Upset the balance of power a bit if we can pull it off.''

The sheriff looked up at the helicopter, frowning thoughtfully. ''Okay,'' he said finally. ''Do it.''

Smiling happily, Sparrow stood up cautiously and grabbed the handle of the helicopter's main door. He tugged and it slid back smoothly. The big man boosted himself up and disappeared into the dark interior of the vehicle. A few moments later, Slater heard a faint whining sound that soon became a regular, clicking whistle. Sparrow reappeared, dropped down to the ground and then scuttled under the belly of the helicopter. He unclipped both the belly tethers and then slid back and removed the tail hitch.

''That should do it,'' he said. ''Coil's on, pumps are on, and there's a quick start for the turbines. Punch the ignition, and you can have her off the ground in under two minutes.''

''Okay. Now what's it going to be, the terminal or that mobile unit you mentioned?''

''Concertina wire around the HQ and guards at four points,'' answered Sparrow. ''You want to get in there, you're going to have to get one of those suits. I say we try the terminal. It's closer.''

''All right.''

The two men eased around the far side of the helicopter, keep-

ing it between them and the fence. Coming around behind the tail
rotor they stopped again, checking out the lay of the land. A
hundred and fifty feet away they could just make out the back
door of the cinderblock building. Slater took the binoculars out
of the pocket of his snowmobile suit and checked the glass-boxed
tower. It was empty.

"Anything?" asked Sparrow. Slater shook his head.

"No. Let's move it."

They came out from behind the rotor and began running for
the rear door. Before they'd made it fifty feet, Sparrow and the
sheriff knew there was something terribly wrong. A siren began
to howl somewhere close by and both men froze. Instinctively,
Sparrow slapped back the bolt on the deer rifle in his hands,
chambering a shell, and Slater's hand went to his gun belt. The
sound of engines added to the racket created by the siren.

"Back!" yelled Slater. They turned around and raced for the
helicopter, crouching down, muscles tensed for the sudden tearing
impact of a bullet. Out of the corner of his eye Sparrow caught a
fleeting movement. Red suit. Still running, he fired a round from
the hip, the big shell exploding out of the barrel with a cracking
thunderclap of sound. Behind him, Slater was firing as well and
Sparrow began to zigzag wildly as the snow-blown hardstand in
front of him suddenly came alive with tiny glowing dots of ruby
light. Within a split second, the universe had contracted to the
still partially open door of the Blackhawk twenty feet away. Make
the door and there was still a chance. Zig. Watch for the deadly
little chips of scarlet, like moving droplets of blood on the snow.
Zag. Ten feet. Eyes on the door. Go through the procedure.
Headfirst, dump the rifle on the fly. Five feet. Into the pilot's seat
as fast as you can, hit the quick start and hope like hell Slater
has the sense to close the door behind him. Did the Blackhawk
have armor? Sure it did. Or did it? Now!

Flinging the rifle to one side, Sparrow dove through the narrow
opening, rolling onto his shoulder, vaguely aware of the glass on
his right exploding into fragments. He landed on the metal-mesh
floor, bruising his shoulder, then rolled and dragged himself along
the floor and into the pilot's compartment. No time for the nice-
ties. Brushing sudden sweat out of his eyes, he leaned forward
and rammed his fist onto the quick-start, heart jumping as he
heard the spooling thunder of the big turbojet begin to moan. He

began switching on, moving without thinking as the rotors began to spin, sending a shivering vibration through the hull. He felt the cabin lean slightly and prayed that it was Slater and not one of the red-suit freaks who'd come aboard. There was a slamming impact as a shell hit somewhere, and taking the collective throttle in his left hand and gripping the cyclic column between his knees, he dragged the bird into the air, hoping like hell that the revs were high enough to get them off. He let his feet touch the rudder pedals that controlled the tail rotor, getting the feel of the machine as it lurched away from the ground. There was a splintering crash and a hole the size of a silver dollar appeared in the windscreen a foot to his right. He hit the rudder and the helicopter canted sharply left, but they were still airborne. He pulled back slightly on the cyclic, letting them climb, and out of the corner of his eye he saw Slater as he pulled himself up into the right-hand seat.

"Two columns in front of you," Sparrow instructed. "Left-hand is the cannon. Red button. Right-hand is the Hellfire pods. Green button. Fire control for the Hellfire is the console on your right. Hit all the switches on the panel. Hands on the buttons. Fire when I tell you, left or right." Just like a drill. Calm and cool. Forget that you haven't done this in a while."

"Got it."

Thirty feet into the air and suddenly the world was spread out below them. Slater brushed his hand over the fire-control switches, all the indicator lights glowing green. He gripped the left- and right-hand columns, keeping eyes front. Directly in front of them, he saw the terminal and the small glass control tower. The helicopter tilted to the left, the horizon pitching up nauseatingly; dimly he heard Sparrow's voice.

"Right!"

Slater squeezed his right thumb down on the green button and instantly felt himself slammed back into his seat as the first Hellfire missile screeched out of its cradle. Without waiting, Sparrow swung the helicopter sideways and down, the ground racing up to meet them. There was a thundering roar from behind them as the Hellfire found its target, and then Sparrow's voice was screaming.

"Left! Left!"

Slater put his left thumb down on the red button and kept it there, watching as a score of tracing lines of smoke ripped down into a running group of figures pouring out of the main entrance to the terminal. Adjusting the cyclic and kicking the rudder, Sparrow leaned the Blackhawk to the right, the cannon shells spewing across the row of parked and tarpaulin-shrouded fast-attack Jeepsters. A fireball erupted directly in front of them like a fist of angry flames and smoke. The concussion battered against the belly of the helicopter and then everything vanished. Ahead of them, there was nothing but a gray curtain of snow, and below them only trees.

"Wanna go back and hit them again?" yelled Sparrow, chancing a quick glance at his colleague. Slater shook his head and sagged back against the seat.

"No," he answered, lifting his voice over the pounding roar of the turbines and the rotor. "We were lucky to get out of there alive. Enough. Get us home if you can."

"No problem!" Sparrow said, his voice jubilant.

And no Karen, thought Slater. They'd hijacked a helicopter and abandoned his daughter. Saddened by their failure and more depressed and frightened than he'd ever been in his life, he stared dully forward, watching as the snow-shrouded streets and buildings of Jericho Falls began forming in the distance.

CHAPTER SIXTEEN

2:35 P.M.

As the Jericho River surged beneath the railway bridge, a fine spray was thrown up, coating the catwalk and handrail slung below the tracks with a thin, treacherous skin of ice. Three times on the long, agonizing way across, Karen had slipped, and once it had only been B.C.'s quick thinking that had saved her from plummeting down into the river. They moved slowly, inch by inch, their nerves shredded, their breathing short and rapid. They were both generating so much body heat that even with the suit ventilation systems turned off, they were uncomfortably warm, sweat trickling down to sting their eyes.

Her eyes firmly on the tiny spot in the distance that marked the far pier, Karen forced herself to continue; after twenty minutes, the spot had become an identifiable square, but still a goal that seemed an eternity away. She kept moving, shuffling her heavily booted feet forward, then sliding her hands along the rail, muscles tensed and teeth clenched, waiting for the inevitable horrifying slip that would mean instant death. Eyes front, locked onto the pier in the distance, she knew there was only a thin honeycomb of ice-coated metal between her and empty air, and if it hadn't been for B.C.'s hand resting lightly on her shoulder, she would have gone out of her mind. Alone, the journey across the narrow catwalk would have been an impossible nightmare.

Then, magically, the high-wire act was over and she was standing on the small platform on the far side. Her sweat-soaked clothing began to dry, and she shivered as the icy cold of the outside began to seep into the suit. B.C. made his way across the last few feet of catwalk and stepped onto the platform beside her.

They were safe at last. She sighed, feeling her legs go rubbery beneath her, and she gripped the handrail hard.

B.C. edged around her slowly and peered downward. The metal ladder was intact, but he saw immediately that it wasn't going to do any good. Karen and Billy had used it in the summer, when the water level was at its lowest. Now, the rungs disappeared into the rushing river. Almost as bad, the lower rungs still above the surface were coated with a thick layer of ice.

He looked up, following the line of iron rungs. They disappeared up into the shadows of the bridge, but he could see a rectangle of sky—some sort of cutout in the railway ties. It was the only way off the bridge, and it would bring them up within twenty feet of the guard. The boy hefted the iron pipe in his hand. Not much of a weapon.

"Shit," he muttered. He bit his lip, staring upward. There was no other way. Frowning, he tapped Karen on the shoulder and leaned forward until the visor of his headpiece was touching hers. "Can you hear me?" he asked, raising his voice.

"Yeah," she answered, her voice muffled. "What now?"

"The water level is too high for us to go down. We've got to climb up the ladder and onto the bridge. Can you manage that?"

"I guess."

"I want you to go up first. The guard will probably see you. I want you to walk back along the bridge, okay?"

"Back the way we came?"

"That's right. Pretend you're sick or something. Stagger, stumble. You can even fall down. I want all his attention on you."

"What if he shoots?" Karen asked.

"Don't worry, he won't," B.C. replied with more confidence than he felt.

"Easy for you to say," she grumbled unhappily. "I was just getting used to being alive again."

"Trust me. It's the only way out of here."

"All right." She put one booted foot on the lowest rung and began moving upward. Compared to their earlier ascent, the climb from the platform to the underside of the tracks was a simple matter of no more than fifteen feet. Karen made it easily, with B.C. right behind her, the iron bar jammed into his belt. Reaching the small rectangular hole, Karen paused for a second, then boosted herself up. B.C. stayed where he was, giving her enough time to play her part.

He looked upward, eyes on the hole, and did a slow count to thirty. At twenty-five he thought he saw a shadow fall across the opening, and at thirty-one he started to move, clambering up the last few rungs and poking his head through the opening. He hung with one hand and pulled the iron bar out of his belt.

Karen was ten feet away, down on her knees, the guard directly behind her, his weapon at the ready. B.C. didn't hesitate. He slithered up through the opening, took three long steps, and wound up, whirling the bar like a baseball bat. He'd spent the last few seconds on the ladder trying to figure out the best place to aim for, and he'd decided on the neck joint in the armored suit as the most likely possibility.

The bar connected with a cracking sound that B.C. could hear even through the helmet, and for an instant, he was sure he'd broken the man's neck. Then, horribly, the guard turned, staggering, swinging the weapon around in his hands as he came. It was all over. Five seconds to live and he couldn't think of one appropriate quote. He squeezed his eyes shut and brought the bar around again, putting every ounce of his strength into the swing. At the last second, he opened his eyes again, watching as the bar struck the guard directly across the throat.

The red-suited figure took a step backward, the weapon dropping from his hands and dangling from its coiled connecting cord. The guard brought both gloved hands up to his neck, head tilted back as he slipped against the low, solid railing of the bridge. The helmet came forward again, and panicking, B.C. lurched forward, taking a third swipe with the bar. This time he hit the visor full on, snapping the man's head back, overbalancing the torso. The guard's feet came out from under him and he did a backward somersault over the rail, vanishing into the swirling snow.

Horrified, B.C. scrambled across the rails and looked over the side of the bridge. There was nothing to see except the dark broad stripe of the water almost fifty feet below. The guard had vanished. Drowned, or maybe even dead before he'd hit the water. B.C. looked down at the iron bar in his hand and then, revolted by the sudden and terrible ease of what he'd done, he threw the simple club over the side. Turning back to the tracks, he saw that

Karen was back on her feet. Reaching around to his backpack, he activated the suit systems again, then crossed over to her and turned her suit on as well.

"You okay?" he asked, activating the suit-to-suit radio link.

"I think so. He was going to shoot."

"I know."

"You couldn't have done anything else," she said, somehow knowing what was going through his mind. "You didn't have any choice."

"Yes, I know that too. Come on. Let's go." He tried to push the vision of the guard's death out of his mind, but it kept replaying in his head again and again. "They'll know he's gone soon. We've got to get under cover until it's dark. We can't stay out in the open."

"Where do we go?" she asked.

"I know a place. Come on."

They kept to the tracks, where their footprints wouldn't show in the newly fallen snow, following the old rail line around the tree-covered foot of Quarry Hill until they reached Overflow Creek, the tumbling stream that bounded erratically down the hillside from the old quarry high above. B.C. led Karen away from the tracks, following the line of the stream until they were lost in the trees. Five minutes later, they reached a small log cabin nestled below a jagged shelf of overhanging granite. From a helicopter, the building, no more than a hut really, would be invisible even in good weather.

"How did you know this place was here?" Karen asked.

"My dad built it. Sometimes he hunts," B.C. explained, his voice tired. He reached up with a gloved hand and found a key hidden above the door. He fumbled with the lock for a moment, and then the door opened. He stepped aside and let Karen in. "Home is the hunter, home from the hill," he said, closing the door behind them. "At least now we can rest for a while."

Sparrow brought the helicopter in over North Beacon Street, and dropped it neatly over the pitcher's mound of the Earl A. Coolis High School baseball diamond, panicking the two elderly guards stationed at the back door of the school and sending up a whirlwind of snow. While Sparrow checked the newly won prize for damage, Slater went into the school and found Jenny, hard at work in the gymnasium sorting out bedding and supplies.

Seeing him, the teacher ran across the high-ceilinged room and threw her arms around him, burying her face in his neck. Half a dozen other people in the gym looked on as they embraced and finally, embarrassed, the sheriff pushed her gently away.

"Come on, Jen, people are looking."

"Let them look," she answered, wiping away the tears flooding down her cheeks. "I thought I was never going to see you again, and we never even said good-bye."

"I'm fine," Slater soothed. "Believe it or not, Sparrow managed to hijack one of their helicopters. It's out on the ball diamond."

"What about Karen?"

"We never even got close," he said, frowning. "We were lucky to get out of there alive. It was a stupid thing to do, really."

"You're damn right it was!" the blond teacher agreed hotly. Then she shrugged, a smile brightening her angry expression. "But I'm proud of you for trying, Jack." She reached out and put the palm of her hand on his stubbled cheek. "She'll be okay, I know she will."

"She'd better be," he answered coldly. "I can't think about that now, though. How are things going here?"

"Well enough. Keeping the panic down is the hardest. Most of the little kids think it's a lark. Muriel Beaman has them all playing games in the auditorium. The old people are the worst. Frightened, confused. And we couldn't get Mr. Semolevitch to leave his house at all. He's the last one."

Slater couldn't help smiling. Like anywhere else, Jericho Falls had its fair share of anti-Semites, but Avrom Semolevitch was universally loved in the town. A Polish Jew born in the wild country south of Kaliningrad on the East Prussian border, Avrom had lived through five wars and fought in three, collecting a dozen scars and a thousand tall tales along the way. He'd settled in the Falls in the late forties, taking up his trade as a shoemaker, his income augmented by his hobby of creating wonderfully human marionettes that had been the joy of children in the town for more than forty years. His small shop on Brock Street, just south of the school, was inevitably full of kids during the lunch hour, and the one person who'd tried to set up a competitive shoe repair store in town had packed up his tools within a month.

"I guess I should talk to him," Slater said, still smiling. Karen had a dozen of the old man's puppets on the toy shelf in her room, and except for the combat boots he'd worn in the army, all his shoes had been custom-made at A. Semolevitch.

"I don't think it'll do any good. But you can try, I guess." She took a deep breath. "What's going to happen to us, Jack? It's not just the old people who are scared. I'm frightened, too."

"They've got a small army out by the airport," Slater said truthfully. "Either we evacuate like this Colonel Wright ordered or they'll walk all over us. The only thing stopping him is this snow."

"Maybe we should do what he wants. Some of the people I've talked to think going along with them would be the best thing. People are getting sick again, and we can't get everyone out."

"I'm doing what I think is right for the town," Slater said, lifting a placating hand. "And I'm not forcing anyone to do anything; this whole thing is on a strictly volunteer basis." He paused and looked at her questioningly. "Why are you bringing this up now? Second thoughts?"

"No. Not really," she answered. "It's just hard to believe that our own army would be doing this."

"It's not our army," Slater said. "It's an evil little pipe dream some psychotic in the Pentagon had that managed to slide through Congress hidden in some appropriation bill that no one looked at carefully enough. These people are on their own, Jen, and they're trying to close the Pandora's box they opened."

"So what do we do now?" she asked.

"Wait for Wright to make his move. If we can hold out for long enough, maybe we'll be able to get someone out to let the rest of the world know what's happening. If we can't do that, we'll get as many people up into the mountains as we can and hope for the best. Sooner or later, the word is going to get out." He looked at his watch and frowned. "With this kind of weather, it's going to be dark in two or three hours. I want to see if I can get old Mr. Semolevitch to leave his shop. While I'm doing that, you get hold of Doc Payne at the Medical Center and find out what's happening there, okay?"

"Sure." She hesitated, then leaned forward and kissed Slater on the cheek. "I love you, Jack."

"You never said that before," he answered softly.

"I thought there'd be time later. Now I'm not so sure."

"I love you too, Jen, and there'll be other times, I promise you." He touched her shoulder briefly, a sad, almost mournful expression on his face, and then he turned away.

A. Semolevitch, Custom Boot and Shoe Maker, was a small, one-and-half-story storefront on the corner of Brock Street and North Beacon, no more than a hundred yards away from Earl A. Coolis High School. The front window was usually covered by a thick, green velvet curtain, with Copernicus, the shoemaker's huge, ginger-colored cat, curled up in one corner. For years Slater had been sure that the cat was some bizarre, stuffed memento of the old man's past, but one day he'd actually seen the animal's ear twitch as it basked in the dusty sunlight filtering through the window. Like Bodo Bimm's haircuts and Chang's french fries, Copernicus, the immobile cat, was a near legendary fixture in Jericho Falls.

Jack Slater pushed open the door, the little brass bell high on the frame tinkling as he entered the narrow shop. He closed the door carefully behind him, squinting into the gloomy interior of the building and breathing in the familiar, thick, sweet scent of leather and shoe polish. To the right, set against the wall was the old man's single-seat shine stand, while the left wall was taken up with a glass-fronted display case full of the artisan's favorite marionettes. Directly in front of Slater was a waist-high counter, and beyond it he could see the floor-to-ceiling shelves crammed with dozens of pairs of boots and shoes as well as Semolevitch's scarred wooden worktables. The front table, set with cast-iron anvils and cutting knives, was reserved for his trade, but the large table at the back, close under the stairs leading up to the garret loft, was strewn with the tools and bric-a-brac that had earned the old Pole the nickname Gepetto among the children of the town.

Slater could make out half a dozen puppet heads on the table as well as crosspieces, delicately joined arms, hands, legs, and feet, and the tiny pieces of brass wire Semolevitch used to hinge them all together. But there was no trace of the man himself.

The sheriff stepped up to the counter and palmed the ringer on the small chrome bell. A few seconds later, he heard the creaking of floorboards above his head, and then Semolevitch appeared on the stairs at the back of the shop. He was a small man, barely five feet, his large head covered with a few wisps of reddish white hair, his nose a leathery, hawklike beak at odds with the gentle blue eyes and the large, smiling mouth. He was wearing bedroom slippers, an ancient, pale green cardigan, and dark trousers held up by old-fashioned leather braces he'd made himself. As always, his shirt was white, the collar fixed with a small, polka-dot bow tie.

"Ah, Sheriff Slater." The old man reached the bottom of the stairs and shuffled down the length of the room. "*Dovitzania,* my friend. And how are you on this wintry day?" The voice was as warm and soft as the piles of leather pieces on the man's worktable.

"*Dovitzania,* Mr. Semolevitch," Slater said, returning the Polish greeting. "Did I disturb you?"

"No, not at all, Sheriff. I was—how would you say it?—woolgathering. The first snow for an old man is often a broad hint at what is to come. It makes me nervous." He seated himself on a tall stool and pulled a worn briar out of his cardigan. Striking a match on the underside of the counter, he applied it to the bowl, then tamped down the tobacco with a callused thumb.

"Jenny came to see you."

"She did. An hour or so ago. She tells me that our town is under siege and that you are trying to evacuate people."

"That's right."

"I hear there is a sickness at large. A plague."

"You might call it that. It affects young people mostly. You have nothing to fear."

"At my age, you have everything to fear," answered the old man, his eyes twinkling behind the thick lenses of his old-fashioned wire-rimmed spectacles. "Everything and nothing."

"Jenny says you won't leave."

"Quite so. It would serve no purpose."

"It could save your life."

"So? My life is here, Sheriff. My life is this shop. I'm eighty-six years old, and here I have more than I ever had in all those years. Past, present, and future all rolled into one. I would have only loneliness if I left here now."

"Aren't you being a little fatalistic?"

"I'm a Jew, Sheriff. More than that, I am a Polish Jew. Fatalism was a word created for us. Your Jenny says there is an army outside Jericho Falls and that this army means to take us all away. To some sort of camp."

The old man sucked on his pipe, one bushy eyebrow rising above the frame of his glasses. "It is a story I've heard before, and a story I will not listen to again. This old man, Avrom Semolevitch, with his lasts and his puppets, you can think him a fool if you like, but he will not run away, and he will not go to any camp. He will go up to his room and put on his tallith and he will read from the siddur, which he knows by heart.

"But he will not read the Alenu, Sheriff, nor the Martyr's Prayer, nor the kaddish, the prayer for the dead. Instead, he will recite the Shema Yisrael. Shema Yisrael, Adonai, el ohanu, Adonai." The old man's voice had risen as he spoke the words and Slater felt a shiver go down his spine. Somehow Avrom Semolevitch had grown taller, and the voice was the voice of a much younger, much angrier man.

"All right, Avrom," Slater said quietly. "I think I understand."

"No," the old man answered, shaking his head. "You don't understand, and there is no reason why you should. But you have a good heart, and I appreciate your coming."

"I'll worry about you."

"I've lived through the Bulgarians, the Prussians, the Nazis, and the Russians. I've had enough, Sheriff Slater. Eighty-six years is a long time, and I've seen many things. The world has become sick with greed and jealousy and fear. I'm no saint, but I've seen too much decay and anger, even in this country. The rot is here just as surely as it was in Hitler's Germany, or as it is in the Soviet Union. For a long time I thought I would go to Israel, but now they have become like all the rest, hard and warlike, ready to protect their interests before their love of man and God."

"You're a good man, Avrom. Maybe you'll have a two-place shine stand in heaven and a couple of apprentices."

"Seraphim to help me nail angel's souls?" answered the cobbler, eyes twinkling. But he shook his head. "The Jews have no heaven, Sheriff, only a release from hell.'' He shrugged. ''But perhaps we shall meet again, you never know.''

''I hope so.'' He held out his hand and the old man shook it warmly. ''Good-bye, Avrom.''

''Shalom, my friend.''

CHAPTER SEVENTEEN

5:30 P.M.

Choking back a scream and sitting bolt upright in the semi-darkness, Karen Slater awakened, eyes wide and staring, heart pounding wildly. Panting, the terrible dream beginning to fade, she looked around the cabin, confused and not quite sure where she was.

The log hut was small, made up of a living room/kitchen and a bedroom barely larger than a cell. Between them was a closet-sized bathroom equipped with a chemical toilet and a shower stall. Overhead, the ceiling was crisscrossed with log beams, bark still intact, and the only lighting came from a single oil lamp B.C. had lit and placed on the rough wood table in the living room area. He'd also managed to light a fire in the old wood stove in the kitchen, and the hut was now comfortably warm.

Karen threw back the old sleeping bag she'd used to cover herself on the couch and swung her feet onto the floor. She glanced out the single window set into the kitchen wall and realized that it was late afternoon. It was almost fully dark outside, the last light of day throwing a pewter sheen into the room. Removing the suits, both she and B.C. had realized just how tired they were and both of them had gone right off to sleep, Karen on the couch and B.C. in the small bedroom.

Hugging herself against the chilly draft blowing in from under the wooden door, she stood up and crossed to the kitchen. Looking out the window, she saw the stream a few yards away, and to the left she could just make out the dark shadow of the rock overhang. The cabin was set in a tiny clearing barely able to accommodate it, and the forest pressed in closely around the modest hunting lodge.

"Hansel and Gretel, lost in the forest," she whispered, staring out into the gathering dusk. She shivered, not from the cold, and hugged herself more tightly. The strange compound at the airport had been frightening, but in some ways this was even worse. The evil that had struck Jericho Falls seemed more ominous and real here in the forest, and she knew that one way or the other, her life had changed forever.

She put the palm of one hand over her sweater-covered belly, pressing gently, wondering if there was life beating there, surprised by the depth of her feeling and its focus. Slowly, she turned and crossed to B.C.'s bedroom, pausing in front of the closed door. She only hesitated for a moment, then lifted the old, black-iron latch and went into the room.

B.C. was sound asleep, huddled under the thick woolen blankets covering the white-enameled iron bedstead. His clothes were piled neatly on a plain slat-backed chair in the corner and his glasses were folded carefully on the bedside table. Karen closed the door softly behind her and went to stand beside the bed, looking down at her friend in the ghostly light.

Without his glasses, he seemed even younger than he was, his tousled hair dark against the pillow, his features relaxed and vulnerable in sleep. Karen smiled gently, amazed that this same boy had been her rescuing knight. Again, she put her hand on her belly, and then, as though in a trance, she began to undress, stripping off the heavy sweater and slipping out of her jeans.

Pulling back one corner of the blanket, she lay down beside him. From the way his body tensed, she knew he was awake and had been ever since she entered the room.

"Hi," she whispered. He rolled over in the darkness, and she felt his bare hip touching hers.

"Hi," he answered, his voice nervous. They lay side by side, listening to the creaking of the beams over their heads until Karen thought she would scream if it went on much longer.

"Aren't you going to touch me?" she asked.

"Do you want me to?"

"Of course I want you to," she said angrily. "Why do you think I took off my clothes and got into bed with you?"

"I thought maybe you might have been cold," he answered.

"They say another person's body heat is the best way to warm up."

"I didn't come here for a first-aid lesson."

"Sorry." Another long moment passed, and Karen knew that if something didn't happen soon it was going to turn messy. She rolled onto her side and slid one hand under the covers until it touched his bare stomach. He shivered, and she felt the muscles of his belly move spasmodically.

"What's the matter?" she whispered.

"Cold," he muttered. He was staring up at the ceiling, his face no more than six inches from hers, and Karen could see his features twisting with anxiety. "I'm—" he began, and then stopped. She began moving her hand in slow, small circles on his stomach, and a few inches away she could sense the first twitching movements of his arousal. "The books all say that—"

"Forget about the books," Karen said. She took a deep breath and slid her hand down over the small wiry patch of hair. She gripped him, surprised by the clearly adult size of his erection.

"Well," B.C. muttered through clenched teeth, trying to make a joke of it. "So you found the old cocktail-weenie at last. My secret is out."

"Shut up," Karen hissed angrily. "You're going to ruin it." Squeezing hard, she brought her mouth down onto his and kissed him, her tongue flicking in between his lips. At first, his response was tentative, but she refused to give in to his fears. Letting his organ go for the moment, she found his hand and placed it firmly on her breast. It had never entered her mind that making love to a boy could be so difficult.

"Look," B.C. said, breaking away from her kiss. "I've never really—"

"I don't care!" she said furiously. "It doesn't matter now! I just want you, okay? I want you really badly!"

Somewhere deep inside him, B.C.'s wall of anxiety collapsed, and suddenly he was with her, matching every motion with one of his own. They seemed to flow together perfectly, and the only hesitation came as he finally entered her. She groaned, and he pulled back, but she shook her head wildly against the pillow, her hands clenching at the base of his spine, pulling him deeper in. For the first time in her young life, she actually wanted a boy to be inside her, and she wasn't about to let him go now.

''Take me away,'' she whispered as he began to move. ''Take me away.'' B.C. didn't know what she meant and didn't care; he was lost in a sea of sensation beyond any expectation and unlike any fantasy he'd ever had. Pleasures joined, they made love like rough young animals, and for a little while, at least, the fear and the darkness were forgotten.

Jack Slater and Jennifer Hale walked along the deserted corridor of the Medical Center, making their way to Rembrandt Payne's office. Jenny had tried to call the Center half a dozen times from the school, but the ringing telephone was never answered.

''I called a dozen times,'' Jenny said, her hand gripping Slater's tightly. ''No one answers.''

''The place is deserted,'' Slater said, peering into each room as they passed. There had been no receptionist on duty at the emergency entrance, and except for a few sleeping patients in the rooms, it looked as though the Center had been abandoned.

''Rembrandt wouldn't have left these people alone,'' Jenny said. ''The other doctors might have skipped out, but he would have stayed.''

''Unless he had a good reason,'' Slater said. They reached Payne's office and he tried the door. It opened and they walked in. Like the rest of the Medical Center, the office was empty, lit only by the pale glow of the doctor's computer terminal.

''Where is he?'' Jenny said anxiously. Slater shrugged and sat down in front of the terminal. On the screen was a list of patients currently admitted to the Center. There were less than a dozen names.

''Hardly anyone here,'' commented the sheriff, scrolling through the names. ''He's got a flag on Bodo Bimm for some reason.'' Jenny came and stood behind him, looking down at the screen. She reached down and tapped out the code sequence beside the retarded man's name. The screen cleared and then began to fill with information.

''It says that Bodo left the Center without checking out and that he might have some kind of natural immunity,'' Jenny said, quickly scanning the information. ''According to this, his blood tests showed no signs of the organism. And look.'' She pointed.

"He still had a couple of tests he wanted to do. Maybe that's why he left the terminal on."

"The lab?" Slater suggested.

"Worth a try."

Leaving the terminal with the information on Bodo still on the screen, they left the office and made their way down to the labs on the main floor, their footsteps ringing eerily along the empty corridors. The labs were vacant, but it was obvious that Payne had recently been in the Histology department. His old twisted briar stood cold in an ashtray, and a large portable blackboard was filled with his neat, schoolteacherish writing. It looked as though he'd been trying to link Bodo Bimm's apparent immunity with the spread of the organism, but some of the words were obscured by a single scrawled name that slanted across the blackboard: LUTHER.

"What the hell does all this mean?" Slater muttered.

"Dr. Payne identified several immune groups," Jenny answered, reading off the blackboard. "Pregnant women, diabetics, people with low levels of male or female sex hormones, and Bodo, who didn't fit any of the categories. And there's Karen's name." She flushed. "He's got it circled with an arrow going back to Pregnancy, and a question mark."

"Karen is pregnant?" Slater said, stunned.

"She's fifteen, physically developed, and presumably menstrual," Jenny said quietly." She's right in the middle of the organism's target range, but she never got the flu or any of the early symptoms. Dr. Payne jumped to the obvious conclusion. She's not diabetic like you, so she must be pregnant."

"That's crazy, she's just a kid!"

"Kids get pregnant, Jack. It's possible." She paused, looking at Slater strangely. "It makes a lot of sense, really. I didn't get sick, either."

"What's that supposed to mean?"

"I've already missed one period, Jack, and the second is a week overdue."

"You're pregnant, too?"

"I didn't want to say anything. I was going to see someone I know in Manchester next week."

"An abortion?"

"I was considering the possibility."

"Jesus!" whispered Slater, dropping onto a lab stool. "My fifteen-year-old daughter gets pregnant and so does my thirty-year-old girlfriend. That's all I need! Grandfather and father at the same time. Christ!"

"If Karen and I are pregnant, it's probably saved our lives," Jenny said. "Karen was sitting across from the Doyle boy when he died. She'd probably be dead by now, or at least as sick as Billy. Me too, for that matter."

"Okay," Slater said, gathering himself together. "Let's leave that for the moment. What about Bodo?"

"According to what's on the blackboard, it really does look like Bodo has some kind of natural immunity. If that's true, then there's a possibility of a serum."

"So we have to find Bodo. Jesus! One more thing."

"He could save lives, Jack."

"And cost them, too," Slater said, looking at the blackboard. "If Bodo's blood or whatever can be used to make a serum, our Colonel Wright would kill to get his hands on the poor guy. Damn! Where is Doc Payne?"

"At a guess I'd say he went to find Luther Coyle for some reason," Jenny answered, gesturing to the blackboard. The sheriff looked at his watch.

"It's already six. Getting dark. We're going to have to make it fast, Jen. Wright's going to make his move any time and I don't want to be stuck in a snowbank somewhere when it happens."

Driving the wide-track four-by-four they'd appropriated from the school parking lot, the sheriff and Jenny Hale crept away from the Medical Center and bludgeoned their way through the drifted snow up to Pineglade Drive and Luther Coyle's ostentatious home.

"No sign of the Meat Wagon," Slater said, climbing down out of the truck. He hitched up the collar of his jacket and walked up the drive to the front door of the house.

"Maybe he walked," Jenny offered as Slater banged the knocker. They waited for a long minute, shivering in the cold; then Slater knocked again. He turned away from the door and glanced at the lowering sky. The overcast had turned to dark steel as the last light faded and the snowfall began to slow down. The wind was still gusting brutally, though, and that might be enough to keep Wright's choppers grounded, at least for the time being.

He turned back to the door and tried the knob. Surprisingly, the door swung open. They stepped inside and closed the door behind them.

"Coyle?" shouted Slater. No answer. He and Jennifer stood in the big foyer, listening. Nothing; the house was silent. "Luther!" Slater yelled. Still nothing.

"Maybe he's sick," Jenny suggested. "He fits into Doc Payne's target group, doesn't he?"

"He should," Slater said, frowning. "He's only fifty-five or so. He looked okay at the meeting, though, and if he was really sick, you'd think he would have booked into the Center."

"There's a light on over there," Jenny said, nodding toward an open doorway to the left. They crossed the floor to the library entrance and looked in.

"My God!" Slater whispered. Beside him, the blood drained from Jenny's face. Rembrandt Payne sat bolt upright in a large armchair on the nearer side of a large partner's desk. His head lolled to one side and even from ten feet away Jack could make out the dark stain covering the left side of the old man's head, turning his snow white hair a rusty brown. There was another, even larger stain spreading like a blossoming rose across the doctor's shirt front. There was no sign of Luther. Stunned and horrified, the sheriff took a step forward. At that moment, without warning, the lights went out and Jenny screamed.

Nothing moved in Jericho Falls, and no light shone. The last gray bar of the hidden sun starkly outlined the sleeping hills and cast a faint silver glow over the town, trees and rooftops capped with ghostly shrouds of snow, the dark line of the winding river cutting through the small valley like a wound. The snow had ceased to fall. Overhead, the cutting winds whirling down from the sea of mountains to the north had torn the overcast to shredded rags, revealing the black night sky and a scattering of stars.

At 5:30 P.M., a ten-man squad from the base at the Jericho Falls Muncipal Airport had moved out in a small tracked vehicle, and just after 6:00 P.M., they reached the New Hampshire Light and Power transformer box at the head of the valley, just off Highway 115A. Although they could easily have destroyed the transformer, they spent almost forty-five minutes working in the small, cinderblock building, recoupling circuits until the main bus overloaded at 6:18. The transformer short-circuited and all electrical current running into Jericho Falls was cut off. This included the trickle current line running to the automatic switchboard of the New Hampshire Telephone Company, shutting off all local telephone connections in the town. Although the Jericho Falls Medical Center had its own emergency generator, there was no one at the facility who knew how to bring it on line, so power was cut off there as well. Three patients in the Intensive Care Unit, all of whom were connected to respirators, died within six or seven minutes of the blackout. The other patients in the hospital, all too ill to move, were suddenly cast into darkness and lay in their beds unattended.

Sitting patiently in the office of the Slumber-King Motel, Bodo Bimm was completely unaware of the sudden loss of power in the town. He'd been sitting with the lights off for several hours, ever since he'd found what was left of Mr. Beavis in his bedroom behind the office. Mr. Beavis had been lying on his bed, wearing his dressing gown, his face and his chest covered with strawberry jam. It looked like jam, and Bodo forced himself not to think that it was anything else. Mr. Beavis had been eating jam in bed. Right out of the jar, because there wasn't any bread or crackers anywhere. And eating the jam had killed him. Bodo sat in the darkness and tore open another bag of potato chips from the display stand on the counter. Bacon Hickory flavor, his favorite. He didn't think Mr. Beavis would have minded.

It was so wonderful, seeing the snow. Bodo loved the first snowfall of the winter. It was clean and crisp, like nice sheets on his bed. Clean as an angel's wing. Now, who had said that to him? It was so long ago he'd forgotten completely, but that was okay, as long as he remembered the angel's wings, the sound of the woman's voice saying the words, and the starched smell of her. Somebody nice from his past.

He stood up and went to the window that looked out onto the highway. A long time ago a lot of men had come, pulling cars out into the road. They were gone now, and the cars were covered in snow, like little hills. Bodo shook his head. He'd tried to think of a reason why they'd want to do something like that, but he couldn't think of anything. But he knew there was going to be trouble, because with those cars there, no traffic would be able to go down the road once the plows came. He smiled. The plows were big though, they'd shove those cars right out of the way! He liked the plows, and that was another reason he looked forward to the first snowfall.

Clean as an angel's wing. Now, that would be something. Having wings, flying up out of the town and looking down. He crammed another handful of potato chips into his mouth, looking up at the sky. He knew you didn't have to be smart to learn how to fly. He'd once heard Mr. Beavis say that pigeons were "the stupidestfuckingcreatures" on God's earth. Maybe he was right, but they could fly. They could soar up as high as they wanted and leave everything else behind, getting smaller and smaller the higher up they went. Bodo smiled at the thought and imagined himself like that, soaring, soaring. He ate some more potato chips and stared happily out at the night.

CHAPTER EIGHTEEN

7:30 P.M.

The withdrawal of the town's electrical power signaled the end of Colonel Wright's siege, and Jack Slater knew it. There was nothing more they could do for Rembrandt Payne, so he and Jennifer Hale left the old man where he was and headed back into town as quickly as they could. Although it was less than two miles from Luther Coyle's house on the Hill to Constitution Common, it took the sheriff almost half an hour to bull the four-wheel-drive jeep through the drifting snow, and by the time they reached Stark Hall, Sparrow Hawke had restored some kind of order to the frightened group of volunteers.

The husky, long-haired man met them in the council chamber, his drawn, tired features lit by half a dozen oil lamps taken from Gaudet's Hardware. He had one of Slater's police walkie-talkies in his hand and on the conference table in front of him was a littered array of weapons, including the stripped-down .50 calibre machine gun from the helicopter.

"Any movement?" Slater asked.

"Not so far," Sparrow said, shaking his head. "I've spent the last half hour or so getting these radios out to as many of the people on point as I could."

"They work?" Slater asked, surprised.

"Yeah. I figured they might. Those bastards out there will have to keep in radio contact once they start to move, so they had to quit jamming all the frequencies. As far as I can tell CB is open, but there's still nothing but hiss all through the shortwave bands. No long-range communications.'' He put the receiver down on the table. ''Where have you folks been?''

''The Medical Center. And Luther's place,'' he added, anger still in his voice. ''Somebody killed Doc Payne.'' Sparrow's eyes widened for a moment.

''Luther?''

''I don't know.'' The sheriff shrugged. ''There was no sign of him at the house. It's a good bet.''

''Any idea why?''

''No, and I can't take the time to think about it.''

''I should be at the school,'' Jenny said. Sparrow pulled a small Radio Shack CB handset out of a box beside the table and tossed it to her.

''Keep in touch with this,'' he said. ''Channel 9.''

''Get as many of the vehicles loaded as you can,'' Slater said. ''Food and warm clothing. When you get the word, start moving people out. Kids and women in the first vehicles. Head up Sherbourne to North Road and wait on the town side of Creek Bridge. You'll be high enough up to see what's going on in town and you'll have the radio. If it starts to look really bad, take the Creek Road into the mountains. We'll rendezvous at the old ski lodge.''

''All right,'' she said, slipping the radio into the pocket of her ski jacket. She put her arms around Slater, hugging him, then kissed him softly on the cheek. ''Good luck,'' she whispered. She turned away quickly, trying to keep the tears back, and walked quickly out of the room. Slater watched her go, knowing in his heart that he'd probably never see her again.

''It's going to be bad,'' Sparrow said, seated at the table. ''No more parlays with the colonel. This is the real thing.''

''I know. We've just got to keep them at bay as long as possible. Until morning at least. Give Jenny time to get as many people out as she can.''

''Then what?'' Sparrow asked.

''I'm not sure,'' said Slater, his voice weary. ''They'll have all the main roads blocked, but maybe we can send somebody out along the old railway tracks tonight. Quincy is about sixteen miles away. Maybe we can get word out.''

''They'd freeze to death in weather like this. And who's to say that Colonel Wright doesn't have the tracks covered? It would be suicide.''

"Got any better ideas?" asked Slater. Sparrow shook his head. "No, I guess not."

"Fine," the sheriff answered coldly. "Then let's get on with it."

Bodo Bimm sat behind the counter in the office of the Slumber-King Motel, the front of his worn old sweater covered with potato chip crumbs. His Silver Surfer comic was spread out in front of him, lit by a single flickering candle. He was proud of the candle. When he had found it too dark to read, he'd summoned up enough courage to go back through the office and into Mr. Beavis's living quarters. He'd found the candle in the kitchen along with a book of matches. Everyone had always told him not to play with matches, but that was stupid, because he knew exactly what to do. He was a fuckin-re-tard maybe, but he wasn't that dumb!

He flipped through the pages of the tattered comic once again, still trying to fathom the meaning of the story. But nothing had changed. The pictures were confusing, and he still didn't know what it was all about. He turned to the last page of the comic. It showed the surfer on his board, soaring high above a range of jagged mountains. Bodo shook his head, amazed at the artist who could have painted such a picture. It really looked like the surfer and his board were going to fly right out of the page, and the zipping white lines behind him really did make you feel as though the board were going fast. Bodo looked up from the comic and stared out the big front window, wondering if there really was a man out there, dressed in a silver suit, able to do what the man in the comic could.

Bodo froze and forgot about the surfer, his heart jumping in his chest. He made a little mewling cry. Something was out there in the snowy darkness. Something moving. He'd seen its shadow, like one of the monsters in the comic, come to hurt him like the one in the red cape had, the one who'd made the pretty girl cry and who looked like pictures of the devil he'd seen . . . where? It didn't matter.

He ducked down behind the counter and huddled there, waiting, the candle flickering on the counter over his head. He closed his eyes and tried to think about something else, something to make the red shadow go away, but all that came was the screaming, gloating devil in the comic. He heard a tinkling sound, barely louder than the rattling wind outside. Breaking glass. His eyes snapped open, and his mouth went dry. He stared into the shadows under the counter, blind with fear, and there it was, resting on two padded hooks: Mr. Beavis's "pride-an'-joy."

The object slung under the counter was a brand-new Daewoo USAS 12-gauge full-auto shotgun. The motel owner had seen an article about the weapon in one of the gung-ho–style magazines Gaudet's carried in its sporting goods department and he'd ordered it by mail. The shotgun looked like the standard Armalite rifle used in Vietnam, but it sported a much heavier barrel and used a 28-round drum-fed magazine.

Bodo had been working at the Gas Bar when the special-delivery package arrived, and he'd listened carefully as Mr. Beavis gloatingly went over its features to Corky White. It had two settings, safety and full-auto, with a second safety behind the trigger. It was Ralph Beavis's intention to keep the weapon, fully loaded, hidden behind the counter in the motel.

A few days later, after buying several boxes of number 4 ammunition, he'd given a demonstration to Corky and a few of the boys, including Bodo. Using the rusted remains of an old Packard out back as a target, he'd put the shotgun on full-auto and squeezed the trigger, unleashing a hail of pellets and a rooster tail of expended shell casings. The barrel of the gun was on full choke and at thirty-four pellets per load, the Packard was instantly peppered with ragged-edge holes the size of dinner plates.

"Just right to scare the living shit out of some bastard who bitches about his bill," as the Slumber-King and Gas Bar owner put it at the time.

Bodo carefully took the heavy weapon down from its pegs. He looked at the side of the shotgun and gently pushed the little bar above the trigger so that the red mark showed. Remembering the comic, and then remembering the horrible headless nightmare he'd seen in the Gas Bar, he reared up from behind the counter, the shotgun tucked into his shoulder, his teeth bared.

"*Ka-boom! Ka-boom!*" he crowed, and then, almost accidentally, his finger squeezed the trigger and the shotgun went off with a thundering roar. The silver-suited member of Colonel Wright's primary infiltration squad never knew what hit him. The pellets from the Daewoo took him high in the chest, half of them soaking into the body armor, but the other half cutting through the vulnerable throat closures below the chin of the helmet.

Standing less than six feet away, the man didn't have a chance. The left side of his throat was blown completely away, and only the nylon grommets of his headpiece kept his head united with the rest of his body. The impact of the shell spun him around and he slammed into the window that looked out onto the highway. The man's arms came up to his throat and then he sagged, leaving a long, dripping brushstroke of red against the glass.

Not quite sure what had happened, Bodo stared at the crumpled silver figure on the floor, then down at the comic book, still open on the counter. He shook his head, realizing that someone like the surfer couldn't have been killed that easily. Frowning, Bodo aimed the Daewoo at the plate-glass window and the uneven strip of blood. He squeezed the trigger, felt the stock of the gun strike his shoulder, and then the glass exploded, a million jagged shards exploding out into the snowy night.

Bodo flipped back the counter hatch and crossed to the body. It really was dead, and this wasn't a dream. Mr. Beavis's little pride-an'-joy had really done the job. Too bad Mr. Beavis couldn't have seen it. Smiling, Bodo went back to the counter and picked up his Silver Surfer comic. He rolled it tightly, shoved it into the back pocket of his coveralls and turned away, slinging the Daewoo over his shoulder, not noticing as the stock of the weapon brushed the candle, knocking it over.

A little confused, but happier perhaps than he'd ever been in his life, Bodo stepped out through the exploded remains of the window. Ignoring the cold wind, he began slogging through the drifting snow that covered the motel parking lot, and then headed west along the Strip.

"Ka-boom! Ka-boom!" he whispered happily to himself, while behind him, the Slumber-King Motel began to burn.

Karen Slater and Bentley Carver Bingham worked their way slowly up the narrow trail that ran beside Overflow Creek and led to the summit of Quarry Hill. It was a difficult climb, but B.C. had chosen it rather than take the longer route along the tracks and around the base of the hill to Old River Road.

Taking the upland trail would cut their distance in half, and B.C. was reasonably sure that there would be some kind of guard detail posted on the highway. Before leaving the cabin, they had armed themselves with a couple of plinking .22s B.C.'s father had left behind at the end of the hunting season, but the light-weight, bolt-action guns were no match for the laser-guided weaponry used by the men at the airfield.

B.C. had also decided to dispense with the helmets for the rest of the journey, even though the weather outside the cabin was bitingly cold. Instead, both of them wore old woolen tuques and long knitted scarves B.C. had found in a box in the kitchen.

Using the radios could very well alert any of the opposition close enough to hear, and it was cumbersome to go through the helmet-to-helmet ritual every time they wanted to talk. At Karen's suggestion, they hadn't left the headgear behind, however, and she'd insisted that they be hooked onto the backpacks; if they did manage to get back to the Falls, she knew her father would be able to make use of the captured suits and the helmet controls.

Squinting against the chill wind, Karen kept her eyes fixed on the back of B.C.'s suit a few yards ahead, pulling herself up the snow-covered trail by grabbing on to the branches of small trees and bushes, fumbling the rifle from hand to hand as she struggled steadily upward. In half an hour of climbing, B.C. hadn't stopped to rest once and she found it hard to believe that the suited figure ahead of her was the same boy who hadn't even been able to rate as a second-string outfielder on the Earl A. Coolis baseball team.

She smiled weakly, breath coming in short, painful gasps as she tried to place her boots in B.C.'s footsteps. Maybe it wasn't so surprising after all: two hours ago he'd proven himself more a man than Billy or any of his letter-sweater friends, and she could still feel the warm glow of satisfaction deep in her belly. Billy might have taken her virginity, but B.C. had made love with her, and she understood that knowing the difference between the two had changed her life forever.

Grimacing, the young woman shook her head. What good was it having your life changed if you could count the rest of that life in terms of hours? B.C. was putting up a bold front, but she knew their chances were slim. Nightmarish or not, the events of the past few days were real and not the pulse-pounding fantasies of a Hollywood director.

In September, just after the beginning of school, Miss Hale had given their class a choice of essay topics and Karen had chosen one relating to the Vietnam War, knowing that her father was a veteran. He'd put her off a dozen times, obviously not wanting to talk about it, until he finally told her one story, about his first day in the war-torn country and his arrival at Bien-hoa Airbase, headquarters of the 90th Replacement Detachment.

"We came in like tourists, in a charter DC-10," he'd said, his voice soft and distant. "It was all like a big game. Nobody really thought about the meaning of the name 'Replacement.' We found out about five minutes after we landed, because it was our bad luck to arrive just as a shipment was coming in from the Qui Nhon medical facility up north. Body bags. Dozens of them, dull black rubber. Dead bodies, that's what we were replacing. Dead bodies replaced with live bodies.

"And the worst of it was the boots. Boots were expensive so they were recycled. All the dead men's boots were lined up on the runway, a long line of empty boots stretching off into the distance, arranged by size. You could almost see the dead men standing in them, like ghosts. So we knew it wasn't a game. We knew it was real. I kept on seeing the boots and wondering if that's how I'd end up, an empty pair of dirty boots on the runway at Bien-hoa. I still dream about it."

She'd never mentioned the war to him again, and he'd never offered, but she knew why he still wore the boots and the leather jacket, and she didn't bother him about how old and worn-out they looked. As long as his feet were in the boots, he was alive.

"Hang on, B.C.," she called out, leaning against a tree, panting for breath. "I've got to rest." He stopped on the trail and turned back to her, his face half-covered by the winding scarf, the hat pulled ridiculously low around his ears. She giggled, realizing that she looked just as silly.

"What's so funny?" he asked, hunching down out of the wind beside her, his knees in the snow.

"Us," she said, sucking in the cold crisp air. "We look like a couple of Snow White's elves."

"Dwarves," corrected B.C. "I'm short enough to qualify, you look more like a high-tech troll."

"Thanks a lot."

"Two minutes," he said. "We're almost at the top. We'll be able to see the town."

"Just let me catch my breath."

"Sure."

They crouched silently in the snow, rifles stocks for crutches, breath puffing up into the night air as the wind moaned coldly through the trees.

"Are we going to make it?" Karen asked after a moment. B.C. shrugged his shoulders. His optimism was gone; he was too tired and they'd been through too much for false hopes.

"I don't know. Maybe. Depends on how badly they want us."

"I'm sorry," she said softly.

"For what?" he asked.

"For being stupid, for not getting to know you better. Sooner. Back there in the cabin . . ."

"Forget it," said the boy, embarrassed.

"I don't want to," she insisted. "There might not be time later. I just wanted to tell you how much it meant to me, Bentley. How much it still means. You've been pretty wonderful."

"Aw, shucks," he said, trying to make a joke of it. "T'weren't nothin'."

"I'm serious." She frowned. "I just wanted you to know . . . I just wanted . . . oh shit!"

"I understand," he said. He leaned over, cold lips barely touching hers. "It was the nicest thing that ever happened to me, Karen. I mean it. I guess I've had a thing for you for a long time, but I never thought—"

"Oh, shut up," said Karen, hot tears welling up in her eyes. "Let's get going before we freeze to death."

It took five minutes to reach the top of Quarry Hill and another ten to cut through the trees along the upper ridge. They stopped again, standing at the top of the long trail that wound down through the trees, coming out eventually at Mill Road on the south bank of the river.

"Oh God!" whispered Karen, looking out over the valley. Below them, Jericho Falls stood in the darkness like a child's toy. The streets were dark, the town lit only by the stars and a splintered moon that shifted through the ragged clouds overhead. Far away, along the Strip, the Slumber-King Motel was an inferno, flames fanned by the wind, sheets of fire and spinning cinders dropping down onto the Gas Bar next door and the buildings on the other side of the road. As they watched, the flames took hold at the Gas Bar and a huge gout of flame reared up into the black sky as the pumps and the storage tanks beneath them detonated. A few seconds later the sound of the explosion reached them and then was torn away by the wind.

"Oh, Jeez, Karen, look!" said B.C., anguish and horror in his voice. A licking wave of flame had spread out from the Gas Bar, torching the trees behind it, a torrent of seething red and orange that touched the autumn forest of the Drake's Farm woodlot, sparking a holocaust that both children knew would be almost impossible to stop. Beyond the fire, at the intersection of the highway and Airport Road, they could see vehicles moving, and here and there, like lancing spears of ruby light, the tracing lines of laser-targeting beams.

The fighting had begun.

CHAPTER NINETEEN

8:05 P.M.

The Storm Warning Contingency Plan, put in place by Executive Order during the presidency of Richard Milhous Nixon and quietly reapproved by each succeeding president of the United States, was designed to deal with any problems arising from the Nixon Administration's decision to continue to manufacture and stockpile chemical and biological warfare matériel as well as to continue to fund research in those areas. This was in direct contravention of the Tripartite accord between the United States, Canada, and the United Kingdom, as well as being directly in opposition to Nixon's own 1971 ban.

The people who devised the original plan, all upper echelon members of the Defense Intelligence Agency working with a small group from the United States Army Chemical Corps, realized that an accident involving chemical or biological warfare matériel within the confines of the continental United States would be a disaster, both in human and public-relations terms.

During World War II, a number of internment camps were established throughout the United States, built to house Japanese and Nazi dissidents, and at the end of the war several of those camps were kept in service, their facilities maintained over the years under a hidden budget within the annual Armed Forces Appropriations Bill. In 1971, six of the remaining nine camps were taken over by the innocently named Army Medical Coordinator's Office, headquartered at the Rock Island Arsenal in Rock Island, Illinois, and referred to as Army Medical Coordination Command: AMCCOM.

All six of the camps were staffed by a combination of Ranger units and specialists from the U.S. Army Chemical Corps, and all six camps were in constant contact with USACC centers such as Ft. Detrick Maryland, Rocky Mountain Arsenal in Colorado, and other bases in Alabama, Kentucky, and Oregon. Through the services of the Defense Intelligence Agency, a communications network was established, allowing the AMCCOM group to monitor the movement of CBW matériel on a minute-to-minute basis.

From the beginning, the senior officers of AMCCOM, operating almost entirely outside normal channels within the army, were aware that time was their most serious consideration, especially when biologicals were involved. In the event of a biological "excursion" it was vitally important that the area of the problem be isolated within twelve hours to prevent further contamination. If local authorities were cooperative, and the biological agent in question was not lethal, cleanup operations could be carried out under the guise of unannounced war games. If the excursion was of a more serious nature, contaminated citizens would be airlifted to the six camps and isolated. In this instance the public would be told that there had been an accident involving radioactive matériel, with an appropriate minor, private-sector nuclear facility as the culprit.

With the upsurge of recombinant DNA work during the middle and late seventies, and the Chemical Corps's involvement with a number of private labs and university research facilities, it became apparent that a more all-encompassing plan was required. AMCCOM, revitalized by the Reagan Administration's desire for increased work in CBW, was assigned additional personnel, including Lt. Colonel James H. Wright, a specialist in small, mobile attack units, much of his experience gained with a number of Special Forces Hunter-Killer units in Vietnam. He was also well versed in CB handling procedures, and had been involved in the Vietnam "Operation Ranch Hand" Agent Orange trials.

Wright literally wrote the book on Storm Warning, structuring a fail-safe hierarchy with the requisite checks-and-balances systems to ease the qualms of a few squeamish members of the AMCCOM group. In fact, the Storm Warning operations manual was a handbook on how to isolate, infiltrate, and depopulate any small American community contaminated with chemical or biological agents. With the aid of sophisticated computers from DIA, Wright was also able to create a CBW transport system bypassing any major urban center, coupling it with a fast-attack plan that would place AMCCOM personnel on site within eight to twelve hours notice.

In addition, by utilizing the cold-blooded escalation procedures within the Storm Warning manual, the AMCCOM unit could be in and out of any problem area within seventy-two hours, leaving nothing behind to indicate that there had been any CBW involvement.

Between 1978 and 1985, Wright established what was virtually a private army, completely outside the control of any established American military unit. Several members of the AMCCOM group worried about the power Wright had accumulated, but there was very little they could do about it. By early 1986, there were thirty-eight private-sector defense contracts in place that involved military CB/DNA, as well as ongoing work at Ft. Detrick, the Dugway Proving Grounds, USAMRDC (U.S. Army Medical Research Defense Command), WRAIR (Walter Reed Army Institute for Research), USUHS (Uniformed Services University of the Health Sciences), and NMRI (Naval Medical Research Institute).

The combined budgets for all of these operations was in excess of two billion dollars, a figure Wright was fond of bringing up when his own relatively small budget of twenty-three million dollars per year was called into question by his superiors.

Beyond that, Wright's revised Storm Warning Plan had proven itself. In his eight years with AMCCOM there had been a total of thirty-three excursions dealt with by Wright and his people, all of them brought to a satisfactory conclusion.

Twenty-eight of these occurred outside of any population center or on military reservations, which made them relatively easy to deal with, but five had involved private citizens. Of the five, three were minor, involving very small communities and nonlethal agents, which were dealt with by telling the townspeople that the accident involved PCBs spilled from large electrical transformers in transit.

Two, however, were much more serious, and as a result, the towns of South Wendel, California, population 96, and Fish Springs, Utah, population 257, had ceased to exist. The South Wendel Incident, logged on the AMCCOM files as Excursion DX/24 occurred in midsummer 1981 and was reported in the press as a freak brush fire brought on by the high temperatures and low precipitation that July.

Of the ninety-six people in the town, fifty-four were reportedly trapped by the raging fire, and the remainder were airlifted out by the Red Cross and helpful military personnel from the nearby Sierra Ordnance Depot. The townsite, thoroughly contaminated by an anthrax spill, was totally burned out. Needless to say, the forty-two survivors, supposedly relocated, were never heard from again. Several weeks after the incident, the infected land was purchased by a hitherto nonexistent branch of the U.S. Department of Agriculture and enclosed by a high, chain-link fence.

Fish Springs, AMCCOM DX/29, occurred in January of 1984. The agent involved was a carcinogenic trihalomethane compound being sent to the Dugway Proving Grounds for testing. Wright's people, posing as Department of Health inspectors, informed the townspeople that their groundwater had become irreversibly contaminated by their own inadequate waste-disposal system. They were told that if they remained in the town, they would inevitably face a much higher than average cancer rate.

Roughly a third of the population moved out of the town during the following year. Utilizing spurious National Health grants, a sophisticated filtration system was put in place for those who remained, and under the guise of installing the system, most of the trihalomethanes were cleaned up.

Since the population had been warned about rising cancer rates and since the majority of those people remaining in the small community were elderly or in late middle age, the resulting deaths over the next three years went unnoticed except by AMCCOM.

Of the eighty-five people who moved out of the town, fifty-six were dead within twenty-two months of the incident, all from cancer. Had they remained in Fish Springs, the statistics would almost certainly have caused suspicion, but the fifty-six, melded into the populations of Salt Lake City, Provo, and Ogden, barely caused a ripple in the annual fatality rate.

AMCCOM DX/35, Jericho Falls, was the largest incident Wright had ever been required to deal with, and QQ9 was by far the most lethal agent. Wright was a soldier, not a scientist, but he knew that QQ9 had to be contained at all costs. His superiors had given him carte blanche without hesitation.

Out of curiosity, he'd run Redenbacher and his cargo through the computer while his group assembled, noting that it was slotted for the P4 lab facility at Detrick. The lab was the only one of its kind in the United States, ultrasecure both physically and militarily, reserved for the most virulent organisms known to man. QQ9 was obviously a killer.

Wright wasn't particularly impressed. For years, he'd predicted a major incident, one of sufficient importance to justify Storm Warning. Now it was here and he couldn't have been more pleased. Nine hours later, the first of his six-hundred-man force arrived at Jericho Falls and began setting up shop. Wright was certain that within another sixty-three hours the problem would be solved, one way or another.

By the time B.C. and Karen escaped from the airport compound, followed quickly by Jack Slater and Sparrow Hawke's embarrassing incursion, Wright had decided that further interaction with the local authorities of Jericho Falls would be fruitless. In fact, he'd learned this at an early stage, but protocol required that he follow his own manual, and if the bureaucratic types he worked for insisted that he follow the rules, then so be it.

Both the escape of the children and the sheriff's hijacking of the helicopter were anomalous and unexpected, but by the same token they were also indicative of a breakdown in the sociological integrity of the town. Wright was no great believer in that kind of hundred-dollars-an-hour thinking, but he had to admit the psychological profiles worked up as computer models by DIA had been remarkably accurate over the years.

According to those models and specific stress-evaluation studies, Wright knew that the majority of people in Jericho Falls had by now moved into what the psych boys called Catastrophe Response Ennui. Cut off from the outside world and frightened by an unseen enemy, the general population had regressed to a state of paranoid lethargy, not too different from Neanderthal families crouched around a fire, terrified by the night sounds around them. By cutting off the town's electricity, Wright had effectively removed the fire.

According to the psychological models, this was a strategically important moment. Frightened, the population would be at its most manageable and, given any show of direct authority, would act like sheep. Wait too long, though, and panic would take hold.

Cross-matching computer input from the satellite link that gave them access to DIA and other government databases, Wright's on-site analysts had given him a breakdown of what to expect. According to their information, there was a total of 3,997 people resident in Jericho Falls. Of these, 1,846 fell into the QQ9 target parameters and would be dead within 100 hours of initial infection. Another 680 residents were in a gray range on either side of the main group, leaving 1,471 residents who would be physically unaffected by the agent, but who would still be infectious to anyone within the target group. Of those 1,471, 782 were under the age of eleven, while the remaining 689 were between 69 and 89 years of age.

Sequestered within those statistics was a small group of immune anomalies, which included eighteen known pregnancies and a few diabetics. Unfortunately, one of these was Jack Slater, the town sheriff. Aided by Luther Coyle, whose air transport company had been used as an AMCCOM courier, Wright's on-site people had been able to monitor computer use at the Jericho Falls Medical Center through the local telephone lines, and Wright had been presented with an odd fact, which he'd relayed to both Ft. Detrick and AMCCOM headquarters in Rock Island.

According to the Medical Center computer, a resident of Jericho Falls with the unlikely name of Bodo Bimm appeared to be naturally immune to QQ9. Detrick and Rock Island responded instantly: whatever else he did, Wright was under strict orders to bring Bimm in alive and kicking. Wright could see that a naturally immune wild card like this Bimm character could be useful to his superiors, but he wondered if they knew how difficult it was going to be cutting one person out of the herd.

According to the manual, Wright's task force had a little less than twenty hours more to clean out the town, stage the appropriate catastrophe cover and disappear. The sudden change in weather and Slater's pigheadedness had already lost him time, and finding Bimm was going to make things just that much more complex.

When the lights went out at 6:18, Wright's first attack group was already in motion. Denied the use of helicopters by the high winds and low visibility, he decided on a straightforward movement up Airport Road, using four personnel carriers to deploy six squads around the intersection of 115A and Woodbank Avenue, locally referred to as the Strip. Outlying surveillance posts had reported activity along Woodbank earlier in the day, including a makeshift barricade of abandoned vehicles, but Wright proceeded anyway.

Instead of striking down Woodbank to the center of the town, the squads had been ordered to work their way through the outlying areas before swinging east. Prior to moving out the personnel carriers, an additional group of ten sharpshooters was sent out on foot through the Drake's Farm woodlot to strike along Woodbank and then up North Beacon Street to Constitution Common.

All were experienced rangers, and three of them were graduates of the Army Snow School maintained by the 172nd Mountain Infantry Division in Vermont. Their immediate objective was to infiltrate the area around the Common, find sniping points, and lay down harassing fire against whatever opposition Slater intended to mount.

Playing it strictly by the book, Wright projected a two-and-a-half-hour time lapse from first deployment at 7:10, and according to his updated weather information, both snow and wind would drop off substantially by 9:30. At that time, with his airborne armor on-line once again, he would open a second offensive, airlifting the bulk of his combat troops to a location just south of the old mill, dividing them between the two bridges over the city and using gunships to lay down covering file as they crossed into the town. Long-range surveillance from the outpost on Quarry Hill had already reported movement, which probably meant the two escapees. They would either reach the town and be corralled there, or they'd be swept up in the first advances of his men. Either way, they no longer represented a problem.

As the main attack group crossed the bridges, the original six squads on the west side of the town would swing east, backed up by the remaining motorized fast-attack armor at the airport, and that would be that.

A neat pincer movement that would have Jericho Falls tied up with a ribbon and a bow well before midnight. The cover had been chosen long before and was already under way. By dawn it would be in place and by late Monday evening the first film of the terrible tragedy in Jericho Falls would be aired on network news; a minor disaster to cover up a major error, a small sacrifice to forestall a monumental catastrophe. According to Lt. Colonel

James Wright, according to his manual, and according to AMCCOM, that represented a perfectly balanced equation.

However, as any mathematician knows, an equation that works in theory does not necessarily work in practice, especially when there are unknown factors involved. At 8:20 P.M., with the snow stopped completely and the wind dying down, the first of those unknown factors came into play as B.C. Bingham and Karen Slater crossed the old spur-line tracks at the foot of Quarry Hill and headed for home.

PART FOUR

HEAVEN'S BREATH
Sunday Night,
November 2

In the event that the cooperation of local authorities cannot be obtained, the Unit Commander, after consultation with AMCCOM Headquarters, may escalate from KHAMSIN/SPRING RAIN to HEAVEN'S BREATH status. When HEAVEN'S BREATH has been invoked, it should be noted that all sub-unit commanders must see to it that their squads are equipped with a proper supply of degradable, standard-issue body markers. All achieved targets must be marked and at the completion of the operation all remaining markers must be counted. Variance in markers used, ruined markers, and accidentally destroyed markers must be reported immediately to the Unit Command Center. Be advised that there can be no stand-down from HEAVEN'S BREATH until all markers have been accounted for and until the number of markers deployed equals the total achieved target figures.

—Lt. Col. James H. Wright
Commander, Special Unit 7
AMCCOM
Rock Island Arsenal
Rock Island, Illinois
Section 4, Number 1, Page 157
BM-31-210

CHAPTER TWENTY

8:35 P.M.

Barry LaGrace, owner of Bear-Bear Roofing and Insulation ("Roof Need Repair? Bear-Bear Is There"), sat huddled at the front window of McKarsky's Barber Shop at the corner of Main and North Beacon, a pair of binoculars glued to his face as he scanned the empty, snow-covered span of Mill Bridge. Leaning against the wall was his old M1 carbine and on the windowsill there was an open box of .30 shells and a Radio Shack walkie-talkie.

On his lap was an old-fashioned twist-handle detonator, trailing copper wires leading down to the floor and out under the door. Behind him, dozing in one of McKarsky's three red-leather-and-chrome barber chairs was Hugh Bates, the semiretired projectionist/owner of the Murray Theater.

Bates, soft-spoken, bald, and given to wearing bow ties, was the opposite of LaGrace. The roofer was built like a turtle, wore a beard that made him look even more French than he actually was, and had a voice like a runaway chain saw. Normally, the two men wouldn't have had very much to do with each other, except perhaps for business reasons, but tonight they were tied together by an intimate bond of fear and anger.

Both men were well into their sixties and outside the QQ9 target zone, but both had lost people to the deadly agent. LaGrace had spent a frantic twenty-four hours with his son, daughter-in-law, and two grandchildren, watching as they died before his eyes. At first, it had seemed like an ordinary flu, but then their temperatures had begun to rise, the two teenage children spiking at 106, his son and daughter-in-law's climbing even higher.

Shortly after dawn, the children began to cough blood, and an hour later, they were dead. By noon their parents had followed suit.

Stunned, the burly, broad-shouldered man had made his way to Stark Hall, where he'd been enlisted by Jack Slater. Now, sitting in the cold, dark barbershop, he had a real enemy to vent his anger on, and with a thousand memories of his family unreeling in his mind, he wanted nothing more than to twist the handle on the detonator in his lap.

Fortunately, almost all of Hugh Bates's immediate family had left the Falls years before, and his wife had been stricken by cancer almost a decade ago, but the deaths of Corky White, his nephew, and Corney Drake, a longtime friend and chess opponent, had hurt him deeply. Worse than that was the sudden feeling that his world had been turned upside down. Hugh Bates was the kind of man you could set your watch by, and for him, routine, order, and regularity were his lifeblood. Dozing in the barber chair, the unfamiliar weight of a shotgun in his lap, the mild-mannered projectionist dreamed of reels of film unraveling in his booth at the rear of the Murray, skeins of celluloid twisting like the snakes of Medusa's head, choking him.

Outside, the falling snow had faded, and the wind was dying. A sliver of moon had turned the approaches to the bridge a glowing silver, while beyond, on the far side of the river, the darkness was complete. Barry LaGrace knew that the enemy was waiting out there, and he smiled, the binoculars still up to his eyes. He gripped the detonator in his lap with his free hand and tried to imagine how it would feel.

Almost half a century ago he'd killed three men in Sicily as his company advanced, and it had made him physically ill. Frowning, the bearded man lowered the binoculars and glanced at the old carbine leaning against the wall. Same rifle. *Bang, bang, bang,* and three lives were snuffed out. It turned out that all three were teenage conscripts who'd been trying to surrender. After the war he'd taken the old rifle and hidden it away, not even looking at it until this afternoon.

The man took a deep breath and exhaled slowly, the gasping, retching deaths of his family like hot bile in his throat. This time it would be different, and he knew he'd feel nothing but exultation. When they came, he'd take out as many as he could by blowing up the bridge, and if any of them escaped, he'd blow their unholy brains out on the virgin field of snow. Digging into the pocket of his old, plaid jacket, he took out a package of cigarettes and lit one, cupping the flame of his lighter and closing his eyes to retain his night vision. He took a long drag, put away the lighter, and picked up the binoculars again.

"Son of a bitch!" he whispered.

The Mill was dark as B.C. and Karen passed, trudging through the drifted snow on the road leading to the bridge, and it was obviously deserted. Ahead of them, just across the river, they could see the night shadows of the town, silhouetted against the nighttime sky.

"Everything's so dark," Karen whispered as their boots made crunching sounds in the snow.

"Except for that," offered B.C., pointing a gloved finger to the west. A mile or so away, below the smaller bridge that led across the Third Chute shallows to Gowan Street, they could see the flickering glow of the fire that was consuming the Drake's Farm woodlot and the Strip. Sniffing, B.C. could detect a faint, sour odor of smoke. It was eerie, watching the fire burn and hearing no siren from Stark Hall, no bleating horns from the VFD pumpers. The fire was burning unchecked.

"Why is it so dark?" Karen asked as they reached the bridge.

"The people back at the airport probably cut the power." Taking her gently by the arm, he guided her onto the bridge. Fifty yards away he could see the unmoving striped pole outside McKarsky's darkened storefront and he felt a funny tug in his gut. He'd had his first haircut at McKarsky's when he was three, and his parents had a grainy old black-and-white photograph to prove it. He'd had the back and sides trimmed two weeks ago at his mother's insistence, and as they reached the center of the bridge, B.C. realized that the trim was almost certainly the last time he'd set foot in the comfortable old landmark.

The soft-nose bullet took him directly in the chest, lifting him up on his heels, then slamming him down to the ground. B.C. was dimly aware of Karen screaming close by, and then his entire being was concentrated on the terrible, white-hot pain just below his heart.

Somehow, he managed to roll over on his side, his cheek

pressed into the snow, and through tear-filled eyes he saw a second bullet impact a yard or so away, throwing up a feather of
snow before it dug its way into the asphalt surface of the bridge.
He could feel cold creeping up through his body, and he blinked.
Consciousness faded for a few seconds, and when he came to
again, Karen was beside him, her face no more than an inch or
two from his, her hands frantically working at the suit closures.

"S'okay," he murmured groggily.

"Shut up!" Karen snarled. Blinking again, trying to make his
eyes focus, B.C. realized she was crying. Looking out under the
crook of her knee, he saw two figures behind her on the bridge.
They were moving slowly, and they both carried weapons.

"Behind you," he muttered, but somehow the words didn't
seem to make any sense. He could feel Karen's warm breath on
his face and that seemed more important. He tried to move his
arm, knowing that he'd dropped his rifle, ashamed that he'd been
so stupid. Now they were both going to die.

"Christ! It's a girl!" A new voice and familiar. Who had a
voice like that, all cracked and rough? Some friend of his old
man's?

"Mr. Bates?" Karen's voice. "Oh, thank God! Help me with
him, please."

"S'not Bates," B.C. warned, consciousness fading again. Mr.
Bates at the Murray didn't have a voice like that. Not that it
mattered, because the pain in his chest was so bad now that nothing else had any meaning. He was dying, but anything was better
than the pain. "Love you," he groaned, taking a last look at
Karen, and then he let himself slip into darkness.

Jack Slater moved carefully down the narrow alley that ran
parallel to South Beacon Street, keeping to the shadows, his
gloved hands gripping the big Stoner automatic rifle from the
police armory. The alley divided the run-down frame houses on
South Beacon from the commercial buildings on the Strip, and a
hundred feet to his left he could see the glow of the fire raging
on the far side of the thoroughfare. Twice he'd spotted roving
groups of the strangely suited men from the airfield, but he'd
avoided them rather than engage in a futile firefight.

As soon as the assault began, it was obvious that their own
pitiful assortment of people wasn't going to be able to do much

more than fight a delaying action. Wright's men were better armed, better defended, and obviously had better communications, even without their air support. He'd managed to get the walkie-talkies to five of the outlying posts he and Sparrow had set up, but by the looks of things, there wasn't much point in going any further. The intersection of 115A and the Strip had already been overrun with Wright's men and with the woodlot on fire, the people he'd sent to Drake's Farm were cut off.

Slater paused and glanced at his watch. By now, Jenny would be moving the first of the school buses out to the North Road rendezvous. The two squads of suited men he'd seen had been swinging north and east, probably trying to come in on the Common from above. If Jenny delayed for any reason, she'd run right into them. The sheriff cursed under his breath and swung around, moving back the way he'd come. He'd lost Karen, and he was damned if he was also going to lose Jenny.

Reaching the end of the block, he slipped between two houses and came out onto Morin Street on the south edge of Frenchtown. Always down-at-the-heels, the neighborhood looked even worse in the cold darkness. Slater looked up and down the narrow street, eyes digging into the shadows for any hint of movement. Nothing. He reached into his jacket and took out the walkie-talkie he'd been carrying, thumbing the transmit switch and keeping his voice low.

"Base, this is Zulu, come in." He released the switch and waited. Base was the council chamber in Stark Hall, he was Zulu, and Sparrow was X-Ray. Keeping the volume down and holding the portable radio up to his ear, Slater waited. For a few seconds there was only the crackle of static and then he heard Sparrow's voice.

"Zulu, this is X-Ray."

"X-Ray, what do you see from the Nest?" Nest was the code name for the lookout in the Stark Hall tower. It wouldn't fool anyone for long, but it was better than speaking in the clear.

"The lady just moved out," came the reply, "and there's something going on at the barbershop."

Slater shook his head angrily. Jenny had been late getting out. He gritted his teeth, praying that she wouldn't run into one of the roving patrols. He tried to brush the thought out of his mind and concentrated on the other half of the message. The barbershop was LaGrace and Bates at the Mill Bridge.

"Say again the barbershop, X-Ray."

"Garbled," Sparrow answered. "A two-man squad attacking? Doesn't sound right to me."

"Me neither. I'm coming back in, X-Ray. I want you to tell everyone you can to pull back toward Brewer and North Beacon. We can't hold the whole town and the fire is out of control."

"Okay, Zulu."

Slater turned off the walkie-talkie, slipped it back into his jacket and moved off again, heading east, making for Constitution Common.

Jenny dragged at the unfamiliar weight of the big, flat wheel, grunting as she eased the long, bright yellow school bus around the turn onto Sherbourne Street. Behind her, snuggled into an assortment of blankets, quilts, and sleeping bags were fifty kids, all of them under ten years old and all of them deathly quiet. For the first time in her working life, Jenny founding herself yearning for the days when it took every ounce of her strength to get a school bus full of children not to run riot.

The other women at the school had done a good job, and the street was cleared well enough to keep the bus going in a straight line. Within the next five minutes or so, the second and third buses would be loaded, followed by a string of smaller vehicles. In all they hoped to move out almost four hundred people.

Jenny bit her lip, trying to keep back the tears. God, how had it happened? Two days ago her biggest problem was how to tell Jack she might be pregnant, and now it seemed as though the world was coming to an end. For the people of Jericho Falls, anyway. Taking a fast look into the side mirror, she could see the glowing horizon to the south.

The Strip and most of Drake's Farm, according to Bess Tilly, who'd gone up on the roof of the school to see where the fire was. She bit her lip harder, tasting blood finally, fighting the terrible urge she had to abandon her charges and go back into town. She was no heroine. She wanted the safety of Jack Slater's arms, and she wanted it now.

But she kept on driving, keeping the cumbersome vehicle in the center of the track cut into the drifted snow. The blizzard had stopped, that was one good thing at least. Or was it? Hadn't Sparrow said something about the snow and the winds keeping the helicopters on the ground?

She made a little moaning sound, deep in the back of her throat, and gripped the wheel until her knuckles whitened. Ten blocks up to North Road, then turn right under the shadow of the ridge and keep going until you hit Creek Bridge. She let the directions fill her mind, repeating them over and over like a prayer.

They struck at the corner of Sherbourne and Arbutus, barely four blocks from the school. At first Jenny thought they'd had a blowout, but then she saw the tracer lines of light spitting toward her out of the darkness. Jenny ducked instinctively and an instant later the windshield exploded, showering her with a thousand pieces of hexagonal safety glass. She dropped out of the driver's seat, rolling painfully down into the well in front of the door; out of control, the bus slewed to the right.

It continued on like some ponderous yellow beast, bumping up over the snow-covered curb, then through a low cedar hedge. It smacked into the screened porch of a large, Victorian house and finally stopped as the engine coughed and died.

All of this took less than thirty seconds, and Jenny barely had time to struggle into a sitting position, back against the doors. She'd twisted her ankle somehow, making it difficult to stand, but she forced herself up, responding to the panicked screams of the kids. Coming up the steps on all fours, she grabbed the big door-opener and pulled herself up just in time to see the rear windows of the bus explode.

One of the children, a girl, was standing directly in the line of fire, and Jenny stared, wild-eyed, watching as the child's body jerked and danced, the right arm dissolving in a cloud of blood before the lifeless body dropped to the floor. The rest of the children were clawing at the windows or crawling down the aisle, and it was obvious that some of them were hurt.

Moaning, Jenny lurched toward them, arms outstretched, feet crunching on the broken glass. There was a tooth-jarring *crump* from the back of the bus, and then Jenny found herself being pushed back as though an invisible fist had slammed into her belly.

The concussion of the exploding gas tank blew her back toward the front of the bus, throwing her against the remains of the windshield. She screamed at the nerve-searing pain and then automatically lifted a protective arm as the surging fireball from the tank blew down the aisle, engulfing the children in a single horrifying instant.

Rolling to the left, Jenny smacked her arm against the door-opener bar, flinging herself through the opening just as the flames reached the front of the bus. She landed on her knees, then struggled painfully to her feet. She kept on moving, blundering forward, faintly aware of the fact that she was in the remains of someone's living room.

Guided by instinct and ruled by overwhelming fear, she battered her way through a sea of splintered furniture, hands over her ears to dull the terrible crackling sounds and the last few agonizing screams still coming from the bus. Then, incredibly, she felt a wash of cold clean air against her cheek and she opened her eyes.

A backyard, fenced, with a gate leading to the alley. Behind her the house was burning, fueled by the torched remains of the bus. Stumbling on, numbed brain refusing to deal with the scene she was abandoning, Jenny crossed the snow-covered yard and reached the gate. She fumbled with the simple latch, pulled it open, and fled, running down the alley and away from the hell behind her.

CHAPTER TWENTY-ONE

9:05 P.M.

Barry LaGrace gunned the red-white-and-blue Post Office Jeep through the heavy snow on Overlook Street, cursing angrily as he juddered the wheel back and forth.

"Stupid God damn kids! What in the name of Jesus, Mary, and Joseph were you two doing out there in the middle of the fucking night, dressed in those suits! Jesus H. Christ!"

In the backseat, Karen sat with B.C.'s head in her lap. He was still out cold, but it looked as though at most he'd have a couple of cracked ribs and a massive bruise. The slug had hit B.C. in the solar plexus, but had been stopped by the body armor in the chest-plate of the suit. LaGrace, horrified when he realized he'd shot a resident of Jericho Falls, was expressing his relief that B.C. wasn't badly hurt by giving the two young people hell.

"You could have been killed!" he snarled. "You realize that?"

"Yes, Mr. LaGrace, we realize that," Karen said. "Why don't you just concentrate on driving, okay? We've got to get B.C. somewhere safe."

"Huh!" snorted the gray-bearded roofer. "Safe? This whole bejesus town isn't safe. Medical Center's out, Frenchtown's going up like a Roman fucking candle. Your dad said it's Americans, but by Christ I don't believe that for a minute, let me tell you. It's the fucking Arabs. First it was the oil squeeze, then the oil glut, then Libya. Fucking bunch of terrorists."

"Just take me to my dad, okay?" She put her head back against the seat and closed her eyes for a moment. All she wanted was sleep.

"God damn kids!" muttered LaGrace. He veered north,

smashing through a bank of snow, and turned up Gowan Street.
A few moments later he wheeled the Jeep into the Square at
Constitution Common.

Stark Hall, lit by an assortment of candles, oil lamps, naphtha
lanterns, and big flashlights, was a madhouse. Fifteen minutes
earlier, the lead bus in the caravan leaving Earl A. Coolis High
School had been attacked on Sherbourne Street. The other vehicles, seeing the flaming wreckage had turned back, making their
way to Constitution Common and the hall. The main-floor corridors and offices were filled with children, senior citizens, and
volunteers, and the auditorium was filling up with refugees from
the outlying sections of the town.

With the help of LaGrace, Karen took B.C., now groggily
awake, to a relatively quiet corner of the auditorium, promising
to return as soon as she could. Swearing, LaGrace went back
outside to the Jeep and headed back to his post at McKarsky's,
while Karen went in search of her father.

Pushing her way through the crowds of crying, distraught people in the corridors and on the stairs, she eventually found him
in conference with Sparrow Hawke in the council chamber. Still
partially dressed in the suit, now minus the backpack, Karen stood
in the doorway, not wanting to interrupt. Sparrow saw her, his
eyes widening, and then her father turned. There was a moment
of stunned silence, and then her father lurched away from his
chair and rushed toward her.

"Karen! Oh God, I thought I'd lost you," he choked out,
sweeping her into his arms.

"No such luck, Dad," she cried, nuzzling into his neck. He
smelled of sweat and old leather, and it was wonderful.

"What about B.C.?" he asked suddenly, breaking the embrace.

"Down in the auditorium. Mr. LaGrace took a shot at him on
the bridge, but he was wearing a suit like this, too. He's going
to be okay, except for a couple of ribs. He saved my life, Dad,"
she added softly.

"How did you escape? Sparrow and I tried to get you out, but
it was impossible."

"We were in some kind of isolation room, with hospital beds,
but they moved us to the basement of the terminal building. It
was B.C.'s idea to cut through the wall. We found . . . bodies

in the cold-storage room Mr. Coyle uses. Officer Dorchester was one of them and so was Corky, the guy who works down at the Gas Bar.'' Her voice broke and she stopped for a moment.

"It's okay,'' Slater said, guiding her to a chair at the council table. He sat her down and waited for her to continue.

"Uh, well, I sort of freaked out then, but B.C. got me back together. We went upstairs and stole a couple of the suits those people wear. After that, we just walked out.''

"Christ!'' Sparrow whispered, sitting across from her. "This B.C. has got balls!''

"No kidding,'' Karen said, smiling weakly. "Anyway, we heard on the helmet radios that they were after us, so we took off. We circled around to the railway bridge and crossed on the catwalk. B.C. killed a guard on the other side. Then we went to his father's hunting cabin on Quarry Hill and waited for it to get dark. We walked the rest of the way, and then Mr. LaGrace shot at us on the bridge. It wasn't his fault, though. We were wearing the suits . . .'' Her voice trailed off. She was pale and drawn, and there were dark circles under her eyes. She blinked, then nodded absently. "Oh yeah. Mr. Coyle is involved in this whole thing. B.C. and I were at the tennis club last night, and he was having some kind of meeting. That's when they caught us.''

Slater stopped himself from asking the obvious question about what they were doing at the tennis club. He patted her on the shoulder instead. "Okay, Karen. I think you've had enough for now. You go down and stay with B.C. and I'll come and see you in a few minutes, how's that?''

"Fine,'' she murmured, climbing to her feet. "We brought both the helmets with us. Thought you could listen in on the radios.''

"Five minutes, no more,'' Slater said. He guided her toward the door and ushered her into the hall. He stood watching for a moment as she made her way to the stairs and went down. Then he returned to the table.

"Quite the story,'' Sparrow said. "She's lucky to be alive.''

"I thought my heart would stop, seeing her,'' Slater said, shaking his head. Then his features clouded. "Any word on who was driving the bus?''

"Jenny. We haven't sent anyone up to check it out.''

"Don't,'' Slater said. He cleared his throat noisily, pulling himself together. "They've got the whole thing figured out. We try getting up Sherbourne, and they'll pick us off."

"It's a squeeze. They're coming in from the north and any minute we can expect them to bring on the big guns from the south, one or both of the bridges. We're trapped, Sheriff, and anybody mobile left in town is coming here. They're going to have us all together, neat and tidy."

"What about helicopters?"

"Wind's down. They could probably use them now without too much risk."

"Shit!"

"That's one way of putting it. I've got the big fifty-calibre from the chopper we took up in the tower. That might stop them for a bit."

"How many people do we have in the hall?"

"Five, maybe six hundred."

"That's all that's left?" said Slater. "A whole town reduced to five or six hundred people?"

"And nowhere near enough transport to move them with. Not that we have anywhere to go."

"I should have gone along with Wright," Slater said quietly. "Maybe it would have been best."

"According to Bess Tilly, there were fifty or sixty kids on that school bus they just torched," Sparrow said, his voice like ice. "Wright and his people are mass murderers, Jack. We're an oil spot they're wiping up. You would have been leading the whole town to its death. This way you can at least tell yourself you tried."

"It's the same result."

"Don't give me that kind of crap," Sparrow snorted. He coughed, the sound thick and deep within his chest. He cleared his throat, rubbing his chest with one hand and then went on. "We're not finished yet. Maybe we can get a few people out, enough to make sure this whole thing gets to the press."

"Maybe."

"What about Karen?" Sparrow asked. "What are you going to do? Sit back and let them come and take her?"

"What's this?" said Slater, cocking an eyebrow. "Your 'one for the Gipper' speech?"

"Survival," Sparrow answered. He stood up and Slater noticed that he kept one hand on the arm of his chair for support. "Survival, my man, that's the last thing we have left. You fight until it's over. And it's not over yet."

"All right," said Slater. "I get the point. It's the Alamo. I'm Fess Parker, and you're John Wayne. What happens now?"

"What's the last thing that bastard Wright would expect?" asked Sparrow.

"Offensive action?"

"Bingo." Sparrow grinned wolfishly. "We attack."

But it was too late.

The first wave of AMCCOM Unit 7 troops reached the southern approach to the Mill Bridge twenty minutes behind B.C. Bingham and Karen Slater. The squad was made up of two twenty-five-man groups spaced two hundred yards apart riding a combination of fast-attack Jeepsters and larger, armed personnel carriers.

A three-man point team took up positions close to the bridge abutments, radioing coordinates back to the commset in the lead personnel carrier. The communications officer in turn passed on this basic intelligence to the single Hughes Apache riding herd on the two groups, half a mile behind and two hundred feet up.

The point team confirmed that there was infrared activity within a small building on the far side of the bridge, and rather than solicit fire, the two ground-force squads paused and waited for the Apache to do the dirty work.

In McKarsky's Barber Shop, Hugh Bates waited anxiously for the return of Barry LaGrace. The man was a boor and a loudmouth, but at least he was company, and staring out into the darkness, Bates was sure he could see some sort of movement on the far side of the bridge.

He sat in LaGrace's chair by the window, the bridge detonator on the floor at his feet. He heard the sound of an engine and stiffened, one hand going down for the detonator, the other reaching for the shotgun he'd been given. He sighed with relief as the cheerfully painted Post Office Jeep pulled up at the curb, and he waved as LaGrace climbed out from behind the wheel.

Suddenly, impossibly, the sun seemed to rise above the bridge and LaGrace and the Jeep were thrown into sharp silhouette. Bates, eyes wide, stood up, jaw dropping as the single roving eye of the Apache's floodlight poured in through the window and then just as suddenly snapped off. Confused, Bates blinked hard, his night vision dissolving into a blinding array of red and green lights that danced in front of his eyes.

In the gunner's seat of the Apache, the co-pilot switched on the Night Vision sensor and the optical relay tube, automatically passing information gathered by the Target Acquisition Designation Sight directly into the heads-up display on his visor.

The array gave him a wide choice of weapons, including a brace of T.O.W. slung on two airfoil struts, a bank of six Hellfire antitank missiles, or the .30mm chain gun under the nose. Given the circumstances and the clear infrared target showing both in front and within the building on the opposite side of the bridge, the co-pilot triggered a single Hellfire, nodding with satisfaction as the seventy-inch projectile spurted out from beneath the belly of the chopper.

The blunt, short-finned missile reached its 625 mph maximum speed within eight-tenths of a second. Traveling beyond the speed of sound, the missile found its target silently, impacting against the side of LaGrace's Post Office Jeep just as the man stepped out from behind the wheel. The twenty-pound warhead exploded with a snapping roar and both LaGrace and the truck were vaporized in a single furious ball of fire. The concussion blew out the front window of McKarsky's, and the wooden exterior instantly caught fire. Inside the relatively undamaged building, Hughes had been blown backward out of his chair, stunned but alive, a hundred razor-sharp slivers of glass glittering brightly in the bleeding ruin of his face.

The pilot and co-pilot of the Apache conferred briefly and, seeing no reason to waste another missile, they veered away to the left, following their predetermined course downriver to cover the advance of the men headed for the lower bridge. Without opposition, the two squads on the ground began to move forward, heading onto the bridge.

Surprisingly, at least to him, Hugh Bates felt very little pain. He crouched on hands and knees, and tried to breathe. His mouth was full of blood and he could feel it dripping down his face. It was obviously going into his eyes, because he couldn't see. He blinked, feeling something hard in one corner of his right eye, and reached up with one hand to wipe it away. It didn't do any good, so instead he began crawling blindly forward, sweeping the floor with his hands, searching for the detonator.

He shook his head, giggling, knowing that LaGrace would call him a coward for blowing up the bridge too soon. Most of the night the roofer had talked about how he was going to wait until the last minute before he blew the fucking commie bastards to hell.

Well, screw LaGrace. Hugh Bates had done enough for one night. He was a movie projectionist, for God's sake, not a soldier. His hand closed around something circular and metallic. The detonator. Good. It really was getting late and he wanted to get a decent night's sleep. Tomorrow he had to drive in to Portland for the new movie. Well, it wasn't really new, of course, the Murray couldn't afford first-run shows. If he remembered right, the one he was getting tomorrow was another of those silly Stallone things. Not his choice of course, but it would play well with the kids.

He pulled himself upward until he was sitting cross-legged on the floor. What would his choice be? He giggled again, gripping the case of the detonator in one hand and curling his fingers around the screw handle the way LaGrace had demonstrated. Under the circumstances what other film *could* he choose?

He sighed, glad that when this was over he could go home, and twisted the handle sharply, sending the necessary trickle of current speeding down the copper wires that still led out the door. It had to be *Bridge on the River Kwai*. The job complete, Hugh Bates fainted and fell face forward, blood from his ravaged face pooling around his mouth and nose, where it would eventually drown him.

Outside, the two squads and their vehicles swung onto the bridge, unaware of Hugh Bates's final moments. The Hellfire missile which had demolished Barry LaGrace's postal truck had also severed the wires leading to the bridge charges, making Bates's last gesture a futile one. The bridge stood and the Unit 7 men moved into Jericho Falls.

Shivering, teeth chattering, Jenny stumbled down the narrow Frenchtown alley. Her ski jacket was a singed and torn ruin, one sleeve missing and a foot-long rent in the front. The force of the exploding gas tank had blown her out of her boots and the heavy socks she wore were soggy from the snow. She'd lost all feeling in her feet now, but at least the cold was keeping her from feeling the pain in her hands, both of which had been gouged on broken glass.

Her mind was numb and she had no real idea of which direction she was going in. As she staggered along the alley, all she could see was the vision of the children dying, all she could hear were their screams of agony as the fire consumed them. Some part of her knew that the fact of her own existence was virtually a miracle, but she could take no consolation from the knowledge. The children had been her responsibility, and she had failed them.

She stopped, her breath coming in tortured gasps, and leaning against a tall wooden fence, she looked back the way she'd come. The flames from the burning house and bus had taken firm hold, lighting up the night sky two blocks behind her. Did they know she'd escaped, and would they follow? She shook her head weakly. It didn't matter. She deserved to die. Half a hundred children were dead, cremated in the ruins of the school bus, and it was her fault. Pushing herself away from the fence, she staggered on, coming to the end of the alley a few moments later.

Jennifer paused again, trying to figure out where she was. In the distance she could make out the dark spire of Stark Hall rising over the flat rooftops of the buildings around Constitution Common. She brushed the back of one hand across her eyes and tried to read the street sign at the corner: Brock and Arbutus—that put her three blocks west of the Common. To her left was a row of pale, Frenchtown houses, to the right was a corner grocery— Anggela's Mini-Mart. Two *g*'s in Angela, the sign bracketed by two big, dark red Coke medallions. In the dark window of the grocery store she could see the dusty cardboard figure of a Phillip Morris bellboy, complete with pillbox hat and toothy smile. Did they even sell Phillip Morris cigarettes anymore?

She heard the sound of an engine, and without thinking, she dropped down onto the ground, huddling behind a dark blue garbage dumpster. A few seconds later a vehicle appeared.

A Jeep but not a Jeep, the open body enclosed by a roll cage with a big long-barreled machine gun mounted on the back. There was a searchlight mounted on the hood and as the vehicle rolled by, the light swung from side to side. There were five men in the Jeep, one standing behind the machine gun, one driving, and three others, all wearing space-age suits that covered them from head to toe.

The searchlight swung over the dumpster, and Jenny flattened herself in the snow behind it. The beam passed on and the sound of the engine receded. They'd missed. Still keeping low, she crawled to the side of the dumpster and looked down the street. The vehicle had stopped at the end of the Frenchtown row and three of the men climbed out. As well as the backpacks, each man had a large plastic container fitted over the chest-plate of his suit.

The three men fanned out along the row, covered by the machine gunner. Petrified, Jenny watched as they approached each door of the row, reached into the chest containers, and withdrew a slightly convex object the size of a dessert plate. There was some kind of lever on the plate which anchored it to the door. Plate fitted, they moved on until every door in the row had been done. With the job complete they returned to the oddly constructed Jeep and drove off, turning onto Arbutus Street.

Jenny lay in the snow for a full five minutes, hardly breathing, waiting to see if the men would return. When she was satisfied that they'd gone for good, she stood up, still keeping to the shadows between the dumpster and the corner store. Frowning, she stepped out onto the sidewalk and looked down Brock Street.

The dark circular plates were clearly visible, clamped onto the doors of each small house. Confused, her mind still recovering from the horrors of the last few hours, she shrugged off any impulse to see what the suited men had been up to. Instead she turned and began walking away as quickly as she could, crossing the road and slipping between two houses on the other side, trying to find a shortcut to the Common. She focused on an image of Jack and prayed desperately that he would be there. In her heart, she knew that she was going to die, and soon, but she didn't want to die alone.

Avrom Semolevitch sat at his puppet-making bench, his best embroidered yarmulke on his head, prayerbook open in front of him. He rocked gently back and forth as he prayed, the words an almost silent whisper. He kept his old gnarled hands flat on the table, supporting him, and his eyes were closed as he spoke the prayer he'd chanted a hundred thousand times before. To his right, there was a single oil lamp without a chimney, flame flickering in the draft that came from under the door.

Drawn by the light, the two night-camouflaged men approached the shop, weapons at the ready, and saw Avrom through the window, his face bathed in the soft puddle of golden light. Without pausing, the man in the lead lifted one heavily booted foot and kicked down the door. He stepped inside, followed by his companion, and both men moved quickly around the counter to stand a few feet in front of his bench. The first man spoke, his voice crackling through the small speaker below his darkened visor.

"WHO ELSE IS HERE?"

"No one," Avrom answered, opening his eyes and looking up at the men. He'd been thinking about home, and his cousin Krysha, a girl with jet black hair and eyes, his first love. A different world and a different time.

"YOU'RE LYING," said the man, poking his weapon toward the old man.

"Why would I lie?" Avrom shrugged. "You've no doubt come to kill me, like all the rest. I would lie perhaps if I were frightened of you, but I'm not."

"STAND UP," ordered the first man.

"I do not stand for such as you," the old man answered.

"THEN YOU'LL DIE SITTING," said the man. "IT DOESN'T MATTER TO ME."

"Nor I," said Avrom, smiling. He lifted both hands, palms up, in a gesture of resignation.

Both men noticed the two small rings of light-colored thread around Avrom's thumbs, but it was too late. The thread, strong enough to articulate the limbs of his marionettes, was connected to the twin triggers of an ancient duck-gun he'd had for years.

The gun, anchored below the table with C clamps, was of a type long since made illegal. It was O gauge, and a single blast from the huge barrel could take out an entire flock of ducks on the water. Intended as a bow gun for a boat, the weapon would have blown off the arm of anyone who'd tried to fire it normally.

Earlier in the day, after his visit from Sheriff Slater, Avrom had thought long and hard about the duck-gun and finally, straining with effort, he'd brought it down off its pegs in the upstairs room and manhandled it down to the shop. He had powder and wads for it, but no shot, so he'd filled the barrel with odds and ends, cramming down nails, screws, and a double handful of the small clips some men liked to have put on the heels and toes of their shoes.

Lifting his hands, Avrom saw the man's gauntleted finger squeezing the trigger of his own weapon, and knew that his own death was only seconds away. It didn't matter, though, because this time he was every Jew who ever was, this time he didn't meekly stand and do as he was told.

"Shalom, schmutzik," he murmured, using the old Yiddish word for filth. He felt a terrible, searing pain in his chest, but before he died he heard the thunderous roar of the duck-gun, and he was satisfied.

The explosion was so powerful that the barrel of the ancient gun cracked the table in half a split second after the hammers of the gun slammed home. A gruesome hail of flying metal blew out from the muzzle at knee height, catching both suited men before they could react.

No amount of Kevlar armor could have withstood such an impact, especially from no more than a yard away. Both men were struck full on, the spinning scythe of makeshift shot hacking through fabric, plastic, flesh, and bone. Screaming, the sound lost in the explosion and muffled by their helmets, the two men, their legs neatly amputated, dropped to the floor.

Blood from a dozen severed arteries began to spurt, pumping across the old floor, but it wasn't enough to douse the flames of the fallen oil lamp. Like the Slumber-King Motel before it, the shop of Avrom Semolevitch, Custom Boot and Shoe Maker, began to burn, the crackling roar of the mounting flames drowning out the last anguished cries of the dying men within.

CHAPTER TWENTY-TWO

9:15 P.M.

Jack Slater responded instantly to the report of the explosion at McKarsky's Barber Shop and ordered the demolition of the Gowan Street Bridge in an effort to stop a possible two-pronged attack on the Common. According to the lookout in the Stark Hall bell tower, at least fifty men had crossed the Mill Street Bridge and now were spreading out into the business district along Main and Whitehill. Slater had fifteen or twenty of his own people in the area, but it was unlikely they'd be able to hold out for long.

Any thoughts Sparrow and the sheriff had about their own offensive went by the board. There was only one thing to do now: get as many people out of town as possible. The two men left the council chamber and headed down the long flight of stairs to the auditorium, but they were stopped halfway down by Dwayne Kennaway, the balding Public Works councillor and owner of K-Way Sanitation Services.

With Luther Coyle absent and Loretta Simms from the school board dead earlier in the day from a sudden heart attack, Kennaway was the last public official in Jericho Falls, by default the acting mayor of the town. From the man's haggard, exhausted appearance it didn't look as though he was enjoying the position.

"They've taken a vote," Kennaway said hesitantly. "I was coming up to tell you about it."

"A vote, Dwayne?" asked Slater, astounded. "There's a war on out there, for God's sake, this is no time for due process!"

"I know, I know," the man stuttered. "But they did."

"Who?"

286

"The people in the hall. Tucker Carlisle and some of his friends started grumbling and then they called a town meeting. They asked how many people wanted to give up. Surrender, I guess you'd call it. They figure if those people out there are really American soldiers, then they've got nothing to worry about."

"That's crazy!" Slater exploded. "They've got to get out. *Now*. We all do."

"I know, I know. You've been saying that. But they're scared. That school bus Miss Hale was driving was full of kids, Sheriff."

"That's right," Slater said, his voice frigid. "And now they're dead."

"They took a vote. It was pretty nearly unanimous. They want to stay."

"So much for mottoes on license plates," murmured Sparrow Hawke.

"I can't just let these people be murdered," Slater said. "I've got to talk to them!"

"Forget it," Sparrow said. "They've made their choice, and you're not going to change their minds. There isn't time."

"What about you?" Slater asked, looking toward Kennaway. The little man took a deep breath and nodded.

"I'm with you."

"How many others?"

"Sixteen, maybe twenty."

"All right. Get them together, right now, and make sure my daughter is with them. She'll be with B.C. Bingham, Charlie's boy. He's hurt, but he can travel. You've got five minutes, Dwayne. Take them around to the fire hall and get everybody onto the rescue truck. There should be enough room if you pack them in. And no lights."

"Where do I go?"

"Off the Common to Fox, and then east to the Creek Bridge at Van Epp. So far they don't seem to be showing much interest in the Hill or Riverside Park. Sparrow and I will meet you at the Medical Center. Got that?"

"Yes."

"Then get going." Kennaway nodded, turned, and headed down the stairs.

"What about us?" Sparrow asked.

"How many could we ferry out in the chopper we stole?"

"Not enough. Eight or nine at most. We'd have to leave the rest behind."

"But it'll still fly?"

"Sure. Full tanks, and the only armament missing is the big machine gun. Why?"

"I want to check the road up to the ski lodge. If it's clear, we can get up there in the rescue truck. If it's guarded, we can do some damage and maybe clear the route for Kennaway and the others."

"And after that?"

"I'm not sure yet. They're not going to let us get away easily, I know that much. For Wright it's all or nothing. Anybody gets away and his whole scenario is ruined."

"You really think we can make it?" Sparrow asked. He coughed hard, covering his mouth.

"No," Slater replied bluntly. "But we've got to try."

"Still hanging in with the 'Live Free or Die' motto?" Sparrow grinned.

"It's all we've got left," answered Slater.

At 9:30, Dwayne Kennaway and eighteen residents of Jericho Falls drove out of the fire hall on Constitution Common and headed north to Fox Street. Three of the passengers, not including Karen Slater, were women in varying stages of pregnancy, and five more were their children, ranging in age from three to eleven. The remainder were elderly or in late middle age, except for Karen and B.C. Bingham. The nineteen people in the large, heavy-chassised utility truck left behind 684 of their friends and neighbors in Stark Hall. Within nine minutes of the rescue truck's departure, all 684 would be dead or dying.

At 9:32, traveling on foot, Sheriff Jack Slater and Sparrow Hawke also left the building, cutting across the snow-covered Common to Woolworth's, and running down the alley to Sherbourne Street and the large, parklike playground of Earl A. Coolis High School. The brick building was dark and deserted, the main doors wide open, a delicate tongue of drifting snow poking into the marble-floored lobby.

At the rear of the school, the large, white-painted Sikorsky helicopter was waiting for them, main rotors moving slightly in the dying wind. The two men climbed aboard and were airborne within three minutes. Barely aloft, and running without lights, Sparrow guided the flat-bellied craft to the north, swinging it carefully above the power and telephone lines that ran along Quebec Street. Ahead of them was the bald line of the Ridge, and beyond that, the bleak, dark sea of the White Mountains.

At 9:39, four helicopters roared over the still-burning remains of Drake's Farm, traveling so low that their backwash actually fanned the flames among the burning trees. Reaching the Strip, they swung east over Brock Street and North Beacon, changing from a box to line formation.

Three of the helicopters were regulation Huey Cobras, while the fourth and leader was the sinister-looking Cheyenne that had eradicated McKarsky's Barber Shop a few minutes before. The Cheyenne was equipped with a variety of target-acquisition and intelligence-gathering apparatus and was acting as a bloodhound for the remaining gunships.

The Cheyenne quickly identified Stark Hall as a major source of infrared radiation and the helicopter gunner quickly relayed the information to his companions in the other choppers. Without interference the four machines thundered over the sloping roof of the Murray Theatre, then swung quickly around the Common, sensors checking for any movement or other potential source of trouble.

For fifteen minutes prior to the arrival of the helicopters, Julius Havelock, owner of Havelock's Pharmacy, had been arguing with his wife Mildred. Mrs. Havelock had no intention of moving from Stark Hall until the authorities arrived and she insisted that Sheriff Slater's belligerent stance had been a terrible mistake from the beginning.

Julius Havelock didn't agree, and although he had deferred to his shrewish wife for the preceding forty-six years, he had chosen this moment to stand up and fight for what he believed. What he believed was simple: the world had gone completely mad and they were now under attack by members of their own armed forces. If there was any other solution, it was that they were under attack by the Russians, and either way, remaining in Stark Hall was suicide. Blotting out the strident sound of Mildred's voice, he buttoned up his thick, tweed overcoat and stomped out of the auditorium. A moment later he stepped out of Stark Hall and into the night air.

The infrared sensors picked up his blurred shape on the steps, and the gunner in the lower seat of the Apache responded instinctively, his finger tightening on the trigger of the Hughes .30 mm chain gun slung under the boxy nose. Julius Havelock, whose last thought was pride in his newfound courage, died instantly, his remains spattered over the graciously arched main doors of Stark Hall.

Working in perfect synchronization, the four helicopters hovered, then banked slightly, until they boxed the compass, standing a hundred yards off from the hall. Each of the machines armed its Hellfire missiles, tilted forward to avoid hitting each other, and then fired almost simultaneously. The result was devastating.

Each helicopter had selectively fired three of its missiles, and all twelve found their mark. The first volley sheared easily into the upper floors of the building, blowing out the council chamber and business offices as well as demolishing the base of the bell tower. Before the crumbling spire had a chance to fall, the second volley roared into the main-floor auditorium, followed immediately by the third sequence.

A total of eight projectiles exploded among the massed citizens of Jericho Falls. Eighty pounds of high explosive detonated in the enclosed area, throwing out almost a quarter ton of shrapnel at near speed-of-sound velocity. Ten seconds later there was no human remain within Stark Hall larger than a silver dollar and any small sliver of flesh or bone that did exist soon vanished in the inferno that followed.

The bell tower, supports demolished, dropped down into the yawning char-pit of the hall, sending up a gigantic cloud of flame and whirling ash that stood like an immense firebrand above the town. It was 9:40 exactly.

At that time, the existing population of Jericho Falls had been reduced to 987, almost all of whom were too sick, too old, or too young to defend themselves, and during the next three hours even those people would be dealt with by the roving squads of men from Lt. Colonel Wright's Special Unit. At 9:50, as the buildings around Constitution Common began to burn, the final element of Wright's plan was brought into play.

Twelve hundred miles from Jericho Falls at Scott Air Force Base, just outside of Lebanon, Illinois, a night-camouflaged KC10A advanced tanker moved down the main runway. Scott was home to the 375th Medical Airlift Wing as well as forty other military airlift command units and the takeoff went virtually unnoticed except by the air traffic controllers in the base tower.

The KC10A was the military tanker/transport version of the civilian wide-bodied DC-10 and had replaced the much smaller KC135 Stratotanker. The 10A, in addition to its own fuel, carried seven specially constructed bags within its windowless interior, loading a total of 131,000 gallons of high-octane aviation fuel.

At 9:53, Eastern Standard Time, the massive, black-painted aircraft lumbered into the air and headed east, following its duly registered flight plan to Pease Air Force Base in New Hampshire.

Jenny awakened, eyes wide, trying to pierce the darkness. Startled and completely disoriented, she struggled up from the pile of laundry she'd been sleeping on, a panicked scream dying in her throat. Remembering, she relaxed slightly and sank back down onto the musty concrete floor.

Three times she'd managed to avoid being captured by the roving patrols, and each time it seemed as though she detoured farther away from the Common. After the last narrow escape, she had gone to ground in a small house on Brewer Street, not too far from the school. She'd gone through the empty rooms cautiously, and eventually she'd discovered an old hunting jacket and a pair of tall rubber boots in the basement. She'd slumped down on a pile of laundry beside an old fashioned wringer washer, intending to rest for no more than a few minutes, and apparently she'd fallen asleep. Checking her wristwatch in the dim silver light filtering through the small window above her head, she saw that it was almost ten o'clock. She'd slept for the better part of half an hour.

And she remembered more. Something had awakened her, bringing her out of an exhausted sleep. What? A noise. And now she heard it again. She froze, listening, eyes rolling up to the bare floor joists above her head. A creaking sound. Footsteps. Someone was walking around upstairs. She jammed a fist into her mouth, stifling a moan of fear. One of the patrols was going through the house, and eventually they'd check the basement.

Terrified, she looked desperately around the cluttered, low-ceilinged room: a wringer washer, woodpile, hatchet and chopping block, clothes, a wicker basket, laundry tubs, piles of old suitcases, and a huge old octopus furnace in the center of the basement, thick, asbestos-insulated pipes running off in all directions. At the far end of the room, barely visible, was a shadowy flight of stairs leading upward.

She'd come down through the back kitchen, and that meant the window behind her probably faced out onto the street. She stood up carefully, wincing as the pile of dirty clothes rustled. She peered up at the window. No escape there. It had been painted over a dozen times, and there were three big nails clewed into the frame and bent across the window. It would take her twenty minutes to open and the noise would wake the dead. The only way out was the stairs.

The footsteps creaked again, this time directly over her head. She stood stock-still and waited, holding her breath. They moved away after a moment, heading for the rear of the house. The kitchen. Swallowing hard, she took three steps forward, eyes on the stairs, and reached blindly for the handle of the hatchet, the blade half-buried in the chopping block. Trying not to panic, she worked the handle back and forth, freeing it. As it gave and came into her hands, the basement door opened and she froze, lifting the hand axe over her head. Insanely, she heard a low voice, singing.

"Silent night, holy night, All is calm, all is bright, Round yon virgin mother and child. Holy infant, so tender and mild, Sleep in heavenly peace, Sleep in heavenly peace."

The words ended, replaced by a melodic humming. The voice had been an incredibly sweet baritone, perfectly modulated and in key, better than any she'd ever heard. But who in God's name would be singing a Christmas carol now?

"Camptown races run all night, doo-dah, doo-dah . . . umm umm, bet my money on a bobtailed nag, somebody bet on the bay!" Feet were coming down the stairs now; squinting, Jenny could see the lowered barrel of some sort of rifle. The man was wearing overalls, not one of the suits. She took another step forward and stood partially hidden by a thick wooden upright.

"Swing low, sweet chariot, comin' for to carry me home . . ." Almost fully down. Jenny stepped forward and began her swing with the hatchet. The face of the man came out of the shadows. "Swing low, sweet chariot—"

Jenny froze, the hatchet stopping in midswing.

"Bodo?" There was no doubt about it, the man on the stairs was Bodo Bimm. Startled, the man cried out and lifted the barrel of the gun. Jenny stepped out where he could see her and dropped the hatchet quickly. Bodo stared, and then his face broke out in a broad grin.

"Hello!" he said happily. "What's a lady doing down in the basement?"

"I was hiding, Bodo. And I was cold."

"Stopped snowin' now," he answered. "Pretty hot at the hall though, that's for damn sure!" He laughed, and somewhere in the sound Jennifer recognized the voice singing the carol. An idiot savant with the voice of an angel.

"What do you mean?" she asked, suddenly frightened.

"Big fire. Few minutes ago. Heli— heli—"

"Helicopters?"

"Yes, lady, that's it. Helicopters. One, two, three, four of them, and they all fired their . . . things all at once and the whole town hall just blew up. *Ka-boom,* a lot bigger than the pride-an'-joy." He lifted the barrel of the gun to demonstrate and Jenny backed out of the line of fire.

"Helicopters attacked Stark Hall?" she asked, her voice strained.

"Yes, lady, and just a minute before that the big truck from the fire station went out. Lots of fires tonight, lady, you bet. Topsy-turvy. The whole town's gone topsy-turvy." Saying the words, he frowned.

"We've got to get away," Jenny said. She reached out and squeezed Bodo's muscular forearm. "Do you understand me?"

"Sure, lady. Where do you want to go?"

"Away from the bad people."

"That would be nice."

Jenny thought furiously. Initially, Jack had wanted her to go to the rendezvous at the Creek Bridge and North Road. That was obviously impossible now, but there was a chance she could still get them to the old ski lodge. It was the only thing left.

"Come on, Bodo," she said quietly. "We can keep each other company. I'll lead the way."

"Sure, lady," Bodo agreed happily. He was used to doing what other people told him, and he was getting tired of thinking for himself. It gave him a headache. "Anything you say."

* * *

Flying low, keeping the silver thread of Mountain Creek below them, Jack Slater and Sparrow soon saw that the road up into the mountains was unguarded. Apparently Wright had considered armed rebellion a remote possibility when he cordoned off Jericho Falls, concentrating all his efforts on the most likely places a panic-stricken population might try to use as escape routes.

From the looks of things, the road was snow-covered but not impossible to navigate, especially now that the snow had stopped falling. The old ski lodge was almost twenty miles due north of Jericho Falls, sitting at the base of Mt. Kineo. The lodge was also part of the New Hampshire Hiking Association's system of cabins and rest stops, which meant it would be fully stocked with basic food items and first-aid equipment. Another twelve miles across country to the west was the northern line of the Appalachian National Trail. If he and the rest of the survivors could get that far, they might be able to follow the trail to the big lodge at Mt. Washington.

After following the mountain road for a quarter of an hour, they swung back toward the Falls. Coming out of the gap just north of the Hill, they could see the furiously burning remains of Stark Hall and the Common.

"My God!" Slater whispered, horrified. "What have they done?" The center of Jericho Falls was aflame, and even as they watched, new fires began to sprout along Main Street and in Frenchtown as the incendiary packages laid by the Unit 7 squads burst into life. Staring at the holocaust, both men realized how close they'd come to dying and both could easily envisage the horror they'd so narrowly escaped.

Tearing his eyes away from the scene, Sparrow wheeled the helicopter around and dropped even lower, skimming the low-pitched roofs of the big Hill houses. He'd been coughing almost constantly for the past twenty minutes, spitting unceremoniously onto the floor. The spit was dark, and Slater was sure the man was coughing up blood.

The pilot dropped the big machine down into the parking lot of the Medical Center. The rescue van was already there, Dwayne Kennaway waiting anxiously. Sparrow kept the rotors turning and followed Slater out of the helicopter and across the snow-blown asphalt to the truck.

"I was just about to leave without you," said the little man as Slater and Sparrow approached. "We almost got stopped twice, and I saw some kind of half-track heading up Whitehill toward the bridge. They'll be here any minute."

"How big was this half-track?" Sparrow asked.

"I'm not sure."

"Probably an armored personnel carrier," Slater said. "Shit! Those things can do at least thirty miles an hour on snow. They'll be on our asses before we've gone ten miles."

"They need to be distracted," Sparrow said. He looked up suddenly, squinting into the distance. "And that's not all. We've got choppers coming." The big man turned and headed back to the waiting Blackhawk. Slater grabbed him by the arm.

"Where the hell do you think you're going?"

"You've got an APC on your tail and choppers on top of that. You get going in the truck and I'll handle the bad guys."

"You're talking about suicide," Slater said.

"I'm talking about facing the inevitable. I got that flu just like everyone else, but I shook it off. I can't shake off what's going on inside my lungs right now. If Doc Payne was right, it's probably lung cancer, and I'll be dead in a couple of days anyway."

"You don't know that for sure," Slater said urgently.

"A body has eight pints of blood inside it. I figure I've already coughed up two or three today. Forget it, Jack. I know when I'm done. Let me play Davy Crockett one last time, okay?"

Slater looked at the man who'd become his friend in such a short space of time and nodded. Sparrow was right. It was necessary, and he was the only possible choice.

"Okay," Slater answered quietly. "And thanks."

"No sweat." He reached into the pocket of his jacket and pulled out a thickly rolled homemade cigarette. Taking out a book of matches, he lit the joint, cupping the flame in his hand. He took a deep drag and held it in his lungs for a moment.

Coughing, he spit out a trail of smoke. "Oh well," he said, smiling weakly and wiping the streak of blood off his lips. "They say dope rots your brain cells anyway." He flicked the joint into the snow, turned, and walked away. A few moments later the Blackhawk was airborne, heading south, its belly skimming the trees. Slater nodded to Kennaway.

"Come on," he said gruffly, refusing to watch the last flight of the helicopter. "Let's get going while we still have time."

Flying as low as he dared, Sparrow Hawke guided the big gunship toward the Creek Bridge at Van Epp Street, struggling to control his coughing and arming the helicopter's bank of rockets as he flew. He spotted the APC and the approaching flight of pure white helicopters at the same moment. Three Hueys and an Apache in the lead. A great white shark and three barracuda.

"Fish for dinner," he murmured to himself. The trick was not getting caught and served up first. Humming under his breath, the long-haired pilot eased the Blackhawk even lower, sweeping down over the bridge no more than ten feet off the ground, the APC filling the windshield in front of him. Unless the approaching choppers wanted to take out their own men, they wouldn't loose the Hellfires under their bellies. Not yet.

The APC was armed with a Browning .50 calibre machine gun on the commander's cupola, but the hatch was closed and Sparrow was reasonably sure the man driving the boxy little tank didn't even know he was there. Which was too God damned bad, because Sparrow would have dearly loved to know that the people in the APC were aware of the bullet they were about to bite down on. Without hesitation, he hit the release button on one of the two remaining T.O.W. missiles and watched as the corkscrew line of smoke and fire slashed out from below, whirling into the darkness.

The wire-guided missile struck the APC directly between the treads, flinging it into the air, surrounded by an expanding sheet of white-hot flame. Above Sparrow and less than three hundred yards away, the four attacking helicopters swung down toward him and the veteran pilot smiled. Chicken hawks, each and every one of them, and never an hour in any real combat situation.

Manhandling the control sticks, he slid the Blackhawk even lower, raking it over the road just beyond the flaming wreckage of the personnel carrier and sending up a blinding cloud of drifted snow. The four attacking helicopters were less than a hundred yards away now, and at the top of his windshield Sparrow saw the lead Apache's tail rotor come up as he looked for the Blackhawk. Anxious. He amended the silent criticism: anxious and outflown. In the last few seconds remaining in his life, Sparrow remembered what that had been like, and the incident that had very nearly cost him his life.

He'd been flying prisoners out of some godforsaken corner of the rain forest. A milk-run back to the intelligence boys in Phu Tai. Easy work for a chicken-hawk pilot who was still getting the feel of what it was like to be "in country." His spirits were up after spending three days inside a concertina-wire fire base, up to his armpits in mud, slime, ooze, and maggots. It was so wet that bodies steamed, fingers whitened, and letters written home were turned to pulp long before they were finished.

The order had finally come to bring the prisoners in, and he'd been airborne in five minutes, not expecting trouble. His worst times were flying medevac into combat zones, so a run back to the brigade's rear-area camp was almost a pleasure.

He had three prisoners in the cargo compartment of the mud-soaked and war-torn Huey. Two of them were women whose husbands were suspected of being Charlies and the third was a man in his late twenties, thin to the point of starvation, his eyes dead and without expression. He'd been taken by a Special Forces group a week before and they hadn't treated him kindly.

One hand had been amputated at the wrist, there was a livid, multicolored bruise that covered half his emaciated face, and one leg was broken. Underneath the tattered remains of his shirt, you could see the soiled bandage binding his broken ribs.

The Green Berets' treatment of the man had caused the delay in getting him back to Phu Tai, since it had taken several days for him to recuperate enough to travel. He was a suspected VC area commander, but no one at the fire base had the expertise or the inclination to interrogate the man to see if the suspicion was valid.

Sparrow didn't think about it. He hadn't thought about that kind of thing for the last three months. Even in that short space of time he'd seen and lived through too much to make critical judgments about anyone's behavior in Vietnam. There was only one truth here: everyone was crazy, and even the ground beneath your feet couldn't be trusted.

A thousand feet up over the endless, rain-soaked jungle, the half-crippled man in the back of the helicopter made his move. He'd been brought on board in a basket litter, his remaining hand cuffed to the metal rail. The two women were handcuffed to an interior strut. Unfortunately, the manufacturers of the handcuffs had designed the restraints for North Americans who weren't on the verge of starvation, and even the smallest closure hadn't been enough to hold the man.

Somehow, he'd gathered enough strength to climb out of the litter and attack Sparrow from behind. It had been more of a shock than anything else and the big man had simply batted the smaller back into the rear compartment. Undaunted, the Vietnamese began tearing at the wires and conduits running along the fuselage.

Since he was flying alone, Sparrow's only defense was to stand the Huey on its nose; eventually, he managed to tip the berserk man out of the open cargo door of the helicopter, the empty litter sliding out after him. He'd flown the rest of the way into Phu Tai in a state of shock, checking back over his shoulder every few seconds to make sure that the two women still manacled to the Huey weren't sneaking up on him.

Hair-raising as it was, the nightmare hammered home a simple lesson: a man who has nothing to lose has nothing to fear. The one-handed VC knew perfectly well that his interrogators at Phu Tai would almost certainly be South Vietnamese regulars, the sort who favored methods like slow castration, fire hoses up the rectum, and low voltage electrocution, to discover what they wanted. It wasn't a question of whether he would die, only when and how. He decided to go out with a relatively painless swan dive from a thousand feet up.

And now Sparrow was the little man in the back of the Huey. He'd told Jack Slater about coughing up blood, but he hadn't mentioned the incredible pain clawing at his guts that no amount of codeine could keep at bay or the hideous oozing sores that covered his chest and back. Two days was being incredibly optimistic—two hours was more like it.

And that was his ace in the hole. No matter how well trained the men in the attacking choppers were, none of them had ever really confronted death. They'd play it by the book, holding formation, trailing him down and trying for a salvo to take him out. Arithmetic. Sparrow was a target, they were on the offensive, and they had the numerical advantage. The Blackhawk could run, but it couldn't hide.

Sparrow had no intention of hiding. As the formation swung

around to follow him, he did exactly the opposite of what they were expecting. The book said he would keep low, weave, and head for advantageous ground. Instead, he throttled back, tilted up, and threw himself back directly into the path of the oncoming machines. At that point, the Apache was no more than seventy or eighty feet above the ground, its three companions trailing slightly behind, just out of rotor range. No room to manuever at all.

A fraction of a second before the inevitable impact, Sparrow leaned over and slammed his palm down on the T.O.W. firing button.

"I made it, Ma," he whispered. "Top of the world."

The Blackhawk's main rotor chewed into the front canopy of the Apache, decapitating the gunnery officer and destroying all the control mechanisms. As the body of Sparrow's helicopter collided with it in midair, the T.O.W. exploded, turning both the Blackhawk and the Apache into a huge, spinning cloud of razoring flak. Both fuel tanks exploded, adding to the airborne land mine, and without any time to react, the other three machines flew right into it. There was a single, huge explosion and then, in a roiling cloud of oily smoke and orange flame, fifteen tons of shrapnel began raining down onto the streets below, the smaller pieces hissing as they ate their way through the dusty drifts of snow.

In the distance, safe now, the faintly visible taillights of the rescue truck disappeared over the Creek Bridge at North Road and turned north, heading into the mountains.

CHAPTER TWENTY-THREE

Midnight

Extracts from the Flight Data Office, Pease Air Force Base, Portsmouth, New Hampshire.

11:22 P.M. Eastern Standard Time:

KC10: "Hello, Pease AFB, this is Tango, Tango, Romeo Alpha out of Scott. How do you read?"

PEASE: "Loud and clear, Romeo Alpha. What's your ETA to destination?"

KC10: "Hold on that, Pease. I'm on classified maneuvers."

PEASE: "Uh, we have no record of that here, Romeo Alpha."

KC10: "I understand, Pease. This is night flight refueling exercise to your coordinates Victor George Seven Nine Three Seven."

PEASE: "Will you require landing at Pease, Romeo Alpha?"

KC10: "Not at present, Pease."

PEASE: "Roger, Romeo Alpha. Keep us advised at fifteen-minute intervals, please. Course and altitude."

KC10: "Sure thing, Pease. Out."

11:56 P.M. Eastern Standard Time:

KC10: "Pease Air Force Base, this is Tango, Tango, Romeo Alpha."

PEASE: "Come in, Romeo Alpha."

KC10: "Sounds stupid, Pease, but I seem to be lost. My Nav's gone crazy."

PEASE: "Happens to the best of us, Romeo Alpha. Ident please."

KC10: "Ident, Pease."

PEASE: "We have you, Romeo Alpha. You're three two five at seven thousand. Stinson Mountain beacon should be on your port side at three thousand."

KC10: "Sorry, Pease, I can't see any beacon. Please advise."

PEASE: "Sure, Romeo Alpha. Hang on for a second. [pause] Okay, Romeo Alpha, try three two zero, zero. That should bring you around. Over."

KC10: "Going to three two zero, zero."

11:58 P.M. Eastern Standard Time.

PEASE: "Come in, Romeo Alpha. This is urgent."

KC10: "Romeo Alpha."

PEASE: "You're way off course, Romeo Alpha, down to four thousand. That's a mountain range you're in, buddy."

KC10: "Pease, I seem to be having trou . . . th . . . draulics." [broken transmission]

PEASE: "Say again, Romeo Alpha."

KC10: "Hydraul . . . flaps . . . not respond . . . shit!" [broken transmission]

PEASE: "Do you wish to declare an emergency, Romeo Alpha?"

KC10: ". . . down there? Advise, Pease."

PEASE: "I say again, Romeo Alpha, do you wish to declare an emergency? You are now down to three thousand. We're losing you, Romeo Alpha."

KC10: ". . . time to dump all of this . . . down somewhere . . . *Oh Jesus there's a town down there!"* [garbled voice transmission followed by loud noise, possibly an onboard explosion. Sound of recorded fire warning and horn. Gear down horn. Gear down siren. Transmission ends 00:00:30 A.M. Eastern Standard Time, Monday, November 3]

Friday, January 6

CHAPTER TWENTY-FOUR

4:30 P.M.

Bundled up warmly in a bright yellow Meteorological Department parka he'd found in the old barracks, Jack Slater dragged himself along the safety line, his head bent low against the incredible winds that blew across the bald rocky summit of Mt. Washington.

The mountain stood at the epicenter of two major storm paths, and some people said that the top of Mt. Washington was the windiest, least hospitable place in the world. For decades, the only people inhabiting the summit had been a crew of weathermen operating the met station, but several years before, the station had been automated. As far as Jack Slater was concerned, you couldn't have asked for a better hideout.

Except for a few brief weeks during the summer, virtually no one came here, and even then the only real way up was the old-fashioned cog-railway that crept up the steep slopes of the mountain from the base station a few miles east of Bretton Woods. There was a toll road, but snow and high winds made it impassable for most of the year, and the narrow footpath cut by the Hiking Association was suicide except in the very best weather. The mountain was the highest elevation in New Hampshire, and from the summit you could see for a hundred miles in all directions. If anyone tried to get them here, they'd pay a heavy price.

The man who'd once been sheriff of Jericho Falls reached the end of the safety line and, struggling, managed to pry open the hatch to the automated weather station. The station was a large, insulated sheet-metal-and-concrete hut built to withstand gusting wind of up to 230 miles per hour. Above it was a tall radio mast and the sides of the hut facing outward were surrounded by a complex array of radio dishes and microwave relay equipment.

Once inside the hut, Slater immediately switched on the big baseboard heaters and then threw off his parka. He'd grown a beard in the ten weeks since their escape from Jericho Falls, and it was heavily streaked with gray. Two months as a fugitive had hardened him, and his body was taut and muscular. His cheeks and brow were burned deep red, and his hands were thickly callused.

Before sitting down at the old metal desk squeezed in among the recording paraphernalia, he pulled a tattered school notebook from under his heavy, chain-stitch sweater and took a pencil out of the breast pocket of his shirt. At first he'd tried using one of the ball-point pens he'd discovered in the barracks on the other side of the summit plateau, but they skipped at high altitudes, and the hundred-yard journey along the safety line was enough to freeze the ink solid.

He sat down at the table and opened the notebook, idly flipping through the pages. When he'd begun the journal it had seemed important, but now he wasn't so sure. As time went on, his hopes of ever truly escaping the terrible legacy of the Jericho Falls siege receded. There was no future, and each day had to be lived for itself. Slater knew perfectly well that their existence at all was a miracle, even if they were forced to live like lepers, their very touch potentially fatal.

FROM THE JOURNAL OF
JACK MONTGOMERY SLATER

November 5,
Mt. Kineo Lodge

I found this notebook in the hut, and it occurred to me that someone should be writing down the story of what's happened to us. I guess I'm elected, because no one else seems to care at this point.

I suppose you could say we were lucky. Twenty of us managed to get out in the rescue truck, and Sparrow must have done a good job because no one followed us that I could see. It took us three hours to get to the old ski lodge, and by that time all anyone wanted was sleep.

At dawn the next day, we had our first miracle. Kennaway and I were trying to figure out some plan of action when we heard someone pulling into the parking lot. I thought it was all over then, but it turned out to be Jenny and Bodo Bimm!

Somehow, they'd managed to get out of town and make it to the Medical Center. Jenny found Doc Payne's old Meat Wagon, and she got it up here on a wing and a prayer in seven hours with Bodo riding shotgun. He was carrying a crazy-looking shotgun we eventually figured must have belonged to Ralph Beavis. I tried to get it away from him before he hurt someone, but it was Karen who finally convinced him to give it up.

Jenny and I talked later and she told me about Sparrow. She and Bodo were about a block away when it happened. My God! What a way to die. But he saved our bacon, that's for sure. She also told me that on the way up to the lodge, there was an incredible explosion from behind her. At first she thought someone had dropped the bomb, but obviously they didn't. I still can't figure that one out.

We've been here for two days now, and that's enough. Kennaway took the rescue truck out this morning and drove it into the woods. There's enough food in the lodge to keep us going for a while, but from now on we go on foot. The short-term objective is to get ourselves as deep into the mountains as we can. If Wright knows we're gone, he'll come looking for us, I'm positive of that.

We'll head west, around the base of Mt. Kineo, and try for one of the huts on the trail.

November 9,
Hut 7
Appalachian National Trail

Snowed again last night, which should cover our tracks. Mr. Cavanaugh said he heard helicopters yesterday, which would be another miracle, since he hasn't heard a damn thing in twenty years.

The hut's pretty small, but it'll do for tonight. B.C. seems to be recovering well enough. Two cracked ribs and a big bruise, but that's about it. I don't think a couple of the oldsters are going to make it, though. We've all been having nightmares.

November 15,
Hut 23(?)
Franconia Notch

Mrs. Eldridge, Mrs. Bailey, and Mr. Cavanaugh are gone. Mr. Cavanaugh had a heart attack, and the old ladies were suffering from exhaustion. They decided to stay with Mr. Cavanaugh until he got better and then they'd catch up. That was four days ago, and we haven't seen them since.

Kennaway was walking point yesterday afternoon about a mile

ahead on the trail, and he swears he saw helicopters. Weather's been poor though, so we shouldn't be bothered by them.

I've got four more days of insulin left. Jenny asked me, and I had to tell her the truth. She wants us to steal some if we get close enough to a town.

I think the children are going to be trouble.

November 28,
Hut 41

A lot of things have happened. B.C. hiked into Pierce Bridge and managed to get me some insulin. Broke into the drugstore there in the middle of the night. The kid's got what it takes.

Brought a newspaper with him. The story was old news on the back pages, but I think we've figured it out pretty well. It looks as though Wright really outdid himself. They call it the Jericho Falls Disaster. Apparently, a big air tanker crashed into the town a few hours after we left. Something like a hundred thousand gallons of aviation fuel. That must be the big explosion Jenny heard. Because it was a military tanker, they cordoned off the town and helped airlift the few "survivors" out. The story is that the tanker was involved in war games being held in the area. Obviously, no one really knows what happened.

Mrs. Simms's three-year-old died. She's about seven months pregnant. I don't think she's going to make it.

Some frostbite, and Kennaway isn't looking good. I can't believe this is happening.

Tomorrow we head east. If we can get to Mt. Washington, we'll be okay for a while. Jenny is definitely pregnant, and Karen thinks she's about three months gone. Pray God we find some sanctuary before either one of them has to deliver.

December 2,
Mt. Deception

Way off the trail. As the crow flies, Mt. Washington is no more than twenty miles away, but it might as well be a hundred.

Last four days spent in hiding. No fires. The mountains are

crawling with soldiers. Sometimes I find myself feeling so angry and frustrated by what has happened.

December 11,
North Fork River

Kennaway and six of the others have disappeared. We heard gunshots, but it was snowing too hard to find out what was going on. Bonnie Lombard miscarried and then hemorrhaged. There was nothing we could do. What I wouldn't give to get my hands around Wright's throat!

December 16,
Mt. Jackson

Every day we seem to lose more people. The Widow Rothwell finally just wandered off. I used to deliver newspapers to her when I was a kid. She told me she always wore black because you never knew when you'd have to go to a funeral. I think she just gave up and didn't want to be a burden. Mr. Farley's gone too. Heart attack in his sleep. The ground is too hard to bury them.

December 25,
Crawford Notch/Presidential Range

A fine clear day. Saw a group of Wright's men on the lower slopes five or six miles back, and there were helicopters again. I don't think they saw us—trees are too thick. Mt. Washington is due north, maybe three days hiking. Merry Christmas.

January 1,
Cog Railway Base Station.

We made it!
Three more gone. Mrs. Simms and the two little ones. Karen

cried over that, but B.C. calmed her down. I think Karen is convinced that the child in her belly is his, and quite frankly I'd be proud to have him for a son-in-law, adhesive tape on his glasses, stupid quotations and all.

Jenny, Karen, B.C., and Bodo. Only five of us left now. When will it end?

January 4,
Mt. Washington Meteorological Station

B.C. and I figured out how to run the cog railway and took it to the summit in the middle of yet another blizzard. The big barracks the Hiking Association maintains was fully stocked, so at least we've got some room, and even running water, courtesy of a full cistern and a blowtorch.

Jenny was on watch this afternoon when the weather cleared for an hour or so. She said she saw people down at the base station. With the little train up at the summit, they're going to know we're up here. We have to have some kind of plan.

January 5,
Met. Station

The poor weather is giving us some time. No helicopters in this wind. We're under siege, though. I want to get B.C. and Karen out of here before it's too late, but they won't go. The same for Jenny. Bodo thinks we're on some kind of camping trip.

Afternoon

I had it out with Jenny. They have to go. It's fifteen miles to Jefferson Highlands, and from there they can steal a car and make a run for the Canadian border. B.C. pointed out that if we are carriers of some kind of disease, we'd just be spreading it further. Christ almighty! What do we do?

Night

It's stupid, but I asked Jenny to marry me. She accepted on condition that I don't try and do anything heroic. Shows how much she knows. They're all asleep now, and more than anything I just want to slip away, leave all the responsibility behind and forget. Just forget.

If the weather eases off, we're going to make a run for it tomorrow. There are skis here. All I need is a telephone, and then maybe we can see justice done. A town died, and someone has to pay, by God!

Jack Slater looked down at the last entry in the journal and shook his head wearily. How pompous he sounded! He must be an utter fool if after all of this he hadn't learned that justice and reality had nothing to do with each other. Still, he was damned if he was going to let Wright win now. If he, Jenny, Karen, B.C., and Bodo Bimm could get off the mountain on skis, using the toll road, they might still have a chance. The thought of teaching Bodo how to ski was mind-boggling, but B.C. and Karen had been working with him all morning, and he'd made a little progress.

He stroked his beard and found himself wishing desperately for a cigarette. He gnawed on the end of his pencil instead. What were the odds on making it out? A hundred to one, a thousand, ten thousand? If Wright's people were down at the base station waiting for the weather to clear, that meant they'd probably be watching the toll road exit and the hiking trail as well. But what was the alternative?

The storm wouldn't last forever, and eventually Wright would be able to bring up one of his helicopters. Demolishing the entire met station would take about five minutes once that happened. He nodded to himself. Sparrow was right. It was better to go out fighting than to just sit there and take it. He took the pencil out from between his teeth and began to write.

January 6,
Mt. Washington Met. Station

This is going to be my last entry. When I'm finished, I'm going to hide this somewhere on the off chance someone other than Wright or his people might find it. Kind of a note in a bottle. We're going to try and get down the mountain as soon as it gets dark. We'll see if we can steal a car in Gorham or Berlin and then drive straight north to the border. There's an old highway that leads into Quebec, and maybe we can get across without being caught. After that, we can only hope that the Canadians believe us. Bodo is our ace in this game, at least if what poor Doc Payne thought was

Slater paused in midsentence, every nerve tingling. He felt a chill draft on the back of his neck and turned slowly, knowing that he'd dogged the hatch down tight before coming into the hut. Behind him, no more than ten feet away, was a tall figure wearing a jet black helmeted suit. The sheriff felt something twist deeply in his belly, and he tried to smile. Things never ended the way you expected, but somehow he wasn't surprised.

"Darth Vader, I presume?"

"I see you still have a sense of humor, Sheriff Slater. Highly commendable under the circumstances, or is it simply bravado?"

"Relief, I think," Slater answered honestly. "I'm tired of running, Colonel."

"And I'm tired of chasing after you." The black-suited man lifted the heavy barrel of the weapon in his hands and gestured at Slater. "How many are there?" he asked.

"Five, if you include me."

"Thank you for being honest," Wright said. "That tallies with my figures. We've managed to keep track of the bodies you left behind. We can't afford any mistakes. The idiot, Bodo Bimm, is he with you?"

"Yes. I suppose Luther told you about him?"

"Correct."

"How is Luther, Colonel Wright? Did he get his thirty pieces of silver?"

"Mayor Coyle has been . . . dealt with."

"Was it that important, Colonel?" Slater sighed. "Was that bug so dangerous that you had to destroy an entire town and everyone in it?"

"Of course," Wright said, the helmet nodding. "It was a recombinant called QQ9. It mutates up to an allergen that causes people to display violent reactions when exposed to a variety of substances, all of them derived from petrochemicals. Exhaust fumes, food fillers, cosmetics, virtually all plastics. The general release of such a bacteria would have devastating results, I think you can appreciate that."

"I guess so," Slater said wearily. It didn't seem to matter anymore.

"I thought it only fair that you should know: you've proven yourself a worthy adversary, Sheriff."

"Screw you," Slater said. "You make it sound as though it was a game. You're a mass murderer, Colonel Wright, nothing more or less."

"Perhaps. And if that is the case, a few more bodies won't make any difference, will they?" Wright gestured with the gun again, and looking down, Slater saw a little green button of light on his chest. "Please stand up, Sheriff. It's time we had an end to this." Then, in the space of a single instant, everything changed, and Slater knew there was one last chance.

Catching a flicker of movement in the open doorway behind Wright, the bearded man reacted instinctively and threw himself to the ground. There was a huge explosion, followed by another, and another.

Ears ringing, Slater rolled to the left and opened his eyes, ready to leap on Wright if the opportunity presented itself. Instead, he saw B.C. Bingham, Ralph Beavis's pride-an'-joy held tightly in his gloved hands. The barrel was still smoking, and what remained of Colonel James Wright was scattered across the floor in front of the desk.

"He came alone. Grandstand play," B.C. said, stepping into the hut. "I was standing guard at the window of the barracks, and I saw him sneak up over the rocks. I came as quickly as I could. You okay?"

"Yeah." Slater nodded, climbing to his feet. "You took one hell of a risk, B.C."

" 'Live Free or Die,' " quoted the boy, eyes twinkling behind the lenses of his glasses. "John Stark." He smiled. "I prefer the 'live free' part myself."

"Second the motion," Slater said, grinning broadly. He

stepped over the splayed remains of the dead man and shrugged into his parka. Looking around, he spotted a place where several electrical conduits crossed each other on the wall, and stuffed the notebook into the space between the wires and the sheet metal. Following B.C., he stepped out of the hut and carefully dogged down the hatch.

They were facing south, and he paused for a moment, staring out over the rolling sea of mountains. Somewhere out there was Jericho Falls, its houses and buildings destroyed by Wright's cataclysmic accident, the air above the gutted, desolate town filled with the sour reek of smoke and ash and death. It had happened there, and it had happened to them, but it could have been anywhere, and Slater knew that it could happen again. Unless they survived to tell their story. He turned away from the snow-girt panorama and clapped B.C. on the shoulder.

"Come on, Bentley Carver Bingham, let's get the hell off this mountain."

AUTHOR'S NOTE

The information described in JERICHO FALLS
regarding Recombinant DNA, epidemiology,
chemical and biological warfare, and allergic reactions is accurate. A compound with the properties of QQ9 exists and is currently under study
by the United States Army Chemical Corps.

Other technical details, specifically the equipment and environmental suits described in JER-
ICHO FALLS, also exist and are now being
manufactured under license in the United States.
All U.S. military installations described in JER-
ICHO FALLS also exist, as and where they are
described.

Jericho Falls and its occupants are, however,
entirely fictional.

—Christopher Hyde